THE OLD WAYS

RK SUMMERS

Inspired
Quill

Published by Inspired Quill: September 2015

First Edition

Contact the author through their website:
www.rksummers.com

Chief Editor: Sara-Jayne Slack
Cover Design by: Venetia Jackson

Typeset in Dante

Paperback ISBN: 978-1-908600-38-7
eBook ISBN: 978-1-908600-39-4
Print Edition

Printed in the United Kingdom
1 2 3 4 5 6 7 8 9 10

Inspired Quill Publishing, UK
Business Reg. No. 7592847
http://www.inspired-quill.com

Dedication

For my Grandfather
George Summers
who told me stories
on rainy days

George Summers
1930-2012

"Look, Grandad. I did it."

Acknowledgements

I hope you can forgive that I can't name you all, but these acknowledgements do need to be shorter than the novel. Still, you all know who you are. You believed in me, you supported me and gave me courage when I thought I was going to fail. And most importantly, you brought me coffee when I was flagging and notebooks when I ran out. You are the best and most wonderful friends I could ever ask for.

And to those who scoffed, who were rude, who told me to give up and stop daydreaming, I have no words for you… except that I hope you fall in a ditch of nettles.

On a lighter note:

To my Mama Bear, who never lets me be anything less than perfect, who dances with me when I'm sad, and who loves me beyond words.

And to my Papa Bear, who does the most accurate impression of Gollum I've ever seen, who brings me chocolate when I'm down, and who raised and loved me as his own.

I love you both so much.

My best friend, Tatty, who puts up with my late-night "I've got a great idea!" texts, and who's not afraid to tell me which of those "great ideas" are actually *terrible*.

Rachael, Laura, and Hannah, my equestrian advisors, for when my own knowledge fails me (which is actually all the time, as I know absolutely zero about horses).

Fiona and EJ, my *editors extraordinaire*! For being kind

with the Red Pen of Doom, even though I was a young author fledgling without the thick skin of maturity to protect me. You two gave my writing the fresh minty breath of life it so desperately needed.

Venetia, who created the spectacular front cover for my debut novel. When I first saw it, I made the most inhuman squeal. It's beautiful, Venetia. Your work is exquisite.

And Sara, who saw an eccentric Northern girl who still believes in faeries and magic, and gave her a chance to achieve what she'd dreamed of her entire life, I can only say thank you.

Faery Blessings on you all.

THE OLD WAYS

CHAPTER 1

The beginning of a war

T HE FOREST SLEPT, silent and still. Spring's first buds were opening to welcome the cool dew of morning, and a herd of white deer stood like sentinels, motionless among the pallid bodies of birch trees. The chill of winter had lessened, and the dusting of frost that sparkled in the pale morning light had melted away. A persistent mist still hung around the graceful trees like a blanket.

The brazen scream of a terrified child broke the silence.

A little girl gripped her mother's hand tightly as they fled through the bracken, her legs too short to keep up without aid. Her mother skidded to a halt, scanning the forest, muttering wildly to herself, "hurry, hurry!"

As if the wind had carried her plea to him, a slim, unkempt man burst through the foliage. A coat of blood painted his teeth red.

"Riaghán!" with a relieved sigh, the mother took a step to embrace him, but he stopped her.

"No time, Bram. I'll carry Thissy, hurry!" Riaghán spat blood onto the ground and swept his daughter into his arms. Jerking his head to indicate their path, he turned and ran, Bram racing after him.

Riaghán's thumping heart pounded in his ears. Thissy

buried her face in her father's neck, her tears soaking his hair. The family dashed between trees, scattering the ghostly deer that blocked their path ahead. Thundering hooves fast approached, drowning out even Riaghán's frantic panting.

They'd been fools to think the forest would offer sanctuary.

"*Papa!*"

Thissy's scream punctured Riaghán's heart. He spun, clutching her tightly to his chest with one arm as a black-clad rider, mounted on a horse of easily fifteen hands, drew within striking distance. He raised an obsidian sword – Riaghán thrust forward his free arm.

"*Tarrthála!*"

Thick branches whipped down with a crack, curling around the rider and lifting him from his horse. The boughs squeezed. A moment later, the limp body dropped to the ground with a heavy thud.

"My thanks," Riaghán nodded to the oak tree. The family turned and ran again. Slower now, exhausted from carrying his daughter and his use of magic, Riaghán dared not stop for breath. He couldn't; not until they were safe.

"Cut them off!" a shout from behind drove terror deep into him. Despite Thissy's desperate sobs, Riaghán was too frantic in his movements to offer words of comfort. Bram tripped over a root and fell into the bracken. Riaghán veered to a halt. He hated the roughness, but blinded by necessity, he dragged her to her feet and pulled her onwards again.

An arrow whistled through shivering leaves, burying itself in Riaghán's shoulder blade. He screamed and dropped onto his knees, clutching Thissy tighter.

Thissy whimpered, breaking away from him as Bram

knelt beside her husband. Riaghán trembled with pain as Bram laid her shaking hands on the wound.

"Keep still, my love," Bram whispered anxiously. In the distance, victorious shouts crept closer as more riders navigated through the foliage. This enclosed thicket bought only a little time. Riaghán silently blessed the confining forest.

"No, there's no time. Take Thissy and run. Hide. Bram, go, now..."

"But I can *heal*—"

"*Go!*"

Bram pulled Riaghán close and kissed him deeply, salty tears stinging between their lips. Thissy pushed herself between them and embraced him. Riaghán kissed her head, clutching his wife and daughter close.

"Papa?" Thissy began, but he shushed her.

"Go with Mama now," he gasped, releasing his daughter and clutching his throbbing left arm. He looked up. "Bram... go to Elphame, to Queen Mab. Tell her he's coming for her."

A sob wracked through Bram as she nodded. She kissed Riaghán one more time, took her daughter by the hand, and fled into the sanctuary of the trees.

Riaghán knelt in the mulch of the forest floor, his breathing laboured. The cold iron arrowhead burned into his faery flesh. He desperately wanted it out, but knew he'd cause more damage by yanking it free.

Jeers of riders soon accompanied their snorting horses. Riaghán didn't raise his head as they trotted to a halt around him. There was no need; he knew exactly who these horsemen were.

"Finally," said the voice nearest him, carrying traces of a

laugh. "I thought he'd never go down."

Riaghán looked up, throwing a slow, cold glare at the finely dressed rider, but kept his tongue still. He prayed Bram and Thissy were long out of sight.

"A fine shot, brother," said another, more sullen voice.

"Should we tell Father it was yours, Corvus? He'd be proud of you, if he thought you'd taken down a seelie—"

"Mothblood bastards," Riaghán rasped. "We'll never submit to unseelie rule..."

"Watch your tongue, leaf-ear!" The huntsman rounded his horse, kicking Riaghán hard in the face. He landed sideways in the springy moss, leaves clinging to his damp hair. His arm throbbed with mounting pain.

"Calm your temper, Malik," Corvus chided. Malik frowned, then his eyes travelled past his brother at the sound of hooves. He straightened respectfully as another horse approached, bearing a rider Riaghán had hoped not to encounter.

His fingers numb with fear, he pushed himself back to his knees. "Prince Erlik..." Riaghán swallowed. The prince wore a slithering black cloak, which put Riaghán in mind of shadows and smoke. The emblem of a great, black dragon proudly reared on the chest of his surcoat.

"Where is she?" Erlik asked. Riaghán stayed silent. Narrowing his eyes, he spat a bloody mess at the ground. The prince scowled, black-gloved hands tightening on his horse's rein.

"Filthy seelie scullion," Erlik dismounted, approaching Riaghán with a slow, dangerous pace. "Where's your queen, leaf-ear?"

"You killed my son, you bastard." Riaghán lowered his head. He murmured, *"Titim gan éirí ort... Mab, cosain mé—"*

to his knees.

Rolling his eyes and tutting in disgust, Erlik sneered at the wounded seelie.

"You think a leaf-ear prayer will save you? You really think she's listening?" Erlik unsheathed his sword. Behind the Prince, Riaghán saw Malik and Corvus glance at one another; these two brothers were just green boys, Riaghán realised. Two hound pups newly unleashed, desperate to prove themselves to their father.

"My sword is newly forged," Erlik continued, pressing its point into Riaghán's throat. "Yet to taste its first blood. You'll have the honour. Unless you tell me where she is. Your queen for your life."

Riaghán remained silent, counting the passing moments in his head. His eyes flickered up and down the blade: he couldn't escape this fate. Gathering what little strength he had left, he staggered to his feet. Erlik took a step back, looking mildly surprised, but amused at this determination.

"To Annwyn with you! Long live Queen Mab!" Riaghán bellowed, thrusting his uninjured arm towards the nearest oak trees. Before he could utter the words to bring them to life, Erlik lunged forward, driving his sword deep into Riaghán's chest.

The seelie gave a choked grunt. Blood sprayed between clenched teeth and over his lips. He fell.

Erlik withdrew his blade and glared at the dead seelie. Malik glanced at Corvus first, then looked at their father with an expression of hope. Erlik snorted.

"Did you expect me to be proud?" he asked his eldest coldly. "*You* let his woman and child escape, then encouraged your brother to lie to me. And Corvus?" The meeker of the brothers quailed. "Don't show your miserable face until you manage to kill at least *one* leaf-ear by yourself. Do you understand?"

The brothers caught one another's eye, faces reddening. Erlik mounted his horse again, pulling the reins. "You're both a disgrace."

He called to the other riders who had been waiting at the clearing's fringe, "Continue the search. I want Mab taken alive and unharmed. And *unspoiled*," he added, menace colouring his voice. "Send word to me as soon as you find the city. Torture every leaf-ear you come across; burn Albion to the ground if that's what it takes. Just find her. *Find her*," he repeated angrily, and pulled his horse away.

Hidden in the foliage, Bram and Thissy trembled at Prince Erlik's wrath. Albion would suffer in a way it had never known. This war was only just beginning.

CHAPTER 2

In which a stag has a narrow escape

B EHIND A PATCH of undergrowth, hidden by his forest-green tunic, Thomas Rhymer pulled his bowstring taut.

Through the trees, a white stag peacefully grazed. The beast gleamed, so cleanly bright it almost glowed in the darkness, velvety antlers bent and twisted like the branches of an ancient tree. Ears twitched. It raised its head, turning towards him, staring with black, doleful eyes.

As he gazed back, Thomas felt his heart beat an uncomfortable staccato against his ribs.

What are you waiting for? Shoot!

But, instead, his hands shook. A bead of sweat rolled down his forehead. Something snapped. He let his arrow fly.

The unharmed creature bounded away, easily avoiding the arrow which, quivering, embedded in a tree trunk.

Thomas stared. He let out the long breath he hadn't realised he'd held, running his now free hand over his face. He couldn't tell; was it relief or fury he felt as the stag escaped?

Pushing his way out of the undergrowth while cursing his indecision, Thomas stormed to the tree to tug his arrow out. Sap bled and slid down the bark like honey.

He'd been hunting for years in these murky forests bordering Ercildoune. Just a *glimpse* of a white stag was a rare occurrence in Caledonia. *I'll never live this down.* He quietly decided he'd keep this sighting to himself.

A childish kick to the tree yielded only a sharp pain in his foot.

Thomas glowered at the tree as though it had done him some personal insult, then turned his back, starting his short trek home, limping on every other step.

Following roughly hewn paths through the trees, he approached a familiar warren of fat, healthy rabbits. As they had dozens of times before, his arrows caught up with them quick enough.

Well, he huffed to himself, tying the catch to his pack, *rabbit for supper. Again.*

Now pleased with himself at having made right his earlier failure, he ploughed on through the bracken until he saw thin wisps of chimney smoke. With a smile, Thomas left the trees' shade, heading up the grassy knoll towards home.

As he drew closer, he saw his younger sister Alissa darning a threadbare tunic in the warm autumn sun, lips pursed, no doubt humming to herself. At his approach she looked up, squinting against the sunlight at her broad-shouldered and square-jawed brother. Despite leaving boyhood behind some years ago, Thomas still bore the fair, wavy hair, pale blue eyes, and crooked smile of his younger days.

Something that made him the sweetheart of girls but the mockery of hempy men.

"Ahh," Alissa said, a cheeky grin spreading across her face. "Our brave knight returns!"

Thomas stopped dead, folding his arms with a sigh, a faint smile twitching the corner of his lips.

"But what's this, Sir Thomas?" Alissa continued, voice exaggerated. She lay down the tunic she had been repairing, and rose to circle him. "No great bounty claimed from your quest?" She nudged him, then playfully clasped a hand over her heart. "I fear our daring champion has failed in his crusade. For shame, Sir Thomas."

"You wound me, Alissa," Thomas gave her a quick smile and continued past, headed for the house. Alissa grinned and watched him go, her hands planted on her hips. The breeze played with her unbraided hair and ruffled her skirt.

"Enough teasing," came another voice from inside the house. "Any luck at all, Thomas?"

Their mother hurried, smiling, into the sunlight. She looked hopefully at Thomas's pack and her shoulders lifted, seeing his modest catch.

"Rabbit again." Despite her words, her voice harboured pride.

"I'll go to town tomorrow—" Thomas began, and at once Alissa appeared at his side.

"May I go with him?" she asked, eyes gleaming. Thomas's shoulders slumped when their mother agreed. Alissa returned to her darning, and Thomas huffed as he entered the house. Margaret followed, unaware – or perhaps ignoring – her children's respective smile and pout.

"Thomas, don't forget it's almost Alissa's name day."

Thomas didn't look at his mother. Instead, he untied the brace of rabbits and laid them out on the table. Margaret's eyes counted them and at last Thomas glanced up.

"I know. That's why I wanted to go into town without her," he replied, trying his grin, but clearly failing to win her over.

"You said you'd already gotten her something," Margaret looked mortified and absently played with the string of prayer beads around her neck, as she always did when she felt uncomfortable. Thomas snorted and shrugged.

"I may have coloured the truth a little, Mother. I know what I'm going to get her, it's just a matter of... *obtaining* it."

Margaret at last gave him a smile.

"You always leave everything to the last hour, just like your father." Twisting the prayer beads, she reached with her free hand to touch a coney's hind leg, then spoke again in a quiet voice. "Fifteen years ago today..."

Thomas's smile slipped. He heaved a sigh and looked away again.

"He said he'd come back with a present for every name day he'd missed," Mother went on. "That wretched war—"

"There never *was* a war," Thomas cut in bitterly. "Father exaggerated. He just left us."

"He loved us, Thomas, you know he did. He had his reasons for leaving, I'm sure, but..." for a moment her words hung in the air. "Well. At least he left us some decent coin. We'd be homeless otherwise." She looked at her son, tensing uncomfortably. "You've been having those nightmares again," she said in a quiet voice.

A disgruntled frown creased Thomas's brow. "It's nothing to concern yourself over," he muttered, turning towards his bed space.

"We can hear you shouting in your sleep," Margaret

said, but he'd already stridden past her. "Thomas, don't ignore me—"

He slammed the thin door behind him.

In the quiet of his own space, Thomas dropped the hunting gear by his door and threw himself down on his bed. He groaned into the down pillow, venting frustration. Emptying his mind of thought, he lay there for a while, and then dragged himself up to finish the rest of his chores while the sun still cast a useful glow above the horizon.

At day's end, Thomas collapsed back into bed, falling asleep the moment his eyes closed.

It was a slumber in which he achieved no rest.

The night terrors were not new. Plagued by them since boyhood, Thomas had often awoken to the sound of his own screams. As he aged, he grew quite accustomed to his dreams, and although they no longer scared him, something about them still unnerved him; some strange, eager yearning.

In these dreams, Thomas saw places he'd never been, yet they seemed as familiar as his own home. Forgotten paths wound through forests he'd never traversed. Misty valleys lay stretched out before him, with cool morning skies blushing pink at the arrival of sunlight.

Yet, every night, as he walked through the woodland, these forests became engulfed in flame. Fire spewed from the maw of a huge black dragon as it stretched its spiked wings skyward. The beast tore through the trees, ripping them up by their roots. And in the valleys, with a roar of its fiery breath, it laid waste to all.

Over the sound of his screams and the crackling heat, Thomas heard others scream for mercy, begging forgiveness from the dragon for unknown crimes.

But this night Thomas dreamt of something new, something that roused greater fear and curiosity.

He stood much taller in this new dream, shoulders broader, blood hot with battle-lust, his arms strong enough to wield a massive sword with a ruby set into its pommel. His steed – a mighty black charger with hooves of finest obsidian glass – stamped and snorted, its eyes gleaming a flaming red.

"*For the queen!*" he heard himself bellow, "*And for Elphame!*"

He charged his steed forward, trampling hordes of soldiers that beset every side, trying to drag him down, realising the young captain would strike a devastating blow to their campaign. Thomas swung his sword in a downward arc, slicing a path of victory for his armies to follow behind.

Ready to announce triumph, Thomas turned his horse. Instead of seeing his cheering army, his eyes found a woman bearing two long, curving swords.

Fear muted all sound. His horse's hot breath steamed in the air. The mount backed up, pawing the ground. Thomas's first thought overpowered him.

Run. You will not survive this.

Her crimson armour gleamed under the wounded sky, the curved swords already dripping blood. Even her ruby-painted smirk masked the hatred behind her eyes, her beauty only a facade.

"*Your father will never take our city!*" he heard himself bellow.

She sneered, "*He already has. Your battle is lost!*"

Thomas woke with a scream, panting, soaked in sweat.

✧   ✧   ✧

NEXT MORNING, THOMAS and Alissa made their way over the hill into Ercildoune: Thomas on Tatterfoal, his faithful gelding, and Alissa on her small grey pony. The warmth of the previous day had melted into a grey, misty morning, another sign of the approaching winter. Thomas wished he'd brought his warmer cloak.

The first bleary-eyed market dwellers were already milling between stalls when the pair arrived. Thomas felt as they looked: exhausted, cold. Far too miserable from his night of restless sleep to enjoy the prospect of wandering around a bleak, damp market.

Only the thought of catching a few stolen words with Úna – a particularly winsome serving maid at the Dancing Kelpie – cheered him.

"Thomas!" Alissa reached over and grabbed her brother's arm. Lost in thoughts of Úna, Thomas started. "Look!"

Thomas squinted. There, where she pointed at the far side of the square, he saw several brightly painted caravans, and silently groaned. *Damn.*

"Can we go over? Please?" Alissa asked, affecting her most innocent smile. Thomas gave her a stony look in reply as he dismounted.

"Please tell me you jest," he said, tying the reins of their mounts to the posts beside the smithy. "It's not like— *Alissa!*"

She'd already jumped off her pony, heading through the market stalls, towards the caravans. Thomas's groan escaped this time, and he followed her, instinctively touching a hand to his coin purse.

Dusky men stood beside the few already-unloaded wagons, full of stormy looks, occupying themselves with chewing on their smoking pipes.

Thomas instinctively inhaled, puffing up his chest with each step. One of the men blew out a mouthful of smoke. Trying to push through to reach Alissa, he walked headfirst into the cloud. His coughing fit and furious glare were met with sniggering.

"Fine, you've seen the caravans, let's go now," he muttered as he reached his sister, who had paused to look around. She tugged her arm out of his grip.

"Not yet, I want to see the fortune teller," she said, standing on her tiptoes to see around the caravans. "I don't see her, can you see?"

Thinking of his God-fearing mother, Thomas said, "A fortune teller? Alissa, Mother will kill you."

Alissa gave him a cheeky smile. "Mother's not here though, is she?"

Thomas cast a longing look back in the direction of their tethered horses, but knew he'd never leave his little sister alone here.

"There she is!" Alissa pointed, and, despite his better judgement, Thomas let her drag him along to a painted caravan, where a tiny old woman sat at a little round table, shuffling a set of well-worn cards.

Eyes alight with glee, Alissa stood before the old woman, watching her lay out her cards.

"Come on, Alissa," Thomas said, coaxing her away. "She's not to be bothered—"

"D'you want to hear yer fortune, lass?" the old woman suddenly asked, voice reedy with age. Thomas blinked when Alissa sat, nodding enthusiastically. Her eyes roved over the gypsy's cards, but the old woman gestured for her hand. Alissa immediately extended it.

Thomas stood by with crossed arms, highly displeased at how this day was unfolding.

The old gypsy stared at Alissa's hand, running her fingers over the palm. Thomas could see Alissa trying to stifle a giggle. *S'blood*, he cursed with a roll of his eyes.

The woman frowned, leaning in for a closer look.

"What's wrong?" Alissa asked.

"Silver Wheel!" the old woman exclaimed. She looked up, taking stock of Thomas, her eyes agleam with whatever she'd seen. "Din't realise you folk came this close."

Frowning, Thomas and Alissa looked at each other. '*You folk?*' Alissa mouthed.

"I'm sorry?" Alissa managed at last to say. Unsteadily, the crone released her hand and stood.

"Get yourselves back whence you came!" She waved her arm, angrily shooing Alissa away from her table.

A low growl escaped Thomas. "Beg pardon?" He stepped forward, one hand alighting on Alissa's shoulder. Three heavily built men appeared from behind the wagon, and Thomas's resolve wilted. "Come, Alissa," he said sullenly. His sister nodded in miserable agreement as she dropped a silver coin onto the table in payment.

"Keep that poisoned coin, pixiekin!" the woman shouted, snatching it up to throw back. Alissa flinched when the coin hit its mark.

The men gathered around the crone, jeering. Thomas stood taller, holding his head high, but the men seemed to take his action as a threat. With flexing fists, they muttered black words and approached.

It took all Thomas had to shield Alissa from the clods of thrown mud as they ran from the caravans.

The pair skidded to a halt once they'd fled out of range.

Both stood doubled over, panting.

Thomas wheezed. He sniffed and stood upright, trying to catch his breath. "Told you... we shouldn't have... gone over..."

Alissa rewarded his smugness with a filthy glare.

SOMEWHERE AROUND MIDDAY, sun replaced drizzle and burnt away the cool mist. More people appeared in the market, taking advantage of the better weather. With Tatterfoal's saddlebag heavier now, Thomas and Alissa untied their horses, mounted, and headed back home.

"I'm sorry you didn't get to see Úna," Alissa mumbled. Thomas said nothing in return.

They'd reached an unspoken promise, it seemed, to not mention the encounter with the crone to their mother. Alissa greeted her with a falsely cheerful grin when they arrived home. Thomas rolled his eyes, but Margaret said nothing about it. *Let her think we've argued.*

Once inside, he hid the skein of silk he'd discreetly bartered for, for Alissa's name day, beneath his bed space. Thomas sat on his bed for longer than necessary, thinking about the gypsy crone.

'Get yourselves back whence yeh came', echoed as he got to his feet. *That old witch, the nerve of her!* Her words circled, unwanted, in his mind as he worked outside for the rest of the day.

Alissa must have noticed his bad mood, because it was only when he stopped to mop his brow that she bothered him to ask if he was hungry.

At day's end, his back aching, his hands sore, Thomas kicked off his boots and rolled into bed.

Maybe tomorrow night, he mused as his last thought, *I'll go for a drink at The Dancing Kelpie and see Úna.*

He rolled onto his back, thinking of the way her eyes lit up whenever he visited her. Eyes closing, he grinned at his last thought before sleep – stealing a few hours at the inn with such a bonny young woman.

✧   ✧   ✧

THE FIRST DREAM sensation came from the deluge of rain, sharp and cold on his face. His dream-self stood on a cobbled street, coughing as pungent smoke cloyed his nostrils and stung his eyes.

Frantic civilians ran in all directions, screaming while half-armoured soldiers defended them as best they could from the legion of invaders.

Thomas's eyes were drawn to the city gates. Mounted on black horses, each accompanied by a score of black hounds, the invading army rode hard into the city, slaughtering screaming people as they tried to flee past them.

The defending army hurled lances and shot arrows, but any weapon that struck true met nothing but ashes.

Ahead of this horror, men and women fled the rampaging army, calling for sanctuary at a great white castle in their city's midst. Rain lashed the citadel. A slash of lightning across the velvet sky preceded a snarl of thunder.

"Nathair! We will not submit!"

Thomas spun around. A few steps from him, a radiant woman stood proud with her bejewelled hand forward, palm outward. A conjured shield of violet shadows protected her from the vicious attack of a single opponent.

Sneering, the dark-haired man opposite her fired bolts

of magic from a black stave carved into a dragon's likeness. The woman never flinched, protected by her magical shield, her moonmilk face twisted into a furious countenance.

Her opponent laughed, his voice echoing eerily in Thomas's mind. *"Afraid of me, vixen?"*

Thomas blinked vigorously through the rain, shaking his head to keep his drenched hair out of his eyes. Eagerness to watch this battle overwhelmed him, even as his heart pounded in his throat.

"Enough of your games, Erlik!" The woman gestured with an easy, measured grace born of furiosity. A bolt of bright magic fired from her palm, striking the man, *Erlik*, in the chest, encasing him in a solid block of ice.

"Mab!" A cry for help on the ashy wind.

Both she and Thomas turned. The white city was ablaze. The castle overrun, dark riders swarming the streets, with more rushing over the black moors like a great wave. Thomas looked back at her. Firelight danced on Mab's face, her eyes wide and her lips thin. Her fingers curled into fists.

Her city was lost.

Thomas looked back at her. Her fathomless eyes fell from the burning castle onto him, glittering like moonlight on ice. *"Come home."*

Despite the raging din of battle around him, Thomas could hear her voice clear in his ear. So close, so real, he felt his mouth fall open.

Swallowing hard, he called, *"Who are you?"* But in the clamour of battle his voice was lost. *"Who are you!"*

Her attention had already left him.

She'd barely begun the journey back towards her crippled castle when, with a scream of rage and pain, Erlik's frozen prison shattered. Panting, he pitched forwards. A bolt of vivid red magic, thrust from his staff, struck Mab, wrapping around her like crimson snakes. The spell trapped her arms. She cried out and tumbled to her knees.

As though the last blow had sapped it of magic, Erlik's black staff gave a violent shudder and shattered. He stared at his empty hand for a moment, eyes wide and mouth open. Yet his face broke into a smirk when he saw Mab kneeling, struggling against her bonds.

To Thomas's horror, Erlik sped to his captive, silent as a phantom, pulling her to her feet, wrapping his lean arms about her. Wickedly grinning, he pressed his sharp-boned cheek against hers.

"It's all mine now," he sneered.

Thomas's growl sounded only to him. A bright flare forced him to shield his eyes. When he straightened again, instead of seeing that storm-sodden city, his eyes beheld Alissa and Mother's bed space.

Both slept peacefully despite Margaret's quiet snoring.

Wondering how he'd silently found his way in there, Thomas crept towards the thin cloth curtain that separated their bed from the kitchen.

And then he saw it: a shadow moving across the floor. Formless, no bigger than a mousing cat, the smoky beast ignored him.

With horrid fascination, Thomas watched the creature make its way towards Alissa, slithering up her blankets in deadly precision to the head of the bed. Thomas's feet had taken root; his throat closed.

The shadow, now bent over Alissa's face, paused. Thomas at once regained feeling in his legs. He lunged to swat the creature away, but his arm passed through shadow. Only a black cloud dislodged, evaporating gracefully into mist.

It leered as it leaned further forward. Rows of needle-teeth gleamed in the moonlight. It kissed Alissa's cheek, then pressed close to her skin. Black shadows seeped into her flesh. Alissa moaned in her sleep. Margaret twitched.

Thomas cast about quickly, his eyes seeking a weapon, *any* weapon. An iron poker lay by the banked remains of the fire. He seized it, thrusting it like a sword into the shadow, only inches from his sister's brow. It screeched above her, a hideous noise pitched between a cat's wail and a babe's scream.

It leapt off the bed, skittering up the wall to the window. Paused to turn, shrieking a warning. Shadows bled from the inflicted wound.

Thomas knelt by Alissa's bedside. The hefty clang of the poker hitting the floor did nothing. She hadn't woken; neither had Mother. Thomas looked up, but the window no longer framed the creature.

Lightning lit the forest outside. Thomas could swear he heard the baying of hounds and a wild, screeching whinny of horses. A rumble shook the house, and with the clap of thunder Thomas's eyes snapped wide open.

CHAPTER 3

In which Thomas invokes the Old Ways

S HEETS TWISTED AROUND his clammy body. Finally untangling himself, Thomas swung his legs over the side of his bed and sat, frowning and running a hand through messy hair. Hearing his mother rattle about in the kitchen, he dragged himself to his feet.

Outside, their cockerel boasted his cry. Thomas bade his mother a brief good morning before sluggishly heading outside to splash cold water in his face. The sharp shock fully roused him from his sleepy daze.

Pushing wet hair from his eyes, he glanced across their little field before returning inside.

Margaret smiled at him, sliding a bowl of sweetened porridge onto the table. He returned the expression and sat down to eat. A comfortable silence lingered over the room.

"I need to fix the scarecrow today," Thomas noted, cheeks bulging with porridge.

Handing him a cloth to wipe his face, Margaret fondly said, "I'll wake Alissa. She can help you after she's eaten."

She lifted the curtain of their bed space. At the table, Thomas absently turned his spoon over and over in his hand, trying to remember the echoes of his dream.

"Thomas! *Quickly!*"

Jolted from his mental task, Thomas almost upended the table in his scramble to his feet. He ripped aside the thin cloth, expecting torrents of blood, a ghastly scene, or some hideous creature.

Instead, Alissa lay peacefully sleeping, her breathing slow and deep. Margaret knelt by her bedside with wide eyes, her hands twisting around themselves, her mouth working wordlessly.

Thomas glanced instinctively at the grate where the iron poker lay, untouched.

"She won't wake!" Margaret gingerly touched Alissa's cheek, then drew back as if burned. "She's ice cold! Why won't she wake? Alissa? *Alissa!*"

His sister didn't even twitch at her mother's loud voice.

His heart thumping hard, Thomas reeled back, throwing out his arm to grab the doorframe. The walls twisted around him.

Taking charge, he forced words past the fear in his throat. "Mother, stay here. I'll fetch the physician."

THE SUN HAD risen high into the sky when Ambrose finally rumbled to their door in his well-travelled cart. Thomas gently coaxed Margaret out of the way, allowing the physician to take the place at Alissa's bedside.

His weeping mother continued to mutter and furiously shuffle her prayer beads as Thomas wrapped his arm around her short, shivering frame.

Ambrose pressed his gnarled fingers against Alissa's wrist, presumably feeling for a heartbeat. The physician gently lifted one eyelid with his left thumb, waved the opposite hand in front of it. Alissa didn't stir. Ambrose studied further: the breath under her nose, the flutter at her throat, the flesh beneath her arms and around her neck. He even pressed the beds of her fingernails. Thomas stared. *What good is this?* At last, Ambrose straightened, sighing.

"She appears to be simply sleeping," his shoulders slumped. "I can find no ailment; she shows no signs of pox or plague." A glance at their hearth, a sniff of the air, thick with the stench of burnt rosemary. "Sweet-root tea might liven her a little. Just a couple of drops to her lips should do the trick. The only other thing I can suggest is to watch her, keep her comfortable. Wait until it passes."

Thomas nodded mutely. His mother fell to her knees beside Alissa's bed, grasping her daughter's hand again, abandoning her rosary.

Ambrose shuffled out after a sympathetic pat on Margaret's arm. Thomas accompanied him in a desperate attempt to escape his mother's weeping.

"I'll have some lavender sent along for your mother," Ambrose said. "It'll help calm her nerves."

Her nerves? Thomas pinched the bridge of his nose.

Clambering onto his cart with a groan of old age, Ambrose paused before taking up the reins. "You know, Thomas," he said, faltering. "You should ask Ceridwen."

Thomas watched him trundle away, his mouth suddenly dry.

Ceridwen Wintersend.

He shivered. Thinking about the old Pagan's secret knowledge made his heart race. A follower of the Old Ways, and a worshipper of their ancient gods. Ambrose had spoken once of finding Ceridwen returning from the darkest parts of the forest with a satchel stuffed with herbs and toadstools. Not even Thomas dared venture where Ceridwen walked with ease.

Thomas chewed his lip.

Knowing his mother's disdain and distrust of Ceridwen's knowledge, he stowed thoughts of her away. Mother would never allow the heathen woman into their house. Not even for Alissa's sake.

THOMAS COUNTED THE passing days on his mother's retrieved rosary. The lavender Ambrose sent did nothing to ease Margaret. She barely slept, nor would she take food; Thomas had to coax her into swallowing mouthfuls of bread crusts softened in small bowls of thin broth.

Exhausted from the extra chores he now tended to, since his mother never left Alissa's bedside, Thomas barely noticed the days growing shorter as winter began to settle in.

AN ENTIRE MONTH crawled by with no change. Like the dead, Alissa slept on. Without her cheeky laughter and playful jokes, the house felt empty. *Eerie and silent.* Thomas sat at her bedside whenever he could, reading to her.

He always made sure Mother wasn't listening before allowing his sobs to escape.

Ambrose's suggestion still fluttered around his ears like a moth. Could Ceridwen really help? Perhaps he should speak to his mother—

No, his rarely-heard reason advised, *she'd never allow it.*

A strained silence had laced their conversations since Alissa had fallen ill. Margaret was more likely to scream or burst into tears at any moment. Were Thomas to suggest inviting a Pagan into their homestead, Thomas imagined her heart would give out there and then.

CREEPING COLD CHILLED the village air. Ercildoune slumbered as dawn broke into the blushing sky.

A hen clucked loudly. Thomas, having escaped his mother's dour sobbing, stood outdoors brushing Tatterfoal with absent thoughts. Skin bristling with gooseflesh, he pulled his cloak closer under his chin.

Suddenly catching sight of a small black fox skulking near the coop, he dropped the iron currycomb at once, grabbing a close-by broom and chasing the fox away with its bristles before it could spook the hens. Tatterfoal snorted at the interruption. The fox, pausing at a safe distance, growled at him before moodily slinking away.

At its movement, something lost in memory burst into recovery.

A shadow. *A creature*. In Alissa's room. *Kissing her*.

His heart leapt into his throat. Thomas threw a long stare at the cottage door, the breeze raising his hair and sending a fresh morning chill across his skin.

As if a whip had lashed across his legs, he bridled his horse and rode to Ceridwen's cottage.

THOMAS KNOCKED THRICE on the Pagan's door, having almost injured himself in his haste to jump up onto her raised threshold; the whole cottage was up on stilts.

No answer.

He banged again. An irritable shout issued from within, "Steady your horse, boy, I'm not as swift as I used to be."

Ceridwen cracked the door and peered between the gap to glare at Thomas impatiently tapping on her doorframe, causing her carved latch to tremble. Thomas saw only a sliver of her silver hair, falling half across a curious brown eye.

"Ceridwen—" He got no further. The old woman opened the door fully. Thomas felt the rush of unexpected heat to his face a moment before he beheld a crackling fire behind her, and a dead crow on her worktop.

"Took your time, didn't you?" she snapped, her voice a peculiar dancing lilt. A Waelisc accent. *Not a Caledonian*, Thomas noted, his ear catching the inflection. "Wondered when I'd hear something. A whole month and not a word? By the Smith, boy, what use are you? Quick now." She turned her back, took the pot off the fire and extinguished the flames with a pail of water set beside it for that purpose.

Thomas watched, half fascinated, half impatient, as she gathered together a collection of bottles and pouches. Ceridwen patted her apron absentmindedly.

"Where did I..." she trailed off, casting a glance about her tiny kitchen. One withered finger touched the crow. A rustle of feathers. An ugly caw. The crow righted itself and stood up, cackling. It fluttered to the mantle and pecked at a bowl with its sharp, clever beak.

"Ah, there it is. Good boy."

Giving the crow an affectionate stroke, she tipped the contents of the bowl expertly into a bottle and slipped it into her leather satchel.

Smoothing out her apron, hoisting the satchel over her shoulder, she turned back to Thomas. He gaped stupidly at her.

"Close your mouth, boy," she snapped, pushing past him with a cluck of her tongue, waiting by his horse, "you're not a trout."

Thomas scowled, grabbing Tatterfoal's reins, as

Ceridwen clambered up behind his saddle.

With a protesting snort at the extra bulk from Tatterfoal, they made their way back to Thomas's home.

Their journey back was short and uncomfortable. Ceridwen kept a tight hold around Thomas's waist, and the smell of her sour breath choked him.

Crossing the bridge towards home, he asked, "Did you know I was coming, Ceridwen?"

The old woman stayed silent for a moment; the motion of the horse seemed close to unseating her. Thomas tugged Tatterfoal's rein, slowing her down.

"I expected you sooner, actually," she said eventually. "I would have thought the Hunt would bring you straight to me. Rode right past my cottage, dirty great beasts, made such a racket. Upset the goat and everything."

The Hunt? Beasts? Thomas resisted the urge to stop the horse and ask her to explain.

"I expect Ambrose dropped my name, did he? Daft old man doesn't know which end of a teapot to hold, but at least he knows who can help when it matters."

Thomas sensed the pride in her voice. He rode on, his head already aching.

THE MOMENT THEY arrived, Ceridwen slid from Tatterfoal's rump as easily as Alissa ever did, entering the house without invitation. Thomas quickly tethered his horse and followed behind, wringing his hands.

Thomas felt like he was intruding on something shameful when he pushed Alissa's curtain aside, seeing Margaret with one hand pressed to her forehead. Her shoulders shook. *Holding Alissa's hand again. As if that alone would wake her.*

At the sound of Thomas's footsteps, she twisted around; her eyes, red and sore from lack of sleep and endless sobbing, drifted towards Ceridwen. Margaret gasped. For a moment, Thomas feared she'd shout, throw anything at hand, order the old woman out. Margaret's trembling hand lifted her rosary and thrust it forward. Weak, it dropped, beads clattering against stone. Thomas's mouth almost dropped open as she willingly moved aside.

"Please wake her," she croaked. A captive animal. Ceridwen nodded.

"I'll do what I can, Margaret. You and Thomas should wait in the other room so I can look her over properly."

Margaret left with a teary hiccough, saying nothing more. Thomas glanced once at Alissa before Ceridwen obscured her frame as she leaned over her. Thomas shuffled out after his mother.

As though waiting for the hangman, the two sat in silence at the table. Thomas half expected an angry outburst from his mother, but she seemed too tired for words.

Instead, her fingers crept across the table and threaded into his. A gesture of thanks, perhaps?

"Did you finish your chores?" Margaret's voice was stretched thin. Weak. Thomas nodded.

"And Alissa's. And yours."

Margaret gave him a watery smile. "You're such a good boy, Thomas." She paused. Then, quietly, "Maybe she *can* help."

Finally, the curtain shifted. Thomas and Margaret leapt to their feet. Shaking her head, Ceridwen stepped into the larger part of the room.

With a sigh, she said, "just as I suspected. It's a changeling."

Thomas and Margaret looked blankly at each other. Ceridwen, with a disdainful sniff, gently pushed past mother and son. "Come, I'll show you. We need to go to the Standing Stones before darkness settles in."

✧   ✧   ✧

THE SUN HAD sunk into the horizon, burning the sky orange and gold. Despite Margaret's desperate wail at the suggestion they leave Alissa alone, the pair had followed Ceridwen to a steep hill past the borders of Ercildoune. Loud, hearty singing rang from the Dancing Kelpie. Thomas's thoughts turned to Úna. *She'll be dancing now,* he thought morosely.

Thomas reached the top first. Ceridwen struggled behind, up the steep hill. Margaret, wearily, came last. Thomas looked around, catching his breath as he waited for his mother and Ceridwen to wheeze up behind him.

Casting the longest of shadows, a circle of enormous stones awaited the trio. A gathering of stone giants. Thomas risked a touch of one of the stones. Warm. Tingling. *Alive?*

"To Annwyn with whoever insisted this circle be at the top of a hill," Ceridwen muttered to herself, appearing over the crest.

A pyramid of kindling sat waiting in the circle's centre, magnificent enough for a king's pyre. Posies lay scattered around the base of the wood.

"S'blood, what is this place?" Margaret blurted, her shoulders hunched, her arms wrapped tightly around herself. Thomas could see her fingers trembling.

"I need to ask her help," Ceridwen said, moving around the wood, striking flint at intervals against the bonfire.

Thomas watched her, silently counting. Seven times she scratched the flint, blowing into the wood. The glowing sparks bit and blossomed, devouring the dried leaves and bracken. Margaret pursed her lips.

"You're not... don't you dare!" she said angrily, "I won't be part of this—this *blasphemy!*"

She stepped back and only Thomas grabbing her arm prevented her from falling down the hill.

The bonfire flared into life. "You think I want to do this?" Ceridwen said. "She's temperamental, I know. But this is the only way I can think to wake Alissa. She's the only one who can help, Margaret. If she ever deigns to leave Albion, mind..." she added.

Shuffling widdershins around the blaze, Ceridwen threw posies onto the fire. The flowers and herbs ignited instantly to ash, sending curling waves of scented smoke spiralling into the air.

"Albion?" Recognition wriggled in Thomas's chest.

Ceridwen smiled mysteriously. "The land beyond the bridge, where Alissa will be."

Thomas looked between his mother and this unnatural woman, his brow creased, silently praying someone would explain in terms he'd recognise.

"I need to speak to Queen Mab. Risky lighting the fire, but—ahh, there we go."

The bonfire's flames blazed a brilliant white, searing into Thomas's eyes.

His heart pulsed in his throat. The flames leapt higher. Despite their warmth, Thomas felt a chill prickle his skin.

Queen Mab.

Her name aroused fear, desire, excitement inside him. *I know that name.*

Thunder growled. Under the iron sky, heaving in the throes of a sudden storm, Thomas looked up and shuddered. The hairs on his arms bristled. Some mad voice inside him demanded he leap into the flames.

A bolt of lightning struck the stone behind him. Thomas jumped away; the rock split in half with a deafening crack. The menhir fell forward.

Margaret screamed, instinct lifting her arms.

Thomas grabbed a handful of his mother's cloak, dragging her out of the way. The boulder slammed into the earth close enough to crush her shadow. Clouds of dust befogged their vision, choking them. Coughing, Thomas blinked the dust from his vision.

A small glow – an insect? – sat calmly on the stone's jagged edge.

A tiny female body took form, glowing with unearthly light. Margaret stepped back, gasping, away from the two pearlescent wings, gleaming like oil on water, fluttering on the tiny faery's shoulders. Thomas stared.

With dismal disappointment, he said, *"That's* Queen Mab?"

Pouting, the creature fluttered towards Thomas and sharply nipped his cheek.

"OW!" he swatted the creature away, scowling. She dodged his clumsy swipe with a nimble flutter of her colourful wings, then childishly poked out her tongue.

"No," Ceridwen sighed. "She's a faery. A seelie. I must have cast the wrong summoning spell." Her voice held a self-berating tone. "Come, we'll talk back at your house."

Ceridwen stepped away from the bonfire with a glance up at the sky. Margaret, suspiciously eyeing the faery, darkly muttered under her breath. Thomas caught the word 'blasphemy' again. Deciding to remain silent, he followed Ceridwen back down the hill, Margaret bringing up the rear. It appeared she wanted to keep her distance from the faery.

Ceridwen beckoned the faery closer. "It's not safe out in the open with a seelie at night."

CHAPTER 4

In which Thomas embarks on his journey

I N SILENCE, THOMAS and his mother sat at the table, watching Ceridwen. She'd assembled a seven-pointed star out of wildflowers and lit the wicks of two half-melted candles. To Margaret's obvious chagrin, the flames burned pure white. Just like the fire had earlier, on the hill.

Sitting cross-legged on the table, the seelie looked curiously around the room, humming a soft, merry tune to herself. Thomas couldn't direct his gaze to anywhere but her. A womanly figurine, subtle curves muted by the glow cast by her pearly wings, a soft gossamer gown hugging her small body. She could easily perch in the palm of Thomas's hand.

Ceridwen closed the window shutters. "What's your name, sweetling?"

Wings twitching, the faery clambered to her feet. Margaret sat in silence with wide, unblinking eyes. Eager for answers, Thomas sat up a little straighter. His skin still prickled, despite the room's warmth.

In a voice far more human than Thomas had expected, she answered, "Thistledown, of Elphame," her eyes on Margaret. "You were trying to summon Queen Mab?"

"Yes, we need to ask her help. A young girl has been

taken." Ceridwen sat down at the head of the table. "Replaced with a changeling."

Margaret stiffened, blanching at having her business so casually spoken of.

Thistledown shuddered. Lifting herself up into the air, her wings fluttered so fast they became a blur of light.

"Oh. That won't be easy. Queen Mab is in hiding. She won't respond to any call or summon." With a shy smile she offered, "I can help, though, as best I can."

Ceridwen nodded, looking to Thomas and Margaret, who stared blankly back. Beaming proudly, Thistledown turned in midair to gaze at Thomas.

"Tell them about changelings first, Thistldown." Ceridwen set both elbows on the rough table. "The luckless souls ought to know."

Thistledown lowered herself again and paced back and forth before her questioner. Thomas noticed she often gestured with her tiny hands when she spoke. He couldn't resist smiling.

"Well," she paused and drew in a breath. She seemed to be steeling herself. "Changelings are left behind in place of mortal bodies when the unseelie take them. Under a cloak of shadows, an unseelie will kiss a human – it's more of a bite, really. They have a kind of poison that draws the Host. That—that's when *they* come…" she trailed off, shivering.

She ran her tongue over her lips, then gulped and continued, "They come in the night, you know, to steal the mortal away. Then they leave a changeling, a wooden doll, and give it breath, but not life, in place of a mortal's body—"

"Oh, Alissa…" Margaret moaned, eyes filling up. She buried her face in her hands. Meanwhile, trembling, Thistledown stared at Thomas.

With a hundred questions tumbling through his mind, only the shortest fell from Thomas's mouth. "What's the Host?"

Thistledown shuddered again. She said nothing.

Ceridwen took over, "The Host, the Wild Hunt, surely you've heard..." she cast a quick frown at Margaret, then muttered something about the *new religion*. "They're huntsmen, the souls of dead men, accompanied by a thousand black hounds, snatching any who get in their way."

His head pounding too hard to think, Thomas ran his tongue over dry lips, staring between Thistledown and Ceridwen. Faded visions flooded his mind: a swarm of dead men on horseback.

"Do they have a leader? Or a king?" he pressed. Ceridwen frowned.

"I'm not sure. I suppose he who governs the unseelie would also control the Hunt. Prince Erlik."

Thistledown's glow dimmed. She shivered again, wrapping her arms around her tiny body.

"*Shh*, he'll hear you," she breathed. Thomas regarded her with concern. Ceridwen was too busy staring suspiciously at Thomas to notice the faery's discomfort. Margaret, who'd been sobbing uncontrollably into her arms, lifted her head, wiping her eyes with the back of her hand.

"Why do you ask?" Ceridwen narrowed her eyes slightly.

Feebly, he explained what he could remember of his dream.

"And there was a woman too, fighting a dark man," he finished. "Some kind of sorcerer, I think. I'm sorry, I can hardly remember. Except that he said, *everything is mine now*."

Ceridwen exchanged glances with Thistledown. Her fast-beating wings fanning Thomas's face, the faery lifted herself up and fluttered in front of him.

"In the war between the seelie and the unseelie," Thistledown said, gesticulating again. "Queen Mab was deposed by—by the Dark Prince. Elphame, our city, was taken over." She addressed Thomas directly now, "Our queen managed to escape, but no one has seen her since; we don't know where she is now. We live in hope that one day she'll return to her throne and drive out the Dark Prince."

Another chill creeping up his arms, Thomas once more heard hounds baying and horses screaming, echoing in his mind. He gulped. The room fell silent for a long time, broken eventually by Margaret's restrained gulping sob.

"S-so is Alissa… one of those—those *demons*?"

Thistledown shook her head at Margaret.

"No, no," she corrected, "Huntsmen are created by the souls of *men*. Mortal women he keeps in the castle at Elphame. She'll still be alive, I can promise you that."

"Then, h-how do we bring her back?" Silence again. Ceridwen fixed her eyes on Thomas, who stared at Thistledown. She gazed back, fidgeting with her fingers, throwing him shy smiles.

"I'll go get her. Thistledown can show me the way."

Ceridwen barely blinked in surprise. Margaret, however, sharply stood.

"You will *not*!" she snapped, furiously wiping away her tears, a palm flat on the table.

"Mother—"

Margaret banged her fist now. "*No*, Thomas! What if something happens? How can we trust this… this *creature*?"

Thistledown pouted, folding her arms. "That's not—"

"I forbid you," Mother continued, her breathing heavy. Thomas glared. "I've lost Alissa, I'm not losing you as well."

"I'm not a child, Mother. I'm going to get Alissa back. You *do* want her back, don't you?"

"You *dare*!? Of course I want her—"

"—then let me go!"

The silence rang. Thomas's hands shook. Mother and son glared; Margaret wilted first. She sat, staring at her hands without properly seeing them.

Thistledown looked awkwardly between both, her trembling wings betraying fright. Ceridwen took a deep breath. She laid a hand on Margaret's shoulder.

"This is the only way to save Alissa, Margaret. I'll stay here awhile, if you like? For company?"

Margaret mouthed wordlessly at her offer, momentarily horrified that a Pagan woman should offer to live with her. Her pride withered. She nodded.

Thomas held out a hand flat for Thistledown. She jumped onto his palm with a little flutter of her wings.

"Will you help me?" he asked, in a voice as soft as her beating wings.

Though her eyes looked nervous, Thistledown smiled. "Of course."

Thomas let her down onto the table and stood. He strode to his room to collect his half-blunt sword. Silently cursing himself for not maintaining the old blade, fastening the buckles of his belt, he headed for the door.

"If you think you can just wander into Albion with no equipment, you'll be dead before you even cross the bridge," Ceridwen barked, tugging his right arm. A stern grandmotherly look in her eyes, she muttered mostly to herself. "Blockheaded *twpsyn*. No food, no weapons…"

Thomas raised an eyebrow, looking down at his sword blankly. Ceridwen took the iron poker from out the hearth and handed it to him.

"Cold iron burns Fair Folk. Take your sword, if you think you need it, but this will help more."

Ceridwen disappeared into the pantry, pulling a leather pouch from her apron, and re-emerged with a clay salt bowl.

Pouring salt into the pouch, she spoke slowly, clearly incanting, "Be *very* careful how you use these. Salt and cold iron harms *all* Fair Folk," a sly glance to her left, "including seelie."

She glanced at Thistledown, who was curiously inspecting the star of flowers like a silver bumblebee. Looking over at the faery, Thomas nodded.

"You're ready now," Ceridwen clucked, raising her voice so Margaret could hear. "Be careful. Listen to Thistledown. And remember, cold iron and salt are your best weapons. Soon as you find Alissa, bring her home. And whatever you do, if you have to enter Elphame, be wary of the Dark Prince."

Thomas nodded, impatient to be on his way. But Ceridwen stared soberly at him. "I mean it, Thomas. Erlik is no stranger to death and chaos. The very mountains fear his wrath."

Margaret's ragged breathing announced her presence. She'd wrapped a thick, woollen cloak around Thomas, fastening it with a horseshoe-shaped clasp. Her cheeks wet, her eyes red and sore. "This'll keep you warm," she said thickly.

She threw her arms around him. Thomas returned her

embrace, willing her to have courage… and faith in him.

"Be careful, my son," she whimpered into his shoulder. "Keep safe. Bring Alissa home."

Thomas gently pushed her away. "I will, I swear."

He pushed open the door, Thistledown following, the moonlight casting the forest in silver.

"Thomas," Ceridwen called just before he vanished into the trees. He glanced over his shoulder to find her eyes boring into him with infinite determination.

"The promises of faeries are fleeting. When you are in Albion, nothing will be as it seems. You must expect the unexpected, and prepare for what is not there."

Thomas nodded, turning his back on the house.

CHAPTER 5

In which Thomas meets Epona

NIGHT MELTED SMOOTHLY into day. With aching legs, Thomas envied the way Thistledown easily flitted between branch and leaf. A misty drizzle cooled his face, so he did nothing to shield himself from the refreshing rain.

Confident in his stride, the pair followed a wide path that Thomas had often traversed when hunting. Until Thistledown stopped in mid-air, pointing. Thomas brought a shaky hand to his forehead and took uncertain, almost drunken, steps.

Hidden by neither foliage nor dimness, as obvious as the sun above, somehow Thomas had never noticed this particular trail before. This path had *always* been straight. If Thistledown hadn't pointed it out, Thomas might have walked past it. As if his eyes didn't want to see. Or his mind didn't want to know it was there. This left fork snaked, twisting into greater darkness with each step.

Thistledown flew closer to Thomas.

Leaves shivered and whispered. Trees grew bent and writhen, like woody crones, plunging back into earth again to form unnatural archways. Unnerved, Thomas slowed. Certain he could see dark shapes skulking between shadows, he spoke up tentatively: "How far is it, Thistledown?" He didn't want her thinking him afraid, so clearing his throat, he quickly added, "I'm worried for Alissa; she's never been so far from home."

Thistledown flew to Thomas to affectionately nip his cheek.

"We've a long way to go. We're not even in Albion yet," she said in his ear. Her soft, melodious voice sent shivers across Thomas's flesh. "By the by, you can call me Thissy. Everyone does."

Pushing through brambles and bracken, they trekked deeper into the wild wood. Thorny bushes snagged Thomas's clothes, scratching his arms, warning him he was unwelcome, their stings suggesting he turn around and never return. Only thoughts of Alissa, alone and afraid in Albion, forced him on.

Then, Thomas heard something jarringly out of place in a dark and cold forest: *laughter*. Mirth strong and clear through the thicket. Thissy tugged a lock of Thomas's hair and pointed his gaze into darkness.

Smoke curled through trees. A flickering light dragged Thomas's attention to a fire's welcome warmth.

A tantalising smell of roasting meat hit their nostrils. Exchanging looks, Thomas and Thissy crept towards light and scents. They drew nearer, trying their hardest to stay quiet. Thomas crouched behind a bush, silently moving leaves aside, and peered through.

A fire crackled high, licking the carcass of a wild pig. People – only men, it seemed – sat, laughing and feasting, as a troupe of musicians played a fiddle, flute and drum. The music pressed on Thomas, compelling his heart to race.

He tore his eyes away and looked at Thissy instead. She glowed pale at the sight.

"Who are they?" he whispered.

She hissed back, "Pagan warlocks. They wander between your world and ours. Oath-breakers, outcasts." Her wings beat faster. "We should leave."

"But what if they know how to find—?"

"Ho there!"

Thomas froze. Clumping boots ended in three pairs of hands grasping and grabbing, dragging Thomas to his feet, out of the bushes. The musician trio immediately stopped with a grating twang. All fell silent. The warlocks threw Thomas into their circle.

"Nosy little thick-skin," one sneered as Thomas righted himself again. Thissy had disappeared. Thomas didn't want to call for her, and assumed she'd hidden out of sight. His hand tensed above the pommel of his sword.

A rustling in the trees behind startled Thomas. Then another, further away. Yet another, on the other side of the fire. Thomas's eyes darted between the shaking leaves.

"You brought friends, thick-skin?" one of the warlocks sneered, throwing a casual glance to the shifting trees.

"Careful, Murchadh," another one warned. Murchadh pulled an ugly face, then nodded to his companion. The other warlock cautiously approached the rustling tree. He thrust his hand between branches. A shrill squeal sounded. His hand re-emerged, Thissy struggling in his tightening fist. Thomas withheld his gasp.

An unsettling pause.

Murchadh burst into snorting laughter and thrust a tankard of frothy amber ale into Thomas's hands.

"Well, there's something you don't see every day. Calm yourself, lad." The warlock's face split into a warm smile as he took a seat on a tree stump. "We welcome all sorts here.

Even the likes of you, little mistress."

The other warlock let Thissy go immediately. She furiously fluttered around his head for a few moments before darting away.

Seeming determined to impress, the musicians picked up their song again. Faster and louder than before, safe in the knowledge there were no more intruders stalking the wood. The other warlocks carried on as if Thomas hadn't interrupted.

Flexing his hands, unsure of how to behave, Thomas sat on a rough tree stump and drank deeply. The ale was cool, crisp, and very welcome to his weary body.

The warlock beside him – Murchadh – slapped his knee to the fast tune on the fiddle. He wiped his hand on his filthy breeches. His shirt was no better, splattered with mud and grease from roasting boar. Leaves tangled his long brown hair.

"What's your name, boy?" Murchadh demanded over his ale tankard, his voice gravelly with an Ériu accent. He swayed drunkenly on his own stump. Thomas gritted his teeth. *That word*, he thought, a muscle twitching in his jaw.

"Thomas Rhymer," he said, drawing himself up. "I'm looking for my sister—"

Murchadh let out a roaring laugh and heavily clapped Thomas on his back. It was all Thomas could do not to fall forwards; he weakly smiled.

"You're not about to find her here, thick-skin. Just me little band of traitors here..." Murchadh lowered his voice, leaning closer. "Heed, though: you need help in this forest, just give us a shout. Me name's Murchadh, but you probably caught that already. Sharp lad."

He clapped Thomas's shoulder again and stood up to

get himself another skinful. Thissy appeared behind Thomas's shoulder like a firefly.

He whispered, "What does thick-skin mean?"

"It means mortal-blooded, but leave that. We can't stay, Thomas. We must go."

"I know, but… wait here, they might be able to help," he muttered, standing up and ignoring her disapproving moan. Manoeuvring through laughing warlocks and hissing pig-flesh he shouted over their clamour.

"Murchadh, I need to ask you—" Thomas pushed through a trio to reach him.

Offering him another tankard of ale, Murchadh beamed "Aye, lad, ask away." Thomas politely accepted the tankard, but refused to bring it to his lips. *Need to keep my wits in this place.*

"Murchadh, I need to reach Elphame, do you know—" he got no further. Murchadh grabbed Thomas's collar, pushing him roughly against a tree. The tankard dropped, splashing ale over their boots.

As though Thomas had blown out a candle, Murchadh's smile vanished. All heads turned towards him. Each thorny warlock glared as though Thomas were something particularly unwelcome.

"You listen here, boy," Murchadh growled, menacing, suddenly sober. "You turn tail and get yourself back home. Before you get caught up in something you don't understand."

Thomas's eyes narrowed.

"I'm not leaving," he said through clenched teeth, "I came to find my sister."

Warlocks closed in. Thissy hid herself behind branches.

"Forget about your sister, thick-skin," Murchadh said.

"If the Dark Prince stole her, you won't get her back. Go home, boy."

A sickening surge of fury rose unbidden in Thomas's chest, blinding him.

His sword in his hand before he even realised, he pointed its blade at Murchadh.

Each warlock doubled over with laughter.

"Think your useless steel scares us?" Murchadh snorted, a dagger clenched suddenly in his fist. He lunged.

Compelled by instinct, Thomas dodged. Ducking sideways in time to evade Murchadh's thrust, Thomas brought down his blade.

His sword bit deep, slicing across Murchadh's shoulders.

He was felled, yet as he groaned on all fours, the flesh knitted. The wound instantly healed. Murchadh gained his feet again, unharmed and smug.

Thomas stared. His face grew hot when Murchadh and his band of warlocks laughed still harder and colder, not at all like their former jovial, drunken selves.

A shrill whisper rang in his ear. Thissy, appearing like a candle moth at his shoulder, nipped his cheek.

"Cold iron, *amadán!*"

Resisting the urge to smack his forehead in frustration, he sheathed his sword and instead drew the iron poker. He realised its weight at once, his arms already starting to ache.

At last, the warlocks adopted wary looks to a man.

A little breathless, Thomas quickly demanded, "Tell me where Elphame is."

Murchadh exchanged uneasy looks with his band. Thomas noticed them eyeing the iron poker.

"We don't know, lad," Murchadh said. His eyes darted to the pure, cold iron. "Nobody knows where that city is anymore. Not unless the Hunt takes you."

"Aye," another spoke out from the fire's far side. "It's the truth."

Gritting his teeth at their patronising words, Thomas probed, "What about the unseelie? Can an unseelie lead us there?"

"If you can find one, aye. But no one leaves Elphame; the Dark Prince forbids it. Lower that thing, will you, lad?" he added, "Before someone gets hurt."

Thomas scowled. "He doesn't scare me, and he won't stop me bringing Alissa home," His iron poker sheathed, Thomas chose a subtler weapon. "As far as I'm concerned, if you're not going to help me, you're as bad as Erlik."

Each warlock hissed at the name, quickly glancing around, as though expecting the prince to appear. Thomas ignored their discomfort.

Without another word, Thomas left the glade, every warlock anxiously staring after him. Thissy, flitting around his head, stayed silent.

Thomas crashed angrily through undergrowth, caring naught for the noise he made, when he heard someone call his name. His hand flying to his sword automatically, he spun around. Murchadh led a white horse by its reins towards them, an apologetic look on his face.

"Listen here, boy—Thomas, because I'm only going to tell you this once. I shouldn't really be telling you at all, but..."

He trailed off. Thomas awkwardly shrugged. Murchadh sighed and, glancing over his shoulder, continued.

"Take Epona, she's an elvish horse, she is. She'll always find you if trouble comes your way. Follow that trail," Murchadh pointed to a dirt track, "it'll lead you to a meadow. Keep going until you reach wilderness. Head for the mountains. I don't know for certain if that's where Elphame is, but it's usually where the Hunt comes from at night. Might as well start there."

CHAPTER 6

In which Thomas Rhymer crosses a bridge

R AIN GREW HEAVIER, a distinct growl thundered overhead. Dark clouds blotted out fading sunlight, the forest's deepness turning day into night. A cool, natural scent of wet earth filled Thomas's nostrils.

Epona tugged against Thomas's pull on her reins; perhaps she wasn't used to him. Perhaps she was merely guiding his hand. Her pearly hooves made no sound on fallen leaves, and her mane shone molten silver against her snow-white coat.

Mounted, Thomas recognized a tiny flickering light in the gathering darkness. Thissy must be ahead, inspecting the path, he thought, and called her name. She darted through the branches, alighting on Epona's bobbing head.

"Stay close, Thissy, I don't want to lose you," he said as Epona tugged left. Thomas let her guide. She obviously knew the way better than he.

Darkness seemed ready to swallow them. Rain dripped out of his hair, under his shirt, sending a chill down his back. He shivered. Epona softly snorted in protest.

Lightning flashed, followed swiftly by a groan of thunder, nearer this time. Thomas's heart vibrated with the sky-quake's closeness. Thissy trembled beneath his dripping hair, below his ear, her wings brushing against his neck, tickling.

At last, the forest began to thin. The sound of gushing water grew louder until it filled Thomas' ears. He ducked beneath a low-hanging branch and walked straight into a spider's wed. He winced at the sensation and flailed to break the silk. When he opened his eyes, he found himself at a stone bridge.

Thissy flitted toward it, her glow pulsing brighter. Thomas dismounted.

"This is it!" Thissy squealed. "The bridge!"

Thomas braved a look into the deep darkness of the chasm on the bridge's left flank, but jumped back almost at once, his head swimming: he couldn't see the ravine bottom. It was as though the bridge connected two floating islands. Thomas wondered where the waterfall he plainly heard might lie.

A flash in the sky, brighter than any lightning. Thissy paused halfway across the bridge. Her glow brightening to a blindingly white light.

"Thissy? *Thissy!*" His voice full of panic, shielding his eyes, her aura became unbearable to behold.

Darkness again. Thomas blinked to rid his sight of dancing pink spots. He cast his gaze upwards, looking for Thissy. His jaw dropped.

She now stood only a head shorter than him. The weak sunlight burst in her flaxen hair, lighting some of the strands into pure spun gold. Thomas couldn't stop staring, nor could he close his mouth. Her lips trembled into a smile, nervous, shy. Her pale pink gown, bound with lilac ribbon around her waist, accented the soft curves of a fully formed woman.

"How—" His throat felt seized. He couldn't form his sentence. Yet Thissy seemed to understand. She let out a giggle, sounding like twinkling silver bells.

"We've crossed the bridge into Albion now," she smiled. Her voice was soft, musical almost. Thomas's skin prickled. "It's nice to take on my proper form, I was starting to—what are you staring at?"

"You're beautiful," Thomas blurted. He then flushed a fantastic shade of crimson. Thissy blushed too.

She glanced at the ground, speaking again modestly, "All seelie are beautiful, Thomas. They say our queen is fairer than all the world's flowers."

Queen? Queen Mab? Thomas suspected hers was the blurred female face of his faded dreams. He severely doubted she could be more beautiful than Thissy, nor did he care to seek her out and discover. Thissy filled his eyes.

Swallowing hard, he walked towards her, crossing the bridge. He offered to help her up onto Epona, but she politely refused.

"The forest will grow too thick for us to ride," she said. "Best we just let her walk behind us."

They carried on, Epona following, leaving the stone bridge behind. As Thissy had predicted, the forest thickened again once the river had been crossed. Trees pressed in around them. Too busy staring at Thissy, Thomas tripped on roots more often than he should have.

Thunder shook the sky again. After the last rumble died away, Thomas could have sworn he heard something out of place; he glanced back to check Epona, who seemed quite unfazed. Some other noise lurked behind thunderous growls. He strained his ears, listening hard. Rumbles rolled over the sky.

There it is again, Thomas thought. *That noise.*

Barely distinguishable underneath the growls, Thomas heard singing. Haunting, mournful voices sent shivers across Thomas's skin, chilling his heart. Coldness filled him until his hair stood on end. Then his eyes focused upwards and ahead, and he drew in a sharp gasp.

High above, white shapes swam with fluid grace between pale grey sky and dark cloud. What Thomas had first thought wings he now saw were actually robes, flowing like fins. Radiant, they glowed, luminescent streaks of shaped light soaring above the trees.

His voice shook, "Thissy?" She stopped and looked over her shoulder, her eyebrows raised in polite confusion. "What are they? Up there?"

Thissy looked up. She licked her lips nervously.

"Come," she said quietly. "We can't linger too long. Night will set in soon; we should keep moving while we still can."

Morbidly entranced, Thomas stared at them, until Thissy gently tugged at his hand. The spirits flitted away like startled fish in a river. He listened hard again for their singing, but none came. They'd vanished. With a sigh, he lowered his head and walked on.

THE RAIN LESSENED. A thick fog began creeping through the trees like wood smoke. It seemed to Thomas that this wood was never ending. The trail that Murchadh had pointed out still snaked through the forest, but without any sign of the meadows he mentioned.

Looking up at the sky, he said, "You never told me what those creatures are."

Thissy exhaled softly.

"Ghosts," she breathed. "Ghosts of elves. They're trapped in Annwyn, in the Sea Without Shore, unable to rest... cursed by their own sorrow. They can never be at peace."

Thomas swallowed hard. He regretted mentioning them. Their comfortable silence had dissolved with the question.

As they entered a clearing, Thissy looked around, "We can rest here tonight. It's too dark for us to continue."

Thomas tied Epona's reins to a tree branch. He started collecting sticks and kindling, bemoaning the fact everything was so sodden after the rain.

Thissy patted Epona's nose. "I've never met an Elvish horse before." Thomas set his armful down in the clearing. Epona snorted, tossing her head. "You must have come far."

"You know how far I've come," Thomas sat down, futilely rubbing two damp sticks together.

Approaching, Thissy chuckled as she sat beside him, "I wasn't talking to you, twit."

Leaning over at once, she nudged it all into an untidy stack. Whispered into the kindling a single word. It began smoking. A spark ignited in the sticks. A crackling white fire soon threw out waves of warmth. Thomas sat back, staring, his mouth slightly open, as she fed branches to the flames.

"Was that magic?" he murmured. Thissy nodded, smiling.

"Simple sparks like this are easy, but I never wanted to learn combative magic. I'm much better versed in healing – I prefer helping people to hurting them."

"Can you teach me?"

"Not many mortals would ask," she said with a giggle. "Most men fear magic. Why would you want to learn?"

His voice grew soft, "So I can protect my family." He twisted his hands. "My mother and Alissa are all I have. I don't want to…"

Smiling, Thissy took his hand. "It's a noble reason, *a chara*." Thissy sat back, looking pensive. "The ability to cast magic doesn't mean we can always protect those we love, you know." Thomas looked up at that, a slight frown knitting his brow.

Thissy took a deep breath, looking up at the sky, "I was just a girl when I lost my father. He died trying to protect me and my mother… she followed him to the House of the Old Gods not long after."

"I'm sorry," Thomas whispered. Seeing Thissy nodding, blinking away tears. "I lost my father too. He said he was leaving to fight in a war, and… well, he never came back."

Thissy gave his hand a gentle squeeze. Thomas returned her watery smile.

"Do you still want to learn magic?" her voice remained hushed. "It's a difficult craft—for a man."

"What do you mean?"

"Well, magic is a woman's domain," she said, gesturing to the fire. "The Heart of Magic is a woman, you see. Men can learn it, but to master it takes years of practice and *enormous* amounts of skill and strength. Women can use magic freely, without physical consequence, because all women have an inherent skill." Thomas creased his brow, already confused. Thissy continued, "But men, you poor things, you have to train. Magic drains you of energy. With every spell you cast, you become weaker until you can barely stand. I think that's why most men prefer to use weapons… still, I can teach you, if you like?" she added sweetly. Thomas laughed, shaking his head.

"You've convinced me otherwise, my thanks," he told her. She smiled, affectionately caressing his hand. Her touch sent a rousing thrill through him. He shifted, suddenly uncomfortable.

The pair sat in silence awhile longer, listening to the quiet crackling fire. Sounds echoed around them. An owl hooted somewhere above. Thissy prodded their dying fire with a branch. Sparks floated upward, dancing and twirling into the air. Neither had forgotten the tantalising scent of roasted meat. When his stomach growled, Thomas cursed himself for not requesting some of it from the warlocks.

"We should go to bed," he decided after a while, trying to ignore his hunger pangs.

Blinking, speechless, Thissy scanned the clearing, her cheeks pink. She anxiously fiddled with her fingertips.

"Oh! I-I'll just—" she didn't finish, but stood up to check Epona's tied reins. Thomas felt his cheeks grow warm. Suddenly realising what he'd said. *Oh no.*

"No! No, I-I meant—I meant we should sleep. Yes, I… I'll sleep over here," he mumbled.

With a shy glance over her shoulder, Thissy tightened Epona's reins on the branch. She nodded, blushing furiously, and gave him a slight smile.

"I know what you meant," she said quietly.

Shifting back, Thomas lay beneath a shelter of trees, their branches and leaves forming a canopy over his head. Thissy curled up in the hollowed tree just beside him, a small concave formed by twisting roots, falling asleep almost immediately.

Thomas leaned back, his eyes roving across those dark clouds for a sign of ghostly elves. But there was nothing. With a sigh, he dropped his gaze. His eyes caught sight of a mark on a tree at the far side of the clearing. Glancing toward Thissy to make sure he didn't disturb her, he stood up to investigate.

It was a carving on the tree trunk, a heart engraved into its bark. It looked immensely old. Thomas ran his hand over the symbol, marvelling at how it had endured. How it gleamed pale under the dying firelight. Even after those who carved it were probably long since dead. He allowed himself a small smile. Backing away, he returned to his makeshift bed. Lying down, leaning against the trunk of a tree, he sighed once. He closed his eyes, hoping sleep would quickly envelop him.

LIKE TINY CRYSTALS, morning dew clung to the undergrowth. The scent of dawn freshness filled the air, cool crisp tendrils of morning creeping through dappled green light around Epona's hooves.

A droplet of rainwater slid from a leaf above, dripping into Thomas's face. He twitched as it splashed on the bridge of his nose. Eyes blinking open, his chest rose with his first deep breath. Thankfully, his hair and clothes had dried somewhat while he'd slept.

Thomas sat up, wiping water from his eyes, as Thissy stirred in her tree root hollow. As quietly as possible, he stood, stretching. Stomach rumbling louder, he cursed his lack of forethought. *Good luck trying to find food here,* he berated himself. *What about Thissy? What do faeries eat, anyway?*

Thomas gazed at her slumbering form, admiring the dappled sunlight falling across skin which looked softer than satin. He had to repress an urge to caress her cheek. Just to see how soft—

A rustle in the bushes. A sharp yet quiet gasp. Intruder. *Danger*.

Startled, he spun to face the source.

His hand on the iron poker, tentatively approaching the bushes, he stretched out to shift them aside.

Hiding herself amongst bracken, a girl no older than Alissa crouched, staring up at Thomas. Wide, round, black eyes, a smattering of russet freckles covering her small nose. Her matted hair, a warm brown colour, looked damp. Her fearful gaze lingered on him for a few seconds.

"Who—" Thomas got no further.

Thundering hooves echoed around him. Thissy jolted awake.

"Thomas?"

With a terrible wail, a sound no normal beast would utter, rearing and plunging with awesome majesty, six black horses burst through the trees behind Thomas. He spun, catching a glimpse of their riders before diving aside, narrowly avoiding being trampled by iron-grey hooves.

Thomas scrambled back to his feet, time enough to witness the riders give chase to the girl, now fleeing for her life into the deepness of the forest.

"*What* are you doing?" Thissy exclaimed. No time to answer; grabbing her hand, Thomas ran to Epona, quickly untying her and throwing Thissy up into the saddle.

Epona gave a protesting snort when they mounted, but yielded to Thomas's tug on her reins. Kicking her hindquarters, they galloped, following the sounds of cracking branches and thundering hooves.

The forest rushed past, woodland becoming a blur of

green. Only the noises ahead gave any indication of the riders and their quarry.

"There!" Thissy pointed into the dimness at a small, scrambling figure. Snorting horses struggled, frustrated, to get through the thickening trees.

Thissy held onto him, her arms tightly locked about his waist, her face buried between his shoulder blades. The horses ahead screamed and whinnied as their riders drove them ruthlessly on.

They pelted through the forest. Branches snatched at Thomas. Epona leapt over a gushing stream, crashing through bracken, leaving a trail of woodland destruction behind her.

Faster!

The gap between the black and white horses shrank. Epona raced neck and neck with a huntsman. Thomas glanced at the rider. His face was hidden behind a black mask. A foul stench of decay, reaching even from such a distance, emanated from him. His horse snorted, a forbidding beast bridled with tarnished silver strapping and rusted chains. Thissy gasped loudly. There was no time to ask why.

Their horses, now galloping side by side, leapt over a fallen log. Both riders slipped. Thomas held on and leant forwards.

"Faster!" he desperately urged. Thomas could see the girl, her bare-footed frame leaping over foliage and ducking under low branches, beneath vines and spider webs. The riders whipped their screaming horses mercilessly. Epona galloped faster than all; swifter than any horse Thomas had ever ridden. Thissy squealed as a branch sliced her cheek. But there was no time to stop.

Ahead, the girl had trapped herself. Surrounded on all sides by woodland debris and fallen trees, she skittered between trees, desperately seeking an escape.

"Thissy, we need—" the thunderous hooves almost drowned his words, but Thissy understood. Glancing over her shoulder, she muttered some ancient word and made a clumsy gesture.

A burst of heat behind them was all the indication Thomas needed. He slowed Epona enough to grab the girl's outstretched hand, and pulled her up to sit with him.

Thomas risked a glance behind. The riders had managed to evade the quickly dwindling flames.

"*Go!*" Thomas kicked Epona's flank and she snorted, racing off again.

The trees ahead thinned. *If we can make it out of the forest...*

Epona snorted, struggling, protesting. Thomas could understand why: she now carried three.

They burst out of the forest into clear air. Thomas grinning, Epona protested against his grip harder than ever. At last, he saw what distressed her.

The sudden ending of the dense forest had a simple enough reason. No trees could grow at such a sheer cliff edge.

Much too late, Thomas pulled hard on Epona's reins. *No use.* The horse and her riders plummeted off the cliff face.

A wondrous sensation: soaring weightless through air. Then the quartet hit the cold, clear water.

Floundering, Thomas struggled to reach fresh air again. Saltwater stung his eyes. Without thinking, he opened his mouth to shout for help. Immediately swallowed a mouthful of briny water. Kicking fruitlessly at the murkiness around him, he sank lower into those unnatural depths, dragged down by steel and iron.

A white hand wrapped around his wrist. Thissy soared through the water as easily as if it were air, pulling him with her. Thomas burst into fresh air, dragging in a hoarse breath.

The riders!

Thomas twisted, treading water and looking up at the cliff edge. Nothing. No riders, no horses. *Safe.*

In silence, Thomas, Thissy and the girl swam for a crescent beach. They crawled out of the surf, collapsing on the far sand. Epona snorted and wetly pawed the malleable ground.

Thissy pulled herself to her feet, muttering darkly in her native tongue, dripping with seawater. She shook herself vigorously. In a blink, as though she hadn't even touched water, she was dry as stone. Throwing a fierce glare at Thomas, she rushed over to comfort Epona.

Thomas lay on his back with the girl beside him, both panting like dogs.

Allowing light and warmth to dry them off, Thomas exhaled heavily, then started to laugh. The girl turned her head to stare at him for a moment, then joined in. Even Thissy gave a reluctant chuckle. Eventually, still smiling, the girl raised herself up on her elbows.

Turning to Thomas, she said, "Silver Wheel bless you, stranger. I owe you my life."

"Think naught of it," he said, waving a hand, still a little breathless. "You should return home before those riders find you again."

Thomas coughed loudly to clear the last of the briny water from his throat, then stood, brushing sand off his breeches. Squinting in the sunlight, Thomas started when his gaze suddenly filled with a mass of brown curls.

"Can I come with you?" she bluntly asked, standing much too close for his comfort.

Thomas staggered back, blinking. "I—what?"

"Can I come with you?"

"No."

"Why not?"

"Because… because—"

"You can't just leave me here!"

Thomas glanced over his shoulder at Thissy, seeking help. She clicked her tongue awkwardly, shrugging. Thomas's brow creased.

"I… I don't even know you," he said, staring at this strange girl as if she were mad. *Perhaps she is*, he suddenly realised. "Just go home."

Thissy made an impatient noise behind him. Thomas turned his back on the girl.

"I don't have a home," she said, trailing behind him like a lost pup. "Can I come with you?"

Thomas heaved a sigh, not stopping his stride across the sands. "For the final time, *no*."

She opened her mouth and breathed silence. Her shoulders slumped.

Thissy took Epona's reins, guiding her away, walking behind Thomas without a word. Dragging her hooves in the sand, Epona trudged along, tossing her head.

"Please," came the girl's quiet voice. He paused. "I don't have anywhere to go."

Thomas stopped dead. He turned. Groaned at the back of his throat at the sight of her pleading eyes.

"Very well," he said, resigned. "You can come with us.

However," he added, because her eyes had lit up, mouth opening to speak, "I'm going to Elphame. My sister has been taken; I'm going to get her back."

A fraction of hesitation. The girl nodded. Thomas couldn't help but notice her round eyes widen slightly. She seemed to be talking herself into something.

"Oh…" Another pause. "Well. Yes, I still want to come with you," she said. "I might be able to help."

"Hmph." Thomas nodded reluctantly.

As they made their way up the beach, "My name is Meri, by the way. Meri Strand."

Thomas looked down at her. She threw him a shy smile. The sunlight glimmered in her wet hair.

"I'm Thomas," he replied, finally cracking and smiling back at her. "Thomas Rhymer."

CHAPTER 7

In which a crow meets an unfortunate end

A BLEAK MOOR lay quiet, a huge mountain overshadowing the rocky hills around it. Weak sunlight cast over the dreary landscape. Feathers shimmering blue-green, a solitary crow flew overhead, fluttering to rest at the mountain's roots. It skittered about on bare earth, morosely pecking hard ground. Casting its sparkling eyes towards nearby rustling, the crow cocked its head. It hopped towards the noise... and disappeared *downwards*.

A low growl. A screech. A throaty giggle.

Something under the earth crunched loudly on the unfortunate bird. Only a few floating black feathers remained above ground.

BELOW THAT PLAIN, in a glittering underground cavern, a tall woman swept up an empty, cobbled street. A corset bound her red tunic tight and two curved swords hung on her belt.

With no hint of smile about her ruby-painted lips, she wound her way through dark, empty streets of the vast city until at last she found herself at a courtyard's guarded gates.

"You heard Abarta got loose again?" one guard

muttered to his companion, not seeing the red mistress approach.

"So long as it stays away from here, it can—"

"Enough," the woman snapped. Her face, hard and cruel, carried a powerful, overbearing expression. "Let me pass."

The guards turned ghost-white. "My lady!"

Both bowing deeply, they stood aside and allowed her immediate passage, before exchanging nervous glances and closing the gates behind her.

The woman ascended the stone steps at the far end of the courtyard. An enormous pair of white beech doors, inlaid with gold, awaited her – as did another pair of guards.

With a curt nod, the guards pushed open the doors. Smirking, the red mistress entered the hall. True, this chamber was impressive, but she had grown bored of its splendour.

Women lounged half-naked over expensive silk cushions around the hall, the once grand chamber reduced to little more than a whorehouse.

The woman in red took no notice of their crooning and giggling. Instead, she strode up the carpet towards a dais, ascending steps to an occupied white marble throne. Uneasy silence fell over the hall.

Erlik reclined idly on the throne with a girl in thin gossamer in his lap, her arms draped around his shoulders. He groaned, rolling his eyes, when the red woman approached, kneeling before him.

"I'm busy, Kali," he smirked, looking still at the girl in his lap, brushing hair away from her face. "Bother someone else."

Rising to her feet, Kali intoned, "This is important,

Father. Someone has left Elphame without permission."

Despite her domineering expression, her voice shook.

Erlik sighed. "I assume from the seelie district?" Still not looking at Kali, he cast his gaze over his plaything. She slid from his lap to the floor beside his throne, absent-mindedly starting to peel red fruit into a silver bowl. "Who escaped?"

"You don't know their names—" Kali sullenly began. Erlik let out a short, sharp, mirthless laugh.

"Don't pretend you care for them," he said. Kali took an instinctive step back. *"Which one?"*

"A—a selkie slave, from the castle," Kali hesitated, then spoke in lower tones. As if hoping he wouldn't hear. "We believe she… knew something about the oubliette."

Erlik's shadowy eyes snapped up to Kali, his features stormy. The girl peeling fruit paused, her hands trembling. She dared a cautious glance up at her lord.

Erlik took a deep breath. "I see…" He stood, stepping down from his throne. Kali flinched but didn't retreat. "And you thought she posed no threat? Just another selkie, another seabitch. Nothing to worry over."

Kali scowled hard, revealing the same frown lines as him. "Father—"

"Surely there would be no danger of her seeking out seelie colonies that have *somehow* escaped your ever-watchful eyes?"

"Father, I—"

"She couldn't possibly have information that could *help* them?"

"But Father, I just—"

"Explain to me how this never crossed your small, dull-witted mind." Erlik folded his arms, a hairsbreadth away from his daughter. The atmosphere crackled. Kali's fists shook by her sides.

"Explain," Erlik breathed. *"Now!"*

"I—I sent six men after—"

"Six?" Erlik snorted with derision and resumed his place on his throne. "A pitiful display. I'm losing faith in you fast, dear Kali. Maybe I should appoint your twin brother captain instead."

A sly smirk played at the corner of his thin lips. Kali gave an irksome twitch, her eyes flashing with hate. Her questioned authority burned her insides with conceited fury.

She spoke now with the bite of annoyance in her voice, "Monstrance's peace-loving filth would drive your soldiers to madness. If you truly think me incompetent, you must know I sent six *Huntsmen*. She still escaped. They said she was helped."

"I don't care, Kali," Erlik said, running a hand through his hair. "Find her, eliminate the problem."

Erlik reclined in his throne, looking pensively around the hall for a change of subject. "Where's your sister?"

Kali sighed. "Morrigan is where you left her. Guarding that leaf-eared canker-blossom *whore* in the—"

Erlik thrust his arm forward, his fingers viciously grasping, squeezing thin air. Gasping, staggering back, Kali choked for breath.

"Unless you want your head on a pike," Erlik venomously spat, his lip curling with loathing, "I suggest you never speak ill of her again."

He tightened his hold. Kali collapsed to her knees, her fingers scrabbling desperately at the air around her throat. Erlik tipped his head back, looking contemptuously down on her.

"Just like your whore of a mother," he said softly. "She

never knew when to keep her mouth shut either. Always such a disappointment. Like you. And your gutless brother."

"F-Father... p-please..."

With an unpleasant smirk, Erlik relinquished his grip. Kali drew in a deep, rattling breath, coughing for air. He paused while she seethed in silence, throwing him an insolent yet wary glare.

"Who was it?" he asked.

Massaging her bruised throat, she croaked, "What?"

Erlik sighed and rolled his eyes.

"Who rescued the selkie-wench, idiot child?" he asked with slow menace.

"A-a man—a boy, they said. Riding one of the elvish horses." She paused. "They tell me he rode over a cliff. There's a good chance they're dead."

Erlik snorted again, "Hmph. That means nothing. Take twenty men this time. If they're not dead, and your *good chance* is only your own stupidity, bring them both back to Elphame. To *me*."

Kali, nodding, stood and bowed, feeling every eye on her. Erlik held out his hand as she turned to leave.

"Kali, little one," every syllable threatening malice, "I don't care that you're my daughter. If you fail again, punishment will be swift and severe. Do you understand?"

Hate burned like witchfire in her throat. Hate of her father, her brother, every filthy leaf-ear, all of them.

Filled with resentment, Kali threw him another sullen nod before departing.

CHAPTER 8

In which Thomas and Meri are kidnapped

"WE TRIED EVERYTHING to wake Alissa," Thomas explained, holding out his hand, helping the two women over sharp shoreline rocks. "Nothing worked. I ended up going to Ceridwen, this batty old Pagan woman in our village. She helped, though. That's when I met Thissy."

Epona had difficulty finding her footing across rocks treacherous with slimy seaweed. Waves lashed seashore like wild laughter, the briny smell filling Thomas's nostrils. Taking in a deep breath, he stopped, and scouted the coast.

"Murchadh said to follow the trail out of the forest. Then head towards the mountains. I'm not seeing any mountains."

Frustration at how far off course he'd taken them by rescuing Meri took hold of him. The girl now stood watching waves lap at her toes, giggling.

"I suppose it would have helped if you'd followed the trail," Thissy said, trying hard to keep an accusatory tone from her voice. "Those mountains could be anywhere."

"I think we're lost, Thissy," Thomas mumbled.

"Take heart, *a chara*. We'll get there." She turned away to continue up the beach.

Thomas gazed after her, unable to stop his eyes drifting

to her swaying hips.

With an awkward clearing of his throat, he turned back to Meri. Arms out, giggling, she still stood in the waves, letting ocean spray flicker across her freckled face.

"Come, Meri," he called. "We'll keep going this way for now."

Black eyes sparkling, Meri turned her head to him. She happily danced over a few rock pools, making her way back to them so they could continue on again together.

ON THE HORIZON, a storm made its way inland. Thomas had a nasty feeling it would hit them sooner than he'd have liked.

"So," Thomas announced after a while, making a great effort to keep his eyes off Thissy. "Why were those men hunting you, Meri?"

She faltered, uncomfortably kicked sand, and picked up her pace. Thomas stared.

"Meri?"

Finally, in a would-be casual voice, she shrugged and said, "No reason."

Keeping her head down, she shuffled on faster again. Thomas snorted in disbelief and caught up with her.

Thomas smiled, "So they saw you and decided you'd make a good throw rug?"

"Arianrhod's Curse, that's *not* funny," she snapped. Thomas's smile slipped from his face. He stopped abruptly and laid his hand on her arm, making her pause mid-stride. She blinked, looking down as though surprised by his touch.

"I'm sorry, Meri," he said. "I wasn't thinking. Who were they?"

When she raised her black eyes to stare at him, he

noticed fear behind her gaze.

"Huntsmen," she said. Thissy flinched. Thomas glanced at her; she shook her head, gesturing for Meri to continue.

"I'm a selkie," she went on. "We've been slaves of the unseelie for centuries. Ever since the Dark Prince came to power, I think. Maybe even before that, back when his brother..." she paused. "The Dark Prince takes our sealskins and burns them, so we can never return to the ocean. And he... brands us..." she hesitated, then shifted aside the neckline of her tattered homespun tunic.

On her shoulder, just above her heart, an ugly red scar burnt into her flesh: a seven-pointed star. Thomas drew in a sharp breath, staring rudely at her brand. Thissy backtracked to take Meri's hand. A small comfort, but a welcome one, by Meri's softening features.

"Some escape, like me," she whispered. "Most are recaptured. Punished. You can't even imagine..." she trailed off again, shuddering, brushing away wetness from her cheek. Thomas watched her, sheer empathetic despair etched on his face.

Frowning, Thissy spoke up. "You're worrying him, Meri." She looked warmly at Thomas. "Fret not, Thomas. Alissa will be well when we find her."

Thomas gulped. Weakly nodding, he wetted his lips.

Yet more silence passed between them. An easy silence. Comfortable. Amicable.

"So..." Thomas addressed Meri, trying to keep his voice steady, "if you escaped Elphame, does that mean you... you know where it is? You could lead us?"

Meri and Thissy exchanged glances.

"I'm sorry, Thomas, I can't." Meri shook her head. "The Dark Prince cast a powerful spell over Elphame, making it impossible to find again to any who leave. Unless an unseelie leads you there. Or you get captured by the Hunt, which is… unpleasant."

Thomas huffed. A small wave of hope had erupted in him, now ebbing away with the tide behind them. He glanced around once more.

"Then we shouldn't delay; come."

HEAVING GROANS RATTLED the air. Shielding themselves against the salty wind, the trio marched on until Meri stopped dead, looking behind. When Thomas realised the young girl had paused, a surge of annoyance welled up inside him.

"I told you we shouldn't delay. What is it?"

In Epona's saddle, Thissy turned and looked back at the pair.

"Run," Meri whispered. She lunged across the sand towards Epona, grabbing her reins to mount behind Thissy.

"Thomas, run!"

Squinting, Thomas saw the air thicken, wavering like rising heat. A troupe of riders astride enormous, screeching birds appeared at the far side of the beach.

Bigger than horses, the birds' feathers gleamed black under dim grey light. Their faces were those of gaunt old women, snarling, screaming in fury; their talons cruel, crooked and sharp.

"Brinewing harpies, Thomas, *come on!*" Thissy shrieked, helping Meri mount up behind her. Tripping over sand, Thomas raced back to them, hurdling onto Epona's rear.

"Go! Go now!" he bellowed.

Thissy dug her heels into the horse's flank. Epona's hooves threw sand up into the air as they galloped away.

Epona may have been one of the fastest, strongest horses in Albion, with elvish blood pulsing through her veins. But she carried three. Even *she* would tire before long.

Harpy wings cleaved the air, whipped into frenzy by their riders' fierce urging. Their pursuers were close now, close enough to be heard shouting, jeering in foreign tongues.

With a great rush of wings, a harpy slammed into the sand before them. Rearing up with a scream of fear, Epona threw her riders to the ground. The harpy tossed her head, shrieking a ghastly noise, somewhere between a raven screeching and a woman crying.

Thomas grabbed Meri's hand, pulling her nearer. Huntsmen? No, these men looked wilder. Criminal. *Outlaws*.

Epona snorted in panic. Thissy scrambled over to stop her from bolting, but the horse seemed too frantic to calm.

Meri swore under her breath as the rider jumped from his screeching mount, landing easily before them. "Well now. What do we have here?" He smirked.

Thomas attempted to stand, his feet slipping clumsily in the wet sand. Laughing, the rider pointed his curved sword at Thomas's chest.

The other men dismounted, one pointing his sword at Meri. Another dragged Epona away. Yet another kept a tight grasp on Thissy's arm.

"Horse meat for supper, boys!" the one holding Epona said. "No more cockles and coalfish for us!"

Still with his sword pointed at Thomas, he laughed. "So, boy. Enjoying your little stroll across *our* shore?"

With a low growl, Meri regained her footing, ignoring the blade pointed at her chest.

"Black breath on you, you worm-ridden bottom-feeders!" she shouted. Snarling, her captor lunched forward and dragged her upright, holding the sword to her throat.

"Still that tongue, harridan," he said, a vice-like grip on her arm. Only Thissy remained silent, her wary eyes fixed on Thomas. He stared back at her, his heart thudding somewhere near his throat.

With a skilful flick, the outlaw shifted his blade up from Thomas's chest, the sharp point under his chin.

"Your seabitch has got real fire in her," he said, leering. "But what about you, boy? You got yourself a spirited tongue to match hers?"

Leaning forward, he hoisted Thomas by his shirt to his feet.

"Shall we find out?" With a nasty smile, he pressed his sword against Thomas's cheek, dragging it agonisingly slowly, slicing his flesh.

Thomas gritted his teeth, grunting in pain. *Don't scream. Don't give them the amusement.* The shallow wound stung, nettle-like, in the salty air.

The riders bellowed with laughter.

Thomas broke free from his tormentor's grip with sudden fury.

Their laughter stopped at once. One still holding Meri hostage, another grasping Thissy, the others lunged at him.

Thomas drew his own sword, iron poker forgotten, thrusting at the first rider that came at him. Anger rather than skill guided his hand, and the sand beneath his feet was unsteady; he slipped often, leaving himself open to clumsy mistakes.

Mcri sprung like a coiled snake, elbowing her captor hard in the face. As he staggered away, clutching his bleeding nose, she seized his sword from where it had dropped, leaping to Thomas's aid.

"Enough!"

Foolishly, Thomas and Meri paused, eyes darting towards the angry bellow.

Thissy.

The last rider had his dagger drawn, pressing into her throat.

Thomas took a furious step. The rider jabbed at Thissy's throat. She sucked in a sharp breath. Thomas stopped at once. *Why hasn't she used her magic?* He glanced at her hands and saw them flexing, then he realised. *The few sparks she could conjure would only enrage him.*

The rider sneered, "Drop your sword, else I'll cut your whore's neck."

Despite rage burning in his belly, Thomas immediately obeyed. The rider gestured at Meri, who reluctantly lowered her stolen sword, scowling.

"You're a troublesome one, boy."

A blinding pain on the back of his head. Someone shouted his name. The world went black.

CHAPTER 9

In which Thomas meets Blackspot Bonney

I N WARMTH AND comfort, Thomas felt pleased knowing he was home; in his own bed, a bowl of hot porridge waiting, his mother bustling in their kitchen, his sister outside feeding chickens. Adventure stories were for children. He'd never even heard of Albion or Erlik or Mab—

Cold water drenched him. He awoke with a start, coughing, spluttering.

Bellowing laughter made Thomas's already aching head pound harder. He groaned, opening his eyes, blinking sleep from his vision.

Harpy riders jeered at him. Meri was strapped behind him, her back pressed against his. His wrists felt raw from where they'd been chafed by the coarse rope they were bound with.

"Are you hurt?" Meri asked.

"No. Are you?"

Meri shook her head. Scanning the area, he found himself in a stable. Epona was nowhere to be found. His heart plummeted.

Thomas twisted his hands within his bonds.

"No use," Meri said, and he stopped squirming. "I've already tried."

Thomas barely listened. With a dreadful rush of terror, his heart dropped like a stone in water.

Trying to keep his voice steady, he asked, "Where's Thissy?"

"They left her behind; no human would dare hurt a seelie. I don't think they even knew who she—"

"Still that wagging tongue," a voice snapped. "Before I cut it out."

Thomas clenched his jaw.

"Let us go," he said through his teeth. His captors laughed.

One – Thomas immediately recognised him from the beach – leaned forwards. His face was scarred like an old map, his teeth just as yellow.

"We don't take orders from unseelie scum," he growled. Thomas narrowed his eyes.

"We're not—" He got no further. The rider struck his face hard. "Shut your filthy mothblood mouth," he said, adding to his companion, "Take them."

The outlaw dragged Thomas and Meri to their feet, slicing the ropes that tied them together but binding their hands anew in chilly iron shackles.

As the riders hauled them through the grubby streets towards a surprisingly colourful market, Thomas whispered to Meri, "How did we get here?"

"Their harpies carried us, look," she nodded at Thomas's waist. Looking down, he noticed for the first time his torn tunic, and three faint scratches on his flesh.

He repressed a shudder.

THIS MARKET WAS much livelier than Ercildoune's. Thomas couldn't keep his eyes still. Colourful birds twittered and sang in golden cages. Dark-skinned merchants rattled amulets and chains, calling their wares from every stall. And, given a wide berth by market-goers, a huge, yawning beast of a golden cat waved its tufted tail, turning its yellow eyes on each person that passed.

"Fret not, madam," crooned its owner, beckoning a patron forward. *Foolish woman*, Thomas wryly thought. *Don't touch that monster, lest you lose a finger*.

Sure enough, once they'd passed, a suspicious growl and subsequent squeal rang through the market.

THE GROUP DIDN'T pause as they walked through the market. It wasn't until they'd moved past the last few stalls and along a side street that Thomas realised where they might be headed. Secluded from the bustling market, a smoky alehouse came into view, wherefrom men came and went, clutching hoods over their faces.

"In there?" Thomas asked, more curious than afraid.

"Aye, *in there*," the rider sneered, pushing Thomas first through the large but surprisingly mobile door.

No one looked up when they entered. Tavern patrons sat draining tankards, or lying slumped over tables in a stupor, or else bellowing for serving girls to bring more drink. Scraggy dogs sniffed morosely at the ground, whining for table scraps, snapping at weaker pups for the best morsels. The room reeked: stale sweat, piss, and ale. A pungent, sweet-smelling smoke from a corner turned Thomas's stomach, making him feel light-headed.

But his rough-handed captor dragged him away and threw him into a storeroom full of barrels.

Thomas stumbled, only just keeping his feet. Less balanced, Meri followed, staggering. Steadying her with his shackled hands, Thomas gave her a reassuring smile. The riders followed, sneering.

His sword pointed at Thomas, "On your knees, mothblood."

They lowered to their hands and knees, like dogs.

"Stay down." The snap of a door closing. Thomas risked a glance at Meri, silently commending her bravery. Though she hadn't shed any tears, her breath sounded ragged. The door opened again. Someone behind them forced their heads down.

The filthy stone floor now his only view, the dull ache in Thomas's head thumped through him again. A low, muttered conversation. Hard footsteps hit stone. Brown leather boots came into view. Thomas didn't dare raise his head.

A rider spoke first, the eagerness in his voice clear enough, "An unseelie with his selkie slave, Captain. We caught them on Achnahaird Coast."

The Captain stayed silent. The suspense of his sentence gnawed at him.

He spoke in a quiet voice, "Captain, I—" The rider nearest Thomas kicked him squarely in his ribs. Hearing an ominous crack, groaning, he collapsed, and drew in a hacking breath.

"Don't you dare speak, *boy.*"

Thomas slowly dragged himself back to his knees, already feeling warm numbness spread up the right side of his ribcage, punctuated with a stabbing pain about a third of the way down.

The silence stretched on. Thomas waited for his judgement to fall. For the captain to say Thomas was to be sold into slavery with Meri. Even killed outright. Alissa would be lost forever.

The waiting agony poisoned him. Thomas dared raise his head a fraction. Instantly, he heard a sword's song, then a sound of metal scraping onto stone; the captain placed his curved sword before him like a walking cane.

Not daring to move his head any further, Thomas squinted to read the name carved into his steel. *The captain's name?* He swallowed hard.

William Bonney.

The captain flicked his sword upwards. Pointed it between Thomas's hastily lowered eyes.

"You kneel before Blackspot Bonney, Captain of the *Allegiance*," came his hoarse voice. "State your business on Achnahaird Coast. Quickly."

Taking a deep breath, "Captain—" he coughed, clearing his throat, and tried again. "Captain Bonney, I'm looking for my sister. She's been kidnapped."

"Kidnapped?" A snort of a laugh. "What madman would dare kidnap an unseelie wench?" The voice took on a sinister tone, a harsh distortion after the laugh. "Should you even think to blame us, mothblood, I'll have your tongue fed to my hounds."

Thomas hastened to speak before the riders could advance.

"No! Captain—I-I'm not an unseelie. My sister neither, we're mortal, both. Alissa has been taken to Elphame," he rushed.

A collective hush rustled around the room. Settled like a blanket. Not a soul moved beneath it. Thomas could almost hear every heartbeat quicken like exotic drums.

Captain Bonney asked, "How do you know this?"

"A wise woman in my village told me," Thomas said.

"Please, I have to find my sister, I promised my mother I would bring her home."

Though he loathed it, as much as he *despised* sounding so helpless, Thomas tried to appear vulnerable, desperate. *Weak.* With luck, he would tug on Captain Bonney's heartstrings. *Surely this man couldn't be entirely heartless.*

Captain Bonney kneeled, taking Thomas's chin and lifting it in a strong grip. Thomas raised his eyes to Bonney's face. His mouth fell open.

Blackspot Bonney let her dark, curly hair hang loose about her tanned face and shoulders. A shark-tooth earring dangled from her left ear. Her right one was missing, leaving only a hard lump of scarred flesh. Captain Bonney's face, weather-beaten and somewhat severe, lit up when she smiled. Hidden laughter danced in her warm hazel eyes.

She jerked her head faintly, indicating Thomas should stand. Rising to his feet, he fidgeted awkwardly for a moment, then stopped abruptly as it sent a shooting pain down his right flank. She was much taller and older than he. Untying his hands, she nodded to Meri that she should stand as well.

"Captain, I need to find my sister," Thomas said. "Will you let us return to that stretch of coast?"

Captain Bonney nodded, her generous smile sparkling with secrets. "What's your name, lad?" Captain Bonney's voice was surprisingly deep. Melodious. Amorous. Thomas suddenly realised another rider must have spoken on her behalf. *Clever way to keep her identity hidden.*

"Thomas Rhymer, Captain," he replied. "This is Meri Strand, a selkie. I rescued her this morning."

Captain Bonney looked between the pair. Her knowing smile widened. A gold tooth winked at Thomas.

"You're a canny lad, Rhymer. You remind me a lot of my own brother, Gods rest his soul. Aye, I'll help you find your sister."

CHAPTER 10

In which Thomas sets sail

"MY FATHER, WILLIAM Bonney, proper noble man he was. Fearsome pirate, aye, but noble. You don't get many like him anymore. He named me after my mother, Mary-Anne Bonney. I hope I do them both proud."

Captain Bonney sliced through the market crowd. Her mere presence seemed enough to deter merchants. A host of pirates followed her, looking bemused, a little disappointed even, at her abrupt liking of Thomas.

"Not easy being a pirate in this day and age," she went on. "But we get by. So long as we sail clear of the unseelie fleet."

Her eyes darkened for a fraction of a second. Thomas took the opportunity to speak when she paused.

"We were travelling with a friend, a seelie," he said, trying to keep pace with Captain Bonney's long strides. "She got left behind when we were brought here, is there any chance we could go back to find her?"

The captain spoke lightly, "Aye, we set sail soon enough. We'll take you back to some caves, by the beach where my crew picked you up. You can look for your friend there."

"Our horse, too. They said—"

"Aye, one of my lads mentioned a white horse. Says she bolted afore they could gut her for meat. You'll have to forgive my crew," she added. "Some of them have spent a bit too long away from civilised folk."

"Epona ran away?" Thomas shared a glance with Meri.

"Could well be. Elvish horse, aye? Clever beasts. Come, no point dallying. I'll get you some equipment. Gods only know why you're wandering around Albion with an iron poker."

THOMAS TASTED SALTY air as they neared the docks. Gulls flew overhead, squawking their peculiar, ululating cries. A massive white sail hove into view.

A brig ship patiently anchored in the harbour. Sunlight bounced off the mainsail, stinging Thomas's eyes.

From the ship deck came the call of, "The *Allegiance* awaits you, Captain!"

Captain Bonney nodded. Turning to her crew, she called an order for them to make ready to sail. Rather than ascending the gangplank right away, she instead led Thomas and Meri to a smithy behind a market stall.

Blackened by soot, shining with sweat, a short man appeared from behind a wide furnace. He clutched a hammer in one hand, a white-hot, unfinished sword in the other. With a nod, Captain Bonney pushed past him, examining a rack of curved swords. She pulled one down and unsheathed it, considering it for a moment, then handed both sword and scabbard to Thomas. Turning the blade over in his hand, he marvelled at how light it felt.

"Fintan is our most skilled blacksmith," she said. Thomas smiled, sheathing his new cutlass. "Elvish ancestry, way back. His blades are fused with cold iron, but they're light enough to use and carry. Clever, hm?"

Fintan reappeared, carrying a dirk and sheath, handed it to Captain Bonney, then bowed himself away. Taking the offered dagger, Thomas examined it.

"You don't know when a little knife will fix a big problem," she said. "Once took down a troll with a steak knife, myself."

Thomas chuckled, unsure if she was jesting, and tied the new dagger to his belt.

THE *ALLEGIANCE* PATIENTLY awaited them, her sails gleaming mother-of-pearl in sunlight. Thomas grew apprehensive. Having never been at sea before, seeing the ship gently bob against tide, his stomach churned at the thought.

Yet Meri, standing on the top deck beside the helm, seemed to be enjoying herself. Watching sailors go about their various tasks, she let sea mist spray her face.

Thomas joined her on the deck, finding Captain Bonney already barking orders to a crewmember.

"Get going, you pox-faced eel-licker," she bellowed. The pirate shot up the rigging like a spider. Captain Bonney watched him, then turned, kicking another pirate's backside to hurry him along. Thomas and Meri watched, desperate to laugh. Neither dared.

The ocean stretched on forever, an unending azure blanket. Thomas found himself wondering what would happen should they keep on sailing. What strange lands he would find! Thinking of the enormous cat in the market place, he grinned at the prospect of such fantastic creatures. Followed swiftly by a pang of guilt. *Poor Alissa. She would have loved that cat.*

A hand on his arm startled him; he glanced down to find Meri gazing at him.

The breeze played with her hair. "Don't worry, Thomas. We'll find Thissy, then we'll go to Elphame together."

Thomas mutely nodded. Captain Bonney approached.

"I'll show you to your quarters, come." As Bonney led them below decks, the ship creaked and groaned, her anchor lifting and sails swollen.

Thomas found his quarters simple yet cosy. He and Meri shared a small room, with swaying hammocks instead of beds.

"You'll have to pull your weight, the pair of you." Captain Bonney led them back to the deck. The port was already shrinking on the horizon. "I'll have no useless barnacles on my ship."

CAPTAIN BONNEY ANNOUNCED it would take at least three days to return to Achnahaird Coast by sea. Since Thomas had no desire to ride a hideous, feathery harpy again, he found no reason to complain.

Yet, after his first dizzying, heaving day – most of it spent holding onto the ship side to keep himself upright – he severely regretted his hasty decision.

AFTER FINALLY FINDING his – albeit a little wobbly – sea legs, Thomas spent his time with a rough brush in his hand, dangerously swinging on a plank of wood hung by two fraying ropes over the side of the ship, scrubbing hard at the crustacean-encrusted hull whenever they hit a calm patch of sea.

His evenings were spent in Captain Bonney's company,

training with a sword – albeit not as fervently as he would have liked thanks to his still-sore ribs. Throughout his youth, his only practice had been against his father's old stuffed training dummy. Now he could test his green skill against a real person, instead of shadows and straw.

"You lunge too quickly," she said, tossing his sword back to him. Thomas's face glowed red after the easy disarming. "Take your time, learn your opponent's weaknesses. Exploit them. Don't go in for the kill right away. That's how I disarmed you these last three times. Come, try again…"

AT LAST, AS their third day at sea dimmed to a close, Captain Bonney announced they had almost reached their destination. A great cacophony of cheering and roaring rang across the water.

Ale barrels rolled out onto deck. The moon cast everything in cool, silvery light. Soon enough, loud, giddy laughter echoed across the still black water. Drink flowed freely, overfilling mugs, spilling onto the deck. Food was plentiful, and for a while, the first time in far too long, Thomas was happy.

Watching the revelry below with ill-disguised jealousy, a pirate stood, lonesome, in the crow's nest. A breeze whispered in from behind a cloud. A shadow passed over the moon. And something dark shifted on the horizon.

"Captain!" he shouted, his voice carrying to the deck below. Captain Bonney looked up. Wordlessly, he pointed to the dark shape appearing over the horizon, heading for the *Allegiance*, gaining speed.

Another ship sliced through the black water like a silent blade.

Captain Bonney leapt to her feet, squinting through darkness. Moonlight reflected against sails. A heavy bell began tolling.

"All hands!"

A flurry of movement. Every pirate with a mug in his hand had now discarded it in favour of a sword. Thomas and Meri dashed to Captain Bonney.

"What is it?"

Bonney pointed.

"An unseelie ship. Get below decks, you two. Leave this to us." The authority in her voice was undeniable, yet Thomas wouldn't miss this chance; someone on that ship would know how to find Elphame. *And Alissa.*

The unseelie vessel sailed toward the *Allegiance* in complete silence: a ghost ship. Captain Bonney's pirates darted around deck, letting down sails, raising the anchor. But the pursuing ship had already caught a breeze.

The crow's nest pirate shouted something to the captain that Thomas didn't understand. Bonney's eyes widened. She glanced over at Thomas, who squinted into darkness at the spectral vessel.

"*Shit...* get below decks, now. It's the *Mantis*," she commanded, turning away. Leaving Thomas to stare, his brow furrowed in confusion.

"Silver Wheel preserve us," Meri whispered, shivering. "Kali's ship. We need to hide below—"

"I'm not hiding!" Thomas said hotly. "I don't care who Kali is. If they know where Elphame is, I'm not missing my chance to find Alissa."

Captain Bonney spun the wheel expertly. No use. The *Mantis*, much too fast, came close enough for Thomas to see each sailor roving around her deck, jeering as they worked to close the remaining distance.

A tall, dark woman in red stood erect on her top deck, arms folded, glaring at Captain Bonney.

"Lower the anchor," Bonney called. "No use trying to outrun this bitch."

Thomas ignored the excited jolting of his heart. Both ships' anchors lowered as the rival ship silently drew up close to the *Allegiance*. A cruel female voice echoed through the night.

"Blackspot Bonney! I, Princess Kali, third-born of the Dragon King, by the might of Tír-Na-Nóg and all its domains, command you to release your fugitive!"

Captain Bonney stepped down from the helm, facing the woman in red across the stretch of boats and ocean.

"No fugitives here, little dragon!"

Meri gave a nervous twitch. Thomas put his arm around her.

She whispered up to him, "*That's* Kali," Meri's face paled. "The Dark Prince's eldest daughter. Trust me, she'll not—"

"Daughter? Erlik has *children?*"

Somehow, though Thomas had never met him, he couldn't imagine Erlik being a fatherly man.

"Seven royal children. Who knows how many more bastards he's sired? Kali is… well, they say she's mad," her black eyes were fearful. "Like him."

"That seabitch you're escorting is an escaped slave. Property of the unseelie court," Kali called through darkness. "Unless you want to go down with your precious *Allegiance*, I suggest you return her."

The *Mantis'* crew had lined up against the starboard, their swords and grappling hooks gleaming in the moonlight.

Glancing back to Meri, Captain Bonney surveyed her with a sweeping, searching gaze. Meri stared beseechingly back, but Bonney's face remained impassive. Thomas shook his head. *Don't…*

Finally, with a smile and a wink to Meri, Captain Bonney turned back to Kali.

"Come get her," she smirked, her hands on her curvy hips. Kali paused.

"Feed the ocean with their corpses!" she called to her crew. "Bring that barking wench to me!"

Chaos erupted on deck.

The crew of the *Mantis* used their hooks to vault over onto the *Allegiance*. Pirates drew swords, bellowed curses, spread mayhem on the deck. Only Kali remained on the *Mantis*. Bonney hurled taunting insults at her before unsheathing two cutlasses and leaping to her crew's aid.

Pulling Meri behind him, Thomas drew his own sword when an ugly, leering unseelie approached. With skills learned from Captain Bonney, Thomas swung his cutlass, carving a defence and thrusting when the unseelie retreated. Meri crouched beside the helm, flinching whenever Thomas dodged an attack.

Clanging steel filled the night, a discord of noise intruding on the silence. Thomas noticed, as he swatted the pirate with the butt of his sword and shoved him over the side, that the unseelie seemed to care little for their targets. Many were dead already. Some others had fallen into the sea. The last few retreated, wounded, bleeding.

Thomas frowned. *Why had this been so easy?*

Dispatching the last with a slice of her blade, Captain Bonney shouted to Kali, "Do you yield?"

A cold wind picked up, filling the sails. Neither ship moved. Kali's manic laughter echoed across black, glass-like water.

"I never do," she sneered.

Laughing again, she vanished in whirl of red smoke. Her laughter echoed louder, closer. Much closer. *Too close.*

Thomas turned around to look at Meri. His eyes found instead a taller, darker, crueller-looking woman.

He stepped back at once.

CHAPTER II

In which first blood is spilled

THOMAS SUCKED IN a sharp breath. Meri scuttled from her hiding place. Leaning coolly against the helm, a smug look lacing her lips, Kali watched her in silence. Without thinking, Thomas pointed his blade at her. Kali snorted with laughter.

Thomas found her simultaneously beautiful and hideous. Perhaps her eyes shone a little too brightly. Perhaps her hair moved too easily without a breeze. Perhaps it was just that unnerving, half-mad smile that caused Thomas's hesitation.

Kali cocked her head, dog-like, her eyes brightening as she judged him with amused contempt.

"So," she said, a victor claiming her reward. "You're the boy who stole our slave?"

Thomas repressed an irksome twitch. Kali smirked, an eyebrow lifting. She sniffed disdainfully. "You smell different. Not quite seelie. What *are* you?"

"My name is Thomas Rhymer," he said, momentarily proud of his steady voice. "I want my sister back."

Kali released a sinister chuckle, regarding him as she would a small helpless animal.

"How charming. A *human*."

Thomas gripped his sword a little tighter, "How did you find us?"

He imagined he could feel the crew's eyes burning into his back, hear Captain Bonney's heavy breathing draw closer. Kali circled the helm, running her hand over the carved wheel. Thomas watched those long, sharp, red-tipped fingernails. *Paint? Or blood?*

"We'll just say West Port is currently burning to ash," Kali easily remarked. "The display was quite magnificent. I imagine its rum-soaked citizens kept our bonfire burning longer than I expected."

"Mothblood bitch!" Captain Bonney suddenly snarled, pointing her sword at her, though not daring to approach further.

"That was feeble," she said, smirking.

"Why do you want Meri?" Thomas didn't trust this game of hers. Too coy. Too slow.

She gave a casual shrug. "We all want what's rightfully ours, little boy."

"I agree. Give me back my sister." The anticipation to strike emanated from her like hot waves. Thomas followed her with his sword, his eyes fixed on hers. Kali laughed once more, the sound a tolling bell over the water.

"Oh, I like you, Thomas Rhymer," she said, drawing one sword. "Alas, I have no control over the Hunt, or those they steal. You'll need to speak to my—*dear* father for that." Her left eye twitched. She took in a slow breath. "For now, my concern is what *we* do. Do we fight to the death over one selkie wench?"

"Gladly," Thomas growled. Behind, he heard Meri let a dry sob escape.

Kali heaved an overly dramatic sigh. "I don't have time

for that, sweet boy."

"What do you propose instead?" Thomas asked. Kali smirked again. Moonlight reflecting on her blade; Thomas saw his own face, mirrored ghostly pale in the night.

Kali shrugged again. "A temporary truce. I will take the selkie back to Elphame. Once she's suitably punished for her escape, I'll speak to my father; ask him to return your sister. Agreed?"

Thomas looked back at Meri. *Could it be that easy, truly?* Could he sacrifice a stranger for his sister? Their eyes held. Hers widened. He didn't know her, really. *Who is she to me? Just a stranger. Alissa is more important. I could have her back by tomorr—*

"I don't have all night, sweet boy."

Thomas turned his attention back to Kali's cruel, smirking, eager face.

"You must be truly mad to believe I'd let her go back with you." He raised his sword. Her eyes darkening, Kali's sneer slipped.

She swung before Thomas was ready. His cutlass shuddered in his hand with the impact. Kali's hand flew faster than Thomas could follow.

Within barely a heartbeat, Thomas knew he would lose.

Kali struck twice, thrice, four times in quick succession, her two blades flashing slivers of moonlight. She left Thomas no room for offence; there was barely enough time to raise his sword against her fearsome attack.

He wanted – needed – to call for help. Yet he found himself unable to take his eyes away from this savage woman, lest he lose the fight. And his *life*.

Her ferocity forced his retreat. Blinking away dancing lights, forced to half-bend over the ship's splintering railings as their swords met and Kali pushed forwards, he pushed her away with every ounce of his strength. Her red-nailed hand crept to his throat.

The black sea churned below: a horrifyingly long way to fall into deep darkness.

This close, Thomas noticed Kali had barely broken a sweat. He glared into her cold, flint-like eyes, feeling her iron-like grip tighten on his throat.

"I'll say farewell to your sister for you, *boy*."

No longer listening, clarity burst into Thomas's mind. It sounded remarkably like Thissy's voice.

Taking one hand off his sword, it seemed for a moment like he had surrendered. A flash of silver. A surprised shriek. Thomas's dirk now bloody. A thin gash marred Kali's cheek.

Her hand leapt to the wound, her shock giving Thomas the window he craved. He shoved again. She stumbled, staring, thunderstruck, at him.

"Cold iron." He breathlessly waved his blade before her. Her cruel eyes followed it. "Stings, doesn't it?"

Raising his sword, he pushed the point against her throat. Immediately her flesh began to burn and sizzle. Hissing in pain, Kali glared at him. Thomas moved his blade away a fraction, not entirely heartless.

"Go now, Kali. And tell your *dear* father I'm coming for my sister."

Her eyes widened, wild with rage. "Thomas Rhymer," Kali growled, backing away, pointing a shaking, furious finger at him. "Three times we will meet; first on this ship. Second in the wake of a dragon's wrath. Third when you are betrayed. That final time, one of us will die."

Kali vanished.

The *Mantis* began to sail away. After a brief silence, a

loud echoing cheer broke out. Meri hugged Thomas hard, and Captain Bonney clapped him on the back.

The crew spent their last nighttime hours on deck, drinking, laughing, discussing their fight with the unseelie, until sunlight broke the horizon. Captain Bonney let Thomas and Meri catch some sleep in the early hours. Her bleary-eyed pirates milled about their ship, grumbling, preparing to sail.

Yet Thomas lay awake, unable to stop his thoughts from drifting to the previous night. Kali had told him they would meet twice more. Thomas repressed a shudder. He couldn't imagine anything less desirable than meeting Kali again.

And who would betray him? Meri? Captain Bonney? Even… *Impossible*. He pushed the thought from his mind as soon as it entered.

Thomas rolled onto his side, unwilling to dwell any longer on Kali's vile words.

Meri sighed in her sleep. Thomas watched her, chest rising and falling with rhythm of her breath, until his gently swaying hammock ushered him into rest.

THE BEACH DREW into sight at last. White sand stretched out like a cloud against the breakers. Thomas and Meri stood on the prow, staring at the caves in trepidation and excitement.

"Lower the anchor, bo'sun!" Captain Bonney strode across her ship's deck, the wind sweeping her hair over her face.

With a great splash and the rattle of a heavy chain, the

Allegiance slowed to a halt. Calling for Thomas, a sailor nodded towards a little boat, gently swinging over the side.

After much muttered swearing and banged elbows, Thomas managed to settle into the small vessel.

Captain Bonney leaned down from the deck above to speak, "I'm staying aboard to see to my crew. Mortimer will take you ashore. You see those caves?" She pointed. "Go through them. When you come out the other side, the rumours say you'll find Elphame."

Thomas smiled. "Thank you, Captain."

Captain Bonney nodded, understanding he meant more. Thomas carefully stood in the shaky boat and held out his hand, which Captain Bonney seized, shaking it, letting out a hearty laugh.

"You're a canny lad, Thomas. Alissa's lucky to have a brother like you." Thomas felt his cheeks grow warm. Bonney beamed at him. Proud, motherly.

Meri and Captain Bonney shared a short yet fond farewell.

"You look after him, pup," Bonney smiled at her.

Meri clambered into the boat – with a little more dignity than Thomas had – her face glowing with pride. Captain Bonney saluted them; her sailors lowered their boat down.

As the black-haired Mortimer rowed them to shore, Thomas saw her wave once more, then turn away and whistle to her crew.

Their journey to shore was relatively quick. Though Thomas had become accustomed to the *Allegiance*'s gentle sway, the constantly rocking little boat was too much. Faintly green by the time they reached land, Thomas leapt out at once, staggering to a nearby rock pool. Laughing,

Meri followed, giving a final cheery wave to Mortimer as he rowed back to his ship.

Meri splashed out of the waves to find Thomas retching behind a boulder. He emerged, considerably paler and shivering. Meri's shoulders shook from holding back a laugh. Wiping his mouth, Thomas turned away, looking around the beach.

"So, how do we find Thissy?" Meri asked. Her voice echoed around the cave mouth, accompanied by a gentle dripping and waves slapping against rocks. Thomas sighed. Out of the corner of his eye, he saw the *Allegiance* shrinking on the horizon.

"Come, we'll try this way first." He walked inland, towards the forest. Hoping Thissy would have sense enough to realise he would return for her.

✧   ✧   ✧

"I'M WORRIED ABOUT him," Thissy said anxiously, pacing the glade. "It's been four days."

Two more women sat by a flickering white fire. Dappled light cast a cool haze over them as gold-red leaves floated down. A protective circle cast around their glade filled the air with a sweet, heady scent.

"Could he be lost?" the fairer woman suggested in a meek voice, as though afraid of speaking too loudly. Thissy shook her head, frowning.

"No, we're close enough to the coast for him to see our fire. He's not stupid, Silverfrost." Sighing, she returned to her seat.

"Perhaps *you* should look for *him*?" the dark-haired woman proposed.

"Shh!" Thissy stood up quickly. "What was that?"

She took a few wary steps. Leaves ahead rustled. Branches cracked. The two other women stood, eyes wide.

Grumbling, pushing past a leafy branch, appeared Thomas.

"… and damn spider webs all over the—" he stopped. Thissy stared. He stared back, equally stunned.

Letting out a loud, joyful exclamation, his eyes lighting up, he rushed at her, then immediately skidded to a halt. Heart hammering, he cleared his throat. Thissy rolled her eyes, then dived at him. Giggling, she wrapped her arms around him. Thomas laughed and, lifting her off her feet, spun her around.

"I knew I'd find you!" He beamed. Thissy laughed too, embracing him again, kissing his cheek as he lowered her to her feet.

"I knew you would! I said, didn't I? I knew it!" She giggled, and this time, kissed his lips.

CHAPTER 12

In which Thomas hears a story

L EADING HIM BY the hand, Thissy explained the glade. "This is a sacred place for seelie, Thomas. Queen Mab created it: a sanctuary against the darkness. Her magic is strongest in all Albion, stronger even than the Dark Prince's powers. No unseelie can enter this circle."

Thissy sat fireside, inviting Thomas and Meri to sit beside her. His cheek burned where Thissy had kissed him.

Noting Thomas' curious gaze, Thissy gestured to the woman with pale eyes and white hair. "This is Silverfrost," then to the one with long dark hair garlanded with pearls and unusual shells, "and Wavedancer. They managed to escape the Purge of Elphame when the Dark Prince took over. They're from a seelie colony in the wilds, making a sacred pilgrimage to the standing stones at Greystanes."

"We're hoping to speak with Queen Mab, if we light the fire there," Wavedancer piped up.

"Thissy told us about your sister, Thomas," said Silverfrost in her faint voice. "You've come so far. We suspect Elphame is near. The Wild Hunt rode by last night. We watched them emerge from the mountain." Thomas felt a chill creep over his skin.

"We need to be more careful now," Thissy went on.

"Close to Elphame, danger will grow. Pirates and harpies are nothing compared to what would happen if we're captured."

"Speak for yourself," Meri mumbled.

At Thissy's words, something in Thomas's memory flashed to the fore.

"Thissy, we met Kali," he said. The warm air suddenly chilled. The seelie women sat straighter, each with an anxious look in her eyes. "Her ship attacked... she..."

Unable to repeat Kali's chilling words, he swallowed hard, running his tongue over his lower lip. Meri leaned forward, her eyes lingering on Thomas.

"She told him they would meet three times," Meri whispered. "She said when they met for the third time, one would die."

Thissy lifted her head in concern. Thomas held her gaze. *I'm sorry. Please, help me.*

Silverfrost spoke instead, thoughtfully, "Perhaps you should stay away from Elphame? Let someone else go in your stead?"

"No," Thomas said firmly, despite the creeping fear around his throat. "I made a promise."

The women nodded, soft sighs lingering in the air. Thissy stood up, kissing her seelie sisters farewell.

"Be brave, Thomas Rhymer," Silverfrost breathed. Wavedancer smiled and waved.

THE AIR HAD grown colder since the trio left the glade, but a sweet smell yet lingered. *Was it protective magic clinging to them?*

Stepping back onto the beach, Thissy stopped to look around.

"Didn't you find Epona?"

Thomas figeted, feeling shame creep warmly around his neck.

"Captain Bonney's crew said she ran away," Meri said.

"We'll waste time looking for her now," Thomas said, swallowing his guilt. "We'll just have to journey on foot from now on."

Thissy approached, taking his hand, as the three turned towards a dark, dripping cave mouth. With a massive sense of trepidation, they stepped inside.

THOMAS, THISSY, AND Meri picked through the dank cave, trying to ignore an unpleasant dripping sound; no easy task to escape the echo.

Meri had already slipped more than once. The soft leather shoes she'd obtained from the quartermaster of the *Allegiance* had proven to be too small, and with nothing to protect them, her feet were soon bleeding.

"Here," Thomas said, removing his undertunic and roughly cutting it into strips with his dirk to bind the girl's feet. Not the perfect solution, but better than nothing.

Thissy's elegant figure illuminated their way. In the dark, her body emitted the same glow her tiny form had. Her doeskin boots skimmed over rocks, barely touching them. Bravely, she walked ahead to find an easier path, allowing Meri and Thomas to catch up at their own pace.

They didn't speak much. With little conversation to interrupt his thoughts, Thomas found himself dwelling on the memory of Kali.

That half-mad warrior woman. Her hair floating about

her face as though caught in a breeze; her dark gaze boring into him, seeing beyond his eyes; that unnerving smile. His thoughts turned to Erlik himself. What sort of man must he be to have raised a daughter like Kali? And what of his other children?

Meri said he had seven! Will I have to fight them all? Are they all like Kali, half-insane, vicious and—

"Are you afraid of Kali?" Meri asked. Thomas stared at her, then reluctantly nodded. She looked up at him, wincing as she put weight on her bleeding feet. "Everyone is. I imagine she gets it from—from her father."

Her voice grew quiet. Thomas suppressed a chill that had nothing to do with the cold cave.

"How did all of this happen? Tell me about the war. Please," he added, when Meri looked uncomfortable.

"We only know stories… some say the Dark Prince went mad. He started to steal souls of men to make his army. The Wild Hunt," she added, when Thomas looked blank. "The Dark Prince stormed Elphame, drove out Queen Mab and her closest advisers, and took over her city. Those seelie who still live there are kept in one huge district, under close guard, taxed to poverty. It's a dreadful place; I've seen, too, the dungeons are full of rebels."

"Rebels?"

"Seelie aren't meant to be walled in like that. There'd be riots, them trying to escape," Meri said. "He used to hold executions once or twice a month to keep them under control. There hasn't been one for a while, though. Some people think Queen Mab contacted him and told him to stop."

Frowning, Thomas said, "That doesn't make sense. If she could contact *him*, why doesn't she answer any summons? From Standing Stones, I mean? Besides, why would he listen to her? If they're at war, shouldn't he hate her?"

"Well… I mean it's all rumour, really… just speculation," Meri drew out, looking uncomfortable again, "Some people say he loves her. They think he took over her city because she fought back when *he* thought she would welcome him. Me, I don't think he's able to love anyone." Her voice dropped to a whisper. "No one knows where Queen Mab is now. There are seelie colonies scattered around Albion, those few who managed to escape, like Silverfrost and Wavedancer. If she's with them, we haven't heard of it. They hope one day she'll return with an army to take back her city and drive out the Dark Prince."

Thomas swallowed hard. *Who is this woman who inspires such faith? And, if she's as powerful as the seelie believe, why is she hiding from a man she could, apparently, so easily destroy?*

After a while of thinking, Thomas spoke up. "Tell me about Queen Mab. Who is she?"

Meri lowered her voice so much, Thomas had to walk closer to hear her.

"Queen Mab is the Heart of Magic itself. Many ages ago, when the Great Smith first forged our world in his furnace, he took the Old Gods from beyond the stars and placed them in the sky above Albion, so they could watch over us in his absence. As a gift, he gave them the very Heart of Magic Itself. They carved it, gave it form, breath, and life. They called her Mab, *she who intoxicates*. Being in her presence is said to be like drinking the most potent wine, one that only the strong-willed can resist. The Old Gods put Mab in Albion so she could guide and protect her people, the seelie. Magic needs people to believe in it to survive.

Since their belief, their faith, in Queen Mab has waned, I suppose she's becoming weaker."

"So what about Erlik? What's he?" Thomas quietly asked. Her eyes betraying her fear, Meri's brow furrowed, shuddering when he said Erlik's name.

"A god who fell."

"A god of *what* though?"

"Cruelty," Meri breathed, a shade of bitterness in her voice. "Madness. Hatred. Fear… we don't know for certain."

Thomas's voice didn't rise above a deathly whisper. "And… what would happen if he found Queen Mab?"

"The Dark Prince will use her to rule both seelie and unseelie." Thissy's pale glow emerged from the gloom, voice shaking. "Albion will be harsher, crueller, and far more savage than it has ever been."

Caught somewhere between horror and fascination, Thomas merely walked on, silent. Even if he found his voice, what could he say?

Thissy returned from the darkness to hold his hand.

CHAPTER 13

In which wicked words are exchanged

DIM LIGHT SHONE through a dark, cold dungeon, gleaming on rusted bars. Its gaunt inhabitants shivered.

A young lad sat on a hard wooden stool in a cell, eyes red from crying, nursing a raw brand on his arm. A girl by the dungeon door kept her head bowed. Her tunic and breeches shone clean and bright in the gloom. A white-horn bow and quiver of arrows lay at her feet.

The young girl raised her face at approaching footsteps. Soft, threatening. The cell-bound seelie drew back into shadows.

A muttered conversation at the door. Prisoners drew further back as their dark-haired captor strode past. At the corridor's end, he fiddled with a lock on a small wooden door. With a quick glance over his shoulder at the girl, who turned away, he slipped inside.

Erlik closed the door behind him, locking it again. With a snap of his fingers, torches flared into life, illuminating a lone prisoner bound by shackles around her wrists, splaying her arms. Her head was bowed. Her soft flesh so pale it seemed to glow in the gloom.

"You can stop dreaming about me, Mab," he said, a

smirk curling his lip. "I'm here now."

He approached her. Queen Mab slowly lifted her head.

"You bring little comfort, *nathair*." She spoke in a biting, bitter voice. But quietly, as if she'd not spoken in so long it was now a chore. Smiling, Erlik produced an apple from nowhere. Stolen from the mortal world.

He buffed it against his coal-black doublet. Mab watched with piercing, glittering eyes. She swallowed hard.

Erlik's eyes, the colour of the ocean at night, glistened with eagerness. Hunger. The smirk on his lips was cold.

"Your presence offends me," Mab said. "Begone."

Shaking his head, patronising, Erlik tutted. "Oh, Mab, you wound me. I've come all the way down here to keep you company, and you thank me with such harsh words?" He moved closer and ran a finger up one of her chains. Mab scowled, keeping her eyes on his apple. "I understand you know something about this... *boy*? That one who rescued our selkie-slave?" he went on. Mab's eyes darted upwards. "Morrigan told me. She said you've been having visions."

"Then she is mistaken; the Old Gods have not spoken with me in a long time." Mab turned her face away. Erlik scowled. "Ask Kali," she added. "I have little desire to speak to you."

Leaning closer to her, he hissed, "You lie. Tell me what you've seen, Mab."

Mab proudly tilted her head back, somehow managing to look down her nose at him, despite their significant height difference.

"I have seen your reign at its end," she growled through clenched teeth, her eyes furiously bright. "Take care, Dragon King, lest you suffer their same fate. *Extinction*."

Rage did nothing to taint those beautiful features. *My*

captive she-wolf. Erlik's smirk grew, his fingers trailing down the chain to her hand.

"Thomas Rhymer—"

"You know his name?" he interrupted. "So you *have* seen." With a soft laugh, he began to pace before her. "Tell me about him, then. What's so special about this thick-skin you've chosen?"

Mab remained silent. She glared, fearless eyes locked with his arrogant gaze. The smirk slipped from his lips.

Menacingly close, he breathed, "Mab."

Still she said nothing.

"*Speak, witch!*"

Mab twitched, yet didn't look away.

"You will discover, as will he," she said.

Erlik frowned. "Stop speaking in riddles."

"Your simple mind astounds me." Mab sighed. "Thomas Rhymer is coming here to take back his sister."

Raising an eyebrow, Erlik let out a thoughtful noise and took a bite of the apple. Mab watched, running her tongue over her lips. Almost instinctively, he put the apple to her mouth so she could share it. She slowly chewed its soft, sweet flesh, eyes closed, savouring the first fresh food she'd tasted in months.

"Say thank you, Mab," he said, gently brushing a stray lock of hair from her eyes.

"Thank you. Now let my seelie out of the dungeon," she followed immediately. "I hear them crying for food at night. Let them go before they starve."

For a moment, it seemed Erlik was about to acquiesce. A compassionate flicker erupted in his eyes. But it died away like quelled fire, and he was smirking once more.

"Don't fear for them, beloved," Erlik said, coolly gazing

down at her. After one more caress of her cheek, he turned to leave, black cloak sweeping behind him like wings.

Calmly, her chains rattling in the silence, Mab spoke up. "You are aware the equinox is coming, yes?"

Erlik stopped, wide eyes darting. Panicking. His lips moved, wanting to speak, but no sound escaped. Spinning around, he lunged forward and pulled her upright. Mab winced. Erlik let go at once. *Gentler! For now.*

"What? What did you say?" he asked desperately, eyes sweeping her face, searching for any bluff or lie. She betrayed none.

"You know I speak truth. The equinox is coming." Mab's uncomfortable wriggle rattled her chains. "The moon is shifting. The days are growing shorter. I know you feel it. I do too."

Working hard to conceal fear, Erlik bit the inside of his cheek. He swept a hand through his hair. Mab looked up into dark eyes, her own secret smirk twitching around her lips.

"I thought I'd be safer. I thought Elphame's power would protect me," Erlik whispered.

"You are fallen, Erlik. You will not be protected."

"Help me, then. Protect me."

Mab blinked, her brow furrowing. She had clearly not expected this.

"If—*if* you let my seelie go, I will find a way to share my power with you. At the equinox, I will keep you safe."

Gazing at her, Erlik heaved a sigh. He held the apple to her lips again, then withdrew it, tantalisingly, when she leaned to bite it.

"Beloved... my beloved, my sweet thing... your price is too high. I'll find another way myself." He offered her his apple again, but once more drew it back, tormenting her. Mab glared.

"There is no other way, fool. Without me, you will lose your strength, become powerless, like a mortal—"

Erlik hissed and grabbed her, dragging her close to him. The chains around her wrists pulled taut, wrenching her arms back. An involuntary cry escaped her lips.

"If you *ever* suggest that I'm akin to those thick-skin pigs," he snarled, "you may just hear of another execution come morning. Do you understand?"

Mab held his glare for a few moments, and then lowered her eyes. She nodded meekly, looking at her feet. Erlik drew in a long breath, gently kissing her brow.

"I suggest you hold your tongue, beloved, lest you find it sliced from your mouth." Mab swallowed hard, watching the dropped apple roll just out of reach. Erlik, following her gaze, made no move to retrieve it. "The Old Ways don't frighten me."

"And Thomas Rhymer?" Mab asked, almost warily. Erlik's laughter tolled hard and cold in the cell.

"Your pet mortal doesn't frighten me either, Mab," he scoffed.

"He will bring an end to your reign, Erlik," she said softly. "If you let my seelie go—"

"Enough!" Erlik raised his hand. "I'm weary of your threats. But..." his voice grew soft, "there's something more I wanted to discuss with you."

Her eyes snapped up to meet his, their matched gaze burned. Erlik ran his fingers over her cheek, tracing her lips with his thumb. His hand slid down to her slender throat. Mab hissed.

"You should come upstairs," he continued, his voice

low. Hoarse. Slow. "Warm yourself by my fire, eat good food and... and sleep in a good bed. With me."

Mab shirked away at once. Erlik's eyes darkened.

"Must you act as though I'm repulsive?" he snapped.

"You *are* repulsive."

Both knew she was lying. Erlik was far from it, with his sharp cheekbones, feathery dark hair and thin lips. Silence stretched between them. *You're too easy to read, my little witch.* He let out a wicked little chuckle. Mab scowled.

"Come, Mab." He let his hands drift down to her waist, pulling her against him.

"Erlik, stop!" her command rang loud. He let go of her at once.

"Beloved, you choose a cold, dark dungeon over my warm bed?"

"Have a care, Poison-Hoarder," she spat. "You may find your *warm bed* besieged with thorns."

Narrowing his eyes, Erlik roughly shoved her away. She stumbled; only her chains kept her on her feet.

"I told you to watch your tongue, Mab," he growled. "Your insolence won't go unpunished. You must learn to obey me; I am your king *and* your master."

"I have no master. No man can tame me," Mab said, proudly tilting her head back. Erlik grabbed her throat, coldly laughing.

"Oh, Mab," he said, leaning closer again. "How tempting a challenge."

He pulled her towards him, pressing those thin lips to her mouth.

CHAPTER 14

*In which Thomas discovers
something terrifying in the cave*

T HOMAS SAT UP at once, eyes wide, breathing fast, his
hair damp with sweat. The two women woke at once,
staring as he gulped down air. Sitting beside him, Thissy
clutched his hand. Her small fingers spread comforting
warmth through him. Meri handed over a water skin.
Thomas gratefully splashed water into his mouth.

"What is it? Did you have a bad dream?" Thissy gently
asked. Thomas swallowed hard, taking deep breaths, and
nodded.

Still shaking, he said, "I—I saw a woman in chains. And
there was a man, he..." Thomas paused. "I can barely
remember now. My dreams fade so fast."

Wiping his face, he stood up. Thissy let go of his hand.
Its absence was a blast of cold air.

"Come, we should keep moving," he said.

Meri peered into murkiness. "I can smell fresh air that
way," she said. Glancing back at Thomas, flicking hair away
from her eyes.

Smiling, Thomas nodded. "Lead the way, pup."

THOMAS STRUGGLED TO remember his dream as he

mechanically followed behind Meri. *There was a dungeon,* he recalled. *A woman in chains.* She had said Thomas's name. Why? And that man, the one with dark hair... Thomas had an unpleasant feeling he'd seen that sneering face before.

Water steadily dripped into the black pool at the source of a stream they had been following, ripples waving the water.

Their pattern broke as a white hand plunged into the pool.

Thomas stopped. He drew his sword. Thissy and Meri stopped too. Both gasped when they saw the creature in the dark.

A young, emaciated woman with ash-grey hair. Her flesh was so thin, so white, Thomas could see blue thread-like veins beneath. She gazed at them with wide, wild eyes, then tilted her head. A pile of bloodied clothes lay beside her. Her thin, skeletal hands were underwater: ferociously, almost involuntarily, scrubbing a black shirt.

"Bean sídhe!" Thissy stepped back.

The phantom opened her mouth to scream. Shrill, cold, hopeless, and utterly mad, her shriek echoed through the cave, vibrating through Thomas like an enormous tolling bell. Threatened to corrupt him until he, like she, was a screaming wreck.

Thomas clamped his hands over his ears, shouting incomprehensible words, trying desperately to drown out her scream.

Then, all at once, it ended. The girl vanished. Thissy stared, frozen, at where the creature had sat, while Meri crouched, clutching hands over her head.

As if fearful of summoning that creature back, Thomas whispered, "What was that?"

Thissy shook her head, bringing herself out of a reverie. Meri got to her feet slowly, shaking.

"A *bean sidhe*. A harbinger of death. That shirt she was washing? It belonged to someone who's about to die. We must have disturbed her nest," Thissy said.

"Nest? You mean—"

"I mean there will be more than one, yes. Come, we must hurry. She's probably already alerted her matriarch."

Meri whimpered.

Eyes darting for any signs of movement, Thomas quickened his pace. After the *bean sidhe*'s screech, silence eerily descended. Meri and Thissy hurried after him, both straining their ears for sound.

AT LONG LAST, a sliver of light illuminating his face, Thomas could smell fresh air. Drinking in cool air, grateful for a change in scenery as sharp, unctuous rocks gave way to a more even surface, the cave began sloping upwards. A sunlit breeze hit them like a gush of clear water.

"We made it!" Thomas smiled. Thissy beamed at him.

A low rumble, rocks scraping. Thomas took a few anxious steps, smile vanishing.

To their left, a skittering cackle echoed from a black crevice. A spidery hand crept from the shadows, dragging a hideous creature from its nest.

A woman, yet not a woman, taller than any human Thomas had ever seen. Skeletally thin. Her long, lank hair half-covered her face. Blood dripped from the unobscured hollow eye. As silently as he could, Thomas drew his sword.

"The matriarch," Thissy breathed. "Quick now... quietly, out of the cave."

Thomas did as commanded, hardly daring to breathe.

His sword felt heavy and hot in his hand. Sweating, he feared he would drop it and startle the *bean sídhe*, yet he dared not sheathe it.

Meri took a step back. The loose linen around her wounded foot brushed against a pile of pebbles.

The tiny rocks sounded like an avalanche in the silence of the cave.

Meri winced, mouthing frantic apologies. The matriarch turned her sightless gaze on them. She opened her mouth wide. Impossibly wide. Jaw stretched to inhuman, demonic reaches.

"*Run!*" Thomas hissed. Thissy and Meri turned on their heels and fled towards fresh air.

The matriarch screamed. The walls vibrated with the pitch and volume. Rocks and debris crumbled into puddles of dark water. Stalactites cracked. Thomas screamed. Collapsing to his knees, he covered his ears. Wet to touch. *Blood.* His heart was about to explode, bones shatter, blood boil in his veins. He squeezed his eyes shut, unable to bear the pounding agony in his head.

Looking back, Thissy gasped, "Thomas!"

She bolted to his side, hoisting Thomas to his feet. But Thissy was unable to bear his weight and he collapsed again, screaming, blood still trickling from his ears. The matriarch threw her head back, screeching harder without pausing for breath. Thomas's eyes rolled back.

A clatter of hooves. The whinny of a horse. It shook away cobwebs in Thomas's mind. Fed him strength. Feebly, he looked up.

Epona!

Racing past the trio and rearing up on hind legs, she kicked at the *bean sídhe*. The matriarch slashed with blade-

like hands. Fearless, Epona rose up again, striking the *bean
sídhe*'s head with her hooves. When her scream turned into
a painful squeal, Thissy plunged her hand towards the dirk
on Thomas's belt.

His blade spiralled through air like a bird in flight. It
struck the matriarch at the base of her throat, to one side.
Her scream died to a pained whimper. She slumped.

Thomas slowly lowered his trembling hands, now
dripping with his own blood. He shook, unable to stand, so
Thissy helped him to his feet. Gulping down warm air as if
he'd been underwater too long, Thomas felt Epona gently
nudge him. He brushed his bloodied fingers against her
muzzle.

Thomas deliriously muttered, "Epona, you're alive. You
clever girl, thank you..." Epona's bright eyes seemed to
smile as he took her reins.

"Come, *a ghrá*, stand, that's it..." Thissy whispered,
gently pulling him up. He obeyed. Now on his feet, legs
shaking like those of a newborn fawn, Thissy and Meri let
him lean on them.

The monstrous cave opened onto a mountainside.
Sloping down to a plain, which lay out like a crinkled map.
A river wound like a ribbon through fern, patchworked with
purple heather.

Groaning, Thomas sunk again. Thissy lowered him
gently to his knees. Both knelt beside him.

"I feel like I've spent a week in an ale barrel," he
moaned, clutching his head. Thissy smiled, then pressed a
kiss on his temple.

"You're so brave, Thomas," Thissy put her hands over
his ears. Thomas felt warmth spreading from her touch. His
head at once stopped pounding. He stood up again,

stretching, relieved for Thissy's healing magic.

"Arianrhod's curse, let's never do that again," Meri said as she stood up.

"It's not over," Thissy said. All three lowered their eyes to the plain. "That's where Elphame is."

Far on the horizon, a sharply pointed mountain rose from the darkness. Cloud crept over the range of smaller hills around it. Wreathed in fog, the silvery stone of the base darkened to stormy grey at the peak.

Meri shivered. Thomas shared it.

Heaving a begrudging sigh, Thomas began the sliding descent, scattering rocks and debris in little dust clouds. The two women followed, Meri stumbling slightly.

Panting, Thomas stared. *That mountain, that's where Alissa is.* He could almost hear her voice. *So close now.*

He looked back, beaming, ready to formulate their plan of attack. Yet Meri's eyes had filled with tears, and she was shaking her head, backing away from the mountain.

"He's in there... No, I—I can't! I can't go back. I thought I could, but—" Sobs took hold of her, her shoulders shaking. "I spent my life trying to escape that wretched place. I can't go back. I can't. *I can't!*"

Annoyance weighed heavy on Thomas, but concern quickly overrode it. He took a step towards her, reaching out, and enveloped her in a tight hug. Her body froze at first, but she finally yielded, wrapping her arms around his waist. A faint seawater smell still clung to her hair.

"Be calm, Meri. You don't have to come with us. But you know I have to go. I can't give up now. Alissa is so close, and she's alone in there."

Wiping her eyes, she whispered, "I know." They broke apart. "I'm sorry."

Thomas shook his head.

"Don't be. There's nothing to be ashamed of. I can understand why you..." He trailed off. He didn't want to admit Erlik frightened him as well. "Well. You can wait here. Once we rescue Alissa—" Thomas looked to Thissy, momentarily distracted. "You're still coming, aren't you?"

Thissy smiled and nodded.

"You must be careful," Meri warned. "The Dark Prince is more than he appears. Silver Wheel protect you."

Nodding, Thomas gently cuffed her chin. She gave him a watery smile.

Meri took shelter in an alcove, the mouth of another cave, gathering enough dry sticks to build a small fire. "I'll keep this fire lit," she said. "There's an old barn at the base of the mountain, you can hide in there. Please hurry. And be careful!"

Thomas turned to gaze at the mountain. A great monster, looming out of darkening mist. First stars began to wink from the gloaming sky, steel-grey clouds threatening to overshadow them.

"Very well," Thomas said, taking a deep breath. "Come."

CHAPTER 15

In which Thomas embarks on a fool's errand

A SICKLE MOON hung high, a silver bow in a velvet sky. Thomas's only light now came from a glowing white fire on Thissy's palm. She had returned from inspecting a curling parchment poster on a barn wall. Though its picture had faded, words beneath still proclaimed a reward for any who brought the fugitive back to Elphame alive.

Inside, cold air wrapped around the pair, far colder than Thomas was used to, even with his highland upbringing. A frosty fog materialised when he breathed out. Despite his first few moments of a childish amusement, now it just reminded him of how deep this unnatural cold penetrated. Nearby, Epona happily grazed on a small pile of hay, left there by the last travellers to use the dwelling.

"I assume you have a plan to enter the city?" Thissy whispered, shivering. Thomas wrapped his cloak around her. She smiled gratefully, huddling closer. A mouse scampered in the corner. Epona raised her head, curious.

"Well, I *had* hoped we'd find a door, but I suppose nothing is ever easy," he said.

Thissy weakly smiled. Breathing warm air into her hands, she said, "You could have just said 'No, Thissy, I don't have a plan'." Thomas threw her a jaunty grin.

"Whatever we're doing, we should do it quickly. The Wild Hunt, you know. I wouldn't want—"

"That's it!" Thomas interrupted. "The Wild Hunt take people back to Elphame, don't they? Back to him?"

Thissy twisted her hands, suddenly uncomfortable, as though she regretted mentioning those fiends at all.

"Well, I—I suppose," she murmured. "But... being *captured* by the Hunt? What if they hurt you? Worst they'll do to me is rough me up and throw me in the seelie district. Who knows what they'll do to you? They may not even take you to the Dark Prince."

"It's our only chance to get inside, Thissy. Please trust me," he said, gazing at her.

She sighed, "Very well..."

They fell into silence. Once quiet descended, Thomas had time enough to contemplate this *brilliant* plan. What if Thissy was right, and they didn't take him to Erlik? What if they just killed him outright? Perhaps if he demonstrated knowledge of their prince, they would take him for questioning. Or torture. Thomas repressed a shiver.

"Is there any way to draw them out faster?" he asked irritably, after a while of crouching in near darkness. Pins and needles crept up his legs.

Thissy sighed, and caused Thomas to frown as she unsheathed a short fruit knife. "How else do you draw a hound?"

A flash of silver and scarlet. Thissy showed him her palm, now split. Bleeding.

A thunderous cracking ruptured the silence.

The earth shook. Thissy grabbed Thomas's hand, her eyes wide, lips trembling. Epona reared up on her hind legs, snorting in fear. Thomas grabbed her reins with his free hand, trying to calm her down as she nervously pawed at the ground.

The earth heaved again. Thomas stumbled. Thissy screamed. He turned, still unsteady, finding her staring in terror upwards. He followed her gaze. A heavy weight dropped into his stomach.

A thick black cloud roiled from the mountain peak, darkening the skies with an oil-like stain. Epona reared up again; Thomas fought to stop her from bolting.

Like a great wave, the cloud rushed down the mountain towards them. A rancid stench of death and decay cloyed the air, heavy and thick.

Abruptly, overtaken by some mad urge, Thomas leapt onto Epona.

Stumbling after him, Thissy cried, "Thomas, what are you doing?"

"No time; come!"

Grabbing her hand, he pulled her up behind him. Ignoring Epona's protesting snort, disregarding Thissy's terrified whimper, Thomas kicked his horse's hindquarters to spur her out of the dilapidated barn and onto the moor, away from the approaching Huntsmen.

Thissy breathed hard and fast in his ear, pressing herself against his back, her arms tightly swathed about his waist. They rode; a lone white horse in a mass of black. New distance stretched between Thomas and the Hunt.

The horsemen drew close enough that Thomas could now vaguely make out each rider in black, accompanied by a swarm of black dogs, red eyes rolling, jaws snapping.

Thomas drew his sword. *Useless.* Thissy clutched him tighter, squeezing her eyes shut. *Now or never.*

"Riders of the Wild Hunt!"

Horsemen raced towards him, their hounds excitedly howling. Flesh. Blood. *Man.*

On a steadfast course to overwhelm Thomas, crush him beneath hammering hooves, the riders galloped full force down the mountainside. Closer. *Too close!*

Thomas clamped his eyes shut, realising at once how foolish this plan had been.

Then, without warning, Wild Hunt turned, veering west. The horsemen thundered away into night, leaving Thomas and Thissy untouched.

Thinking of Meri, Thomas's heart dropped, hoping she'd have sense enough to hide during the night, especially with her wounded feet. As the last few riders passed, Thomas watched them gallop away, shoulders slumped, disappointment and embarrassment colouring his face.

"Well," he sighed. "I suppose it *was* a stupid plan."

Thissy grabbed his arm so tight it hurt. "Thomas…" she whispered.

An echo of hooves. Thomas looked back to see a dark figure slowly, somehow condescendingly, approaching on horseback. His mount, black like those of the Hunt, looked much larger, more impressive. Regal.

Thomas tensed, readying himself. *Is this Erlik?* The unknown rider stopped a short distance away. His coal-black horse, plumed with an extravagant ebony feather, snorted and pawed at the ground.

Silence. The stranger drew a gleaming sword, raising it above his head.

A flash, clouds rolled with thunder. A flickering ribbon of lightning struck the ground between Thomas and the dark stranger. Thissy tightened her grip on Thomas's waist.

She whispered in his ear, "It's Malik, his first born… be

careful."

Thomas's heart pounded so hard, it hurt. *More of Erlik's mad offspring?*

The lightning flashed again, illuminating both horse and rider. Malik: tall, dark-haired and good-looking, a few years older than Thomas. His black eyes narrowed with curiosity and amusement, though his lip curled spitefully. Prominent gold trimming stood out against his black surcoat, his hair falling in waves to his shoulders.

"So," Malik sneered, arrogance and vanity hanging about him, "You're Thomas Rhymer? My little sister has told me about you. How amusing that Kali has been bested by a *boy*."

Thomas swallowed his angry retort. "I've come for my sister," Thomas said, trying not to let his voice quaver. From anger or fear, he couldn't tell.

Malik laughed. "Really? Why?"

Thomas stared. How could he be so heartless? Malik had a sister; did he care nothing for her? *Although,* Thomas thought, *if Alissa was anything like Kali—*

"As it happens," Malik went on. "My father wants to meet you. Dismount. Lay down your sword and any other weapons. We'll take you to him."

As Malik spoke, several Huntsmen appeared behind him, though Thomas hadn't heard them approach. *Stay silent. Don't ask too many questions.*

Mustering the coldest glare he could, Thomas dismounted, handing Epona's reins to a rider. Laying his sword at his feet alongside his iron dagger, he felt the leather bag against his hip. *Salt.*

Still saying nothing, Thomas stood straight, unwillingly allowing his hands to be bound.

One rider pulled Thissy down from Epona with unnecessary force. Her squeals lanced through Thomas.

"If you hurt her," Thomas quietly threatened as her hands were also bound, "I'll make sure you pay."

Malik raised an amused eyebrow. "Don't worry, thick-skin. I'll take good care of her."

Turning his back, Malik led his soldiers and captives into the mountain.

CHAPTER 16

In which Thomas and Thissy enter Elphame

FLANKED BY TWO horseback soldiers, his hands bound with thick rope, Thomas felt like a slave being led to market. As they approached a fissure in the mountain it appeared to expand, swallowing them.

Thomas had to allow these unseelie to lead him deeper, Thissy by his side. Epona was guided alongside one of the skeletal black horses.

When the thick darkness suddenly flashed hot-white and Thomas at last managed to adjust his eyes to the glare, he gaped.

A decrepit city of dirty white stone lay stretched out before the group, still some way off within the mountain. Towers, blackened with ash and smoke, choked on tendrils of ivy and weeds. Their spires stabbed out from the city. A mighty white castle sat, like a monstrous beast, at the other side of Elphame. Although no breeze disturbed this crooked city, ragged flags and banners fluttered on poles around the castle.

The group stood on an outcropping, wherefrom stone steps led down to city limits.

Thomas couldn't help but stare, trying to take it all in. Glancing right, he saw Thissy approach, bound by the same long coil of rope, her face a picture of despair.

"Oh! Look what they've done to our city!"

"Hold your tongue, girl," Malik snapped. "Why don't we take a shortcut, hm? Through the leaf-ear district, I think."

With a wicked smile, he turned his horse away. His soldiers followed, tugging their prisoners roughly along.

Malik led them through back streets. The further into the district they walked, Thomas saw how the houses fell further into squalor and disrepair. Lanes narrowed, became more crooked. Beggars lined the streets; Thomas felt a hard lump stick in his throat when he noticed children among them.

Silent tears wetted Thissy's cheeks as she clutched Thomas's arm. He realised with a jolt that these tormented, hungry beggars were *her* people. Thissy could have easily been amongst them. It was hard to imagine the seelie as the proud, powerful race she had described.

Faces appeared in shutterless windows and at doors, devoid of hope or happiness. A few curious children stepped into the streets to eagerly watch their procession, and were quickly ushered back inside by anxious parents.

That white castle loomed closer; the imposing, ashen walls burned into Thomas's sight, much like the *Allegiance*'s white sails. Far sooner than Thomas liked, they arrived in the castle's courtyard.

Malik dismounted, pausing to regard Thomas, raising an amused eyebrow, then turned away, pulling his two captives up a set of stone steps. At the top, he pushed open the grand doors with his free hand.

A massive dark hall lay beyond the doors, its walls lined with braziers that burned with milk-white flame. A purple carpet stretched from their feet to a raised dais at the hall's end, where an impressive, empty marble throne sat. Stone columns interspersed along the walls, twisted with vines. In an alcove to their right, a statue of a dancing woman stood proudly in a pool, clear water cascading from her hands.

Thomas stared around the hall in fascination, every flicker of his eyes forcing him to appreciate more detail. He only noticed that Malik had turned away, down a cool corridor towards another chamber, when his wrists were sharply tugged forward by the taut rope. Thomas quickly tried to rearrange his expression from heightened awe into calm nonchalance.

Thissy shivered.

"What is it?" he whispered. She shook her head, unable to speak.

Malik opened the doors to the next chamber; easily as big as the entrance hall and lavishly furnished with tapestries and paintings, instead of a throne, a long table dominated this room, groaning under a hundred dishes.

A stunning stone fireplace, large enough to roast an ox, blazed with faery fire, warm waves washing over them. Despite this, Thomas felt a chill rake his blood with icy fingers; a man sat at the table head, gazing at his visitors through wickedly amused eyes.

After a sip from a silver goblet, he stood. Much taller than Thomas, his slender figure cut an arrogant stride towards them. *This is a man who will not be intimidated.*

Thomas felt Thissy shiver, pressing closer, as though she wanted to hide behind him.

With a sigh, Erlik stood in front of Thomas. Thomas had expected him to be much older. The sight of a man only ten or fifteen years his senior was too unnerving.

"I've come for my sister," Thomas said. His voice sounded youthful, foolish, in the silence.

Thomas tried holding Erlik's dark gaze, but it was like trying to stare down a wild dog. *Sooner or later, it's going to bite.*

"Untie them, Malik," Erlik said. "Have you no manners? Anyone would think I raised a barbarian."

Malik smirked. Drawing a short knife, he sliced away the ropes binding Thomas's wrist. He moved to Thissy to cut her rope, standing far too close for Thomas's comfort. Malik leaned closer, smelling her hair.

"I'll come find you later, hm?" He gave her a wink, running a hand along her waist. Thissy pulled away and shuffled closer to Thomas.

"You're dismissed, Malik." The prince motioned carelessly to his son.

Malik nodded curtly, offering a mocking bow to Thomas and Thissy, then left.

"Well," Erlik said, beckoning them, pointing at two places at the opposite end of his table. "Thomas Rhymer. I heard you were young. I didn't expect a *boy.*"

Ignoring the condescension in Erlik's voice, Thomas and Thissy shared a nervous glance as they sat down. Thomas saw Erlik's eyes lower to their clasped hands.

Though the table was laden with food, Thomas ignored his hunger pangs. He noticed Erlik wasn't eating either. Suspicion flickered through his mind.

Thissy sat straight-backed, rigid in her chair. Breathing fast and staring, unwaveringly, at the wall. Erlik kept glancing at her, apparently amused by her fear.

"I added another place," Erlik poured red wine into his goblet, gesturing to an empty seat beside Thomas. "There's one less in your party." He set his bottle down. A dull thud. "So where's the barking seabitch who ran away?"

The air became chill at once. Lingering malevolence hung in his tone.

"We left her behind. On Achnahaird coast," Thomas lied, without hesitation. Thissy's hand twitched within his.

"A fascinating lie. Tell me the truth this time. Where is the selkie?" His hand stroked his goblet's stem. Had he looked up, he would have registered the look of wild panic that passed over Thomas's face.

"I'm not lying," Thomas insisted, injecting confidence into his shaking voice. Erlik heaved a sigh.

"I *created* lying, boy. I know when someone employs my own tricks. For the last time, *where is the selkie?*"

Thomas stared into those oceanic eyes. *No use. No matter what I say, he'll see right through it.* Thissy squeezed his hand in reassurance.

Hating himself, he said, "M-Meri left us. Just before we were brought to you."

Thomas lowered his gaze to his lap. *I'm sorry, Meri.*

"Little coward," Erlik laughed. "I suppose every disobedient dog dreads its master's wrath. The Wild Hunt will take care of her."

A knot tied in Thomas's belly as Erlik, pushing his chair away, stood. With an arrogance found in victorious men, he approached.

"I must thank you, thick-skin," he said coolly. Reaching Thissy, he leaned over to pour out a goblet of wine, almost brushing her shoulder. Far too close to her for Thomas's liking. He could feel her hand become clammy, trembling. Her eyes were too bright, too wet. Terrified.

Don't be afraid. I'm here.

Offering her the wine, Erlik went on, "You've brought me another one for my little leaf-ear village. I assume Malik took you to see them. Dirty creatures, aren't they?" He gave an unpleasant snort of laughter and gestured to Thissy. "Run along and play with your friends, little mongrel."

In a movement so abrupt she almost disrupted their table, Thissy leapt to her feet, her chair legs scraping harshly. She snatched the goblet from Erlik's hand.

Throwing wine over him, *"Nathair!"*

Thomas held his breath.

Erlik didn't flinch. The red liquid stopped, floating in mid-air, a bizarre globule of wine. Smirking, Erlik waved his hand towards a wall. The wine followed his command, splattering sanguine against white stone.

"How peculiar," Erlik darkly said, lowering his arm, advancing on Thissy. Now realising how rash her actions had been. "That all you filthy leaf-ears should call me that. Do you even know why? Because of your *queen*."

Thomas noticed Erlik's eyes briefly glisten with something other than anger.

"She called me *nathair* when I defeated her. Should I show you how?"

Raising his hand, Erlik clenched it into a fist. Thissy gasped, clutched her chest. Fell to her knees, unable to draw breath.

"Thissy!"

Thomas leapt from his chair. Laughing, Erlik lowered his hand. Thissy drew in a ragged breath. Thomas stood in front of her.

"How noble," Erlik sneered. "A knight coming to the rescue of his lady."

Ignoring Erlik's cruel laughter, Thomas swung at him.

Erlik vanished, reappearing faster than Thomas could have prepared for. Erlik knocked Thomas' fist off-course. He seized Thomas's throat with icy fingers, squeezing under his ears. Thomas choked. Erlik dragged him close. Thomas did his best to dislodge the hand, but his vision had already blurred. A red haze descended over his eyes.

Erlik smirked, "You have such a *nasty* temper. I hate to admit it, but you quite remind me of myself. Unfortunately for you, that's where the comparison ends. You're so... fragile. Mortals always are. I can crush you as easily as any leaf-ear."

Erlik tightened his grip. Thomas's eyes shuttered closed.

"C-crush me then, coward!" Thomas choked out. With a furious, guttural snarl, Erlik threw Thomas away. Impossible strength for a man with such a slender build.

Thomas hit a wall with bone-jarring force, and slid down the stone.

"Be silent, idiot girl," Erlik growled at Thissy as she let loose a sob, advancing on Thomas. Taking a deep, calming breath, the prince approached, smirking. Thomas weakly lifted his head. Cracked his blurred eyes open. Saw Thissy shake her head in horror, fretfully conjuring hesitant sparks at her fingertips. Erlik waved his hand at her, a simple and dismissive gesture. Thissy's magic extinguished. She staggered back, gasping, her powers drained like water through a sieve.

"It does you no favours to fight me," Erlik said patronisingly to Thomas, as through addressing a stubborn child. "When I hold your sister and your... *companion*." Erlik returned to the table.

Glaring, Thomas struggled to his feet. Every inch of him ached. Erlik's smirk broadened, watching Thomas groan as he straightened. Thissy appeared by Thomas's side, her arms around him, warmth billowing from her touch. She let him lean on her, limping back to the table.

Painfully, Thomas fell into his seat. Erlik watched the pair with narrowed eyes, amusement clearly growing.

"Now," Erlik announced, glancing between them. "Would you like to see your sister?"

Thomas froze.

Erlik raised an eyebrow, "Well?"

"I-I—"

He immediately regretted that stammer when Erlik sneered. *Idiot! He's mocking me. Don't waste this chance.*

"Where is she?"

"Somewhere in the scullery," Erlik said. "Don't ask me which one she is, I'm terrible with names." He paused, idly toying with a knife from the table. He heaved a mocking sigh. "I hope none of my sons have taken out their frustrations on her yet. How embarrassing *that* would be."

Red fury clouded Thomas's vision.

That's my sister, you son of a bitch! If your animals have touched her—

He heard himself growl. He wanted to lunge at Erlik, to hurt him, *destroy* him. But the prince was speaking again, and Thomas strained his muscles to not move. Yet.

"You know, no one comes looking for them. The ones we take. I believe you're the first." A pause, then Erlik threw a wickedly smug look at Thomas. "And the only reason I've allowed you to come so close is because I wanted to meet you. You're a curious beast. You just keep... getting in the way. Why, for instance, did you rescue that selkie?"

Thomas's eyes raked the hall. Searching for a door, an escape. Erlik waited, staring, for an answer. *Keep him talking.*

Keep him thinking he's in control.

He tried to shrug. "I—I don't know. She was in trouble."

Erlik let out a harsh bark of laughter. "No one is *that* noble. Although..." His eyes wandered to Thissy as he cruelly smiled. "I see your gown is ripped, leaf-ear. Perhaps he's not as noble as he likes to think?"

Thomas recoiled, looking, not at Erlik, but at Thissy. She squeezed his hand tighter. Reassuring.

"I'd never hurt her," Thomas said through clenched teeth.

Erlik's dark eyes crinkled as he sneered. "We'll see." Erlik lifted his head. A hound catching a scent. Thomas's heart dropped. The prince gestured towards the doors, which immediately swung open.

A malicious grin contorting his handsome face, Malik approached. Behind him, two Huntsmen half-dragged a struggling figure. Thomas didn't need Thissy's gasp, nor did he need her tightening grip, to recognise her.

CHAPTER 17

In which a forest comes to Thomas's aid

"MERI! WHAT HAPPENED? Are you hurt?" Thomas wanted to stand, to run, break her free of the Hunt and escape. Erlik's eyes halted him.

"I-I'm sorry, Thomas," Meri moaned. "They caught me by surprise. I tried to—"

"Enough." Approaching, Erlik leaned towards Malik, not taking his eyes off the quivering selkie.

"Do what you like to her, then take her to the dungeon. Don't put her in with the leaf-ears." Erlik paused before turning away. "Oh, and send someone to fetch the Rhymer girl from the kitchens. If she's aught like her brother, she'll be fair-haired and witless."

"Stop!" Thomas stood up. "If you hurt them, I'll—"

"You'll *what?*" Erlik cut him off with a laugh. Malik paused, eager to watch. "Do you know nothing, boy? I can make you suffer with just a snap of my fingers. I don't even need to use magic. I have *every* advantage against you. You still think you're in a position to make threats?"

"*Enough!*" Plunging his hand into the pouch on his belt, Thomas easily uncorked the bottle with his thumb and threw the handful of salt at the Dark Prince. Erlik shrugged coolly, laughing.

"Salt will work against some of those... *lesser* beings," he said with a nasty smile at Thissy. She trembled, scrubbing her arms where a few stray grains had caught her. "But I am a *god*. It is no threat to me."

A crushing hand on Thomas' shoulder made him spin, finding Malik snarling, bestial, drawing back a fist.

Thissy swung a heavy plate at Malik's face. The resulting clang and crunch gave Thomas opportunity to steal his sword. Malik staggered away, clutching his bleeding nose.

Erlik flicked his hand at Thissy again. Like a ragdoll, she flew through the air, slamming into a column.

"So, *amadán*," Erlik said coldly, stepping towards Thomas with grim determination. "I hope killing your sister will be as enjoyable as killing you."

Erlik grabbed Thomas's wrist, twisted it, and kicked his legs out from under him. Thomas grunted when he hit the floor and struggled to catch his breath. Erlik merely looked amused at his determination as Thomas weakly got to his feet.

A shriek rang behind Thomas. Foolishly, he risked a glance over his shoulder.

Malik had Thissy.

Taking advantage of the distraction, Erlik skilfully lunged and grabbed Thomas' throat again, pointing his now-unsheathed blade against Thomas's pulsing chest. Yet, just as Erlik was about to plunge his blade into Thomas's heart, his eyes flickered away. With a wicked little smile, he lowered his sword. Thomas gulped, exhaling in relief. Erlik stepped back. The sounds of scuffling died away.

"Father?"

Yet another of his?

Thomas blinked. A young girl appeared at Erlik's side. Lifting an arrow from a quiver strapped to her back, she nocked it to a bow of white horn.

"This is Morrigan, my youngest," Erlik said, smiling down at her. Thomas's breath caught in his chest. Erlik seemed... fatherly, even *loving*, towards her. "She's beautiful, isn't she? Nothing like her mother, of course. She gets those good looks from me. She's quite the archer too."

Morrigan aimed her arrow at Thomas. The room fell silent, save for the sound of Thissy's breath, whether from fear or exhaustion, Thomas couldn't tell.

Erlik smirked as Morrigan stretched back her bowstring.

"People usually run," Erlik advised.

"I'm not leaving without Alissa."

Leaning closer to his daughter, Erlik whispered, "Shoot him."

Morrigan hesitated. She stared at Thomas past her arrow point. Thomas could have sworn she smiled at him.

"Do it, Morrigan."

She blinked. Faltered again.

"Foolish girl," Erlik snarled, grabbing an arrow from her quiver. Roughly pushing past her, he approached Thomas, who took a wary step back. Out of the corner of his eye, he saw Morrigan scuttle out of the room.

Erlik vanished into smoke. Reappearing behind Thomas, an explosive agony ripped through him as Erlik pierced his side with the arrow.

His scream rent the air. Pain coursing through him as the serrated arrow sliced into his flesh. He collapsed to his knees. Delirious, lost in burning, crippling agony, he grabbed Erlik's cloak. Pleading. Erlik pulled away from him, a look of disgust on his face.

"Take them all to the dungeon. Let them watch him suffer."

Huntsmen appeared, flanking him.

A great rumbling echoed throughout the hall. Frowning, Erlik bent at the knees, steadying himself against the tremors. Huntsmen warily drew swords, as if their blades could stop the earth trembling. Plates of food, goblets of wine, rattled off the table. Spilled their contents over the floor. Thissy and Meri broke free.

Erlik stared around, his left hand grasping his hair, something akin to panic.

"No! No, don't you *dare!*"

The stone floor cracked. Blackened, ancient, twisting roots clawed out of the earth, snaking upwards, surrounding the Huntsmen and Malik, forming a cage of interlocking roots and branches.

Hunters hacked with their blades, but the trees grew too thick, too fast, entrapping them in a thorny prison.

Snarling, Erlik lunged for Thomas, hands clawed like a beast. Thissy and Meri lunged towards Thomas, shielding him.

A writhen root sprang forward, snapped around Erlik's wrist like a whip, and yanked his arm back. More roots emerging from beneath ensnared Erlik's legs, pulling him back from Thomas.

"*Boy!*" he bellowed. "I'll hurt her for this!"

Through blurry eyes, Thomas vaguely saw Erlik's struggle against the roots. He desperately grabbed Thissy's arm. The simple movement crippled him; he screamed, panting hard as sweat beaded on his forehead.

"I—w-we… need—I can't—*Alissa…*"

"We'll come back for her, I swear it," Thissy said,

dragging him to his feet. "We need to go. *Now*."

Meri threw Thomas's arm around her shoulders. With their combined strength, they heaved Thomas to his feet. The three staggered to the door. Erlik and his men still struggled to free themselves. Thissy grabbed Thomas's confiscated weapons from the floor as they passed.

"*Stop them!*" Erlik screamed in fury. But the grand entrance hall had emptied. There was no one to impede them.

Epona, already awaiting them in the courtyard, bent low so Thomas could clamber onto her. He could feel his blood pumping, thick, stinging sensations travelling through his already-aching chest to each limb.

✧   ✧   ✧

"THOMAS, YOU MUST stay awake," Thissy said, trying to stop her voice shaking. "Keep your eyes open."

Groaning, Thomas gasped short, gulping breaths. He swayed on Epona, so unsteady Thissy feared he would fall.

"The arrow—w-we need to get the arrow out," she said to Meri. Thomas fuzzily saw Meri look around as she kept up with the horse. "We're not far enough away to stop, yet. We need to put more distance between—"

"There!" Thissy cut her off with a muted look of apology at her sharpness, and a wave of a slender hand. Thomas had to lift his head slightly to see – then his vision swam and he succumbed to the darkness.

"THOMAS, LOOK AT me," Thissy whispered, her voice coaxing him back to consciousness. Thomas grunted as the sharp corner of a rock made itself known by digging into his side as he lay on cold earth. Meri quickly knelt beside him, grasping his hand. "Keep looking at me; don't look anywhere else, just at me."

Thissy took hold of the arrow shaft. Thomas understood at once what she was about to do; he gripped Meri's hand tighter, his eyes widening.

"No... n-no, Thissy, please, don't," he mumbled. He stared up, past her to the roof of the cave they must have found while he'd been unconscious.

"I'm sorry, Thomas. I'm so, so sorry," she whispered. And pulled.

Thomas's scream bounced and echoed. He fell back into Thissy's lap, gulping down air, piteously moaning. She wiped blood from her hands before touching his cheek to turn his head to face her.

"You're so brave, Thomas." She offered him a shaky smile. He returned it, weak in his agony. His face suddenly contorting with pain, he sucked in a sharp breath when Meri pressed his wound to stem the flow of blood too thick and dark to be untainted.

"I'm sorry! I'm sorry, I'm sorry!"

From the other side of the moor, a cruel breeze rattled over the mouth of their cave. Thomas shivered. Thissy brushed tears away from his cheeks, then away from hers when she felt his flesh icy cold at her touch.

"Arianrhod's curse, Thissy, can't you heal him?"

"I... I can try. I won't be able to heal it fully; it's too deep. Besides..." Thissy paused. "I don't know how to heal whatever poison has corrupted his blood."

"We should go back for Alissa," Thomas muttered deliriously. Thissy shook her head.

"Hush, now," she whispered. Carefully, avoiding

catching torn flesh, she hovered her hand over his wound. A warm glow erupted on her palm. Thomas trembled. Blood stopped slowly pumping out of the wound. It scabbed over, creating an ugly, half-healed pockmark. Meri pulled a face.

"That's the best I can do for now," Thissy said, holding herself shakily upright with a flat palm on the unforgiving ground. "I could try again tomorrow. We'll rest here tonight, and then..." she trailed off. Thomas weakly nodded, barely listening. Epona stood at the cave mouth.

"I'll keep watch," Thissy offered. Thomas closed his eyes, drifting into an uneasy sleep. Thissy rested a hand on his chest to make sure he kept breathing.

CHAPTER 18

In which Thomas falls into the hands of the Old Gods

THISSY HAD NOT slept. She gazed at the mountain, wondering if the Dark Prince still struggled, fighting to unbind himself from the grasping roots.

She allowed herself a smile. *I'd recognise that magic anywhere.* Thissy offered up a silent prayer of thanks.

Thomas stirred in his troubled sleep. His breathing shallow, uneven.

Night air wrapped colder around her. Thissy took in a deep breath, shivering, and then drew in a sharp gasp.

Like a galleon at sea, heading for their cave, a ghostly white shape soared through darkness.

Her heart thudding, Thissy gently slipped out from beneath Thomas' head and lowered him back to the ground. He slept on, undisturbed. She glanced at Meri, who still snored quietly beside him. Epona lay sleeping at the cave mouth.

The shape grew closer, close enough for Thissy to make it out. A barn owl.

Warily, her eyes narrowed. Fluttering to a stop, it hopped across the ground. Round black eyes glittering like coal in the full moon circle of its face. A flash, and as the owl rasped an eerie call, its shape grew into a girl in white.

Thissy glared at her. Harsh. Unforgiving. Her eyes glistened with angry tears. "What do you want, mothblood?"

Morrigan pouted. "No need to be so hostile, leaf-ear." That word sounded odd from her lips; Morrigan seemed too young to use such words.

"Why are you here?" Thissy asked. Sighing, Morrigan took a nervous pace forwards, her hands raised to show she meant no harm, eyes downcast. Hostility wilted when her eyes found Thomas, lying prone.

She said, tentatively, "I—I've come to help." Before Thissy could stop her, she'd stepped past, kneeling beside Thomas. He frowned in his sleep. Thissy's eyes blazed as she glared at the young princess.

"Stay away from him!" she snarled. She took a threatening step, but Morrigan quickly raised her widened eyes, her lips and hands trembling.

"I just want to help. Please, let—let me help. I promise, I won't hurt him."

Thissy paused, her fists clenched, then nodded slowly. "Very well. But if I see one *ounce* of foul play—"

"I know."

Morrigan chewed her bottom lip. She inspected Thomas's wound for a moment, then glanced at his face, twisted in a grimace of pain. She pressed a hand to his forehead, the other hovering over his wound.

"What—"

"*Hush!*"

Morrigan closed her eyes. Thomas immediately began jerking, shivering like a fever had taken him. Morrigan took no notice. Thomas moaned, twitching, in a fitful sleep. A flash of light illuminated the pair. Morrigan dragged in a hoarse breath, her eyes flashing black for a brief moment.

At last, Morrigan got to her feet, panting. Thomas had stopped shivering. Thissy's heart leapt into her throat. Dashing past Morrigan to kneel beside Thomas, she swept his hair away from his face and checked his wound. Only the tear in his tunic remained; his skin whole, unbroken. Thissy looked incredulously at Morrigan.

"I—I don't know what to say," she admitted. "Why would you help?"

Morrigan gulped, shrugged, and turned away. "It doesn't matter. Don't tell my father, or he'll have my head."

Thissy could only stare, her gratitude unspoken, as Thomas rolled over onto his side, his breathing slow and deep. Thissy nodded. Morrigan gave her a weak smile.

A third flash. The barn owl ruffled its feathers.

Wordlessly, Thissy watched her leave. She sat beside Thomas, her fingers curled next to his, and her eyes scanning the horizon for any more *surprises* in the night.

✧　✧　✧

DAWN BROKE WITH welcome crispness. The surrounding area looked less forbidding, less monstrous, in daylight. Had thousands of black-clad Hunters truly marred the landscape only last night? No hoof or paw-prints remained.

Thissy slowly woke, rubbed sleep from her eyes and sat up. She momentarily cursed herself for allowing sleep to overcome her. Meri still curled beside their burnt-out fire, deeply asleep. Thissy gazed at this picture for a few moments, before her heart skipped. She leapt over the fire to shake Meri awake.

"Meri, wake up!" she hissed. *"Meri!"*

She jumped at the abrupt awakening, staring with tired eyes at Thissy. "Ugh," she groaned. "Is it morning already?"

"Thomas is gone."

Meri's eyes snapped open.

The two hastened to the cave mouth, desperately scanning the moors. But other than Epona just before them, no other living creature lay in sight.

"His sword, look," Meri said, pointing. "His sword is still here. *Arianrhod's curse*, you don't think the Dark Prince took him?"

Thissy twisted her hands, chewing her lip.

"No, if he'd been here, he'd have killed us. Or taken us t- wait! No, look!"

She pointed. Thomas approached, the carcass of a white deer slung over his shoulder. He dropped his kill as soon as he entered their cave.

"Breakfast," he said. With barely a smile, he dropped to his knees and began dressing the deer with unwonted, unnatural ferocity. Meri pulled a face, dry retching.

"Thomas?" Thissy said. He didn't look at her. Merely grunted, still carving the carcass. Meri turned away, clasping a hand over her mouth. Thissy pressed her lips together and swallowed hard.

"Do you—" She cleared her throat. "Do you remember what happened last night?"

Thomas threw her a filthy look. "Of course I do. You think I'm a fool?" he sneered. Thissy drew back at once. She approached Meri, who wiped her mouth.

Thissy whispered to her, "His blood yesterday, it bled dark. You don't think—"

"The arrow was dipped in the Dragon King's Poison? It makes sense – the Dark Prince didn't go for the kill when he stabbed Thomas with it."

Thissy nodded silently. After a glance at Thomas, she explained Morrigan's late night visit, and sudden desire to aid them.

"She must have healed the flesh, but he's still—"

"How does Morrigan even *have* that power? *Curse*, do you think—"

"When you shrews have finished gossiping," came Thomas's voice right behind them. They jumped, turning to face him. "We should get moving as soon as breakfast is done. I want to get home as soon as I can."

"Home?" Meri repeated. Thomas wiped his bloody arms on a scrap of cloth.

"Yes, *home*. That place where I live, Meri."

Meri, scowling at his sarcasm, folded her arms.

"What about your sister?" she asked. Thomas shrugged.

Not sounding remotely upset, he said, "She's gone. I can't do anything more for her."

Thissy stood adamantly before him, her hands planted on her hips. For a moment, she swore his eyes flashed black. But then she looked again, and they were blue. Shining and cold.

"I'm going home," he said again, speaking slowly, sarcastically. "I don't care what happens to you two. Stay here and rot." Thomas gave a cold laugh. It didn't suit him at all. He pushed Thissy away. "*You* can crawl back to Malik and be his whore."

Thissy sucked in a sharp breath and Meri hissed *"Thomas!"* but he ignored both and continued. His voice grew quieter, angrier with every breath.

"I saw how you looked at him. Admit it, you're quite taken by that princeling, aren't you? Well, what about *me?*"

He advanced; Thissy retreated. Thomas raised his voice. "Am I not good enough, is that it? You want a prince? Is a farmhand not good enough for *Her Majesty?* I don't know why I bother. You're a heartless bitch who—"

Thissy slapped him.

Thomas staggered. When he straightened again, he looked confused: an upset child. His hand clutched the healed wound on his side. He took a nervous step forward. "No... no, Thissy, I'm sorry. I'm so sorry," he whispered, his eyes wide and frantic. "Please forgive me... I don't know why—"

Thissy stepped forward and took his hand. Tried to keep her voice from cracking as she explained the darkness of his blood and the poison making its way through his system.

"Don't push us away," Meri said.

"We'll fix you, *a ghrá.* I swear," Thissy mumbled into his chest as she embraced him.

Epona nudged Thomas with her muzzle. He let go of Thissy and Meri, glancing back at her. "What do we do now?" he asked. "I need to go back for Alissa."

"If we seek out a seelie colony, they might be willing to help. So long as you offer help in return," Thissy said, picking up Thomas's weapons and handing them over. He accepted with a grateful nod.

"Will you be able to find them?" he asked.

She smiled. "I should be able to. But we need to fix you first."

Thomas inhaled deeply. Kneeling down, he gathered up the remains of the deer carcass and carried them to the mouth of the cave. *Might as well feed the carrion-eaters,* he thought morosely. Gazing at the sightless black eyes of the dead animal, he'd suddenly lost his appetite.

"I think there's a village nearby," Meri piped up. "Their wise woman may be able to help – with the poison, I mean."

"We can only try."

Thomas mounted Epona, both women refusing to join him.

"We're fine. You're still injured, Thomas. You ride, and gather your strength," Thissy said. Thomas huffed, but said nothing.

CHAPTER 19

In which Thomas fights a dragon

"**Y**OU SNEAKY, UNGRATEFUL, *treacherous* little whore!" Erlik bellowed. He struck Mab across the face with the back of his hand. Pulling her upright, he roughly shook her. "You helped him escape! I know it! I could *smell* it! Your filthy earth magic, you scheming—you deceptive—"

"*Father!*" Morrigan shrieked, running forwards.

Mab glared back, her lip broken, bleeding. Erlik panted hard, his eyes wide with fury and madness.

Morrigan gazed up at him. "You said you weren't going to hurt her."

Sighing, Erlik shook her off. "Begone, Morrigan. This doesn't concern you."

Morrigan ran her tongue over her lip. She glanced at Mab, who gave her a weary, yet reassuring nod. With a sigh, Morrigan hurried out. The door closed behind her.

Erlik paced slowly. He watched Mab with a sinister gaze.

"Why did you—*how* did you—" Erlik cut himself off with a snarl when Mab gave a breathless laugh. "Stop mocking me!"

"Do you think I am not aware of what happens within my own castle?"

Growling, Erlik lunged at her, wrapping a hand around her throat and leaning in close.

"What a wife you would make," his lips grazed her pointed ear. His hand roamed down to her waist, pulling her hips closer to his. "So clever. So defiant. You excite such... *desire*. My resolve won't last forever. You can't keep tempting me and expect me not to give in. I've been patient," his voice was surprisingly, deadly calm. "But I'll eventually take what is mine. I will tame you. You'll see, my little she-wolf. You'll be mine."

THOMAS, THISSY, AND Meri wandered through the woodland. Trees grew tall and thick around them, shafts of sunlight penetrating through to bracken. Birds swooped between branches, twittering, disturbed by these strangers in their forest.

Before long, the three arrived at a set of unguarded gateposts.

"This is it," Meri said. A small village – no more than a handful of dingy streets, where a few scraggly chickens hungrily pecked at muddy ground – lay beyond.

THOMAS NOTICED PEOPLE averted their eyes as the three made their way to the centre of the village. Muted conversations stopped altogether.

"Are you sure about this?" Thomas asked Meri. She glanced around, frowning.

"There's a free-house at the end of the road. We can ask in there," she stepped around patches of thick mud. Holding hands, Thomas and Thissy followed her.

Meri approached the tavern, but it appeared to be bolted closed. Peering through the boarded windows, she knocked. Thomas looked around. Something on the ground caught his eye. Something red and wet on the stone steps leading up to the tavern. He knelt down, inspecting it closer.

"Thomas?" Thissy asked. Meri quickly stepped back from the tavern.

Thomas drew his sword. "We need to go."

At once, several doors burst open. Soldiers spilled out of houses, surrounding them, brandishing spears and swords.

A mad, mirthless laugh echoed around the street. Thomas felt his heart plummet. Kali pushed past her soldiers, surveying Thomas with cold, cruel eyes. A long scar marred her cheek.

"Very good, Thomas Rhymer. I was wondering when you'd make it. Do you see how I speak only truth?' Kali said. "We have met in the wake of a dragon's wrath." Her words rang cold around the empty street. Thomas raised his eyebrow, looking around, unimpressed.

"Well," he said dryly. "These people look quite unburnt after a *dragon* attack."

Rather than look offended at his insolence, Kali instead gave a sharp laugh, unfastening her cloak. She threw it aside, bearing the emblem on her tunic: a red dragon. Thissy whispered a curse in her native tongue.

"*Kali* is the dragon. We call—*him* the Dragon King. That makes her—"

"Little dragon. Captain Bonney knew, remember, Meri?"

Kali sneered. Thomas took a step toward her.

"This is between us. Let them go free, and we can settle this properly," he said, sheathing his sword, raising his hands in peaceful gesture. But Kali laughed again.

"Have you learned nothing? I don't do things *properly*. Take his women!"

She clicked her fingers for effect. Her soldiers moved forwards as one. When the ensuing scuffle cleared, he was alone in a circle of watching soldiers. Thissy and Meri were bound, struggling against the soldiers' grip.

"Let them go, Kali!" Thomas said, drawing his sword. She let out her harsh laugh again. *She's so much like Erlik. Those eyes—*

"I don't think I will, sweet boy," she replied. She unsheathed one of her swords, approaching him. "I need to repay a debt," she went on, running a finger along the scar on her face. "I could take it out of your hide. Or I could take it from one of them?" She pointed at Thissy and Meri. "Never skinned a selkie bef—"

Thomas didn't let her finish. He lunged forward. Kali, momentarily hesitating, brought up her sword.

Kali staggered back, her eyes wide with surprise at Thomas's new strength. At this rage he'd apparently kept hidden. Their swords collided; locked.

"You—"

Thomas's arm shuddered. A ripping stab tore through him. Had his wound reopened? Screaming, he fell back, away from Kali. Through a haze of agony, he heard Thissy cry his name. He braced himself on all fours, panting like a hound. His sword lay abandoned beside him.

Kali laughed, eyes bright, standing victorious over him. Thomas looked up. Kali paused.

"Oh, I see you've met my sister?" she sneered. Thomas tried to stand. Pain clawed him again. He groaned, collapsing.

Kali laughed, cold and cruel. She swung her sword.

"Your battle is lost."

Her words pierced the fog of pain muddying Thomas's head. Kali brought down her sword, slicing in a wicked arch towards his neck. He rolled aside, grabbed her ankle, and pulled, bringing her crashing down. She grunted, dropping her weapon. Thomas seized it blade-first. Feeling the stickiness of his blood spurt from his fingers, yet suffering no pain, he grabbed the hilt instead and pointed Kali's own sword at her.

Kali stared up at him, wide eyed, as Thomas wielded her sword with apparent ease.

Meri and Thissy – her magic still drained from the previous evening – could only watch, dismayed.

A smirk that wasn't his slowly spread across Thomas's face. He raised Kali's sword high. She bowed her head, shoulders shaking. Was she sobbing? Thomas didn't care. A moment before he brought the sword down, she raised her head, her eyes flashing. Not sobbing; *laughing*.

"Do it!" she cackled. "Do it, boy, go on!"

Thomas faltered. *Why?* Kali got to her feet, her breast heaving, gasping in mad excitement.

"Morrigan got to you first. Poisoned you, didn't she? Now you're drowning."

Thomas's arms shook with the effort of holding her sword. Kali stepped closer, her wide eyes locked onto his face.

"It's not poison, clever boy," she whispered. "It's blood. Do you want to know whose?"

Every sound muted, except his own rough breathing. Slowly, Thomas lowered the sword.

"His?" he asked. He gazed deep into her murky eyes.

Smirking, she nodded.

"You're bound to him now in ways you can't even imagine—"

"*No!*"

Thissy drove her elbow into her captor's belly. He buckled with a groan and she threw herself from his grip. "Thomas, don't listen to her!"

Kali pushed Thissy aside and stepped around her, taking her place. Thomas glanced between them. Burning pain spread from the healed wound in his side.

"I can take you back to Elphame." Kali purred. "To your sister. You can become *my* champion." Kali smirked, brushing her fingers through his hair. Thomas grabbed her wrist.

"Become your champion?" he repeated with a sneer. "You mean become part of the Wild Hunt? I don't think—oh..." He tipped his head back. "I understand now, Kali. I understand *you*. I know what you want. His little warrior. Always trying to impress him. And always failing. *That's* why you want to take us back. So you can prove you're not a worthless failure, that you *can* do something right. Well, it won't work, Kali."

Icily, she pulled her wrist back. "You're soft, little mortal boy. You're weak and fragile. I can break you."

She pressed her lips to his, breathing dragon fire into his mouth, down his throat, into his heart, blazing a mighty furnace inside him.

CHAPTER 20

In which water flows the wrong way

THOMAS RODE ALONGSIDE Kali on a horse that wasn't Epona. Neither spoke. He didn't look back at Thissy or Meri – bound again and forced to walk behind the mounted pair with the common footsoldiers.

Back through the forest they rode, until moorland once again stretched out, that forbidding mountain stabbing skies in the distance. Yet Kali and Thomas directed their horses away, heading deeper into wilderness.

"Where are they taking us?" Meri whispered.

"To Elphame," Thissy whispered back. Then, noting Meri's confused look, she went on, "The Dark Prince must have moved it. It's why no one can find the city. Dark magic," she grimly added. "Unseelie can find it, always, because they can feel his presence. Or *hear his call*, as they like to say. I suppose that's why Thomas knows where to go. He can hear the call now, too. I can't imagine the pain he's in."

"He looks fine to me." Meri glared at Thomas' back.

"Perhaps. But can you imagine what will happen—"

A sword point jabbed into Thissy's back, silencing her.

"Keep talking, wench, and you'll not live to find out. Now *move*."

✧   ✧   ✧

THISSY FELT READY to collapse with exhaustion when they reached their journey's end. The grass was sodden, mud unpleasantly squelching beneath her aching feet.

Kali dismounted her horse, clambering up on a boulder to look out over an expansive loch. An unpleasant smile curled her red lips as she gazed at the still water.

"Melusine!" Kali called, her voice echoing a hundred times. Nothing happened. Kali scowled. "I know you can hear me, Melusine. Show your scaly hide or I'll drag you out of there and hang you up to dry!"

The loch's tranquil waters bubbled. A greenish light shone beneath its surface. The silence grew heavy, thick with ancient magic. Unearthly singing echoed from the loch and sent pleasing chills across the skin of all who heard it.

A dark head broke the surface of green water with barely a ripple. Naked, save for a few slithers of waterweeds, a merrow rose from the water. A beautiful, silent demon. Her hair clung to soaking shoulders like a black cobweb. She smiled so mysteriously it was nigh impossible to guess her intentions. *Friend or foe?*

The merrow – Melusine – approached Kali's rocky harbour, her silvery, scaly tail glistening beneath the surface. Thin, membranous gills on her arms and tail fanned out underwater. More of her kind appeared around her, silently emerging from water. *Ghosts.*

"Ask what you will," Melusine's strange voice chimed, echoing, across the loch.

"Grant access to Elphame," Kali commanded. Melusine said nothing, her disdain obvious.

Her silvery, liquid eyes cast over Kali's party until they

finally rested on Thomas. The merrow tilted her head and beckoned him nearer. Scowling, Thomas dismounted and approached.

"Come close," Melusine said. "So that I might whisper in your ear."

Kali narrowed her eyes, suspicious, but Thomas kneeled on the pebbly beach, leaning in to hear. Melusine smiled, her eyes moon-silver bright, and pulled herself up onto the bank. Her belly pressed against cold, hard earth, her tail thrashing in shallows.

Quiet enough for only him to hear, she said, "Annwyn will beckon on your long journey. Accept your fears, Son of the Old Ways, but do not let darkness consume you."

Thomas felt a curious chill thrumming in his blood, though the loch shore breeze was warm. He stared at her, but Melusine said no more.

Instead, she beckoned him close, and then pressed her lips to his. Cool, pale fingers wrapped in his hair. The taste of loch water filled his mouth. Trickled down his throat. Quelled Kali's fire within him.

"I said *enough!*" Kali pulled Thomas away. He fell back, blinking, shaking his head. Melusine hissed. For a moment, her beauty vanished: her teeth pointed fangs, her eyes black as velvet night—

"Open the way to Elphame," Kali snarled. "Or I swear I will skin you alive!"

Melusine's glimmering tail flickered as she retreated down to the depths. The other merrows vanished after her.

Thomas mounted his horse again, hesitant, uncertain of himself and his purpose. Did he come to rescue Alissa? Or return to Erlik?

The loch bubbled again, sloshing, parting. The water,

between blades of sodden grass, drained away. The loch floor became visible, strewn with slimy plants and rocks, revealing an eerie walkway to a dripping stone arch.

Without waiting for Kali, Thomas kicked his horse's hindquarters, heading fearlessly into that shadowed, watery path. Kali's soldiers followed, but she pushed past to ride beside him.

Thissy and Meri trailed behind, casting nervous glances to the watery walls. The shimmering faces of merrows appeared there, some wearing mysterious smiles, some clutching long spears.

"Rhymer and I will enter first," Kali said. "Follow after with the women."

Thomas had already passed under the archway and vanished.

Darkness and cold shrouded him for a few moments, until the water receded with a great splash, revealing stone walls, cobbled streets, and a looming white castle.

WHEN THEIR GROUP reached the double doors, Kali dismissed her soldiers, taking hold of Thissy and Meri's binding rope.

Without waiting for Kali, Thomas dismounted and ascended the steps. He pushed open the castle doors, striding up the long carpet. Kali stalked behind him, dragging Thissy and Meri.

Erlik sat on his stolen throne, deep in conversation with his eldest. Malik noticed Thomas first. Frowning at his distraction, Erlik looked up. A wicked smirk cracked his face. After a moment of hesitation, Thomas fell to his knees, bowing.

"I'm impressed, you recognise your king," Erlik said

when Thomas stood tall again. Malik raised an eyebrow. But before either could speak again, Kali pushed past Thomas, her dark eyes sparkling with victory.

"Father," she announced, pride dripping from her voice. Pride that turned quickly to contempt when she acknowledged her brother. "*Malik.*"

He rewarded her unwilling salute with a snort of laughter and a mocking half-bow. Kali returned her attention to Erlik.

"Oh, dear me, what happened to *you?*" Erlik smirked, eyeing her scarred cheek. Kali's eyes flashed, but she simply turned to point at her catch.

"Father, look. I've brought you that runaway selkie, a rogue leaf-ear, and Thomas Rhymer," she said, a child trying to impress her father.

Erlik's smirk slowly slipped, replaced with a look of restrained fury.

"You brought him here? Through the lake?" Erlik asked quietly. Malik's smirk spread into an unpleasant grin. "Tut tut, little sister," he said softly. Kali ignored him. Her proud smile disappeared.

"That was what you wanted, wasn't it? You wanted him brought here." Her voice broke. Malik let out a soft, derogatory laugh, clearly enjoying Kali's humiliation.

Erlik sighed. "Did you let Melusine speak to him?"

"I—I d-don't—"

"Don't answer, I already know. You, idiot girl, have ruined what I tried to do."

Kali mouthed wordlessly. Erlik stood, ignoring Thomas, and approached his daughter. Thissy and Meri drew back, but his eyes were fixed on Kali. She thrust the rope into Thomas's hands.

Erlik's voice was barely a whisper. "You've failed me again, worthless child. Begone from this place."

Kali's eyes swam with furious tears. She turned and ran from the hall, leaving a pounding silence behind. Erlik sighed and finally turned to Thomas, who folded his arms, still holding the rope binding Thissy and Meri.

"Well," he said, half-circling Thomas. "She's gone. Now let's see if you're truly mine. What say you, Malik?"

Erlik stepped away and Malik approached. He stood uncomfortably close to Thomas, who recoiled in subconscious dislike, tipping his head back.

"Your blood is strong, Father."

"And?"

Malik paused. "Pure."

Erlik gave a satisfied smile.

"Come, we'll rectify Kali's mistake," he said, his voice echoing around the hall as he gestured for Thomas to follow his long strides from the hall. Wordlessly, willingly, Thomas obeyed the silent command, pulling Thissy and Meri along behind by their rope.

Malik's eyes darted around the room. Once his father was out of sight, he turned and vanished down a corridor.

CHAPTER 21

In which storm clouds gather

THE AIR GREW cold as they ventured deeper into Elphame, until Erlik stopped at a wooden door. He pushed it open with a grating creak. *A dungeon.* Thomas followed him inside. They passed a dozen cells, each bearing several shivering seelie prisoners who stared from the shadows. Thomas gazed at their pale faces. Each slunk back into darkness when Erlik approached.

Ignoring all, Erlik strode on until they reached another wooden door, smaller, studded with heavy bolts. Erlik touched its rusted lock. The door unlatched with an echoing click, then swung open. Erlik gestured and Thomas entered first, tugging the rope so Thissy and Meri followed.

Once he'd entered, Erlik locked the door behind him and clicked his fingers. Torches flared into life, light gleaming on chains that bound the cell's lonely prisoner. Thomas's heart pounded in his chest.

Her moonmilk skin bruised and cut in places, the cruel marks did nothing to diminish her unearthly beauty. Thick, dark hair fell in bounding waves to the small of her back, tangled, dishevelled. Her rose-tinted lips curved into a faint smile.

"Queen Mab?" Thomas whispered. Slowly, Mab

nodded. Her deep, fathomless eyes wide with curiosity, a fire dancing within, glittering like moonlight on ice.

Thomas had never seen anything so beautiful, yet so sad. Mab held herself with royal dignity, even chained in ignoble conditions. Thomas resisted the overwhelming urge to fall to his knees in respect.

"I thought she was hiding," Thomas said softly.

"A cunning deception," Erlik said. "Do you really think I would announce that I have the Queen of the Old Ways imprisoned? The rebellions would begin before I could even think of her ransom."

Meri clutched Thissy tightly.

More to herself, Thissy asked in a soft voice, "Why can't I sense her? Seelie can sense Queen Mab at all times. I can't feel her presence—"

"My magic is blocking hers, foolish girl," Erlik said. "And yours, for that matter. Else all those filthy leaf-ears in the district would sense her too. I can't have that."

"You're evil," Thissy whispered.

"Hardly. And yet, you talk far too much. You two, I think, should be locked up." He snatched their rope from Thomas's hand and dragged them out of the cell. Thomas stared at Mab, ignoring their shouts. Erlik returned alone.

"How you could stand those shrieking harpies, I will never know," Erlik said, locking the door again.

"Why did you bring me here?" Thomas asked, his voice cold. Erlik smiled, almost fatherly, and drew a long, thin dagger. He pressed its hilt hard onto Thomas's palm.

"You must be tested. What better way than this?"

Erlik pushed him towards Mab.

"Pain is powerful encouragement. Mab has a strong will, but it can be broken."

"Encouragement for what? What do you need from her?" Thomas asked, apprehensively eyeing Mab. Erlik lowered his voice.

"Locations of her seelie colonies in the wild, as many as you can obtain."

Thomas looked down at the dagger.

"What damage would this do? Surely she—"

"It's enchanted," Erlik said impatiently. "Stronger than a normal blade."

Erlik's eyes flickered past Thomas to Mab. Thomas thought for a moment he saw pity in those dark tunnels. They held each other's gaze. Thomas glanced at Mab, but she said nothing.

"Whenever you're ready, boy," Erlik said. He stepped aside, leaning against a wall. Casual. Watching.

Thomas approached Mab. The dagger hilt felt slick in his hand. He lifted the blade as his eyes danced over her various wounds. Had this dagger already pierced her? Was that why she stared at it with such apprehension?

"I warn you," Erlik's soft, threatening voice drifted from the shadows, "I'm not a patient m—"

"*Father!*"

The door almost burst off its hinges. Hysterical shouting accompanied the banging on the door.

Rage passed over Erlik's face. He unlocked and threw open the door, revealing Morrigan, breathless.

"*What?*"

"Father—th-the seelie…" she panted. "They're rebelling!"

"Then cull them, Morrigan! Send Malik and Corvus if you're too—"

"No! Father, we—we need you!"

A muscle twitched in Erlik's jaw. Thomas glanced at Morrigan, but her eyes were fixed on her father. Beseeching.

"Very well," he snapped. He turned back to Thomas. "When I return, you'd better have what I want, boy, or I'll make you both suffer. Do you understand?"

Thomas nodded.

"Morrigan, stand guard outside. No one is to enter or leave until I return."

Erlik slammed the door shut behind him. The room fell silent. Thomas looked down at the dagger. The blade glinted in the near darkness, reflecting his pale face. His hand trembling, Thomas whispered, "What should I do?"

Mab tilted her head. "You should lower Erlik's dagger." She spoke in a slow, precise way, considering each word. Thomas paused and looked down. Mab gave him a catlike smile, though still a little apprehensive.

"He told me to hurt you."

"Are you going to obey?" she asked. Her chains quietly rattled in the heavy silence as she shifted. Thomas's eyes followed their links. Shackles around her wrists had left her flesh raw. Thomas's heart leapt into his throat.

Those manacles are cold iron.

"Alissa is waiting for you," Mab went on. Thomas looked up, startled, ashamed. "Do not abandon her, Thomas. I know what he told you, what he did to you, but you are not like him. Yes, his blood is now in you. But do not let his darkness consume you."

Thomas shook his head. Pain built in his temples, burning a furnace in his brain and he raised his free hand to press the heel of it into his eye. Something dark rose in him: a terrible desire. It urged him to raise that knife and silence her.

But Erlik didn't want her dead—

Plunge the blade into her breast.

Thomas didn't want her dead either. He couldn't kill her—

Drown her words with screaming.

He couldn't—he mustn't—

Do it! Do it now!

With a scream of anguish, he raised the dagger. Swiftly brought it down in an arc across her chains. Mab closed her eyes but didn't flinch away.

The chains around her wrist rang when they shattered.

Mab opened her eyes, lips curving into a smile. The dagger loudly clattered to the floor, its magic spent.

"Forgive me," Thomas said, breathless, staring at Mab. "I was—I—"

Mab smiled, rubbing her aching arms.

"It is good to feel freedom again," she said. Her voice echoed. Floating. Slow. Deep. Thomas held his head in his hands, groaning as the room span.

"Thomas?"

"My head… what's happening?" he moaned, collapsing. On his knees now, he curled up, biting his tongue so hard he tasted blood. But it was necessary to stop the scream that built in his chest. Mab kneeled beside him.

"If the Dragon King's Poison is not purged, it will kill you," Mab said, stroking his hair. "I can help you. But you must help me in return. I want my freedom again." Her eyes sweeping over his face, she put her hand over his heart.

"The Old Gods are kind this day." She leaned over him. Parting his lips with her thumb, Mab moved forwards, her lips lightly brushing his. *Cold. Too cold!* A long curtain of her dark hair tickled Thomas's cheek.

Thomas convulsed. He shuddered, gasping for breath, his eyes rolling back in his head. A black cloud rose from between his parted lips. It billowed in the air, twisting and writhing. Mab inhaled. Thomas arched in agony when Erlik's poison left his body, then slumped back to the ground, half-conscious.

Slowly, Mab straightened. Her eyes closed. She shivered. A slight smile pulled at the corners of her lips. She tilted her head back, and exhaled the smoke. Her lips trembled, gooseflesh prickling her arms.

"Most potent, *a rúnsearc…*" she breathed.

At once, Thomas sat up with a ragged gasp, coughing. His bloodshot eyes found Mab and he stared at her. She offered him her mysterious smile. He nodded.

"I owe you my life."

CHAPTER 22

In which Thomas encounters a different dragon

"CAN'T YOU USE magic to unlock the door?" Thomas paced Mab's cell. She patiently watched him and shook her head.

"Erlik locks this door with more than a key. I cannot overcome his powers this time," she said. "I have spent too long underground."

Thomas let out a low growl of frustration, resuming his anxious pacing. Silence reigned for a while.

"A rebellion will not distract Erlik for long," Mab pointed out. "He will return soon."

Thomas nodded, casting his eyes around the room, seeking a weapon. *The dagger!* It lay abandoned by the door, undamaged. Thomas grabbed it, shoving it into the empty sheath on his belt. He threw Mab a smile. She nodded in reply. Then, sharply, her head turned to the door.

"It is time," she said. Thomas nodded. *This is it.* Mab instinctively flexed her hands. The lock rattled. Clicked. The door creaked open.

"Come, my lady, quickly." A young man, barely older than Thomas, beckoned them.

"Who—"

"No time, come!"

Thomas narrowed his eyes, then followed the stranger. Watched him unlock another cell door. A flicker of movement caught Thomas's eyes.

Muttering in low voices, Thissy and Meri sat hunched in a corner.

"Thissy! Meri!"

Both looked up. Their faces brightened. The stranger unlocked the gate on their cell and entered. Immediately, he approached Thissy and helped her to her feet.

"Are you hurt?" the stranger asked her.

After a glance at Thomas, Thissy shook her head. The stranger beamed, running a hand through her hair. A jealous knot tied in Thomas's belly. An unexpected growl escaped his suddenly dry mouth.

"Who are you?" he asked, watching this stranger carefully. Meri and Thissy gave Thomas a brief, welcome embrace.

"My name is Monstrance, if it matters," he said. His large eyes reminded Thomas of someone, though he couldn't quite recall. "I've freed you; why are you still here? Get out, go on!"

"The queen!"

"She's here!"

"Queen Mab! Look!"

Mab had stepped out of her dank oubliette. Excited mutterings and whispers rewarded her presence. Seelie pressed against the bars of their cells, wanting to see her for themselves. Monstrance anxiously shushed them, then turned to Thomas.

"Go on, get ou—"

"Are you ready?" The voice startled Thomas, and he spun around to see Morrigan on the stairs, staring at him with wide eyes.

"*Damnú air*, Morrigan! Never have I met a girl so silent when she walks." Monstrance smiled. "Aye, do it now."

Morrigan took a deep breath, then screamed, "Treason! Prisoners escaping!"

She dashed out of sight.

"Good girl," Monstrance muttered, then grabbed Thomas's arm. "Come, you need to get out, now."

"But—"

"There's no time, Thomas! We can come back for your sister, but we have to leave, *now!*"

The sound of a heavy tolling bell above them spurred Thomas into fast agreement. He dashed for the steps leading up into the castle, followed swiftly by the others. The seelie cheered, applauding Mab's escape; she paused only once to look at them.

"I will return to Elphame. I will save this city, I swear it," she said. Only when Monstrance tugged on her arm did she follow. The group ran out of the dungeon, into the heart of the castle.

Monstrance led their way, running through corridors and foyers. No one impeded their progress. *The rebellion*, Thomas remembered. No sooner had the thought crossed his mind when shouting voices echoed around them.

"*Run!*"

The group fled, dodging daggers and arrows thrown and shot by the castle guards who came upon them. Vases shattered. Tapestries ripped. An arrow skimmed Thomas's arm. Flesh caught, sliced. No pain. *Keep running!*

"Thomas?" A familiar voice. He stopped dead. *Foolish!* Meri crashed into him.

"Thomas, what are you *doing?*"

"Alissa!" he screamed. His sister stared at him, wide-eyed, from a corridor. She took a step, about to drop the silver platter she bore and run to him. The horde of guards rounded the corner, shoving her out of their way, nocking more arrows.

"Thomas, come *on!*" Thissy desperately called.

"I'll come back for you!" he bellowed, stumbling back. Had she heard? He felt Thissy tug his arm.

Dashing through corridors, their group finally burst through a set of heavy wooden doors into a stable. Monstrance slammed the doors shut as soon as Thomas and Thissy got through.

A familiar white horse whinnied and pawed, eager to run the wilds.

"I made sure she wasn't harmed," Monstrance said, mounting a bay horse. Despite himself, Thomas smiled. Mab held Epona's reins out for him. One foot in the stirrup, he mounted. She snorted, happily tossing her head.

A shout came from behind the stable doors, which heaved with effort before bursting open.

Five horses escaped the stables and galloped to freedom, leaving behind several stunned, anxious soldiers, each dreading the wrath of their master.

CHAGRIN GNAWED AT Thomas's insides as they rode free. His heart had leapt upon seeing Alissa, dreams of returning home bursting into his mind. But they'd been swept away almost instantly. Only a thick lump in his throat prevented his ashamed moan from escaping. He'd betrayed Alissa. He had the chance to rescue her and lost it.

As the five horses rode from Elphame, their riders found themselves on a sprawling purple moor, wild and windswept, dotted with gnarled trees. There was no sign of Melusine's loch.

Finally, after what felt like hours, Monstrance slowed his horse to a stop and allowed the exhausted beast to rest. The others, catching up, dismounted. Thomas glared at him, needing to vent his guilty conscience.

Mab reached him first. Monstrance lowered himself to his knees at once, his head bowed.

Sharply, Mab said, "Monstrance, Erlik will have your head for this."

Monstrance sighed, his eyes closed. Mab's face broke into an affectionate smile.

"But let him seethe. *I* am proud of you," she said, gesturing that he should stand. He did so, returning her smile with a hint of smugness at the bewildered expression on Thomas's face.

"I... I don't understand," Thomas said. Thissy took his hand. He glanced at her. *Unhurt.*

"Thomas, this is Monstrance. My eyes at the heart of Elphame," Mab said, flashing him her catlike smile. "Thankfully, Erlik had no idea of his allegiance. We could never have escaped without him."

"Morrigan helped, obviously," Monstrance said modestly. "We organised a riot in the seelie district, and Morrigan was to raise the alarm about your escape, so no one would suspect her involvement."

"You look familiar," Thomas pressed, squinting in suspicion. Monstrance heaved a sigh, awkwardly shuffling his feet.

"You're quick. Most people don't notice it straight

away," he mumbled.

"Monstrance is Erlik's fourth-born. Kali's twin brother," Mab said. Thomas stared at him again. And the longer he looked, the more obvious it became.

Those same large eyes had stared at him with such hate, such madness. That same dark hair had moved without a breeze on the deck of a ship. That same mouth had sneered, had laughed at him.

Thomas took an instinctive step back, his hand flying to his stolen dagger. Monstrance raised his hands to show he was unarmed. Mab, too, raised her hand, but to stop Thomas.

"Enough," she said sternly. "Monstrance is not your enemy. He has never taken up arms against us, and has helped me since I was imprisoned. He brought me information when I could not see past the walls of my dungeon, and gave his father false news about my seelie and their colonies. Trust him, Thomas. I do." Her tone signalled an end to the discussion.

Thomas sighed. "Very well. But what do we do now? Alissa is still in Elphame." A bite of shame gripped him. Monstrance cleared his throat.

"There's a seelie colony not three days from here. We can rest there and gather strength before returning," he said. Mab smiled, nodded, and mounted her horse again.

Monstrance immediately approached Thissy to help her mount. Thomas watched him touching her.

"Thomas, can you help me, please?" Meri called. His eyes fixed on Monstrance, he reached over and helped the selkie tighten the straps of her saddle.

"Do you trust him?" she asked quietly. Monstrance had mounted his horse, gazing at Thissy. *Is that adoration?*

Thomas growled a sigh and looked at Meri, scowling.

"No. But what choice do I have?" he said, mounting Epona. Muttered to himself, *"Mothblood..."*

Mab spurred her horse into movement. Monstrance and Thissy followed. Meri and Thomas glanced apprehensively at each other before pulling their horses' reins, galloping away.

CHAPTER 23

In which Elphame suffers the fury of the Dragon King

"**Y**OU DO IT, go on," Malik muttered. Corvus stood opposite him, eyes darting between Malik and the floor. His chewed fingernails took the brunt of his nerves. Malik folded his arms, drumming his fingers.

"To Annwyn with that," Corvus said. "You're first-born, you should do it. He favours you over me, he's less likely to—I mean, I'm not afraid or anyth—"

"*Liar!*" a black crow on his shoulder cawed, ruffling its shimmering feathers. Frowning, Corvus flicked its beak.

"Quiet, Lilith," he said. Malik chewed his lip.

"He's going to find out eventually. Better to do it now than later," he said.

Corvus exhaled a slow, deep breath. The brothers stared at each other, then turned their gazes into the hall.

Erlik had quashed that seelie riot with only his presence. Once news had spread that the Dark Prince himself was approaching, the rampaging crowds had dispersed too fast for Malik or Corvus to find the instigators, yet half a dozen seelie had been imprisoned.

Their punishments remained undecided.

A shrill giggle rang from the end of the hall. There, Erlik dallied with a serving girl who'd fetched his wine. He stood up and bade her follow, smirking.

"We should do it together," Corvus said.

Sighing, Malik nodded. "Aye."

Both stepped out of shadows, into Erlik's path. He abruptly stopped, staring them down. Taller than both of them. The serving girl immediately lowered her eyes.

Corvus cleared his throat, then said weakly, "Erm…"

Erlik narrowed his eyes, shifting his gaze to his first-born. Malik promptly looked at the floor.

"Father…" Malik began.

Erlik scowled. "One of you had better speak quickly."

Malik's eyes darted around. Erlik. The floor. Corvus. Back to Erlik. He cleared his throat and gulped. "Queen Mab has—has escaped."

The silence that followed built, growing louder, tenser, with every passing moment. Sensing rage, the serving girl took a wary step away, nervously running her tongue over lips.

"What?" Erlik's voice betrayed no emotion. Malik and Corvus glanced at each other again.

This time louder, braver, "Queen Mab has escaped."

Erlik narrowed his eyes. "When you say 'escaped'," he asked, a nasty edge to his voice now, "do you mean she's out of her dungeon and wandering around in the garden?"

"N-no, she… she's gone," Malik appeared to be fighting the urge to back away. Corvus swallowed hard.

Erlik clenched his hands. A muscle twitched in his jaw. The serving girl quickly bowed and moved towards the door. Erlik grabbed her wrist and pulled her back.

"Do you mean to tell me," his voice a deadly whisper, "that after everything I've done for her, everything I've done to keep her safe, she's *left?*"

"The boy, too," Corvus said. Erlik's hands trembled. He closed his eyes for a moment, but his rage couldn't be contained. Fury and frustration overtook him. He slapped the serving girl hard. With a sharp squeal, she fell to the ground, her face now decorated with a bleeding lip.

Erlik roughly shoved past his sons. Malik and Corvus followed, leaving the girl to tend to her lip.

ERLIK FLUNG THE dungeon door open and stormed inside. Whatever excited muttering buzzed inside stopped at once. Open doors of empty cells creaked in the darkness, like they were laughing at him.

"Oh. You clever little witch..." Erlik said through clenched teeth.

Malik and Corvus entered, but stayed as far away from him as they dared.

Without turning to face them, Erlik growled, "How?" Furious disgust etched on his face. Malik and Corvus shared a glance. Neither wanted him to know the truth. The dungeon resonated with silence.

"Answer me!"

"They were helped," Corvus said. He swallowed hard, looking to Malik for help. Erlik ran his hand across his forehead, down over his face.

"Then who was it, whoreson?" he asked, his voice shaking with the effort of controlling his temper. Corvus narrowed his eyes.

"It—I don't know," he said. Erlik spun around and grabbed Corvus, throat. No magic required to hurt him.

"You lie! Tell me!" Erlik bellowed, dragging Corvus closer, inches apart.

"Father!" Malik shouted, but Erlik waved his free hand.

His magic sent Malik sprawling against a wall, groaning.

"F-Father—please—" Corvus, eyes rolled back; he was on the edge of losing consciousness.

"Who was it?" Erlik asked again.

"M-Mon—Monstrance!" Corvus choked out.

His name echoed. Erlik let go, and Corvus fell to his knees. Gulping down air, he massaged his bruised throat as Malik knelt beside him, helping him back to his feet.

"He will pay for this." Barely a whisper, his voice shivering through the darkness, Erlik stormed out of the dungeon, leaving silence in his wake.

The brothers stared at each other, their eyes overcast in fear and sorrow for their younger brother.

"What do you think Father will do to Monstrance?" Corvus asked as they left the dungeon, avoiding the halls their father frequented.

"I don't know. Arrest him. Execute him, most likely," Malik said miserably. "Foolish boy; what did he *think* would happen?"

Corvus heaved a sigh. He stopped to glance out a window, as though hoping to catch a glimpse of Monstrance or his company.

"Gods light your way, lost brother."

BLINDED BY RAGE, Erlik stormed through his halls, higher and higher, until he reached the topmost chamber.

It was dark, filthy, neglected, and freezing at the tower peak. Erlik didn't care. Two clay statues guarded the door, clutching swords, bearing strong, proud expressions. Spiteful, childish, he pushed them over. They smashed against the stone, scattering clay shards. Erlik threw open the door.

"Out!" he spat. Without a word, the two guards who stood inside left. The door slammed shut.

Erlik sniffed disdainfully, looking around. On a pedestal, a large onyx box sat, silent and patient. Erlik approached, placing his pale hands on either side of the box. He pushed open the heavy lid.

A silver dagger lay inside. His fingers caressed its blade, admiring how it gleamed in the dim light. A smile formed on his lips.

Mab had given him this dagger, once upon a time, as a gift. On the blade in fine, curving letters, her name still shone clearly. Instead of his own reflection in the blade, he imagined he could see her face, smiling. It had been a long time since she'd smiled like that at anyone. Erlik lifted the dagger out of its box, gazing at Mab's smile. Her moonlight eyes danced over his face.

Erlik threw his head back, releasing a furious, guttural scream of hatred and heartache. The dagger burned white-hot in his hands, yet his anguish overrode any pain.

Elphame trembled at its foundations. Every inhabitant, seelie and unseelie alike, turned towards the castle, staring in fear at that immense tower.

Debris began crumbling from its spire. As Erlik's scream died, a bolt of lightning, born of his wrathful magic, struck the tower.

Large pieces of the ruined tower rained down on Elphame, crushing houses and people. Erlik had no care for them. Alone he stood in the cracked remains, breathless, glaring at the fleeing citizens below.

His eyes burned, hands shaking; the red-hot dagger had

seared his flesh.

"Are you listening, Mab?" Erlik bellowed to the sky. "Do you hear them screaming? Do you feel their pain? Do you feel *mine?*"

Panting, feverish with madness, Erlik knelt down. Slicing his arm, he painted a seven-pointed star on the stone with his blood, then plunged the dagger into its heart.

The star glowed red, fluctuating from bright to dim. The dagger trembled. As though attached to a rope, it yanked itself out of the earth, returning to Erlik's outstretched hand.

Bone-white, sharp-nailed fingers crept out of the stone. Another hand followed, dragging a head and torso behind it. At last, the white, clammy creature tore itself free and straightened. It clicked, hissed, and snorted, unable to speak, blinking its small eyes at Erlik in curiosity and subservience.

"Find Mab. Bring her back to me," Erlik said, looking disgusted at this creature's mere presence. "Kill her companions if you like. Just bring her back. *Unharmed.*"

The creature cocked its head abruptly. Twitching, it made hacking, guttural noises at the back of its throat.

"Mab has escaped," Erlik replied, somehow understanding this monstrous creature. "My traitorous bastard son helped her. Murder him if you want, I don't care. In fact, I invite you to. Last, so he can watch the others die."

The creature gave him a menacing smile. Or as close as it could manage. It leapt onto a half-destroyed wall. Crawling across it like a hideously overgrown spider, it prepared to jump out onto rooftops far below.

"Abarta," Erlik said, stopping the creature before it left. "You have your orders. But you know exactly what I'll do to you if you hurt Mab."

Abarta hissed and snorted in reply, a brief flicker of fear erupting in its beady eyes. It turned away from its master, gracefully leaping from the window. Erlik watched his creature leave.

Hate bubbled in his chest. Monstrance had always been a weak child. Sickly. Fragile. *He should have been drowned at birth.*

Hate against Mab, for leaving him when he'd cared for her, looked after her, kept her safe from this terrible world. The greatest betrayal. *How dare she? How dare she leave me? After everything I've done for her?*

But most of all, out of all those treacheries, the mortal boy who had tricked him. The thick-skinned human *pig* who had wormed his way into the heart of Elphame. *A maggot to steal my most prized possession away.*

His name burning, blistering, an unbearable madness in his mind.

Thomas Rhymer.

CHAPTER 24

In which Queen Mab offers some calming words

T HOMAS HAD NEVER seen clouds form so quickly. The sky darkened, a menacing black storm looming overhead. Monstrance slowed his horse and allowed the others to catch up.

They'd been riding for hours, still on ferny moorland with rust-coloured soil and jagged rocks. Thomas spotted a farmhouse in the distance, a few horned, hairy cows dotting the fields.

A flash and a quiet rumble. Mab looked around, her eyes exploring the moors as though expecting Erlik himself to appear.

"We should find shelter," Monstrance suggested as the others slowed to a stop behind him. A hard, cold wind picked up and rain began falling in sheets. Thomas nodded in silent agreement. Epona fretfully snorted when a thin ribbon of lightning slashed the sky, thunder rattling louder. Monstrance jerked his head towards the farmhouse Thomas had noticed earlier. Nodding wordlessly, the others rode towards it.

THOMAS KNOCKED ON the little wooden door. This house reminded him of his own, with its warmth hearth and simple comfort. Another pang of guilt racked through him.

A creak and the door opened, revealing a short man with narrowed eyes, one blue and one green, and a balding head. When he scrunched up his face against the bitter cold, staring at this odd, huddled group in bewilderment, Thomas could see several missing teeth.

"Forgive us for bothering you, sir," Thomas said in the politest voice he could muster. "Could we stay here until this storm has passed? We'd be happy to offer something... erm, in return..."

Thomas trailed off. The words had left his mouth of their own accord, yet he had no money to offer. Monstrance tugged a heavy ring off his finger and offered it.

"Real silver," he said. The farmer took Monstrance's gift, inspecting it. It must have pleased him, because he grunted and nodded. He opened his door fully and gestured inside, still squinting at the ring. Thomas smiled, thanking him even as he dripped rainwater onto the floor.

A fire, blazing cheerfully in its grate, sent forth waves of warmth into the house. In the corner, a tethered goat bleated as the farmer curiously peered at the strangers he'd just allowed into his home.

Once they'd stepped in from the rain, Monstrance and Thissy vigorously shook themselves and were stone dry at once. Thomas couldn't help but feel a little jealous, squeezing water out of his dripping hair. Meri shook her head like a dog, spraying them all with water again. She grinned apologetically at Thomas. Mab looked as though the rain hadn't even touched her.

"M'name's Deepwick," the farmer grunted. "You lot need food?"

When they nodded, Deepwick gestured to a wooden

table, indicating they should sit. His back to them, he poured ladlefuls of stew into carved bowls, then turned and set them down on the table.

Thomas, Monstrance, and Meri began to eat at once, thanking Deepwick for his hospitality with bulging cheeks. Deepwick merely grunted in reply.

Thomas took a spoonful of hot stew, only to catch Thissy's eye. She was smiling at him, playful yet genuine. She raised an eyebrow and pointed to the corner of her lips. Thomas cleared his throat and, blushing furiously, brushed away splashes of food around his mouth. *Animal,* he thought, *be more civilised.*

Deepwick, although at first unnerved by his faekind guests, offered honey cakes and berries to all, as well as a bowl of milky porridge each. Mab began to smile more, stroking a black and white collie that emerged from a corner.

The fire spat sparks as logs crumbled. Deepwick sat in the corner, whittling, watching his guests.

"We should get going soon," Monstrance said when all had finished. As if in response, rain pounded harder against the window, and thunder shook the little house. Meri gave a low moan, her shoulders slumped. Standing, Mab approached the window to look out onto the moors.

"I don't think this storm will pass tonight," Thomas said.

"Got bed space," Deepwick grunted. All eyes turned to him and he jabbed a thumb upwards. Getting to his feet, he motioned for Thomas to follow, then led him up the rickety stairs into a loft with space enough for a few people. Thin blankets and pillows lay piled in a corner.

"We can stay?" Thomas asked. Deepwick nodded, but

rubbed his thumb and forefinger together.

"Got coin?"

"Oh. Well, I... I don't really have anything else to offer, I'm—" he said. Deepwick leaned uncomfortably close, tapping Thomas's silver horseshoe clasp.

"That'll do."

"Oh... this was my father's," Thomas said quietly. Deepwick shrugged.

"Then you's'll be out on your arses in the pissin' rain."

Sighing, Thomas unfastened his clasp. After a moment of hesitation, he handed it over. Deepwick grinned and descended the steps again. Thomas threw his cloak over his arm, following him back down.

"There's space in the loft for us to sleep," he said. "We can't go anywhere in this weather; we'll drown before we get anywhere. We'll head out again in the morning."

A murmur of agreement hummed around the table, followed by a scraping of chairs as everyone stood. One by one they ascended to the loft.

Still a little annoyed about the loss of his clasp, Thomas followed the others upstairs. Meri had already curled up under blankets when Thomas entered. Mab stood by a window, her arms folded, staring out into the grey night. Thissy made up a bed and bade them all goodnight. Monstrance crawled under a blanket beside her.

Thomas approached the window to stand beside Mab. Lightning illuminated her face and, for a brief moment, her wintry eyes flashed white. "This storm is Erlik's doing. He knows we have escaped," she said, still gazing onto the moors. "His wrath will be swift and terrible. We must be ready for when the Dragon King breathes his fire."

"Why do you call him that?" he asked. Mab hummed

for him to elaborate, her head cocked in a bird-like way. "Thissy said the seelie called Erlik the Dragon King. Why?"

A miniscule smile twitched Mab's lips for a passing moment.

"If you had seen his soul as I have, you would call him a dragon, too."

Thomas stared at her. A terrible, crushing weight suddenly bore down on him. How could he possibly hope to accomplish his task? Why had he thought it would be so easy? Mab turned to him, a frown creasing her brow. Did she know what he was thinking?

"You should rest, Thomas," she said. He gave a soft sigh of agreement and turned away to bed, on Thissy's other side. He resisted an urge to drape his arm around her and pull her closer to him.

As Thomas pulled a woollen blanket over himself, his last sight before sleep was of Mab, staring onto windswept moors with a strange expression. If Thomas had known her better, he might have called it fear.

✧   ✧   ✧

A WILD, BELLOWING laugh roused Thomas. He sat upright and scanned the room; everyone was still deeply asleep save Mab, who still stood by the window. Had she stayed there since Thomas had gone to sleep?

She said softly, "Did they wake you?"

Thomas nodded. The storm had blown itself out. Now a clear sky allowed moonlight to cast a soft blue glow over the moor. Thomas stood and crept to the window. Mab stepped aside to allow him room. As a bellow of neighing laughter came again, Thomas looked down.

There, a strange collection of creatures danced below their window, a circle of crushed grass beneath their mismatched feet. They looked like goats, but stood upright on their hind legs, dancing madly, cackling with wicked glee. Their braying laughter echoed against stone walls. As Thomas watched, some transformed into giant black stallions or enormous dogs with blazing yellow eyes.

"They are called *púca*," Mab quietly said. "Unpleasant beasts. They have been known to accompany the Wild Hunt, feeding on whatever scraps they can scavenge."

One *púca* beat a large drum in a fast tempo. Another took on a centaur's form to accompany the drum with a fiddle. Their music was dark; fast and forbidding, yet oddly thrilling. Thomas's skin prickled. He tore his eyes away from the dancing creatures to glance at Mab.

"Harvest is upon us," Mab went on, her face caught in moonlight. Its light made her both beautiful and terrifying. Ancient. Powerful. "Everything must thrive and fade in its own time, like the passing of winter into spring. There will come a time when we will be forgotten. Mere fragments on the edge of dreams."

Thomas stared at her, but she continued before he had a chance to ask her meaning.

"The equinox is drawing closer," she said. She looked up, her eyes brightened by the glow of the moon, the ghost of a smile on her lips. Thomas gulped. "This is when you must strike. This will be when you will rescue your sister, and help set my seelie free from Erlik's tyranny."

Thomas balked, a trace of panic on his face. "What?" His hands slipped from the window ledge. "I—I have to fight him again? I only want Alissa back. I'm no soldier, I can't fight—"

"Shh, you will wake the others," Mab soothed. She reached out and cupped his cheek. Thomas repressed a shudder; her talon-like nails were unnervingly close to his eyes. "You do not have to be a soldier to win a war."

"But I have to be a soldier to fight in one! I can't do what you ask."

"If not you, then who? Thomas, you must understand. If you do not help us, then all hope is lost," she said. Thomas stared, his brow furrowing, and Mab sighed. "Once a century, the autumnal equinox falls under the moonstate of Godsbane. When that golden moon rises, magic rests. All faekind become powerless."

"I don't understand," Thomas said. Mab smiled.

"Erlik is fallen. He is no longer a god. He is powerful, yes. But still vulnerable. The Old Gods would not have sent for you at this time had they not thought you capable. Strong enough to be my champion."

Thomas's voice dropped to a whisper. "What if I fail?"

"You will not be alone. I will help you. Unlike Erlik, I look after my own kind," she said. Mab quickly lowered her hand and cleared her throat, looking down at the *púca*.

"They are disbanding now," she said. "You should go back to sleep."

Thomas slowly nodded and returned to his scratchy blanket. The others breathed deeply, undisturbed.

"What about you?" Thomas asked, watching Mab gaze at the dispersing *púca*. She turned her head, throwing him her enigmatic smile.

"Go to sleep, Thomas. There is much to do tomorrow," she said quietly, and Thomas sank into his pillow.

CHAPTER 25

In which the sky burns

D AWN POURED IN through the window, bringing the fresh scent of a new day. Outside, a cockerel flourished his cry. Rubbing his eyes, Thomas sat up, spotting Mab still by the window. She turned to smile at him.

"Did you sleep at all?" he asked. She shook her head.

"I have no need of sleep. 'Tis a luxury I am denied."

Thomas blinked. It quickly occurred to him how ancient Mab seemed. How lonely it must be, patiently guarding their frail mortal lives as they slept. Being the only creature awake, with no one to talk to, only her thoughts for company. Had she stayed this way for the thousands of years of her life? He suddenly understood why she looked so alone.

Thissy, Meri, and Monstrance began to wake, yawning as they threw off their blankets. Mab paced.

"We should be on our way as quickly as possible," she said pointedly as they descended into the farmhouse. "Erlik will have dispatched many bounty hunters. We must reach the colony before they find us."

Deepwick led his goat into the kitchen on a thin rope, a bucket of her milk in his other hand.

Setting the bucket down, Deepwick said, "Been feeding

chickens. You's lot leavin'?"

"Yes, thank you, Deepwick," Thomas said. The farmer grunted, bustling around the hearth.

"I will check on our horses," Mab said. She fixed her eyes on Thomas. "Be quick in your discussion."

Thomas watched her go, feeling a prickle of shame around his neck. How did she know he was going to question Monstrance?

"My father will know of my involvement by now," Monstrance said. "I can't go back to Elphame. Father would kill me on sight. If we are indeed heading for the seelie colony, I would be grateful if I could come with you."

Meri and Thissy shared a glance. Thomas narrowed his eyes.

"I don't think that's a good idea. Considering who you are. Where you come from," he said cagily. Monstrance frowned, leaning back in his chair, folding his arms.

"I know who I am. Do you think I'm *proud* to be his son? And if you remember, you never would have escaped if not for me," Monstrance said. "Besides, have you seen me send any messages? Have I asked you about your plans? About yourself?"

"Not *yet*," Thomas snapped.

"Why would I help you escape only to trap you again? Do you really think the unseelie are so petty?"

Thomas angrily stood. "Who knows how you mothbloods—"

"Enough!" Mab's voice rang from the door. They all turned to her. Thomas avoided her eyes, yet she appeared to have more pressing matters on her mind.

"Come outside, all of you, now," she said, and turned away. With a quick glance at each other, Thomas and the others followed her urgent gait.

THE STABLE DOORS had been flung wide open. No horse, save Epona, could stand. The elvish mare gently nuzzled Monstrance's bay horse.

Mab approached Epona, leading her away from the bay horse so Monstrance could tend to it. "Epona, tell me what happened."

Sounding distressed, Epona snorted and pawed at the ground. Mab stroked her muzzle, soothing her. Thomas patted her neck and looked around the stable, confused. The others tended their lame horses.

"Are you certain?" Mab said, and Epona nudged her with another snort. Something akin to fear passed over Mab's face, and she turned to Thomas.

"Go, tell Deepwick to take only what he needs and run," she said, urgency colouring her voice.

"What is it? What's wrong?" Monstrance asked, standing straight.

"Erlik has sent Abarta."

Monstrance paled. Nodding, he beckoned the others to follow him back inside. Thomas didn't move.

"Who's Abarta?" he asked. Mab looked up at him, her dark eyes full of disquiet.

"I will tell you once we are safe. There is danger here. I will see to the horses. Go inside and help Deepwick."

Thomas nodded and followed the others into the farmhouse.

The kitchen was empty, with Deepwick nowhere to be seen. No tethered goat. No black and white dog. Thomas walked upstairs, checking the loft. No one. *He must have already left.*

Heading back downstairs, he caught sight of Thissy's face; she looked unnerved.

"What's wrong?" he asked. She sniffed, her terrified eyes darting around the room.

"It's here," she whispered. "We're too late."

A strange noise above them, like a cat choking on a hairball. Deepwick dropped from the ceiling, a thick coil of rope around his neck. Thissy threw her hands over her mouth. Deepwick swung, eyes bulging, his body limp. Thomas drew his sword to cut him down, despite knowing he was already dead.

Something – white-bodied and sinewy – rushed at Thissy, wrapping an arm around her, using her as a shield. Its hands clenched around her throat.

"Abarta—" Thissy choked.

"No!"

Thomas pointed his dagger at the hideous creature. It let out a guttural giggle and pulled Thissy closer, shaking its head. It squeezed, claws puncturing the soft flesh of her throat.

Meri swung a heavy pan at the creature's head. The ringing *clang* echoed hard in their ears. Abarta gave a shrill squeal like a burned child, and let go of Thissy. She immediately stumbled forwards, gasping for breath.

Growling, Abarta lifted Meri and flung her across the room. Her small frame slammed into a wooden support. It snapped, bringing down a large chunk of the ceiling. Meri slumped, buried under remains of wooden beams, plaster, and stone.

"*Meri!*" Thissy took a step forward, but Thomas threw out his arm to stop her. Abarta gazed between Thomas and Monstrance, flexing its pasty, clammy hands.

Thomas lunged, his dagger raised high. Grinning, Abarta grabbed his blade, crushing its metal in its fist. The beast lashed its clawed hands, slashing his chest, leaving three gouges that stained the tattered remains of his tunic. Cold air angrily bit at the open wounds. Thomas screamed, dropping to his knees.

Monstrance raised his hands in a gesture of peace and said calmly, "Abarta, stop this."

Thomas stared incredulously up at him. "You're *reasoning* with it?" he gasped.

"*Quiet!*" Monstrance hissed, his face twisted with anger. For a moment, Thomas had to blink to clear his sight, thinking it was Erlik who stood before him.

Menacingly, Abarta grinned. Thomas clutched Thissy closer as she crouched to heal his wounds as best she could. He felt naked, vulnerable without a weapon. *I hope you know what you're doing, Monstrance.*

"Go back to my father and tell him you failed. Tell him you couldn't find us," he said. Abarta paused, blinking. It cocked its head like a dog.

Thomas saw its intention sooner than Monstrance, but before he could shout a warning, Abarta grabbed the unseelie and threw him hard against a wall. The farmhouse shook, dust falling from its already damaged ceiling.

Groaning, Monstrance tried to heave himself to his feet. Abarta stood over him, triumphant. Its hand raised to deliver a killing blow, eyes glinting with victory.

"*Enough!*" Mab's voice once again rang from the doorway. Waves of fury emanated from her. Abarta looked up. Its small eyes widened, and it grinned.

Approaching slowly – *meekly?* – it held out its hand to her. Clicking and grunting in its terrible, guttural language.

"What's it saying?" Thomas whispered.

"It says if I go back to Erlik, it will not harm you anymore. It will let you go free," Mab said scornfully. "It lies. It always lies."

Abarta gave a throaty giggle. It lunged at her. Mab narrowed her eyes, her lip curling into a wolf-like snarl. She raised her hand. The heat of the room vanished. Thomas struggled to catch his breath for a moment. Abarta stopped. Blinking, it looked down.

Ice had formed over its bare feet. Frost slowly crept up its legs. Abarta raised its eyes to Mab, whimpering like a child. Mab glared back at it: hard, pitiless.

Ice slithered around its waist, and Abarta squealed in pain. It arched forward, desperately trying to escape the freezing prison. Mab's magic crackled higher, encasing its shoulders, neck, chin, head. Fear and horror frozen on its face.

Mab slowly curled her hand into a fist. The ice began to crack. Deep fractures ran like rivers along its frosty surface. With a final snarl, Mab clenched her fist tight. The ice, and Abarta, exploded into a thousand tiny, sharp shards.

Mab slowly exhaled into the otherwise silent room. Thomas now understood why she was feared as much as respected, and made a silent vow to never become her enemy.

There was no mercy in her.

"Thomas, help Monstrance," she said. "Thistledown, help Meri. We have lingered here too long."

Thissy began to dig through rubble to reach Meri. Thomas gingerly stepped over splinters of ice, offering his hand to Monstrance. The unseelie gave him a grateful nod.

"Thomas..." Thissy said quietly. Thomas looked at her.

She sat with Meri's head in her lap. Her eyes, full of tears, fixed on him.

His heart thumped painfully in his throat. Icy numbness spread through him.

No.

Thissy looked down at Meri's still form, gently stroking her soft brown hair. Cradling her body. Thomas swallowed hard and looked away, trying to choke down his tears. No use. They overwhelmed him in a hot wave, prickling the back of his throat. He turned away, hiding his face in his hands. Thissy wept silently, rocking back and forth.

Mab approached her and gently took her hand.

"Come, child," she said, in a voice far kinder than Thomas had ever heard from her. "Let her rest."

Thissy let Mab guide her out. Monstrance followed, blinking his eyes dry. Thomas couldn't face leaving. Meri could have been sleeping. *Too still.*

He knelt down beside her. He stroked her hair away from her face, wiping blood from her mouth.

"I'm sorry, Meri," he whispered. "It doesn't mean much now. But I-I'm truly sorry..." he couldn't finish. Kneeling beside her, he buried his face in his hands and sobbed.

AT LAST, EMPTY and aching, Thomas got to his feet. His eyes sore, he left the farmhouse to find the others waiting for him. He glanced at Thissy but quickly looked away; her sorrow brought back his own despair. He fought hard to keep his tears from spilling again.

Mab waved her hand. A blaze sprang up around the farmhouse door. Thomas watched the flames climb higher, devouring the wood and thatch. His heart ached in his chest. He half expected – and for a moment, truly hoped – to see

Meri stumble out, crossly chiding them for leaving her behind.

Thissy took his hand. Thomas looked down at her. Gazing at him, she offered a weary smile and leaned against his chest. He wrapped an arm around her. Words failed both.

"Here," Monstrance said in an empty voice. "This is yours."

Thomas looked at him. He lifted his hand to take what he offered. Monstrance dropped the horseshoe cloak-pin onto his palm. Thomas stared at it. A hollow exchange for Meri's life.

"Thank you," Thomas said quietly.

Monstrance nodded and turned away. Mab approached on a grey horse, leading three others by their reins, including Epona.

"I thought they were lame," Thomas said thickly, desperately seeking a different subject. He separated Epona's reins and climbed up.

"They are. These are Deepwick's goats and pigs, reshaped with faery glamour," she said. Thomas mutely nodded, casting one last, long look at that blaze.

"Come, we must go," Mab said, and kicked her horse into a gallop. The others followed. Thomas came last, leaving a burning farmhouse, a dead assassin, and their fallen friend far behind.

CHAPTER 26

In which Elphame takes over the underground

OORLAND AGAIN. THE group had stopped to allow their horses respite; they'd galloped for miles without rest.

Monstrance sat on a grassy hillock, legs crossed. Gingerly rubbing the back of his head, he groaned and checked his hand for blood. Mab stood behind him, her hands in his hair, inspecting him for injuries. Monstrance flinched.

"*Ow!*"

"Stop fretting," she said with a hint of a smile, laying his hair flat again. "'Tis only a little graze."

Monstrance gave her a disbelieving raised eyebrow. Mab smiled and sat beside Thomas. Her powerful woodsmoke and wildflower scent stung his nostrils.

Thomas sat staring at nothing, absent-mindedly fidgeting. He had no more tears to shed. *What good would tears do anyway? It wouldn't bring her back. Nothing would.*

He felt empty, useless. Thissy glanced at him more than usual, eyes still red. He couldn't bring himself to meet her gaze.

"You must not blame yourself, Thomas," Mab said. He nodded again, wordlessly. "The creature that killed her is dead; there is no need for vengeance. Thoughts of revenge will only poison your mind."

"What was that creature? You said you would explain when we were safe," he said emotionlessly, still staring at grass. The others looked up. Mab slowly exhaled.

"A dead assassin, and no longer a cause for concern. 'Tis best not to dwell on what has passed."

"Father could bring it back," Monstrance said. "He's done it before. Perhaps you should explain, just in case you're... not there to help, next time?"

He trailed off. Mab frowned at him. Monstrance sheepishly turned his face away. Thomas lifted his gaze to her.

"Very well," she said. "Abarta was one of Erlik's many failures. Centuries ago, Erlik thought to dabble in necromancy. This art is dangerous: a deadly game of chance. Once Idath, the Lord of the Dead, has claimed a prize, he will never relinquish it. Erlik sought to change that."

A shiver went around their group. Mab pressed on. Thissy shifted closer to Thomas.

"Whether he wanted to humiliate Idath, gain more power or knowledge, or whether he was genuinely interested, I do not know. What I do know is that his first attempt went terribly wrong."

Monstrance opened his mouth to interrupt, but Thissy shushed him.

"His subject had been a young seelie. Captured, subjected to all kinds of torture. Alas, he was not strong enough to survive Erlik's vicious interrogations. So Erlik attempted to resurrect him. Perhaps to garner yet more information out of the boy. But although Erlik managed to bring him back to life, the boy lost his mind at the sight of what he had become."

Thissy let out a whimper. Thomas looked down at her. Her hands trembled, her eyes round and fearful.

"No…" she whispered, too quiet for any other to hear her.

"Erlik named him *Abarta*, a 'doer of deeds', and gave him strength beyond his control. He took away his free will, so that he could only ever be summoned. It would never stop until it had accomplished its master's command. When Abarta came for you, you knew Erlik wanted you dead."

Thomas felt a shiver creep up his spine, tingling into his scalp. He could tell by her dark eyes that Mab told him this not to frighten, but to warn. *Warn me of what Erlik is capable of.*

Sighing, Mab got to her feet. Monstrance sat beside Thissy, fidgeting. His arm twitched as though he longed to wrap it around her. He put his hand on her shoulder, offering her a scrap of cloth to dry her eyes. Thomas glared at him.

"We should keep moving," Mab said, turning around to address them all.

"My lady?" Thissy said cautiously, standing. "Why would the Dark Prince send Abarta? Does he want to kill you now?"

"No, child. Yet I believe he has no hesitations about killing any of you. Even his own son." Mab cast her eyes to Monstrance. He merely grinned.

"In blood only, my lady. I'm glad it's the only thing we share. *You* have my loyalty."

"Thank you, Monstrance. No seelie of mine will bear ill intent towards you, I assure you. A man cannot choose his father, but he can choose his companions. Come, we have lingered long enough."

Monstrance wordlessly nodded. Thomas, finding his thoughts numbed when riding, was eager to be on the move.

They clambered onto their horses again. As Mab settled herself into her saddle, her magnificent grey gelding snorted. Stroking its neck, she leaned forwards, whispering in its ear. Thomas watched her. Frowning.

"They are not familiar with such labour," she explained, sitting upright again. Still gently stroking her horse's mane. "Magic is, after all, only an illusion."

Mab gave her secretive smile again and galloped away. Despite himself, Thomas felt a bubble of warmth in his chest. Epona snorted.

"I don't know." Thomas smiled, patting Epona's neck. "She talks in riddles."

Epona snorted again – in agreement, perhaps – and galloped after the others.

✧   ✧   ✧

ELPHAME HAD MOVED again.

Deep underground, its citizens curiously gazed at their city's new foundations.

Hewn from the rocks, dimly lit by a muted glow. An underground cavern glimmered with hundreds of subterranean waterfalls. Steps and bridges connected cliffs to platforms. Its inhabitants stared in wonder – and confusion – at this recent addition to their city. No disruption, no noise, no stone out of place. Nothing to suggest anything had happened. Had these two cities always been this way?

Giants roamed the underground. Pointing at this strange sight, muttering amongst themselves, wandering out of their caves and niches. Elphame's sudden appearance had rattled them.

IN HIS CASTLE of stone, King Argus, tallest and most fearsome of all, sat on a massive throne. Listening to the reports from his scouts, he recognised the Dragon King's magic at once.

"Ambassador Gidal, go to Elphame. Speak with Prince Erlik," he rumbled to another giant. "Find out what he wants. If he intends peace, which I doubt, I will allow him and his people to stay. Otherwise, I will remove him. I want no part in this war of his. He will not endanger my people on its behalf."

Ambassador Gidal nodded. When he left the castle, all eyes followed him until he entered Elphame with an unseelie escort. The muttering intensified. Every question the same: what did Erlik want here?

UNSEELIE GUARDS LED Gidal to Elphame's castle. *I see stories of Elphame's beauty have been vastly over-glorified*, he thought.

Gidal's guard escort abruptly stopped outside the castle, the only part of Elphame that remained pristine.

"You will wait," a guard said, "while I announce you."

Gidal nodded and patiently obeyed. He shifted his weight from one foot to the other. Glanced around the courtyard. The whole city seemed... *grey*. Its inhabitants as broken as their home.

At long last, as Gidal dubiously wondered if he'd be granted an audience at all, an unseelie guard emerged from the hall.

"Prince Erlik will see you," he said. "Show your respects when you enter."

Nodding, Gidal stooped beneath the doorframe and entered.

Prince Erlik sat on a throne of onyx, his head gently resting on his hand, tapping his fingernail on the armrest. Anger clouded his eyes: a silent, tired fury. Gidal wondered of the swollen underground rivers, and the flooding the giants suffered in their caves and hollows. Had Erlik's bad mood affected the weather so much?

Erlik said nothing, glaring at Gidal as he approached. He raised his head as Gidal drew nearer, somehow managing to look down his nose at the giant, despite Gidal suspecting Erlik would be half his height, should he deign to stand.

"Prince Erlik," Gidal announced, briefly lowering himself to one knee. Rising again, "Lord of the Unseelie Court, Dark Prince of Elphame and Dragon King of Tír-Na-Nóg."

Erlik sighed at his long string of titles. He wearily pinched the bridge of his nose, already looking irritated with this discussion.

"What do you want?" he asked. Uncomfortably warm in this cavernous hall, Gidal shuffled his feet again.

"I am Gidal the Earthbreaker. I have come as the emissary of King Argus, King of the Underworld."

Erlik said nothing. He stared in disdain as Gidal cleared his throat.

"King Argus requests your intentions. I have come to inquire of why your city has..." he paused, thinking of how best to proceed; Erlik's temper was ephemeral at best. "Er, *invaded* ours. Should you bring war to our realm, King Argus will not tolerate your presence."

Gidal put his hands behind his back, awaiting Erlik's reply.

Erlik took a deep breath. He lifted his head off his arm with the patience of a rearing cobra. He leaned back on his throne, surveying this giant.

"Begone, gargoyle."

His voice was quiet, yet like his expression, it promised wrath should the giant not comply with the threat. Gidal took it in his stride. He had known this arrogant prince would be difficult, but he wouldn't fail his king.

"I am to return to King Argus with—"

"I heard you the first time," Erlik said. "Listen, Grendel—"

"Gidal," the giant quietly corrected. Erlik ignored him.

"Return to your king. Tell him to come bend his knee if he wishes to surrender. I will stay here awhile. Make your peace with that, and leave."

Gidal's face darkened.

"King Argus will not tolerate this insolence. He will ensure you pay with your city in ruins and your body in pieces."

Smirking, Erlik watched the irate giant storm out, knowing what would occur once Gidal relayed his message. *Goading that fool had been so easy. It's a wonder they've managed to construct a city so vast...*

"Addercoil," Erlik called. An advisor crept forwards. "Ready the Wild Hunt; we're about to have visitors."

✧   ✧   ✧

GIANTS MARCHED ON Elphame in one terrible force. Some carried weapons; most merely picked up huge boulders and hurled them at the white castle.

Watching from his balcony, Erlik smirked. *What audacity.* Their boulders smashed through Elphame's walls. Screams echoed from the city centre. Had Erlik cared, he would have pitied their plight.

A bell tolled hard through the city.

Unseelie soldiers burst from Elphame, overwhelming the stronger giants with their greater numbers. A stalemate. The underground trembled with the skirmish. Rocks torn from walls bombarded the swarming unseelie. Roaring, felled giants threatened to cave in the shaking cavern. Yet, despite the unseelie efforts, a couple of giants broke free, tearing through Elphame's defences and into the castle.

The castle doors slammed open, creating a thunderous rumble. Three giants stomped towards Erlik.

"Gentlemen," he said, throwing back the last dregs of wine. He turned to face them. "You've made such a mess of my city."

Without waiting for them to shepherd him out, Erlik strode past, out of the castle. Flanked by his enormous escorts, he crossed the battlefield, through the massacre of both his unseelie and Argus' giants marching toward that stone castle where a giant king awaited him.

The massive doors didn't hinder him. With a wave of his hand, they swung open. Sweeping into a dark chamber, up towards a throne with his black cloak slithering behind him. The only show of respect Erlik offered was a mockingly exaggerated bow.

King Argus glowered, not impressed with his insolence. Erlik smirked back, his arms folded. An arrogant child. He made a disapproving noise.

"Are we done?" His voice rang in the grey silence: deep,

impressive.

One giant laid a heavy hand on Erlik's shoulder. Was that to stop him escaping? Erlik looked down at the hand. Cast his gaze up to the giant's stony face, then across to King Argus.

The king nodded, emotionless. Erlik stumbled when the giant holding him pushed him to his knees.

Yet his smirk widened, his black eyes now bright with mischief, his face no longer overcast with stormy looks.

"Do you know who I am?" King Argus asked, staring down at this smug prince with severe dislike.

Erlik took a deep breath and spoke to a giant beside him, "Your king has forgotten his name. Care to remind him?"

The replying blow sent Erlik reeling. White stars burst in front of his eyes, yet he laughed, wiping blood from his mouth. Argus sat back, a vein throbbing in his temple.

"Kill him," he commanded. Grinning, satisfied, his giants nodded. They raised their clubs high above their heads, preparing to bring them down in a flurry of execution. Erlik didn't move, his wicked smirk stretching into a menacing smile.

"I'm not so easy to kill, dirt-kisser."

The three giants stopped, frowning at each other. One blinked hard and dropped his club. He put a hand to his face, finding it wet and red. Blood seeped from his nose, his eyes, his mouth. He dropped to his knees, a low, pained groan rising to a scream. The others backed away from Erlik as he turned his gaze on them. They choked as blood filled their mouths, dripping from their noses and eyes.

Erlik got to his feet, calmly brushing dust off himself. Argus' eyes wide with horror as he shifted on his throne, eyes darting. The Dragon Prince approached the throne. Slow and dangerous.

"You answer to me now. And your people will cower before me."

CHAPTER 27

In which Thomas finally understands

LAUGHING, ERLIK DODGED a giant, swinging fist. Pillars lay smashed on the stone floor of the ruined hall, destroyed by King Argus' rage and frustration. Erlik twisted his hand. A dusting of black smoke, and a shining silver sword appeared. Argus bellowed, bull-like, and charged at him. Erlik nimbly dodged the rampage and flicked his sword, slicing the back of Argus' knees. Roaring with pain, the giant king collapsed, panting.

Erlik stood over him, casually prodding him with his sword, puncturing his skin with each jab. Welts popped blood, rivulets running red across his body.

"I want command of your army," Erlik said, pointing his sword beneath Argus' chin, pressing into his soft, loose flesh. "I want control of your city. I want your fealty in the coming war."

Argus repaid Erlik's smirk with a glare of pure hatred. "You want a lot of things, mothblood prince! Is that why Mab ran from you? Because you demanded so much of her?" he snarled. "Oh yes, mothblood. We all know she ran from you when you approached."

Erlik's face suddenly darkened. His mocking smile vanished. "Have a care, dirt-lover," he said, a low, threatening voice. "Your next words could be your last."

"Why would she welcome you? *Kinslayer*—"

"*Silence!*"

With a scream of fury, Erlik hurled a fistful of black lightning towards Argus. Too slow to dodge, the bolt of dark magic struck him, square in his chest, and lifted him off his feet with the force.

Argus groaned, twitching, trying to find his feet again. Erlik approached and stood over him. Trembling with rage, he raised his sword.

"I hope Idath butchers your soul in Annwyn," he spat. "Give my brother my regards."

He brought his sword crashing down with awful finality, the blade cleaving flesh and bone.

Miles away on a wild black moor, Thomas awoke with a start.

✧ ✧ ✧

A POISONOUS YELLOW moon hung in the sky, curving like an archer's bow. Thomas and the others had taken shelter in a circle of standing stones.

Thomas sat up. His eyes found Mab, slowly circling the cairn like a patient feline. Their fire had dimmed since everyone had fallen asleep; the dying embers cast a bloody glow over her dark eyes. Grim shadows danced over the surrounding stones.

"You see him in your dreams?" Mab asked. Her eyes fixed on those last few embers. Thomas nodded and she continued. "I see him too. You are not alone. I know such visions are frightful, but you must not be afeared. He is too far away to hurt you now."

Thomas put his head in his hands. *It's not easy to forget that twisted face.*

"What is it?" Mab asked. "Are you still troubled?"

Thomas snorted. Mab cocked her head in her familiar gesture, and curiously gazed at him. Sighing, Thomas lowered his hands but kept his head bowed. He spoke to his knees, "I don't understand. Why can I still see him? His blood is gone. I'm not poisoned anymore—"

He looked up, his heart pounding. The horrible thought had just occurred to him. What if he *was* still poisoned? What if he turned on them, as Erlik predicted he would?

With a soft rustle of silk, Mab sat beside him. Close enough for her mystical scent to again wash over him. She swept her eyes over his face and sighed.

"I understand this must be hard for you. You were dragged out of your certain, comfortable life, and plunged into Albion's icy waters," Mab said. "You and Erlik were bound by blood when he wounded you with Morrigan's arrow. I could purge you with every form of magic I possess, but I could not break that bond. It is part of you now."

Thomas felt sick. Tainted, unclean.

"But I could see things before Erlik stabbed me. Before I came to Albion, even. I saw visions of your war. Your defeat," he said. An angry flush crept over Mab's cheeks. *Perhaps I was a little too blunt*, Thomas thought.

"That is harder to explain," she said, twisting her hands. Thomas frowned. He'd never seen her so uncomfortable.

"Try," he said, voice colder than he intended. Sharply, Mab looked at him. He blinked at the fierceness in her eyes and quickly corrected himself, "I'm sorry. I—I meant… can you try to explain? Please?"

Mab sighed. "I suppose you must learn one day," she said. "Very well... what do you know of Albion?"

Log embers crumbled, spitting fireflies of ash into the air.

"Not much." Thomas shrugged. *What did that have to do with anything?*

"And of the seelie? Of Elphame? What do you know?" Mab pressed. Thomas frowned.

"Only what Thissy and—and Meri told me," he said. His throat stuck when he said his friend's name.

"Then what do you know of your father?"

It took a few moments for her words to penetrate his understanding. Why would she mention *him*? He scowled, his fingers tightening into a fist.

"What about him?" he asked in a low voice. "He left us. He said he was going to fight in a war, and he never came back. Why does it matter?"

His hands now shaking, Thomas chewed his tongue to stop himself saying more.

"Your father loved you, Thomas," Mab said, sounding more like his mother. "That war he spoke of, the one he left for, was ours. Against Erlik. Your father was a seelie of Elphame."

What?

"That's impossible."

"Why is it so? Have you not noticed, you are oddly comfortable here? You have seen wondrous beasts and monsters, yet they have not surprised you. You know you belong here. This heart beats with seelie blood," she said. She put her small hand on his chest, where his heart thumped hard and fast.

Thomas looked up at her slowly. His eyes and mouth

wide.

"My—my father… was a *seelie*?" Thomas said. Mab nodded again, her fathomless eyes steady on him.

"I remember the day well. Tamlyn had been hunting. He followed a stag just a little too far; crossed the bridge without realising. He found her there, your mother: young and beautiful, a fragile mortal. He loved her at once."

Thomas balked; a young man, a mysterious hunter, emerging from the forest. Approaching his mother. A young woman, then.

"Tamlyn was a good man. He wished to stay with her and raise their family. He came to me and asked to leave Elphame. I was reluctant, of course. Love invites only heartache and grief. But he pleaded, and I relented. Tamlyn took his leave of Elphame, abandoned his faery heritage, to live a mortal life with a mortal woman he loved. And their children."

Thomas drew in a shuddering breath. He wasn't sure if he wanted to hear more.

"I believe he never told her where he had come from, what he really was. Perhaps he could not bear to think of what sorrow it would bring her, to discover her beloved was not born a mortal man."

"Does that mean I'm…" Thomas couldn't finish.

Mab smiled. "Half seelie, half mortal. What you see in your dreams are not visions or prophecies. They are your father's memories. You inherited more than his cloak pin."

"So why did he leave? If he loved us so much?" Thomas's anger flared up again.

"When Erlik's army first attacked, and our war began, Tamlyn knew he could not sit idle while his people suffered. He returned to Elphame to fight for his city, his queen, with every intention of returning to you when the war ended. But, of course, war is a fickle beast, and Idath will take whomever he chooses from the battlefield. He did not survive."

Thomas felt the skin around his eyes grow cold with drying tears. They sat in silence for a while, until the eastward sky began to pale.

"How did he die?" Thomas croaked. Mab broke her gaze from the lightening sky to look at him.

"Does it matter? He is at peace now, resting for all eternity in the House of the Old Gods." Mab stood up. She sighed. "We should be leaving. These moors are dangerous, even without Erlik's hunters tracking us," she said. Thomas frowned. *She's hiding something.* He stood up, put his hand on her arm and stopped her.

"Mab, tell me," he said. She froze. Raised her eyes to him. Perhaps she found his touch offensive. He retracted his hand at once. "How did my father die?" he asked again.

Mab sighed again. "You are already burning with vengeance over Alissa's capture. If I told you, how far would you go—?"

"It was Erlik? He killed my father?" Thomas interrupted, his voice rising in anger, hands shaking. Thissy stirred in her sleep.

"Shh," Mab whispered, glancing at her before continuing. "No, Thomas. Erlik did not engage seelie on the battlefield. He faced only me."

"I don't care! *Tell me!*"

Mab inhaled slowly. "Kali killed your father."

A powerful beast rose in Thomas' chest, screaming, demanding revenge. Forcing something hot and sickly up his throat. He swallowed a hammering desire to scream in anguish and fury. But he couldn't quell the sour burning deep in his heart.

"Mothblood bitch!" He spat on the ground. Storming to Epona, he grabbed her reins, dragged her to her feet, mounted her. Mab quickly stepped in front of him.

"Epona, let him down," she said, stroking the horses' muzzle. Epona gratefully snorted, kneeling, lowering Thomas back to the ground. Thomas glowered at Mab. Yet he quickly remembered who he was looking at, and averted his eyes.

"Be calm, Thomas—"

"*Be calm?* She killed my father! I've *hated* him all these years and it's *her* fault!"

"Yes, she did. But Kali is far away. You will waste time hunting her. Your chance for vengeance will come, but not now," she said.

Thomas heaved a great sigh and dismounted. "Very well," he said, glancing towards the rising sun. "We should wake the others. We need to be on our way."

Mab narrowed her eyes, as though suspicious, but said nothing more. She walked over to coax the others awake, while the sun rose over them.

A storm raged inside Thomas's skull. Kali, Little Dragon, that mad woman, had slaughtered his father where he lay. He remembered now, he'd seen it happen in his dreams.

And now, according to her prophecy, they would meet again. Her words echoed in his mind. *On that third time, one of us will die.*

"Thomas?" Thissy's voice broke through like a blast of cold air. He shook his head to clear it. The others had mounted their horses; the sun had fully risen. Thomas must have been lost in memory. He once more clambered up onto Epona.

"Stop daydreaming, Thomas. Come," Thissy said, smiling.

He found himself boiling with anger. How could she be so calm when all he felt was anguish and hatred? Yet she'd done nothing wrong. He smiled, although strained, and apologised.

"We're not far now," Monstrance said, tugging his horse's rein. "We should reach the colony before sundown."

Mab nodded. She glanced at Thomas. Lost in his own thoughts, he stared into the distance. Monstrance didn't notice his distraction and kicked his horse into a gallop. The others followed.

CHAPTER 28

In which a queen returns to her people

ERLIK TAPPED HIS fingernail on the arm of his throne, glaring so fiercely at the quivering seelie that his tired eyes ached with pressure. It took all his self-control not to incinerate this wretch where he stood.

"Sire," the seelie said, in a shaky voice. "The winter is coming. Nights are growing colder, and days are becoming short. The small amount of firewood you've allowed for each house is not enough to sustain us each week. Our children and elderly are falling ill. Already the weakest have begun to perish. We beg you, my lord. The seelie district needs aid."

Taking in a slow, deep breath, Erlik lifted his head. Looked down at the seelie, his black eyes glittering with curious malice.

"What's your name, leaf-ear?" he asked. The seelie balked, looking around the hall, anxiously twisting his hands.

"Greytamer, sire."

Tipping his head back, Erlik leaned back, still tapping his finger on his throne. An irregular heartbeat. Seelie names irritated him to no end. *Far too superfluous.*

"Greytamer... what do you do? For a living?" he asked.

Greytamer swallowed hard.

"Swineherd, sire."

"You have a family?"

"Aye—yes, sire. A wife, a-and two children."

Hatred of the seelie bubbled in his chest like poisonous bile. Erlik's glare burned into Greytamer for a long time. He suddenly sat up straighter. Greytamer flinched. Smirking now, Erlik stood up.

"Very well," he said, slowly approaching the quivering seelie. "Each household will receive more firewood a week."

Greytamer smiled in relief, hastily bowing.

"Thank you, sire. You are most gracious," he said. He turned away, ready to be escorted out by unseelie guards.

"Of course, you realise," Erlik raised his icy voice. Greytamer turned back, his smile slipping. "Taxes will be raised to accommodate this luxury."

Greytamer stared, horrified. Erlik smirked, folding his arms, and sat back on his throne.

"B-but sire," Greytamer pleaded, approaching Erlik again. "We can't afford higher taxes!"

The guards pulled him back. Erlik shrugged.

"That's the price to pay. Freeze to death at night, or starve to death during the day. Your choice," Erlik said.

Forgetting himself, Greytamer spat at him, "Tyrant! How are we supposed to feed our children?"

"Feed them with pigswill, swineherd," Erlik sneered. He turned to one of his guards. "Go to Farmhand's Nook, find his family, put them in the dungeon. Tell the executioner to sharpen his axe." Erlik looked at Greytamer. "Three days, leaf-ear."

"*NO!*" Greytamer lunged against the guards' grip, as if

hoping to attack Erlik. The prince merely laughed.

"Don't worry, you'll all be together," Erlik said. "Lock him up."

Guards hauled Greytamer away, the seelie screaming curses. Finally, his voice died away and silence fell in the hall once more.

"Allow his eldest to escape. Make sure the child knows what's happening," Erlik said to his guard captain, who looked at him quizzically.

"Sire?"

"The best way to lure a she-wolf is to threaten her cubs."

❖   ❖   ❖

THE SETTING SUN cast a soft golden glow over the moors. A wide river wound through fields, its surface shimmering like glass in dimmed light. Castle turrets, reflected in the water, thrust into the sky like spears.

In a quiet hall of the castle, a powerfully built old man bent wearily over a map, his hair a mane of moonlight down his back. The parchment, worn at its edges, had some areas crossed out with thick black lines.

"Elder Lightfoot," a soft voice said. Silver-haired Lightfoot turned, scanning his friend's face for any trace of good cheer. He found none.

In a tired voice, the old man asked, "Any news, Firestrider?"

Firestrider sighed. He had a harsh face, features carved into a permanently bleak expression. A thin scar ran over his left eye, his shining red hair streaked with grey.

"None, *a sheanchara*," he said, with a sad shake of his

head.

Lightfoot sat down heavily, hiding his face behind his hands. Firestrider turned the map around to stare at it.

"Elphame is moving more than usual," Firestrider said.

"Indeed. I believe the Dark Prince is on edge," Lightfoot mumbled through his hands.

Firestrider squinted at the map. "He moved it under Rostherne Mere?" he asked. Lightfoot nodded without looking out from behind his hands. "Didn't Melusine protest?"

Firestrider set the map down. Lightfoot lowered his hands, revealing an old man; far too old, too tired, to lead the seelie in such dark times.

"Perhaps. I suppose she didn't want to risk her people's lives," he said. "We know he has no qualms about slaughtering an entire race."

Both seelie stared at each other. Neither wanted to voice their fears, but they knew their list of allies grew shorter with each passing day.

Breaking the grim silence in the hall, the doors crashed open. Lightfoot's head snapped up, his hands flexing, prepared for an attack. A young lad ran into the hall, out of breath, eyes alight.

"Eld—Elder Lightfoot," he gasped, clutching a stitch in his side. "Qu... Queen Mab... has arrived." His words echoed.

Without another word, the two elder seelie scrambled for the door, dashing out of the great hall, along a corridor, and stopping at a balcony overlooking an antechamber. Below, seelie had gathered, muttering excitedly.

The doors opened wide. Swirling mist poured in, tinged gold and red from dying sunlight. Silence fell.

Hooves sounded against stone, and the Queen of the Old Ways emerged from the golden mist, bareback upon a magnificent grey gelding. Her ancient, glittering eyes swept the chamber, and her seelie fell to their knees.

Others appeared behind her. Mab smiled as a few seelie curiously looked up. "Arise, my seelie, and pay respect to my companions, who helped me escape from Prince Erlik," she called. It had been so long since her voice rang in their ears that none of them even flinched at his name. "We have come to begin the uprising against a tyrant, he who calls himself king in our city. The fallen one who subjugates *our* people in *our* city. We will stand for his cruelty no longer. We will return to Elphame. We will overthrow the Dark Prince. And we will take *back* what is rightfully ours!"

Braziers and fireplaces burst into purple and black fires that sent waves of arcane scent billowing into the air. Seelie broke out in roaring applause, cheering for their queen. Mab's proud smile shone in the firelight.

CHAPTER 29

In which the seelie discuss their fate

THOMAS RESTLESSLY PACED his bedchamber. Despite such lavish, distracting furnishings, his mind raced with thoughts of Mother; was she still sitting by Alissa's bedside, watching, waiting for her to wake? Thoughts of Alissa still in Elphame, alone and afraid.

It seemed impossible to think that only a few days ago, Thomas had stood in his own home, unaware of any world beyond his own. Unaware of faeries, of Mab and Erlik, of—

A knock on his door broke Thomas's daydreaming. Turning, he saw Thissy enter his bedchamber. Smiling, she looked beautiful in a new pale green gown.

"Are you coming down?" she asked. Thomas smiled, nodded silently and followed her. They headed down a hallway towards spiralling stairs.

Thomas kept quiet as the pair made their way through corridors. Just before they entered the great hall, Thissy put her hand on his arm.

"What's wrong, Thomas?" she asked. He blinked, then smiled.

"Am I so obvious?" he laughed. Thissy gave a little smile.

"You've been quieter than usual. What's wrong? Is it…"

She took in a deep breath. "Are you thinking about Meri?"

Thomas sighed. He took both her hands and pressed them close to his chest. His heartbeat quickened. Thissy's cheeks flushed pink.

"I miss her, but... there's something else, Thissy," he said. She frowned, curious. "Mab told me about my father. Who he was. Who—*what* I really am. My father was a seelie. And I'm... I'm half-seelie."

Thissy blinked. Her eyebrows lifted into her hair. Thomas continued before she could speak.

"Mab says I belong in Albion. But I miss my home, my *real* home. I miss Alissa and Mother. I feel like I'm forgetting them."

Thissy stared at him, her eyes full of sadness. Thomas slumped under her sorrowful gaze.

Thissy asked quietly, "You want to go home?"

He stared at her and ran his tongue over his lips. "I—I thought I did. I thought all I wanted to do was find Alissa, take her home and... and never look back," he said. Thissy sighed and lowered her eyes. "But being here, being with you, it's made me see things differently."

Thissy looked up again. Her eyes sparkled. Smiling, hesitant, Thissy wrapped her arms around him. Thomas gently brushed strands of hair from her face, gazing down at her. Thissy stood on her tiptoes, closing her eyes, her breath coming faster, in short bursts. He leaned closer to her.

A click. The hall's door opened. A seelie emerged and cleared her throat loudly. Both Thomas and Thissy jumped and broke apart at once.

"Her Grace is waiting for you, my lord, my lady," she said. His cheeks burning, Thomas nodded.

Others had already gathered around a large table in the

hall. Mab sat at its head, regal and imperious. Monstrance looked up when they approached. His eyes travelled between Thomas and Thissy, noting their flushed faces. Scowling, he lowered his head again.

"Morale had been low before your arrival, Your Grace. The seelie didn't have the courage to take war to Elphame," Lightfoot was saying, as Thomas and Thissy took their seats. "Our soldiers are few. Only yesterday we received word that Captain Shatterblade is dead. Your arrival will have lifted their spirits, but faith will only get us so far."

Mab took a deep breath. "How many seelie stand ready to fight?"

"Two hundred strong, my lady," Firestrider said. "We were unsure if we should summon allies here, before we learned of your imprisonment. We assumed, like many others, that you were in hiding. Now that you are with us, we will send emissaries to our allies and begin building our army."

"Have we many allies left, though?" Monstrance asked, raising his head. A scowl twisted his face. "My father has decimated any who stand opposed to him. Whoever is left would now be too fearful to come to our aid."

"What about Captain Bonney? Can't she help?" Thomas asked. All eyes turned to him. He averted his eyes. Nervous, wishing he hadn't spoken. *They all look at me the same way. Like they recognise me. Like I'm... familiar...*

"Her ship will be the other side of Ériu's Isle by now. And with West Port burnt down, her resources are low," Firestrider said, then added in a mutter. "Besides. *Pirates...*"

"We could send word to the *Fianna*," Monstrance quietly said. An awkward hush fell over their table. Everyone avoided looking at him, save Mab, who gazed at

Monstrance with fierce pride. Lightfoot made a rumbling noise at the back of his throat.

"Oathless mercenaries? No, no, it's a bad idea," he said.

"It may be our only choice." Monstrance reclined in his chair, shrugging.

"We don't have the wealth to buy an army."

"Erlik will be ravaging their lands as well as ours," Mab put in. "Perhaps they will fight for their own survival, rather than for our coin?"

"They're a formidable force, Your Grace," Lightfoot said. "But the *Fianna* are notoriously flighty. They change alliances as easily as the wind."

"Then what—"

The hall doors burst open. A dirty, bedraggled child, barely older than ten, ran in screaming, pursued by half a dozen seelie guards.

"Forgive the intrusion, my lady," one said, quickly bowing to Mab. "The boy slipped by us."

Mab nodded. She looked down at the boy sobbing uncontrollably at her feet.

"He's going to kill them!" he squealed. "They said— they said he's going to kill them!"

Mab slipped down from her chair and kneeled, so they were at the same height. The boy took her offered hand and stopped sniffling.

"Calm, child. Tell me what happened," she said in a kind, yet firm voice.

The boy nodded. "Th-the D-Dragon King." He sniffed, wiping his eyes on his sleeve. "Papa went to ask him for more firewood, but then some men came. They took Mama and Rosy away. Please, please, he's going to kill my family!" The boy started wailing again.

"Have you come from Elphame?" Mab asked, incredulous. "Alone?"

The boy nodded, wiping his eyes with the back of his hand. "Stole a pony," he mumbled, the faintest hint of pride in his voice.

"You are brave, child," she said, her taloned fingers surprisingly gentle in his hair. "Go with these men, they will take care of you." She beckoned a guard and watched him lead the boy from the room.

The door snapped shut. Mab faced her court again, each one avoiding her eyes. She gripped the table edges so hard her knuckles shone white.

"My lady?" Lightfoot tentatively asked, leaning towards her. Mab took in a deep breath, casting her gaze at each member around her table.

"I believe this boy is a messenger." Mab stood up, circling the table. "Erlik is cruel, but he is no fool. He has little interest in mindless executions. This is a lure."

"You can't return there, my lady! It's—"

"I know the dangers, Firestrider."

At once, half a dozen pairs of feet bore their owners' weight, as each one around the table leapt up, shouting voices overlapping.

Narrowing her eyes, Mab raised a hand. Purple fire flickered at her fingertips. Furious indignation died in their throats, and all mouthed wordlessly like fish in a pond. Silenced, they all sat meekly back down.

"That is much better," she said, her enigmatic smile tugging the corners of her lips. "It is my duty to defend my people, down to the smallest child. Erlik knows this; he is exploiting it. This is a game to him. Thankfully, I know how to play."

Thomas cast a glance around the table. All looked resigned. *Why is no one questioning her?* He couldn't let her go back, it would be madness.

"I will return to Erlik and stop this execution, along with any others he may have planned. Use this time I buy you to recruit allies, as many as possible. I will leave at dawn."

Thomas got to his feet, glaring. "You can't do this," he growled. "He'll kill you."

Calmly, she folded her arms. "He will not."

"What if you're wrong?" he said. The others sucked in a collective sharp breath.

"Thomas, *hush!*" Thissy whispered, urging, desperate. She tugged his arm, trying to get him back to his seat. Instead, he pulled his arm out of her grip, kicked his chair aside and approached Mab. All eyes followed him. Lightfoot and Firestrider tensed.

"Why is it so important *you* go back?" Thomas snapped. "Why not one of us?"

Mab's voice grew icy, "Is that what you propose? Tell me, then, Thomas. What do you suggest I do?"

Thomas could have sworn the room's warmth vanished. Gooseflesh pimpled his arms. Yet he ploughed on. "You should hide and let us fight for you. There's no reason for you to go back to him."

Mab's eyes were blazing now, the flaming braziers dimming, plunging the room into darkness.

"Hide? Allow others to fight and die on my behalf? I see. And you think Erlik will give up?" she asked. Her voice was cold now. *Too cold.* Thomas swallowed hard. Had he gone too far? Mab got to her feet. Frosty waves crept from her, engulfing him. Thissy shivered. Thomas took a nervous step back.

"I—I only meant—"

"Erlik is willing to slaughter *children* to get to me," she hissed, her voice a slither of wind through winter branches. "Do you believe he will think twice about slaughtering any of you? How long do you think it will be before he inflicts his wrath upon the rest of Albion? I will *not* abandon this world to his tyranny."

"My lady—"

"Any man who uses fire to kill a dragon is a fool," Mab said. "You cannot think to outsmart Erlik. He is cunning and he is ruthless. More so than any of you can imagine."

Admonished, ashamed, Thomas fell silent. He slowly sat back down, his stare fixed on his hands.

Warmth crawled back into the room. The fire regained its light. Mab inhaled, slow and deep, and turned to face the rest. All eyes avoided her gaze. Silence fell around the table.

"Perhaps you should all get some rest," she said with a sigh. "This night has lasted long enough."

Chairs scraped as everyone stood up. They filed out one by one, until only Thomas remained. Thissy paused, waiting for him, but he bade her goodnight, and she left without a word.

Thomas waited until she'd shut the door behind her. He turned to Mab.

Her back was still to him when she said, "Go to bed, Thomas."

"What happened between you and Erlik?" he asked, his anger flaring. Mab slowly looked over her shoulder at him.

"Why do you ask me this?"

"You said I was bound to him by blood. But you have visions of him, too. *Why?* What did he do to you?" he asked, approaching her. Mab turned to face him. What was that look in her eyes? Sadness? No... regret, perhaps?

"You ask impertinent questions. 'Tis not your—"

Thomas grabbed her wrist. *"No,"* he spat. "I don't want to hear that it's not my business, or that it's too complicated, or that I won't understand. I won't let you go back to *him* knowing he's done something to you, something he could easily do again."

She glared. He withdrew his hand with a yelp of pain. Through frosty eyes, Mab watched him put his burnt fingers to his mouth. Thomas's heart pounded bitterly in his chest. Did he hate her, or himself?

Her wintry eyes quelled the red-hot anger in his heart. He sighed.

"I'm sorry," he said after a long, thoughtful pause. Shaking his head, he turned away, too ashamed of himself to face her. "I don't want you to put yourself in danger."

He heard her sigh. Stealing a glance, he found her sitting back down at the table, gesturing for him to join her.

Taking his hands, healing his burns, she said, "Erlik and I are bound, not by blood, but by love. This is how I know he will not kill me," she said.

Thomas stared at her. *How could anyone love that monster?* A smile twitched on her lips. Perhaps she knew what he'd been thinking. Her eyes were fixed upon the table. He considered asking her if she loved him still, then quickly thought better of it.

"You must understand, this was many years ago," she said. "Erlik was not as he is now. I had been... *promised* to Idath, his brother. As you can imagine, the Lord of the Dead did not make for good company. He was cold, heartless as stone. I felt nothing for him. And I believe he felt nothing for me." Mab paused, releasing Thomas's hands. "Erlik was different. He did not treat me the way others did. Not as a tool to shape the world. Not a voiceless, soulless creation. Not a magical substance to which he could become addicted. He saw me as a woman, and treated me as such."

Thomas looked down. Admittedly, he had always either thought of her as a queen or a powerful sorceress. He'd never considered her a *woman* before. This peculiar vulnerability didn't suit her.

Mab went on, "Erlik was strong, clever. Gifted in magic, silver-tongued." A soft laugh, then. "A little roguish, perhaps. He was always kind to me. Considerate. And I adored him."

"It seems impossible. How did he become... like he is now?" Thomas asked, enraptured. Mab sighed.

"He and Idath quarrelled often. I am uncertain of the cause of their arguments. I only know there was no love between these two brothers. Perhaps it had been my confession that drove Erlik to do it – I had admitted my feelings for him. Perhaps Idath could not bear the thought of losing to his younger brother... he always was a proud, stubborn man."

She paused now. Thomas didn't press her.

"Their bitterness grew into hatred. Hatred turned to madness. And madness consumed him... consumed them both, perhaps. Yet Erlik struck the first blow. Idath was not fast enough. Erlik had killed his brother before I could stop him."

"He killed his own *brother?*" Thomas asked, barely able to manage louder than a whisper. Mab gravely nodded.

"Love is vicious," she said. "I broke with Erlik that day. For his crime against his brother, he was punished. Cursed.

The Old Gods cast him out. I believe he holds me responsible for his banishment. But I know in my heart he will not kill me. No man can tame me."

"I... I'm sorry, I had no idea, it—" Thomas said quietly. Mab pressed her fingertips to her lips.

"You have no need to ask forgiveness, Thomas," she said. "Your loving heart, your compassion, they make you strong. They make you *human*. I am proud to call you my champion."

Thomas gulped. Her glittering, crystal eyes pierced him. She stood and Thomas mentally shook himself.

"You should go to bed, Thomas," she said.

"Will you be safe? When you go back?"

She smiled. "I cannot say for certain. But do not fear for me. You are needed here."

She turned to leave again. Thomas stopped her once more. With a slightly impatient sigh, she glanced down at his hand holding hers. "What is it, Thomas?" she asked. He paused.

"Be careful, Mab," he said, and raised her knuckles to his lips.

Mab flinched slightly.

His face flushed, Thomas pulled away. He stared at the floor, shuffling his feet. "I'm sorry," he mumbled. "I'm not sure why I did that... I—that was an accident, I'm sorry."

Mab sighed. He looked up, grateful to see her smiling.

"Another woman owns your heart. You and I both know who." She gave him a searching look.

She knows how I feel about Thissy. Thomas felt his cheeks warm.

"Now that you know who and what you really are, you will feel the pull of magic much more strongly than you once did. That is why you kissed me. You do not have feelings for me; fear not. You are merely attracted to magic. But you must control it, you understand?"

He nodded, meek now. He ran his tongue over his lips, chewing the insides of his mouth.

"Go to your chamber and rest, Thomas," she said, a smile colouring her voice. "Tomorrow, we both take the first steps of our journey."

CHAPTER 30

In which Thomas Rhymer looks into his soul

GREY MORNING BROKE night's darkness with fresh, cold crispness. The sun had yet to rise, and Mab stepped out of the castle doors, cloaked against early morning frost. Allowing the doors to close behind her, she stepped onto the grass. A chill nipped her fingertips.

Mab glanced at the paling sky; a few stars still blinked at her. Her hood fell back, sending waves of dark hair tumbling around her shoulders.

She closed her eyes, crossing her arms over her chest. The slowly receding fog that preceded dawn tingled with ancient magic.

"Cosantóir," she breathed. Lowering her arms, a pulse of magic rippled from her. Grass waved, yielding to the rush of magic, tender and frosty in the mist. The ground at her feet birthed a spray of white heather that blossomed into a bush, encircling the castle like a moat.

This will keep you safe, Mab thought, picking a stem of heather and fastening it to her cloak.

With a satisfied smile, she turned away from her ring of flowers, approaching the stable to untie a horse, knowing that the slowly rising sun would soon wake her seelie. A few goats and pigs miserably bleated and snorted in a corner.

Mab's magic, no longer needed, had faded from them.

She loosed a horse's rope and mounted the beast. He nervously pawed the ground, but Mab patted his neck. Reassuring him. Reassuring *herself*.

"Come, Aonbharr," she said. "We have both faced worse."

The horse snorted. Mab tugged his reins into movement, and Aonbharr set off, passing over the protective circle of heather. Mab's cloak billowed behind her like wings as she galloped back across the moors to Elphame.

THOMAS SAT UPRIGHT. Panting, he fell out of bed, banging his head on the side of his four-poster bed, dashed to his window and looked out.

His head throbbing, he saw a lone figure riding away on a grey horse over rolling plains and mountains. A crowd had gathered beneath his window, curiously inspecting a white circle that had apparently sprung up overnight.

Thomas moved to the trunk at the end of his bed, pulling on his shirt and breeches as fast as he could. Tugging his boots on as he went, he staggered out of his room, only to crash into the woman standing there.

"Thomas, there you are," Thissy said, beaming. He flattened his ruffled hair. "Come quickly!"

She led him out to the castle's front steps and pushed her way through the crowd to the fore.

Thissy pointed to springy bushes of white heather at her feet. "Look! Queen Mab must've summoned them to protect us while she's gone."

"Gone?" a seelie beside her repeated. "What do you mean? Where's she gone?"

"Oh! I—er…" Thissy stammered.

"Queen Mab's gone again? Why?"

"Gone? Where?"

Thomas pulled her away from of the murmuring crowd. They followed, gathering around her like worried sheep.

"Why has she left us again?" someone at the back piped up. Their muttering grew to panicked shouts.

"Queen Mab has left to defend Elphame." Lightfoot's voice silenced that distressed crowd. He stood on the top step, gazing down at them.

"Will Queen Mab be safe? She hasn't gone back to… *him*?" someone else asked. Lightfoot glanced at Thomas before he answered.

"Such details are not important. But know this: we will now rise from our repression and show the Dark Prince the strength of our—"

"What strength? We barely have an army!" another voice called.

"Shatterblade is dead; we have no one to lead our soldiers!" someone else shouted. Objections swarmed like scurrying rats. Lightfoot cast his eyes to Thomas as he and Thissy moved away from the crowd.

Thomas shook his head frantically, shrugging, but it was too late; the seelie had seen Lightfoot glance at him. Silence fell. All eyes burned into Thomas.

"Him?"

"But he's just a boy," a seelie at the front said.

Narrowing his eyes, Thomas opened his mouth to object. Yet words failed in his mouth. They were right. His mind rang with promises he'd made. *And broken.*

The look on his sister's face when he'd left her behind in Elphame…

He thought of Mab. They were wasting time by arguing amongst themselves. She had called him *champion*, yet he felt so undeserving of such a title. Soft fingers threaded into his. He looked sideways to find Thissy gazing at him. His heart pounded in his throat.

"Your—*our* queen has returned to Elphame. She has left to save the seelie Erlik has under his thumb."

A shiver reached through the seelie at his name. Thomas creased his brow. How could they fight against a man they so feared?

"Mab is risking herself to save our people, and we would stand around, thinking of reasons why we shouldn't fight? Despair and self-pity won't best a dragon. Fear and hatred won't best a dragon. Courage will! Strength and unity will! How much longer will we stand around arguing? Will we let him win?" he asked. A few seelie dolefully mumbled. Thomas scowled at their despair. "He's murdered and oppressed the seelie. He's destroyed the lives of so many. And now he has our queen!"

Their muttering ceased at once. Anger rippled.

"Mab may have left us for now, but she's still guiding us," Thomas went on. A new bubble of pride overcame his fear. "Erlik thinks we're weak. He thinks he can break us. But will we turn and run? Will we admit defeat? No! Because we stand together. We will rise from the mist and the moors, stronger than ever. So I ask you again: *will we let him win?*"

"*Never!*" a seelie at the front bellowed. A few joined in with his enthusiasm.

"The Dark Prince," Thomas scoffed. The seelie jeered. "Why should we fear his name now? Erlik's age has come to its end. It's time to bring Elphame back to glory, and drive out this shadow he's cast over Albion for far too long. Sharpen your swords, my friends. Fletch your arrows, tighten your bowstrings, and summon your courage. It's time to take this fight back to Elphame. For Queen Mab!"

As one, the seelie raised their arms, cheering.

"For Queen Mab! For Queen Mab!" they chanted. Thomas stared down at the army, *his* army, a fire blazing in his chest. He looked to Thissy, her face glowing as she beamed at him and nodded firmly. His heart leapt into his throat and he suddenly realised something that had been gnawing at him for a while. Something that he hadn't quite understood until now.

I love her.

ACROSS THE MOORS, cheers echoed until they reached Mab's heart. She sharply pulled on her horse's reins, looking back from whence she'd come. Though now too far away to see the castle, she heard and felt the outcries of her people. And she smiled.

CHAPTER 31

In which the Dragon King regains his pride

S KIES GREW STORMY as the day wore on. A grey horse galloped over meadows, fields, and moors without rest. Sweat coated the beast, yet Mab urged it on. Relentless. With hope, with luck, with an enormous amount of kindness from the Old Gods, she would reach Elphame before the execution. Her breath caught in her throat whenever she imagined what would happen if she failed to reach her city in time. *No,* she told herself. *He would not...*

The sun had rolled well towards its horizon when a mountain range finally came into view. A scar on the world.

Approaching a flat boulder at the foot of a mountain, she scanned the rock face for a fissure, an entrance she knew led to the underground city of giants. She dismounted Aonbharr and he gave a grateful neigh.

"How did you know it would be here?" he said. Playfully smirking, Mab patted his nose.

"My own city, Aonbharr?" she said. The horse grumpily tossed his head.

"I never understand your magic," he snorted. Mab gave him another grateful stroke, then turned to examine the rock face again.

After a few moments, running her hands in the air over

a deep fissure, Mab said, "The way is through here."

"Are you certain you should do this?" Aonbharr asked, nervously pawing the ground. Mab looked over her shoulder at him. She stepped back, guiding him away from her magic.

"I saw this day approaching many moons ago," she said. "I knew then I could not escape it. I have seen what will happen when I enter this mountain, and I have accepted the consequence. What will happen in these coming days could change the fate of Albion forever."

Closing her eyes, Mab raised her hands. A cruel, hard wind picked up, dragging her hair across her face. The ground rumbled and Aonbharr whinnied, rearing in fright. Mab felt a potent, malicious power resist her own. Water crashing against a dam. *Erlik's power.* She almost faltered, but managed to keep herself steady, forcing tendrils of her magic deeper into the rock.

Mab kept her eyes shut through the sound of a loud, splintering crack. Clouds of purple flame billowed at her fingertips. Her hands trembled. The cold ache of magic tugged hard on her heart. Her mind furred, dizzying.

The crack split further until at last it was wide enough for them to slip inside. Only then did she lower her arms, panting, her head swimming and her heart thumping.

"You did it," Aonbharr said softly. Awed. "You moved the mountain."

She stroked his nose, "You should return to the colony, Aonbharr. There are fewer places less suitable for an elvish horse than underground."

"We say the same of you, my lady," Aonbharr nudged her gently. "I stay with you."

Mab smiled and nodded, grateful. Taking his reins to

guide him, she headed into that dark mountain. Aonbharr resisted at first, but Mab kept a reassuring hand on his neck. She conjured a dancing purple and black flame on her palm, lighting their way in the pitch black.

A path led them down, further into deep darkness. The mountain rumbled around them again as the fissure closed, trapping both in the underground cavern. Mab suddenly felt its suffocating darkness and closeness. Her breath caught in her chest. Her heart pounded painfully hard in her throat. Visions of a black and silent oubliette threatened to overwhelm her. But she pressed on, forcing those sickening images away.

At long last, the darkness began to lift, and Mab found herself staring at the majesty of an underground city. She found it hard to appreciate such magnificent craftsmanship when Elphame's glaring white walls gleamed in the darkness, demanding her gaze. Mab drew a deep breath.

Elphame's castle loomed out of shadows, crouching beastlike at the highest reaches of the city. Its dark windows appeared to her like eyes, watching for her, knowing she had returned.

ERLIK STOOD ON a balcony above the castle's courtyard, gazing down at the gathered crowd of seelie. Some wept, or bayed for his blood; most stood silent in fear and sorrow. Three figures stood on a raised platform, hooded and bound. The smallest figure shook like a leaf. A tall, muscular unseelie stood nearby, face hidden behind a white mask, clutching a massive axe.

Erlik's eyes scanned the crowd, seeking a flicker of her

midnight cloak, a faint trace of her earth magic, a glimmer of her moonlight eyes. Nothing. He shook his head. Disappointed, he sighed and leaned forwards, nodding to his executioner.

He grabbed the tallest seelie first – Greytamer, perhaps? – and forced him to his knees, bending his head over a wooden block, exposing the back of his neck for the cool kiss of a blade. The crowd grew restless.

"Down with the Dragon King!" came the cry from the seelie mass. Erlik's cold eyes snapped to the voice, yet he remained silent. He signalled to his guards. At once, they pushed through the crowd, dragging the one defiant seelie out of sight before he could incite further rebellion in the others.

"Carry on," Erlik called down to the now silent courtyard. Nodding, the executioner raised his axe high. Each seelie held their breath. Erlik narrowed his eyes. With a cruel swish, that wickedly curved axe cleaved the air.

"*No!*"

The axe wrenched, dragging its executioner with it, by a thick, sylvan root. Metal struck wood instead, the blade missing its target. The crowd gasped, looking around. Erlik grabbed the balustrade and leaned forwards. At last, he saw her.

Mounted upon a grey stallion, having at last emerged from the gates of the courtyard, her glittering eyes fixed on him. With her arm raised, commanding the roots of the earth, Mab glared up at Erlik with that intensity he'd always adored. Slowly, she lowered her arm. The crowd, realising what had happened, began to applaud and cheer, swarming towards her. But she had eyes only for Erlik. His heart jumped into his throat. He laughed, cold, clear, and sharp.

His audience fell quiet, looking up at him.

"Behold," he called down scornfully, gesturing to her. His voice rang in the silence. "Your queen and saviour, come to depose me."

Mab smoothly dismounted, eyes still on him. Erlik beckoned her. The seelie parted to allow her through, each one bowing as she passed.

✧   ✧   ✧

ERLIK SAT EASILY upon his stolen throne, a hungry smirk on his lips. Mab stood in the middle of the room, her black cloak shimmering against firelight. Icy as a statue in winter. Unafraid. Unfeeling.

"I received your message." Mab's calm voice echoed in the empty hall.

"Obviously," he said, standing up. "You wouldn't be here otherwise."

No longer smiling, Erlik approached her. Circling her, a lion judging its prey. He kept his hungry eyes on her. Mab carefully watched him. *He is more dangerous now.*

"You're clever," he went on. "Tricking the boy into helping you escape. What did you offer him? Power? Riches?"

"Freedom," Mab said. Raising a cocky eyebrow, she sauntered to a table, where she poured wine into two of the goblets. Erlik's eyes drifted to her backside. "Freedom from your control. From your... *taint.*"

"My taint?" Erlik repeated, approaching her. "Such harsh words, beloved."

Turning, Mab handed him a goblet. Ruby wine gleamed in the firelight. He slid her cloak off her shoulders, letting it fall around her feet.

"It *is* a taint. I should know, I have tasted it." Mab smirked when Erlik casually took her goblet, swapping it for his own. After raising a toast to her, he took a swig of wine. He returned to his throne, comfortably reclining. Watching her. Noting how she lowered her undrunk wine.

"You *are* clever," Erlik said. His voice clear in that silent hall. "But what should I do with you now? Now that I have you back." He smiled wickedly at her.

Mab stood stoicly, a patient she-wolf.

"I am sure you will think of something," she said in a biting voice. Erlik's brow crinkled.

"I won't put you back in the dungeon," he said. "The leaf-ears—"

Mab hissed. Smirking, Erlik raised his hands in apology.

"The *seelie* know you're here; there's no reason to hide you away."

He stood up again and approached her. She took an instinctive step back. Amused, Erlik chuckled, and continued towards her. Mab tipped her head back, an eyebrow briefly flicking up. Her heartbeat quickened. Could he hear it?

His eyes wandered up and down her frame.

"You know there's always a place in my bed for you," he breathed, trailing his fingers along her collarbone, tangling in her hair. She pushed his hand away.

"I will have my own bedchamber," she snapped. Erlik grabbed her wrist, holding it up to face height, frowning.

"There's something… I can smell something on you."

Erlik leaned closer, his eyes dark and narrow. He coursed his free hand to her throat, towards her face. His thumb traced the outline of her rose lips. He paused, looked down at her hand.

"Who kissed you?" he asked. A scowl dented his brow.

"I am not your—"

"The boy?" Erlik grabbed her arms and shook her. Then, with a distinct air of disgust, "You let a *mortal* kiss you?"

"You hold mortals in such low regard, yet you have no qualms toying with their lives," Mab retorted. Her face had flushed from anger, not embarrassment. Thomas's kiss had been nothing to her: an act borne of confusion. Erlik's eyes seared into her.

"Because that's all they are: playthings of gods," he sneered, roughly forcing her face up to his. "You filthy little whore, you—"

Mab slapped him hard. Stunned, he stared at her for a moment, blinking. Then responded with a vicious backhand.

Mab staggered back with the force of his blow, reeling. Stars burst into light in her eyes.

Slowly, she turned her head to look back at him. Erlik glared back, panting.

Mab raised her hand and touched her stinging cheek. For a while they were silent, merely staring at each other. Unspoken memories hung in the air.

"Well," Mab said at last, wiping blood from a neat cut on her lip. "I see your manners have not improved over the years."

"I could do worse," he growled. He began to circle her again. Slowly. "I could have done *much* worse to you, after what you did to me."

"And what did I do to you?"

"You destroyed me!" he grabbed her again, spinning her

around to look at him. His fingers bruised her arms, leaving purple hearts in her milky flesh. "I was banished because of you! You told me you loved me, but you *left* me!"

"You found company quickly enough," Mab said, a trace of bitter resentment in her voice. Erlik blinked, momentarily distracted.

"What? Oh…" he snorted out a cold laugh and let go of her. "Well, of course, what did you expect?" he took her hand now, his voice beseeching. "I never loved them, you—"

"*Love?*" Mab repeated, almost laughing. "What do you know of love?"

She stared up into those dark eyes. Her heart skipped. He looked hurt by her words. *Do not be fooled. It is a cruel trick.*

"How can you say that?" he asked. "After everything I've done for you? For *us?*"

"You are heartless," Mab said. Erlik took her hand, placing it on his chest, over his racing heart.

"Am I?" he asked. He brushed Mab's hair away from her face with his free hand. She gazed at him. Then, as though to prove a point, he took his hands away from her. Hers remained on his chest.

"'Tis heavy with hate and anger. How remarkable you are not weighed down by it, like a stone in a river," she said, taking her hand away, folding her arms. "If the world were just, your face would be as twisted and withered as your heart."

Erlik smirked, toying with her hair again. "Such kind words, Mab. That you still think me handsome after all these years."

Mab narrowed her eyes.

"I tire of your glibness. I will retire to my chamber," she

said. "Do *not* follow me." She pushed his hand away and once more strode past him.

"Mab," he said. She paused. "Do you love me?"

A long, solemn silence followed. Mab took in a deep, slow breath, glancing over her shoulder at him. He gazed back, hope in his eyes. He swallowed hard.

"Do you love me?" he asked again. Softer this time.

Mab said nothing. She turned away and left the hall, leaving Erlik to sit on his throne, brooding and seething in lonely silence.

CHAPTER 32

In which a traitor is made known

"I CAN HEAR his call. Father has moved Elphame again," Monstrance muttered, opening his eyes, looking around at the seelie. Each stared at him patiently. "It's underground, in the city of giants."

"A clever move; we can't attack there. There's no possible route for an army to enter the mountain," Lightfoot put forward.

"Perhaps we should wait until Father moves it again?"

"We could draw them out. Fight on open ground," said Firestrider, poring over a crinkled map.

"When's the equinox?" Thomas asked, bending over the map, glancing at Lightfoot. The elder looked taken aback at this question.

"Less than a week," he replied. Thomas made a thoughtful noise at the back of his throat.

"Is that enough time to gather our allies?" he asked. "Mab told me that's when we should strike."

Silence met this announcement.

"Are you mad, thick-skin?" Firestrider asked, a half-formed laugh in his voice.

Thomas blinked at the seelie in surprise before straightening up.

"Mab said it would be the best time to attack," he explained, glancing at Lightfoot. "Because Erlik and his unseelie would be weak—"

"Aye, but what about us?" Firestrider replied, standing up and walking around the table to face Thomas. "We would be as defenceless as them under equinox moonlight."

"We don't have time to waste," Thomas said. "Mab is risking herself to protect us and buy us time."

"Thomas is right," Monstrance said. All eyes turned to him now. "But the equinox can offer something more."

The seelie stared at him. Monstrance stood and approached to look at their map. He moved a quiver of arrows out of the way, placing it with the accompanying yew bow leaning against the side of the table.

"The strength of my father's army lies not in his citizens or soldiers, but in the Wild Hunt," he said. "Father commands the Hunt as his own personal army, with Malik as their captain. Unseelie soldiers are little more than city guards."

"Whenever you feel like explaining, mothblood," Thomas said impatiently. Monstrance flushed, scowling.

"My point is, *leaf-ear*," Monstrance snapped back, "The Wild Hunt are just shadows: shades of men, not alive, not dead, just… wraiths. But under the equinox moon, their magic is stripped away, and they are shown to be tangible, killable men." He smiled now. "When that moon rises, they'll be more helpless than a rich man in a den of thieves."

Thomas made a noise between a thoughtful murmur and a sigh, reluctantly impressed, and glanced at Firestrider. "What more reason do you need?" Thomas said. "We take the battle to *them*. We need to work quickly."

"Very well," Lightfoot said, standing up. "I'll send—"

The hall's doors crashed open, inviting a cold breeze in.

Mab stood framed by creaking doors. An odd, cooling mist seeped into the hall, pooling around her boots.

Thomas stared. Why had she returned so soon? Behind him, the seelie quickly got to their feet. Each face registered bewilderment.

"My lady?" Lightfoot said, his face blank. He blinked several times, perhaps thinking his eyes were lying. Mab turned to him, an unnervingly sweet smile lighting her face, and started to laugh. Mad, wild, and cold.

The seelie stared hard. Each one backed away from her as she approached, her gait awkward and limping, shuffling like a beggar.

"Erlik must have done something to her," Thomas whispered to Lightfoot. "She's not right."

Before Lightfoot could whisper his reply, Mab lunged forwards. She grabbed Thomas's face, pressing her sharp nails into his cheeks, forcing his eyes onto hers.

"You are he who stood with me! On foaming tide where merfolk hide!" she said in a singsong voice, still madly grinning. Thomas's brow furrowed, now uncertain, as Mab leaned in closer, staring deep into his eyes, her nails digging into his flesh. She giggled.

"See what you have seen before, Little Dragon at a city door!" Mab took a step back. Thomas's mouth dropped open.

"No…"

Mab's pale skin darkened. Her sleek hair turned shaggy, onyx black. Her amethyst gown became tattered remains of a shirt and breeches. The final remnants of her beauty faded, revealing a cruel, wide-eyed woman, smirking the same way her father did.

Seelie scrambled to grab weapons, but Kali laughed manically. Her head twitched with every step she took.

"I tell the truth, you see? *You see?*" she squealed. Thomas backed away, hiding himself in the small crowd of seelie. Kali watched his every move. Grinning, she cocked her head. "Ooh, is Rhymer boy afraid of me?"

"*Kali!*" Monstrance pushed through the seelie. "You shouldn't be in here!"

Kali hissed at him like an angry cat. Their brown eyes met, the resemblance enhanced now that Thomas saw them together.

"Treachery! Most heinous treason! Monstrance has lost his sense and reason!" Kali sang at her brother. She shook her head quickly, her face twitching, eyes blinking. *Madness.*

"Kali, please. You're not well," Monstrance said in a placating voice. She stamped her feet and squealed, an irate toddler. "You need to let me take care of you."

"Kali is not mad, though she seems to be," she said, shaking her wild head again. Thomas tried to avoid her eyes, but she swept her gaze over their huddled group and sought him out. "Come out, come out and play with me!"

Thomas didn't move. The group pressed closer around him. Thissy placed her hand on his forearm, steadying him. Kali hummed to herself, swaying where she stood.

"Crush the moon and drown the sun," she mumbled, dancing, turning on the spot, giggling. "Pluck the stars out, one by one."

"She's sick," Monstrance whispered urgently. "Please, let me take care of her!"

"How did she even get in?" Lightfoot asked, his eyes fixed on the madwoman.

"Whisper, whisper, whisper, whisper, it won't matter

once Father's kissed her..." Kali sang to herself.

"I know how," Thomas said darkly. He turned to Monstrance. "*You* let her in."

Monstrance blanched. His eyes widened, his mouth falling open. Attempting a smile, he said, "T-Thomas, why would you—"

"She said I would meet her again when I was betrayed. It was *you*. You helped her get in, get past the circle. She couldn't have managed it by herself. You're the traitor!"

Monstrance opened his mouth to retort. But his face flushed. Thomas knew his accusation rang true.

"I told her to stay hidden..." Montrance's voice was quiet. "I didn't want anyone to find her. I need to take care of—"

"I want you gone, mothblood."

Shivering now – whether with anger or fear, Thomas wasn't sure – Monstrance had gone pale. His eyes wide, bloodshot.

"No, Thomas, you don't understand."

"I don't want to hear it, get out!"

"Thomas, maybe we should do something..."

He looked down at Thissy as she spoke. Her eyes were fixed on Kali, still swaying like a willow in a storm. Thomas turned to face Kali. Then, as though his heart and legs had made this decision on their own, he stepped out of the group. Kali's gaunt face lit up. Metal sang against leather when he drew his sword.

"No!" Monstrance rushed forward, grabbing him his arm. "Please, don't!"

Thomas caught a fistful of his collar and threw him away. The unseelie staggered. Firestrider caught him and held him fast.

"Thomas, please!" Monstrance begged. "She's my sister! Aren't you trying to save *your* sister? Let me save mine!"

"Don't you dare compare Alissa to Kali!"

"Are we going to play now, Rhymer boy?" Kali asked, shuffling forward. She only had one of her two swords left hanging at her waist. "To dance and play! What joy, what joy!"

She giggled, unsheathing her sword. Thomas approached, hand steady. Up close, Kali looked dreadful.

Her filthy, matted hair hung lank around her face. Sun-darkened skin stretched gaunt across sunken cheeks and empty eyes. Madness had robbed whatever beauty she had. The scar Thomas had given her shone white through the dirt on her face.

"Thomas, be wary," Thissy breathed. Kali's eyes snapped to her.

"Witchling, witchling, say no more!" Kali squealed at her. "Lest you speak what I deplore!"

She started a dash to Thissy, but Thomas swiftly raised his sword, pressing it against Kali's hollow jaw. A thin trickle of blood slid down his blade. Kali hissed in pain.

"It's cold, it's cold, it burns us folk!" she shrieked, retreating from his sword. "Like kissing fire and catching smoke."

"Begone, Kali," Thomas said. Angry blood thumped in his ears. "Begone and I won't follow you."

"But Kali has crossed fern and fells," she said, pouting. "Under falls and over dells."

Thomas glanced back at the group. Firestrider still held Monstrance, but all eyes were on him now.

"Tear the flesh and break the bone," Kali mused, staring with deep interest at Thomas. He looked back at her, unsure of himself. "Will Kali then be welcomed home? If Kali kills the Rhymer's son, will Rhymer's song at last be done?"

A wave of hot fury cascaded over Thomas. Roaring, he raised his sword and lunged at her. Kali squealed, more excited than afraid, and nimbly dodged his clumsy thrust.

"This battle you can't hope to win, when a battle rages still within," she said, her eyes flickering to the healed wound in his side, where Erlik had stabbed him with the poisoned arrow. Foolishly, Thomas faltered. Kali at once took advantage of his hesitation, leaping forwards, sword raised.

Her strike almost shattered both blades. Those watching flinched as Thomas and Kali clashed again and again.

Kali may have been a fierce fighter before, but now madness had taken her. She fought without limits, without need to pause for breath, taking every opportunity she could to duck beneath his defences. She nicked his shoulder, pierced his arm, and sliced his thigh. Yet Thomas still fought back. *I will not relent!*

He swung his sword at her legs. Kali fell on her back with a grunt, dropping her sword.

"No," she moaned, and began to cry, child-like. Thomas stopped. He blinked. Guilt nibbled him.

Perhaps she—

Kali screamed and swung her blade upwards, slicing down his wrist and into the back of his thumb.

Yelling in pain, Thomas flexed his hand, suddenly realising he couldn't hold the weight of his sword. His heart pounded in his throat, choking his gasp. Unsteadily, Kali got to her feet.

She cackled, "Liar, trickster, cheater of death! A moment then, to catch your breath?"

Through a red haze of pain, Thomas transferred his sword to his left hand, though its unfamiliar weight made him hesitate. He raised his sword, pointing it at her face.

Monstrance struggled to free himself.

"Don't kill her!"

Thomas ignored him. Why *shouldn't* he kill her? She would easily kill him, given half a chance.

Kali bared her teeth. She lunged, and Thomas brought up his own blade. Kali deflected it with a violent swing. She pitched her clenched fist at him. He dodged. Not quick enough. Her strike glanced off his jaw. He staggered. Seeing him unsteady, Kali kicked him hard in the stomach.

The force of her kick like a smithy's hammer, Thomas fell with a grunt. Kali bounded forwards, a mad grin splitting her face, aiming her sword for his chest. His eyes widening, Thomas rolled away.

Kali released a frustrated scream. Her sword had plunged into the floor where Thomas had been only a moment before. Her blade sunk deep into stone as though it were soil. She tugged desperately at it.

Panting, Thomas looked up. Saw her struggling. He kicked her legs from under her. Kali shrieked and fell in a sprawled heap.

Thomas pushed himself to his feet with his sword. He advanced on Kali, raising his sword to point it at her.

Kali's lower lip trembled. *Is she about to cry? That childish trick won't work again.*

Thomas glared, hatred like he had never known coursing through his body.

This pitiful, wretched creature was the reason he had

grown up fatherless. A solemn, empty silence blossomed through the hall. Barely anyone breathed. All eyes were on him. Thomas could only hear his own furious heartbeat.

Until a voice – not his, not Thissy's – floated into his head.

"You and Erlik were bound by blood… I could purge you with every form of magic I possess, but I could not break that bond. It is part of you now."

Thomas's hand shook. He swallowed hard, sweat beading on his forehead.

Did Erlik's blood still surge through his veins? He had sensed there was… *something* not quite right inside him.

Fear in Kali's eyes burned into him. Her tremulous breath seemed louder. Thomas stared into those dark pits.

I'm not like him. I'm not…I'm not…I'm not!

A loud clatter. Thomas threw down his sword.

"Leave, Kali. Go now, and don't return. If we ever meet again, I will kill you. Do you understand?"

She slowly nodded. Thomas's hands shook, tears pricking the corners of his eyes. He blinked them away and took a deep breath.

"Kali," Monstrance said. Firestrider had released him, now assured he wasn't about to help her murder Thomas. He took one step, then shook his head and stopped mid-stride. "Go, Kali. Run away."

"Thomas!" Thissy breathed, and pushed through the crowd to run towards him. He sniffed and threw his arms around her, buried his face in her neck. Her hair caught those tears that managed to escape as she held him.

A piercing scream, more animal than human, rattled through the hall.

Kali!

Thomas barely had time to speak. He thrust Thissy away, out of danger, and spun around. No weapon. *Fool!*

Kali had leapt to her feet again, Thomas's sword raised high above her head.

A twanging bowstring. A meaty thump.

Kali staggered, drew a ragged gasp, her eyes wide. She made choking, guttural noises at the back of her throat. Her fingers lost their grip and she dropped the sword. A shivering wail escaped her open mouth as her eyes took in the shaft of an arrow.

Kali fell to her knees, trembling. Thomas stared. *How...* He turned. His jaw dropped.

Monstrance clutched the bow so tightly his knuckles had turned white. Its string still quivered. Silence rang loud, and all eyes were on Monstrance.

Kali whimpered and collapsed back. Dropping the bow with a woody clatter, Monstrance rushed to her side. He lifted her into his arms.

"K-Kali..." he moaned. "I'm sorry... I'm sorry, I'm sorry..."

"Little brother..."

She looked up at him. She smiled, raising a trembling hand, gentle as she touched his cheek. Madness dwindling at journey's end, Kali closed her eyes, and her chest fell with her final breath.

CHAPTER 33

In which a wolf is tamed

E RLIK STOOD ON a white stone balcony, surveying his city. A warm breeze lifted thin gossamer curtains, like ghosts, behind him. His black eyes narrowed as he watched merchants set up a market below his balcony. Many stalls heaved with potions, trinkets, and weapons.

Glaring into Elphame's inner city, Erlik took notice of a small girl – fair-haired and white-clad – drifting through the cobbled street below. His glare softened. *Morrigan. Good girl.*

Erlik smiled to himself. Morrigan picked up a gleaming obsidian dagger. Her conversation with the merchant was brief. She handed over a fistful of coins and tucked the dagger into her belt, continuing on through the market. Erlik couldn't help noticing her miserable expression. *Why is she so sad?*

Erlik sighed, running a hand through his hair. A breathy moan, and Mab approached him from behind. She locked her arms around his waist, resting her head between his shoulder blades.

"Come back to bed, my handsome prince," she cooed. He turned, looking down at her. Her thin gown was bound tight and lush around her, accenting those tantalizing curves. He stroked her warm, silken cheek, and she purred, wriggling with pleasure.

"Disrobe for me," he said, returning to his bed to watch her, drinking deep from a wine cup. Giggling, Mab slowly unfastened the strings of her gown. She let it fall in a ring around her feet. Erlik sighed, feasting on her naked form. Until she swayed, an alluring dance meant to entice, and he rolled his eyes.

He tutted in disgust, "Don't do that." Then, draining his cup, "She doesn't act like that."

Pouting, Mab dropped her arms by her side. She huffed a sigh, puffing out her cheeks.

"Well, how *does* she act, then?" she asked, picking up her gown and pulling it on. Erlik closed his eyes. He took in a deep breath and leaned back.

Opening his eyes, he looked down at her, "Like a queen, not like a whore."

Frowning, Mab waved a hand over her face.

A red-haired girl stood before him, a little taller than the real Mab. She crawled over the bed towards him.

"If you wanted to bed a queen, you shouldn't have invited a whore to your chamber," she said, lying beside him, nuzzling his neck.

Erlik closed his eyes again. He imagined Mab standing over him now, wearing that half-exasperated, half-amused smile.

"You're right," he said pensively, stroking her bare back. He sat up suddenly, disturbing his whore's ministrations, and strode to the door, pulling on a shirt as he went. The girl stretched out on his bed, watching. Erlik stumbled, the wine affecting him more than he'd realised. He rubbed his eye with his knuckle.

"I'll be here, then," she said in a singsong voice, rolling

onto her back. "If she doesn't want you."

Scowling, Erlik grunted, slamming the door shut behind him.

✦   ✦   ✦

BY A CRACKLING fire, Mab sat on a plush chaise longue, reading a book she had read a hundred times over. She lifted her gaze with a sigh, casting it about her elaborate bedchamber.

Leafy plants in stone containers stood beside the bookcases lining the walls. A pair of imposing statues sat either side of a blazing fireplace. An ornate chandelier hung from the ceiling, barely casting any light around her chamber. The huge four-poster bed, hung with lavish furnishings, took pride of place in the middle of the room.

Mab lowered her book at the hard knock on her door. Rolling her eyes, she stood. Before she could reach it, the door opened and Erlik stepped inside, closing the door behind him with a snap. Mab narrowed her eyes, suspicious. What did he want now?

"I'm lonely," he said, approaching her.

Oh.

His wine-heavy breath choked her. She grimaced, expelling a short puff of air through her nose.

"You are *drunk*," she retorted. Erlik grinned. Mab took his hand and guided him towards her chaise longue.

"You're such a rare beauty…" he slurred as Mab gently pushed him to sit down. He grinned at her, his nose crinkling. She rolled her eyes. Waving a hand at her bedside, she conjured a silver pitcher and goblet. He watched her pour a cupful of crystalline liquid.

"Here," she said. "Drink up."

He took the cup and threw back its contents. Mab sighed, pulling a face at his drunkenness. Water spilled around his mouth. Mab wiped his lips with a scrap of cloth. *Like taking care of a child.*

He looked up at her, blinking, sobering.

"You act like such a fool when you are drunk," she said.

"That's not fair," he said, his brow set in a frown. Again, she said nothing and turned away. Erlik followed her like a dog behind its mistress. Mab put the empty cup on her bedside table. She turned to face him again, then sucked in a sharp breath when she saw how close he'd come, how he towered over her.

"Do you love me, Mab?"

"What do you want me to say?" she snapped suddenly. "You would not believe me, no matter what I said. Should I say yes, you would call me a liar. Should I say no—"

"I would call you worse," he finished for her, smirking now.

"What do you want, Erlik?" she asked. "Why are you here?"

He sighed, gazing at her. Completely sober now, thanks to Mab's drink. "I want *you.*"

Her eyes snapped to his.

"Why must we fight?" he went on. "You must know by now that I'm stronger than you. Why won't you submit to me?"

"Because no man can tame me," Mab said.

Erlik gave his wicked chuckle. "I am *much* more than a man."

Mab laughed now. *Such arrogance!*

An angry flame erupted in his eyes. His smile slipped.

"You mock me?"

"You say you are more than a man, yet you are driven by the most primitive of desires," she said, glancing downwards with a smirk. Blinking, an eyebrow raised at her boldness, Erlik recovered quickly.

"Well, I can hardly be blamed for that, can I? At least I know what I want," he said. "You, in my bed, ready and willing."

"I would rather spend a night with an ogre," she retorted.

Erlik laughed again. "I had no idea you were so insatiable."

Mab narrowed her eyes. Anger bubbled in her breast. The goblet on her bedside table exploded, firing out shards of glass, a puddle spilling on the floor. Erlik calmly glanced over.

"Is that the extent of your power? Breaking glass and spilling water?"

"I could break bones and spill blood instead," she growled. Erlik gave a short, sharp laugh. Mab glared up at him. *I could hurt you if I wanted to.*

"Should I show you *real* power?" Erlik said, and stepped back. Mab frowned. *He would not...*

He flicked his hand at her – a cruel dismissal – and a bolt of crackling lightning struck her chest, pinning her against the wall. There she hung, suspended by shackles of lightning, glaring at Erlik in deepest rage.

"Let me down!" she demanded.

"My pinned butterfly," he laughed. "Oh, my sweet Mab, how does it feel knowing your power can never match mine?"

"*Nathair!*" she spat.

Mab narrowed her eyes at Erlik's feet. The floor erupted in spitting flame. A rearing, fiery serpent rose up, encircling him. He stared at it, blinking stupidly for a moment, then laughed again.

"Mab," he said. "Would you—"

"*Lonsaigh!*"

Hissing, spitting, the snake flickered out a long, writhing tongue of flame. It struck Erlik's chest, a fiery battering ram, and threw him across the room.

His magic spent, the lightning shackled around Mab's wrists vanished. She did not fall far, but her legs buckled when she hit the ground. She collapsed onto her hands and knees, her blazing serpent crumbling to ash.

Erlik looked up sharply, as did Mab, throwing back tousled hair from her face. She reclaimed her feet first. Screaming, frustrated, she launched herself at him.

Erlik grabbed her mid-sprint. His fingers dug roughly into her arms. He threw her hard against the wall and pressed himself against her.

"Shh," he whispered, soothing, almost, yet still pushing her harder against the wall with the length of his body. "Hush now… Gentle, my little she-wolf…"

"*Let go!*" she screamed, fury twisting her face. He laughed. He took both of her slender wrists in hand, lifting her arms above her head.

"Such hostility," he said, rubbing his face into her neck. Panting, Mab squirmed against his grip.

"Let go," she breathed.

"I think not," he said. His lips brushed the tip of her pointed ear. She shivered, that simple touch sending a wave of reluctant pleasure rippling through her.

"*Oh…*"

He wrapped his arm around her waist, pulling her hips against his. He was close enough now to count the lashes framing her wintry eyes, brushing his fingers down her throat, ghosting over her chest, slowly caressing her breast.

"Stop me." His voice was soft.

A dare? Or a request?

Mab's eyes snapped open. She writhed harder, and Erlik nuzzled against her more. His hand drifting, pushing, demanding all of her at once.

"Stop me, Mab."

Her heart pounded quicker, her breath catching in her chest.

Wriggling a hand free, she lashed out a burning palm and slapped him across the face. Ashen sparks flew from the contact. Remarkable strength for a woman of such small frame.

Erlik staggered back. Gently, he touched a finger to his split lip. He hissed when the torn skin dragged.

"Marry me," he said suddenly, running his tongue over his bleeding lip.

Mab faltered. *Not this again.*

She said, wearily, "Erlik—"

"Marry me, Mab," he repeated, approaching her. She didn't retreat. Her brow instead creased in confusion. Erlik hungrily ran his tongue over his teeth. "We're equals, you and I," he went on. Taking her hand, he pulled her away from the wall. She tugged her hand out of his grip. "Matched only by the gods who sent us down to this grey, barren land. Marry me, and rule by my side as my wife. My queen."

Borne of bewilderment, Mab gave a soft laugh.

"What madness has taken you now?" she scoffed. Erlik

scowled. "You tortured and bullied my citizens. You ransacked my city. You have forced my people into hiding. You held me prisoner in my *own* dungeon. Marry you? I have far better things to do."

Erlik heaved a rough sigh, running a hand through his hair. "A pity," he said, and lunged at her.

Wrapping his hands around her face, he kissed her hard. She squirmed, trying to escape the brutal embrace. But, with a growl of frustration and anger, Erlik grabbed her throat and lifted her, slamming her against the wall again. He pushed his knee between her legs. His free hand crept up her satin thigh, nails raking her soft flesh.

"*No!*"

The chamber door burst open. Corvus stumbled in, a screeching crow circling his head like a black cloud.

He stopped short, taking in what he'd interrupted. His face turned red. Erlik looked up, letting go of Mab at once. She collapsed, gasping for air.

Mab looked up too. She saw Corvus, eyes travelling over his father's bleeding lip, the remains of her half-destroyed room; at last his gaze came to rest on her.

Their eyes met. His stare softened – pity, perhaps? – until Erlik approached with a sour look. Corvus blanched.

"What do you want?" Erlik hissed, wiping blood from his lip. Corvus paused before answering, his eyes still fixed on Mab.

"I... I heard noises. I thought—"

"You thought you could intrude on an intimate moment between me and my beloved?" Erlik said.

Behind him, Mab made a derisive noise, massaging her bruised throat. Erlik threw her a filthy look.

"I'm sorry," Corvus said. Quiet. Mab looked up at him

again. Had he aimed his apology at her? Or his father?

Erlik paused, narrowing his eyes, glancing between his son and Mab. She looked away. Silence fell over the room.

"Was there something you wanted to tell me, Corvus?" Erlik asked.

"Oh!" Corvus started. His face paled. "Y-yes. The... the execution has been carried out. Those three seelie you chose are dead."

Erlik smirked, nodding, and raised his voice. "Perfect," he said, glancing over his shoulder at Mab. "Thank you for informing me. You're—"

"Dead?" Mab repeated, struggling to her feet, horrified and dismayed. "*Why?* I came back to you!"

Turning, Erlik looked down at her, feigning innocence.

"Punishment, beloved. You, for leaving. And them, for rioting during your escape," he said coolly. "It's your own fault. You should have known I wouldn't tolerate insolence."

Mab swallowed hard. Speechless at his lack of empathy, his blinding cruelty, his sheer *arrogance*. Her heart pounding hard in her throat, suffocating her, she wanted nothing more at that moment to rush at him. To break him into a hundred pieces. To shatter that spiteful, contemptible smirk.

"You... *murderer!*" She screamed, running at him. Once more he grabbed her, holding her wrists, forcing them down.

"Don't test me, Mab," he said darkly, his voice low. Deep.

"Father, don't," Corvus said quietly. "Don't hurt her."

Both Erlik and Mab looked at him.

"You're dismissed, Corvus," Erlik said, watching as Mab regained her seat by the fire. "Leave us."

Corvus didn't move. A flush deepened in his cheeks. Erlik turned. Seeing him still there, he gave him a piercing glare.

"*Now!*" he shouted, clipping the back of his head. Corvus flinched. Pausing only once to gaze at Mab once more, he left.

The door snapped shut behind him.

Erlik turned back to Mab. She stared into the flickering flames of the hearth, dancing pure white. Erlik's face suddenly obscured her view, staring beseechingly into her eyes.

"I *am* sorry, my sweet," he said, yet there was no sorrow or pity in his voice. "It had to be done."

He touched her hand. Flesh sizzled, and he retracted at once.

"Do not touch me," she said. Quiet, weary.

"A proposition, then," he said quietly, a familiar smirk reappearing. "If you become my wife—" His words were punctured by Mab's venomous hiss. Erlik began again. "If you become my wife, your leaf—your *seelie* will be safe."

She looked into his eyes. The dark pits gleamed with mischief and menace.

"But if you refuse," he continued. "I will destroy every single one I can find, down to the last child. I will mount their heads on spikes to line the castle walls. I will give their fingers to my dogs. I will leave their rotting corpses for carrion-eaters to pick at. Do you understand?"

Mab looked away. Too disgusted to look at him. He tapped his finger impatiently on her hand. She closed her eyes. Her head twitched. Erlik raised an eyebrow.

"Do you understand?" he pressed, when she said nothing. Opening her eyes again, Mab sighed.

She knew this was no lie. He would stay true to his word. His hatred of seelie-kind was matched only by his hatred of losing. Silence stretched on forever. Mab could see no end, no escape. *It is the only way.*

"I understand," she said. Erlik smirked.

"Good girl. Now," he got to his feet, looking down at her. "Let's do this properly. Mab, Queen of the Old Ways... will you be my wife?"

She shook her head, briefly. More of a resignation than a refusal.

"Very well," she said.

As soon as her words had escaped her mouth, a thin band of silver formed on her finger. She stared at it, this ring that now bound her to him.

A milky moonstone set into a delicately forged leaf design. It would have been beautiful, in other circumstances.

"Swear to me they will be safe," she said aloud, staring up at him with narrow eyes.

"I swear on my own blood, your seelie will not be harmed. So long as you behave," he added.

"And Thomas?"

Erlik's victorious smirk slipped. Bowing his head, he heaved a resentful sigh. "Safe as a virgin amongst eunuchs," he said.

"Release his sister so he may go home," she said. "Then I know he will be safe from you."

"*Fine,*" Erlik snapped. "The Hunt will relinquish their hold on his fool sister. He can take her away and they can leave Albion forever. Fair?"

Mab nodded slowly in compliance. Satisfied, Erlik offered his hand, pulling her to her feet. He guided her to the balcony, and both stared out into Elphame.

Mab's eyes found those ramshackle rooftops of the seelie district. *Perhaps now I can protect them. If I am here—*

Erlik wrapped his arms around her, pulling her closer. Mab kept her hands on his chest, as though she longed to push him away.

Erlik gave a contented sigh; his eyes closed, and rested his cheek against the top of her head. Mab bit her tongue, holding back the furious tirade she desperately wanted to hurl at him.

"Think of it this way, beloved," Erlik said, stroking her back. "It's only forever."

Mab sighed in vengeful silence.

CHAPTER 34

In which someone is given a weighty task

"COME ON, LITTLE crow!" Malik laughed, dodging Corvus' clumsy lunge, slapping the flat edge of his sword against his brother's leather-clad backside. Corvus tripped, staggering into a pile of hay. He emerged, huffing, straw in his hair, pushing himself up with his sword. Malik swung his claymore. An expert, of course. Chuckling, he pulled his brother to his feet.

"Your head," Malik tapped his sword point against Corvus' temple, "needs to be as quick as your feet," tapping his ankles now. Malik clapped his shoulder, messing up his hair.

Grinning, Corvus playfully shoved him away. "You're in trouble, then," he said, readying his sword again. "Once more?"

Malik shook his head, sheathing his blade. "No more today. I need to train some new guards," he said. "Catch your breath. And sharpen your sword; here." Smiling, Malik threw Corvus a whetstone from his pocket. "We can practice again tomorrow, when you've come up with a better way to beat me."

Both brothers' dark eyes crinkled with smiles. Laughing, Malik left his little brother alone. The courtyard now silent, eerily so after their clashing blades. Corvus sat down on a stone bench, scraping the whetstone along his blade's edge.

Hearing familiar voices above, he looked up. His father and Mab stood on the balcony. Corvus' sharp eyes could just make out something silver glinting on Mab's left hand.

What is that? A ring?

Corvus took in a deep breath, gingerly rubbing the crown of his head. He sheathed his sword and pocketed the whetstone.

Corvus' only resemblance to his father and brother was his hair: thick, dark, and unkempt. He always had a playful smile lingering on his thin lips, despite his somewhat sad eyes.

Standing, stretching, his body aching from Malik's vigorous training, Corvus picked a rogue strand of straw out of his hair.

"Leave me alone!"

Corvus started. *Morrigan!*

Scrambling to his feet, he rushed to the archway, following his sister's shrieks of fright and pain. Then, silence.

"Morrigan?" he called.

Another voice answered: brash, arrogant and mocking. It was undeniably Astaroth, his youngest brother.

"Stupid little pig-lover!" Astaroth said. Though Corvus couldn't see him, he could picture his sneer. "Why don't you go frolic with the leaf-ears?"

Corvus skidded into the stable. Morrigan cowered in a corner. Astaroth slowly advanced on her, black war axe clutched in hand, laughing as he kicked her hard.

"*Astaroth!*" Corvus bellowed. His brother looked up, then staggered back, eyes widening. A snarl curled his lip.

"Next time, little sister!" he spat on her.

He fled. *Coward.*

As Astaroth melted into shadows, Corvus kneeled beside Morrigan, who had curled into a quivering ball.

"Here," he said, pulling her to her feet and embracing her tightly. "He didn't hurt you too much, did he?"

Morrigan shook her head, breaking away from him. Corvus smiled down at her.

"Brave girl," he said. "Come. We'll keep out of his way for a while."

Casting a nervous glance towards the shadows into which Astaroth had vanished, Morrigan nodded.

Corvus' crow, Lilith, fluttered down from a rooftop, alighting on his shoulder, and playfully pecked his hair.

Brother and sister walked in silence. They had almost crossed the courtyard when light footsteps echoed against stone walls. Corvus quickly put his hand on Morrigan's arm to stop her.

Mab stormed through a cloistered corridor around the courtyard, fury blazing in her frosty eyes, apparently so lost in thought that she hadn't noticed Corvus or Morrigan. Both watched her pass, her airy black gown, slashed with purple silk, billowing around her ankles.

Corvus marvelled at how... *delicate* she looked, despite that anger raging in her eyes.

She strode past without so much as a glance, vanishing from sight.

"I like her," Morrigan said. A simple, child-like comment, full of innocence. Corvus looked at her, bewildered. "She's always so nice to me."

"She's not *nice*, Morrigan," Corvus said, an incredulous laugh colouring his voice. "Don't you remember those stories Father used to tell us about her?" He glanced at those shadows where the elfin queen had vanished. "She's heartless. Cruel, he says. You mustn't go talking to her. She'll put you under one of her spells."

"I don't believe that," Morrigan said, wrinkling her nose. "She can't be as heartless as he says. If she was, why would he love her so much?"

Corvus looked down at her, abruptly seeing sense in her words.

"The seelie love her," Morrigan continued, walking on. Corvus ambled beside her. "They wouldn't love her if she was a tyrant. I think she sacrifices a lot for her people. We shouldn't judge her so quickly."

Smiling, Corvus ruffled her fair hair. She playfully batted his hand away.

"Stop being such a sage; your hair will go grey," he laughed. "I suppose you're right. We *should* be kinder to her."

A comfortable silence stretched out between them. Their short walk had brought them to a rear balcony that overlooked, not Elphame, but a glittering darkness of the cave. Sparkling waterfalls cast dancing spots of light against stone.

"Do you think she loves Father?" Morrigan mused. Corvus felt his cheeks grow warm. A fist clenched around his heart.

"I don't know," he said, a little too quickly. "I think she's afraid of him."

Morrigan looked at him, eyebrows raised in surprise. Corvus nodded.

"I know, it's strange," he went on. "I'd never imagine her to be afraid. But the way she looked when I walked in on them, she—"

"You *what?*" Morrigan yelped.

Lilith screeched, flapping her ebony wings. Corvus jumped, quickly, anxiously, casting his eyes about, checking they were still alone.

"Gods, Morrigan, be quiet!"

"I'm sorry," she whispered. "I meant… why did you—"

"An honest mistake," Corvus said, stroking a flustered Lilith to calm her. "I heard noises; I wanted to make sure—" He flushed harder. "I—I wanted to make sure he wasn't… doing something he'd regret."

"You know he hates it when we interrupt," Morrigan said, her voice meek. "What happened? Did he hit you again?"

Corvus nodded, eyes fixed on his feet. He rubbed the crown of his head once more.

"He was furious. But Mab was… she…" He trailed off into silence.

Morrigan narrowed her eyes. "Mab was what?"

Corvus kept his eyes on his shuffling feet, his face burning. "I—it's hard to explain," he mumbled. "I saw her… in a way I've never seen her before."

"Oh. *Oh!*" Morrigan's eyes widened. She too lowered her gaze, speaking instead to her feet. In a curiously high-pitched voice, "You mean—you saw her sky-clad?"

"No!" he said, again, far too quickly. *Fool!* "Gods—no! No, I meant—I didn't see her *naked*… I meant… well, I…" *Gods, this is not going well.* He ran a hand through his hair. "I was just doing what he told me. He said I had to go to him – when he was with Mab – and tell him that three seelie were dead."

"Are they?" Morrigan interrupted, looking anxious. Corvus smiled, cuffing her chin.

"No, don't you worry. They're alive. He just wanted me to lie." He paused, his treacherous thoughts drifting back to Mab. "I don't know why. Mab, she... she was angry, of course. But not just angry, though. Sad. Hurt. I've never been so ashamed. I felt like I'd just broken her heart. I felt *sorry* for her. And gods, she was so b—"

"Morrigan."

A voice behind them. Both spun around. Their father approached. Corvus' heart plummeted. Toxic fear clutched his throat. *Had he heard?*

"Father," Morrigan acknowledged, beaming. She curtseyed respectfully.

"The dagger. Give it to me," he said. Her bright smile slipped for a brief moment. Slowly nodding, Morrigan handed a shining black knife over. Corvus caught a reflection of his face in the obsidian blade. Pale, wan, and terrified. Erlik examined the dagger for a moment. Corvus held his breath. But his father's face broke into a warm smile.

"Clever girl. Well done, Morrigan," he said, still staring at the weapon, fascinated by its design. He sheathed the dagger, tying it to his belt. "I knew there was a reason you were my favourite. Now, have either of you seen Malik? I have a task for him."

"I could do it," Corvus said at once, satisfied his father hadn't heard his confession and eager to show his worth. Erlik cast a cold eye over him.

"You?" he said, sounding amused. Flushing red again, Corvus swallowed hard. He ran his tongue over his dry lips, unable to meet his father's gaze.

"I—I only thought—"

"Very well, Corvus. I'll give you this chance to prove

yourself."

Corvus stood up straighter. *Yes! At last! I'll—*

"I want you to watch over Mab," Erlik said. Corvus sucked in a sharp breath. His father spoke slowly now, clearly enough for his instructions to be heard. "She is not to speak to any of the leaf-ears. She is not to be touched by any man except me. She is not to leave the castle without you or myself in attendance. She is to be kept safe and unharmed. Am I understood?"

Corvus' lower lip now trembling, he gulped. Nodded shakily. "I—y-yes, Father."

"Morrigan." She looked up at him. "You may also speak with her. She will be your new mother; you must be kind to her."

Morrigan nodded, smiling. "Yes, Father."

Erlik's gaze travelled past them both. Morrigan and Corvus turned to see the source of his distraction.

Mab, standing on a large stone balcony, her hands resting on balustrades, stared past Elphame's boundaries, into the darkness of a now empty cavern. Erlik gazed at her. Something that could have been adoration crossed his face.

"Corvus, be careful what you say to her. Her temper is not to be trifled with," he said, then swept past. Morrigan neatly stepped aside for him.

Corvus watched, a jealous clench in his belly, as his father approached Mab. He muttered something in her ear. Whatever those hissed words had been, they must have offended; she spun around, gave him a withering look, and stormed out of his presence.

Erlik watched her with a smirk, his eyes never leaving those swaying hips.

"Corvus?" Morrigan asked. Corvus blinked. Shaking

himself, he stared down at his sister. With a swift smile, he wordlessly ruffled her hair again, then took off after Mab, leaving Morrigan to gaze after him, a confused frown on her face.

✧ ✧ ✧

"COME, THOMAS. COME with me."

Though the voice was gentle, Thomas couldn't bring himself to move. His eyes fixed upon Monstrance. What could he say? How could he hate him now? How could he send him away? Monstrance had taken hold of that bow again – he stared at it with such disgust now – and Kali's body had been moved out of sight. Wrapped in a linen shroud, placed in a quiet chamber. Yet its absence hadn't saved Monstrance the horror of realising he had taken a life. His *sister's* life.

Thomas wanted to console him. To thank him. To beg his forgiveness. Something. Anything to fill this gaping silence.

"Thomas?"

A small, warm hand entered his. Thissy stared at him, her shoulders slumped, her eyes full of pity. "You can't blame yourself. Monstrance chose to... well..."

Thomas wanted to speak, but the words stuck in his throat. He nodded, the only thing he could do. Thissy sighed, briefly squeezing his hand, and stood on her tiptoes to kiss his cheek.

As she turned away, Thomas took a step towards Monstrance. *Say something.*

"I'm sorry," he said at last, quiet enough so his voice wouldn't echo.

Monstrance started. He stared back at Thomas for a moment before answering. "As am I." He sighed. "Thank you, Thomas. For... for not making me leave. I don't think..." He trailed off again. "Kali forgave me. She forgave us both. I've set her free from her madness. She's in the House of the Old Gods now." He almost managed a smile then. "She wants me to ask you to forgive her. For what she did to you, to your father."

Thomas felt his mouth fall open of its own volition.

"W-what?" he said. "What do you mean? She's... still alive?" He couldn't stop his eyes from darting anxiously, as though expecting her to come bursting into the hall again. But Monstrance shook his head.

"No, I..." he paused. "My father's mother, Maniae, was patron of the dead. She taught me to reach into Annwyn, or the House of the Old Gods. How to hear whispers of those who—who've passed from this realm." Monstrance made a strange movement. Trying to repress a shudder, it seemed. "It's hard to bear sometimes. Those in Annwyn especially. I try not to venture there too often. Such anguish... Idath's realm is cold."

He released his shiver this time. "But my Kali isn't in Annwyn, thank the gods. She's at peace. My sister flies free."

Thomas sighed quietly. Monstrance sniffed and leaned back, staring at the ceiling, blinking fast. Tears sparkled in the corners of his eyes.

"I think I need to be alone for a while," he said slowly. "I'm sorry, Thomas. I mean no insult."

Thomas nodded, understanding, and watched him push away from the wall and amble away, his head hanging.

Thissy's hand found his again. He looked down at her, finding comfort and warmth in her green eyes.

"Come. I'll clean you up."

Thomas looked to the side and saw Thissy gesturing to his bloody hand, comfort and warmth in her green eyes. Thomas touched the gouge. A vicious sting sent bursts of white-hot pain shooting up his arm. Clenching his teeth to repress a groan that threatened to escape, he nodded. *Another scar,* he thought bitterly.

ENTERING HIS BEDCHAMBER, Thomas felt a rush of giddiness swamp his head. *I must have lost more blood than I'd realised.*

Groaning, he sat gratefully on his bed, holding his bloodstained hand away from his clean bed sheets. Thissy busied herself with a jug of water by the window, casting glances over her shoulder at him, an endearing smile on her face.

"Stop squirming, you'll make it worse," she said.

Thissy approached, carrying a clay bowl and a cloth. She kneeled opposite him, soaking the rag in water. Thomas braced himself.

With a reassuring smile, Thissy pressed the wet cloth onto his wound. Ice-cold water sent a wave of dizzying pain through Thomas. With every application, his pain gradually subsided, even as the chilly water turned red.

Thissy worked in silence. Thomas caught himself gazing at her, quite enjoying how her brow furrowed and her lips pressed together when she concentrated.

"It's deep. A shade too deep for me to heal, *a ghrá,*" she said after a while. Thomas started, blinking. "I'll have to stitch it first." Though she'd spoken calmly, Thomas tensed.

"Stitch it?" he repeated, trying to keep his voice steady. Thissy nodded, getting to her feet.

"Don't worry, it won't hurt." She took out a bone

needle and some flax thread from a dresser by the wall. She approached him. Thomas shrank back, withdrawing his hand. A childish action, but he didn't care. Smiling, Thissy took his hand. Her gentle touch soothed his fluttering nerves. Anxious snakes squirmed in his belly. Taking a deep, shaky breath, he turned his face away when Thissy threaded her needle. She pushed its point into his skin.

Thomas became far too aware of the needle slipping in and out of his flesh, though it was less painful than he'd been expecting. Everything suddenly seemed ten times louder: his own breathing rattling in his chest, Thissy's gentle hums of concentration, the low rumble of moving seelie below—

As Thissy gently pulled thread through his flesh, Thomas felt a flash of pain and fear. Not his. His stomach lurched. The room darkened, spinning. Two voices – both horribly familiar – echoed in his head:

"Mab, Queen of the Old Ways, will you be my wife?"

"Very well."

CHAPTER 35

In which a sword is reforged

"*T*HOMAS!*"

Thissy grabbed his arms, shaking him. The clay bowl fell, smashing on the floor. Red water spilled, darkening the stone floor.

Thomas blinked, his vision returning.

"What happened? You're shaking," she said. Thomas gulped down shuddering breaths. He stared at Thissy, seeing right through her. Then, with a rush of energy, he leapt to his feet and dashed to the door.

"Thomas, what is it?" Thissy called urgently. But he dared not stop. He bolted through halls, scanning every room he passed.

Not there. Not there. Not there. Where is he?

At last, as Thissy caught up with him, he spotted grey-streaked red hair disappearing down a corridor.

"F... Fire... Firestrider..." Thomas clutched a stitch in his side, panting. "Where's Lightfoot?"

Firestrider appeared to note the desperation in Thomas's voice at once. He jerked his head, indicating Thomas should follow, and led him to a chamber at the corridor's end. Without bothering to knock, Thomas burst into the room. He found Lightfoot there, hands clasped behind his back, gazing at an enormous, ragged map covering a wall, lost in thought. Startled, his hand flew to the claymore at his waist when Thomas staggered into his room.

"She's marrying him!" Thomas blurted, clutching a bedpost to keep upright, leaving behind a bloody smear from his half-stitched hand.

All three seelie stared at him. Thomas stared only at Lightfoot, willing him to understand, to believe him.

"What?" Lightfoot broke the stunned silence.

Taking a deep, slow breath, Thomas swallowed his exhaustion. "Mab is going to marry Erlik," he said slowly.

"How do you know this?" Firestrider asked, frowning.

Thomas looked at him, gesturing weakly to his head. "I—I could hear them... hear them talking, in my mind."

"How is this possible?" Lightfoot asked at once.

"Thomas shares a bond with the Dark Prince, Elder Lightfoot," Thissy said. "Blood-bound by a wound inflicted by Morrigan's arrows. Thomas dreams of him sometimes. He can see what he's doing."

Lightfoot's eyes narrowed, his hand tensing on the hilt of his sword. "You share a bond with him?" he repeated.

"What does it matter?" Thomas snapped. "We have to save Mab, now!"

Lightfoot nodded. "Very well. We have to work quickly. Firestrider, send emissaries to all of our remaining allies at once. Thissy, to the stable. Send Epona to the other elvish horses in the wild. We'll need the swiftest mounts."

Nodding, Firestrider left straight away. Thissy paused, gazing in concern at Thomas. He gave her a reassuring nod and a swift kiss on her cheek. With a slightly apprehensive smile, she too left.

"Come," Lightfoot said, once they were alone. "We have something for you."

He strode past, holding the door open for Thomas to follow.

As they walked through the corridor, Lightfoot spoke, "These are dark days, Thomas. We've waited a long time for the Old Gods to send us a champion."

Thomas tried his hardest to calm his frantic heartbeat, but Erlik's voice still echoed eerily in his head. *Why are we wasting time? We need to go for Mab now!*

At last, they reached the front doors. Stepping out, the sound of clanging metal and an overpowering smell of burning wood assaulted his senses.

Lightfoot gave him a quick, reassuring smile and headed out in front of him, leading the way to a makeshift smithy, set up along the side of the castle wall.

Thomas felt sweat pebble on his forehead as he approached. Furnaces spat floating sparks into the air as a dozen blacksmiths struck hammers against white-hot swords. Thomas paused to watch one dip a blazing blade into water before it enveloped its maker in clouds of hissing steam.

"This way, Thomas," Lightfoot called. Thomas followed his voice.

"Our smiths have been working on this for you," he said, holding out a long wooden box. Thomas frowned, confused, and opened its heavy lid with unsteady hands.

Inside lay the most beautifully crafted sword he'd ever seen. Its hilt was carved with silver dragon scales, the pommel glittering with a huge, blood-red stone. Thomas lifted the sword out of its silk-lined box. *Much lighter than it looks*. Furnace fires danced on the blade and refracted from the stone. His face reflected back at him. He looked up at Lightfoot, who returned his bemused smile with a proud look.

"I know this sword," Thomas said slowly, his mouth suddenly dry. *I've held this sword. In a dream, long ago.*

"Mab left us a requisition to forge this blade. A replica of one that belonged to a very brave seelie. Skilled in battle, quick of wit. Tamlyn, I think, was his name." Lightfoot smiled. Thomas's eyes darted up.

"My father?"

Lightfoot nodded. "It's a perfect likeness," he said.

Thomas ran his palm along the flat edge of the blade, admiring it. His eyes gleamed. *My father's sword.*

"You like it, milord?" a voice behind him. His words punctured Thomas's thoughts. He spun, finding a blacksmith staring at him, awaiting his approval.

"Indeed, it's magnificent," Thomas said. He smiled. Yet it felt forced; something gnawed at him. Shame?

The blacksmith beamed, proud, and walked away. Thomas turned to Lightfoot and handed the sword back to him. Laying in its box again, Lightfoot frowned, "Is something wrong?"

"Why did he call me that?" he asked, sighing. "I'm no lord. Nor a knight; I'm not even a squire. I can't be Mab's champion. I've never been in a real battle."

Lightfoot sighed too, but with a smile. "Mab told me you had your doubts. If she believes in you, I believe in you, too."

"Belief doesn't matter if I don't have skill," Thomas replied. His voice grew louder, more heated. "What good is faith, Lightfoot? Faith won't defeat Erlik! No matter what I told the seelie, I'm not ready for this. I'll never be ready for this."

The blacksmiths threw him dubious looks; Lightfoot gave them a reassuring smile. "Pay him no mind," he said, leading Thomas away, into the main hall of the castle again. He said in a low voice, "Thomas, enough of this. Listen to me now. I *know* you can do more than you think. Look at how far you've come already! You say you're no knight, but you've already fought the Dark Prince—"

"I barely escaped with—"

"You rescued our queen from his dungeon—"

"Monstrance was the one—"

"Not to mention overcoming that poison he inflicted on you."

"But Lightfoot, I've failed in what I came here to do in the first place! Alissa is still trapped in Elphame! And instead of trying to rescue her, I'm hiding here, plotting a war that could get you all killed. What good is that?"

"Thomas, look around. This is where you *belong*. I knew your father; he wouldn't want you to think like this," Lightfoot said. He paused. "I think you should rest for a while. You're upset. You need some time to think."

He beckoned to a young lass on the balcony above. She dashed down the stairs and bowed to Thomas when she reached him. Thomas sighed, once again extremely uncomfortable.

"You don't need to do that," he mumbled, his face beet-red.

"Vervain, can you help Thomas get some rest?" Lightfoot asked.

Thomas frowned. "I don't need—"

Vervain blew gently over him. Sweet breath rushed at him, and at once, Thomas felt an irresistible urge to fall asleep. His eyelids were suddenly so heavy he could barely keep them open.

"That's... not fair..." He yawned, staggering, and grabbed a banister to stop himself falling over.

"You could've waited until he was in his chamber," Lightfoot said sternly.

Vervain chewed her fingernail. "Whoops..."

"Too late now."

"It's easier if you don't fight it, milord," Vervain kindly said to Thomas.

Thomas sighed, trying to blink his eyes open, but it was useless. "Don't... call me..."

Without another word, Thomas's eyes rolled back. He slumped down into a deep and heavy slumber.

CHAPTER 36

In which Mab indulges in a stolen moment

A MASSIVE GARDEN, rich with greenery, lay before him. Hedges grew into a wild maze that led astray those unfortunate souls who deigned to wander in. Trees sagged under the weight of their leafy branches, casting dark shadows over the emerald garden.

Past thorny hedges and imperious trees lay a deep pond, a stone island in its centre, displaying a small cairn of rocks. A grave marker, perhaps? Stepping stones formed a path through the water.

Under a sheltering grove of trees, on a wooden swinging seat, Queen Mab sat waiting. For *him*.

Thomas walked through the garden, past a weeping willow dipping its branches into a winding brook, somehow knowing which path to follow to reach her.

Mab raised her head, beckoning him with her mysterious smile. "Thomas, at last," she said. Her seat swung lazily, her gown billowing around her boots. Returning her smile, Thomas took a seat beside her. They sat in easy silence, watching a couple of sparrows peck the earth near their feet.

"Do you like my garden?" she asked finally. "I come here to think sometimes. 'Tis quiet enough."

"It's beautiful," he said. He didn't want to break this comfort, but it must be done. The question fell from his mouth before he could stop it. "Mab, why did you agree to marry Erlik?"

Mab's eyes snapped up to meet his.

"I know what you must think—"

"I told you not to leave us," he said, his voice bleak. "I *told* you he would hurt you."

"I know, Thomas," Mab snapped, then sighed her apology. "I know. He will not hesitate to hurt me again. But what is done is done. I must stay here and be his wife. He will kill all of my seelie if I refuse now."

Thomas stared at her. She bore an unusual expression. True, she was unforgiving as always. Yet now, sadness – and pity – lingered in her eyes. Thomas glanced down at her hands, where a strange silver ring wound around her finger.

"What is this place?" Thomas asked finally. Mab glanced at him, then cast her gaze around at the garden.

"*Gairdín Síoraí*; the eternal garden," she said. "What you see is how it appeared when I ruled Elphame. I believe you would rather see it bountiful? Sadly, it is no longer so…"

Thomas nodded, braving a smile. Silence fell between them again. Thomas noticed Mab kept twisting the ring. Perhaps she longed to remove it. Thomas's tongue burned with questions, but he dared not press her further. He suspected her temper already bubbled just below its breaking point.

"Oh, I almost forgot," Mab said suddenly. "Erlik has released your sister."

Thomas's mouth fell open. "What? Really?"

Mab nodded, her lips curving upward. "He swore to me he would release her," she said. Thomas's heart, having leapt into his throat, plummeted. How could he trust Erlik's word? Yet Mab went on, "Unfortunately, I do not know where. He told me she would be released onto moorland. I have no way of tracing her. You could send Epona to seek her out."

"Lightfoot sent her to fetch other horses for the army," Thomas said despondently. "I don't think she'll be back for a while."

Mab nodded in understanding. "Then I suppose you can only wait. From what I hear, she is a resourceful and clever child. I am certain she will come to you." She placed her hand on his. Thomas glanced down. That silver ring caught the sunlight, gleaming white.

Noting his gaze, she said, "This is a Binding Ring." Mab held her hand up so Thomas could examine it. "It bears magic more intricate than Erlik comprehends. A Binding Promise works both ways." A knowing smirk pulled at her lips now. "Indeed, I belong to him now. I must obey him, or suffer terrible consequences. But he must also uphold *his* oath. If he harms even one seelie, I am free from the Binding."

Her eyes widened ever so slightly, apparently willing him to understand. Thomas had no clue of her meaning. He took her hand, running his thumb over the ring. At once, it burnt white hot. He yelped, withdrawing his hand. Mab sighed.

"Erlik is a complicated man." She smiled. "He will offer a rose with one hand and bear a sword with the other."

Thomas said nothing. *The way she speaks about him...* He frowned. *The way she says his name...*

Mab abruptly looked up. A figure strode along a path towards them.

Thomas's heart skipped over a beat. He thought for a fleeting moment that this approaching figure was Erlik. He neared, and Thomas saw only a stranger, younger than the prince, more vulnerable looking. Thomas didn't recognise him. Yet Mab tensed, and Thomas knew this approaching figure must be unseelie.

"You must go now," she said quickly.

"How?" he asked, his brow furrowed. His voice was low as the figure grew closer. How was he meant to leave when he couldn't even remember getting there?

Mab huffed an impatient sigh, pressing something cool and delicate into Thomas's palm. "You must wake," she said, then pinched his arm hard.

Thomas immediately opened his eyes.

❖   ❖   ❖

As CORVUS APPROACHED Mab sitting alone, he couldn't help but admire how her form glowed when she sat in her deep, meditative trance.

The garden was a pitiful sight: trees either dead or dying, no birds twittering in them, no bees to visit those withered grey flowers. *I remember Father saying once,* he thought, *that Mab had always liked flowers. Maybe I should have brought her some.*

Corvus sat beside her as Mab blinked open her eyes. The glow around her faded away.

"Can I help you?" she asked coldly. Corvus gulped before answering. He uncomfortably squirmed under her icy gaze.

"My father has asked that I watch over you, my lady," he said, trying to not sound as shy as he felt. Mab fired him an angry glare.

"I am not a child," she snapped. "I do not need to be watched day and night. Or does Erlik think I will fall into the pond and drown?"

Corvus balked. "I… I didn't—I meant—" He floundered. *This is harder than I thought.* "I-I'm your… personal guard."

Mab tipped her head back, narrowing her eyes. She cast a suspicious look over him.

Corvus twisted his hands. The silence was crippling. *This is not going well. Say something!*

"Why are you out here by yourself?" he asked. Mab didn't look at him. Her gaze was fixed instead on her city's rooftops.

"I wanted some time alone," Mab said, though her voice had lost its sharp edge.

"Oh… of course. Forgive me, my lady," he said. He looked down at his hands. Silence descended again. Not sure what else to say, Corvus instead lost himself in staring at her.

He suddenly understood why his father desired her so deeply. How easy it would be to fall obsessively in love with this dark, mysterious, powerful woman—

"How discomforting," she said curtly. Corvus felt blood rush to his cheeks. Could she hear his thoughts? Worse, had he spoken them aloud without realising?

"I—w-what is it, my lady?"

"You have accompanied Erlik on many occasions," she said. Corvus withheld his sigh of relief. "How many of my seelie have you captured? Even killed?" Her voice had grown icy and harsh again. Corvus gulped hard. *Oh.*

"I… I try to avoid hurting them, when I can," he said

quietly.

"I do not believe you," she said. "You are Erlik's son—"

"You trust Monstrance; why don't you trust me?" he asked, much sharper than he'd intended. His eyes widened. Before he could stammer his apology, Mab raised her eyebrows and smiled, looking impressed. Corvus' heart bounded in surprise.

"I suppose I could learn to trust you," she said. "Especially after what you did earlier today. Interrupting your father's clumsy attempt at seduction."

Awkward now, Corvus cleared his throat, twisting his hands again. Mab gave him a brief smile.

"No need to be so bashful," she said. "We both know what he wants."

"He's not subtle about it, I suppose," he said without thinking. Mab laughed: a deep, throaty sound. Corvus smiled shyly.

"I think that's the first time I've ever heard you laugh," he said, his cheeks burning again. "It—it's nice, a nice sound. You... you should laugh more."

"Perhaps if I am given reason to laugh, then I shall," she said, casting a dark glance at the castle. Smile slipping, Corvus sighed. He put his hand on hers, startling himself.

"It must be so hard for you," he said quietly. Mab looked at him. "We've learned to stay out of his way when his temper gets the better of him. Although... maybe if you're here now, he'll be happier. Maybe he won't get angry as often."

"I..." Mab paused. "I do not think it will be so easy, but I appreciate your words. Thank you."

She stood up. Again, Corvus marvelled at how small she was. For such a powerful creature – *woman,* he corrected himself, *not creature* – she seemed more of a porcelain doll. Her delicate features only reinforced this image.

"Come," she said, beckoning him. "I want to show you something."

Mab led him to the maze, vanishing into a green haze. Though he quickened his pace to catch up, she'd already disappeared into the hedges. Corvus stopped.

"My lady?" he called, his heartbeat pounding in his chest. Surely he hadn't lost her already? *Some guard,* he cursed himself, scowling.

"This way, Corvus," her voice whispered from a nearby corner. He turned, following the sound. But she had already gone.

Follow me.

As in a dream, Corvus obeyed, chasing after her ethereal voice. A mischievous laugh echoed. *Vixen! She's toying with me.*

At last, he reached the end of his pursuit, catching up with his elusive quarry.

Mab stood, statue-like, in a green-cast glade. Moss made the ground springy, the scent of the earth filled his nostrils. Trees grew bent and gnarled, sheltering them beneath wooden arms. Corvus stared, and Mab smiled at him.

"I've never seen this place before," he said in barely more than a whisper. "Where are we?"

"Somewhere safe," she replied, circling this secret glade. Corvus watched her closely.

Though her heavy gown was rich with deep purple and black, Mab didn't look out of place in this green forest sanctuary. Corvus couldn't take his eyes away. This must be how she'd looked before his father had overpowered her. *Intoxicating.*

Mab gave him a mysterious smile. Corvus swallowed around a lump in his throat. He exhaled sharply, his belly in knots.

"You trust me, then?" he asked, his voice brittle. "What changed?"

Mab approached slowly, her steps silent over moss.

"The scar on your hand," she said. Her eyes glanced toward it. Corvus' fingers twitched.

Trying hard to tame his trembling, Corvus extended his arm and Mab took his hand, curiously examining that odd-shaped scar. Corvus blinked. How could her touch be so soft? Mab ran feather-light fingers over his palm. His own hands seemed large and clumsy in comparison. What tormenting magic could she put those hands to?

"This mark was made by cold iron." Her voice came as a swirl of cold air. Corvus started, then nodded.

"Punishment," he breathed. He forced his eyes anywhere but her.

"For what?"

Corvus hesitated.

"I… I was young, just a child…" he said, voice uneven. His eyes fixed on the trunk of a nearby tree, not truly seeing it. "Kali and Monstrance had just been born. As much as I loved Malik, he never had time to play with me. I was lonely. Father never cared much for me. I wanted a friend. Someone to talk to…" Against all better judgement, despite everything he had told himself, he looked up and gazed at her. Instead of frost or fire, he found pity.

"Go on," she said.

"There was a boy, a selkie. A slave. He used to help his father clean the stables. I spoke to him often. His father was kind, even…" He paused. "Even to me. But my father didn't approve. He said I shouldn't associate with them, that they were animals. But Wynn was my friend. I knew my father would never allow me to see him again, so I..." Another pause. Mab took his hand. Corvus thought he felt lightning spark between their entwined fingers. "I helped Wynn and his father escape one night. I told them to run far away, and never return to Tír-Na-Nóg."

"Oh, Corvus," Mab whispered. He nodded, finding that once he had started this tale, he wanted to finish it. *Tell her everything.*

"Father knew," he said. "He'd found out. He was *furious.* I had disobeyed him, and I had to suffer the consequence. He dragged me into the courtyard, and... he had a—a piece of iron. A tiny fragment. An arrowhead, I think. He put it in my hand. He made me stand there all night."

Mab's hands had instinctively clenched around his. She sucked in a sharp breath.

"Corvus..."

"It burned... *gods*, it burned me," he said. "I would've been there longer had Malik not begged for my forgiveness. Father relented, for Malik. Not for me. Never for me. He made me keep the scar, as a reminder of... of what he does to people who disobey him."

Staring straight at Mab now, Corvus could see empathy in her eyes. His heart jumped into his throat, beating hard against his windpipe. *Hard to breathe.*

"Oh, Corvus," she said again. "Sweet Corvus." She raised her hand and brushed cool fingers against his cheek.

"I understand what pain you suffered," she said. "I *shared* it. The chains that bound me in the dungeon were cold iron. We are not the first to feel its sting, nor will we be the last."

Corvus blanched. His hand fisted around his scar. He could survive the touch of cold iron. But Mab? True, she had weathered it already, but his father could put her through a lot worse than the cruel kiss of cold iron. He would hurt her. *I must protect her. I must keep her safe from Father...*

"I'm sorry," he said aloud. "I—I had no idea. I could have done something, if I'd known—"

"But you did not," she smiled. "It has passed now; we cannot change what has been done." She lowered her eyes to her hand, where she twisted that accursed silver ring. Corvus longed to remove its poison from her.

"Thank you for listening," he said softly. "No one ever really has time for me." He'd leaned closer to her without realising. Now barely a breath from her. His eyes fixed on her mouth. Those perfect lips: plump, rose-coloured and begging to be kissed. Her eyes were lowered, their stare not fixed on him. What would she do if he kissed her? Would she kiss him back? Or strike him down for such impudence?

What man would dare kiss a queen without her permission?

Father would.

"We should return before we are missed," Mab said, and Corvus abruptly drew back. He inhaled deeply as Mab stepped past, nose burning with the scent of magic: a powerful aroma of flowers, woodsmoke, and night. Intoxicating, yet terrifying. Skin prickling, Corvus shivered and followed her out of her secret glade. Once they'd returned to the garden, Mab paused.

"Thank you, Corvus," she said. "For your company today."

Uncertain of what to say, Corvus bowed to her. Mab turned away, gliding out of that wilted garden.

After making sure she couldn't hear him, Corvus sat, groaning. His head in his hands.

Fool.

CHAPTER 37

In which the Black Heart has his moment of glory

ARK EYES WATCHED both Corvus and Mab. A shadowed face twisted with a cruel smile as Mab walked away, her graceful gait barely skimming the ground. Corvus sat again, either dejected or embarrassed. *Both, perhaps?*

The watcher grinned in wicked delight.

"Oh, my dear brother," Astaroth's low voice carried a sneer. "How disobedient of you."

Slipping away noiselessly, Astaroth followed Mab at an easy pace, hidden behind waxy leaves. Unseen. A ghost in the dark.

Mab hummed a haunting melody to herself as she strolled out of her garden. The smell of her magic filled his nose. *Filthy.* He had caught her scent easily. He'd always been the best hunter of all of his brothers. He would recognise a leaf-ear's stench anywhere.

Just wait until Kali hears about this!

Mab stopped dead. Astaroth paused, onyx eyes glittering like beetle wings.

Your disgusting leaf-ears call me the Black Heart. Would you like to see why, witch?

Mab turned back slowly, as though she had sensed

someone watching her. Frowning, she squinted into the dark foliage. Astaroth held his breath. After a few moments, however, she apparently decided she'd imagined it, and turned away again. Astaroth exhaled slowly.

His grip tightened on his black war axe. Its serrated edge glinted unpleasantly in the half-light. He would enjoy seeing terror blossom in her eyes when he cleaved her with this axe. *Oh, what delicious sweetness... what wondrous joy, to taste her fear.*

"Whist, little witch," he hissed through the leaves. His voice barely a whisper, it carried on a breeze and caught Mab's ear. She stopped again. Astaroth's smirk split his face. He wished she would face him. He wanted to see that fear in her eyes.

Yet when Mab spun around, her face showed no terror. Astaroth bit down a sigh. *She's harder than the other dogs.*

"Who is there?" she called, voice cold.

Be afraid, you stupid bitch. I want you to beg.

Flicking a gesture at her, a rush of magic tugging his chest, a spurt of fire erupted at her feet. Mab stepped back quickly, a sharp gasp escaping her, and smothered the sparks on her gown's hem.

Using this as a distraction, Astaroth finally stepped out of the bushes, brushed himself off, and approached. At the sound of his footfalls, Mab looked up sharply. Her eyes narrowed. A rush of ruthless excitement flooded him.

"Oh, I hope I didn't startle you, my lady," he said, voice dripping with bitter contempt. Mab glared; she obviously knew he meant to mock her.

Leisurely – not wanting to rush this – Astaroth strode toward her. He stopped short when Mab took a hesitant half-step back. His face twisted into a malevolent grin.

Those hollow cheeks and sunken eyes made his face unnervingly skull-like. Mab repaid his look with narrowed eyes and turned away. Astaroth rushed to walk beside her.

"Have I offended?" he asked. Mab ignored him, quickening her pace. Astaroth frowned. "Very well, we don't have to talk."

"I would rather you not accompany me, Astaroth," Mab said icily.

"A pity, because I *will* accompany you," he said with a faint trace of anger, his voice a guttural growl. Mab said no more.

They maintained an uncomfortable silence until they'd left the garden. A pebble path led them toward a round stone balcony. Mab approached its edge, resting her hands on the balustrade. Astaroth stood beside her, leaning against it with familiar pride.

It wasn't just arrogance that Astaroth shared with his father. He'd also inherited his sharp, angled features.

"Have you seen much of my little sister, witch?" he asked, looking down on her. Mab said nothing in reply. With a ghost of a sneer, Astaroth went on, "Hmph, I think you two would get along well. She's always harboured some ridiculous pity for your *mongrels*. I sometimes wonder if her mother was a leaf-ear."

He paused now, watching her reaction. Mab's hands had clenched tight; her knuckles were white.

"I wouldn't put it past Father to have raped a few women from the district," he said in a low voice, leaning closer, making his words sting in her ear. "I enjoy their company from time to—where are you going?"

Mab had turned away with a disgusted look. He leapt up, standing before her so she couldn't proceed, leering at her. Yet his eyes held hatred, not lust.

"I knew you'd come back," he hissed. "I could smell your stench as soon as you crossed the gates. I'd know it anywhere. Why is Father so obsessed with you?"

"Perhaps you should ask him, should you ever find yourself brave enough," Mab spat.

Fury cloyed at him. "You call me a coward?" Astaroth snarled. A vein pulsed in his throat. He grabbed for her, but Mab batted his hand away.

"Touch me again and I will break you," Mab said. Astaroth growled. His hand tightened on his axe. Mab's eyes flickered to the whitening knuckles, yet she didn't retreat.

"Such fire," he said. "Imagine what I could do with your magic…" A manic glint appeared in his eyes now. "This will be *glorious*. Not only will I destroy you, but I will finally take what's rightfully mine. Even my father and brothers won't—"

"You will be dead before you try—"

Astaroth laid a stinging backhand to her cheek, silencing her. Mab staggered back several feet with the force of it.

He laughed, a cruel, harsh bark. "Take your last breath, witch!"

Astaroth heaved his war axe above his head, an executioner now. Mab coolly tipped her head back, eyes widened. In those brief moments before Astaroth's axe cleaved the air, Mab lifted her hand, staring at her trembling fingers. Both fear and fury etched on her face.

With a roaring laugh of victory, Astaroth brought his axe down. Mab dodged, a shriek escaping her. Metal struck stone and Astaroth snarled.

Mab lifted her hand again, thrusting it toward him. Nothing.

"Too afraid to use your filthy magic?" Astaroth laughed as he rushed to her, barrelling into her with a broad shoulder and knocking her to the ground. He raised his axe one more time. Dazed, weakened, Mab pinched her eyes shut, her hands thrown up in reflex.

"NO!"

The slapping sound of flesh catching an axe handle; the heavy thud of a dropped weapon. Mab slowly opened her eyes.

Facing down a disarmed Astaroth, Corvus stood over her, sword unsheathed and pointed at his brother. The heavy axe lay discarded.

"Begone, Astaroth," Corvus growled. "She's under my protection."

Breathless, Astaroth ran his tongue over his teeth. "Is that what you're calling it, Corvus?" he hissed, taking a step. Corvus pressed his sword point into his chest, and Astaroth stopped. *"Protection?"*

Corvus swallowed and lowered his sword.

"What are you talking about?" His voice wavered. Did Astaroth know how his feelings towards the Queen of the Old Ways had blossomed in so short a time?

Astaroth smirked again. Leaning close to whisper, looking up at his taller brother, "Does she know? About you? About your desires?"

Corvus fought not to look back at Mab. He heard her stir behind him.

"How much you want to touch her?" Astaroth breathed. "Oh, Corvus. What would Father say?"

"Say no more!" Corvus hissed. He swallowed his fear, his brow twitching.

"You're her guard now; it's perfect," Astaroth went on. His face lit up. "You can get into her chamber whenever you want. She probably won't even complain. She wants to be touched, look at her. You can break her in for Father. You know once he's had her, she'll be damaged. He'll shatter her."

Against his will, Corvus looked back at Mab. It wouldn't hurt, really, would it? To have her before Father did? Astaroth was right, in a way.

Father won't be gentle with her. But I will. I could teach her. I won't make it hurt.

Mab appeared at his side. Her dark eyes fixed on Astaroth. Corvus looked down at her. *I would be her first.* A chill nipped his arms. He shifted, suddenly uncomfortable.

"Maybe when Father's finished, he'll lend her to me," Astaroth mused. Corvus' eyes snapped back to him now. "But when *I'm* done, I won't give her back. I'll slit that pretty throat of hers."

His hands now shaking, Corvus glowered at his brother. "You won't touch her."

Astaroth sneered. "You won't either."

Mab pulled Corvus away. Her touch on his arm pulsed through him.

"Begone, hag-seed," she hissed at Astaroth.

He let out a sharp laugh. "Nasty little viper, isn't she? I wasn't talking to you, *whore*." He spat at her feet.

Enraged, Corvus grabbed him. Swinging a fist at his brother's jeering face, he punched him square in his sunken jaw.

Astaroth staggered back, coughing, then straightened.

"Keep your mouth shut, Astaroth," he spat. "If you go near her again, I *will* kill you."

Astaroth laughed again. He put his hand around the nape of Corvus, neck, then gently slapped his face in what could have been a gesture of brotherly affection, had both not despised the other so deeply.

"You won't always be there, Corvus. I'll get her one day," he said, backing away.

With a bruise blossoming on his jaw, Astaroth picked his axe up, smirked, and turned away.

"Who knows," he called back, not bothering to turn around. "Maybe you will as well!"

Corvus ignored him as he vanished from sight. Instead, he turned to Mab.

"Are you hurt?" he asked with genuine concern. Mab shook her head, staring at her hand. "What is it?"

Mab didn't reply at first, still gazing at her trembling hand.

"I—I do not understand," she said. "I could not use magic against him. How is this possible?"

Corvus took her shaking hand and turned it over. Her eyes roved until they found that glittering ring on her finger.

"Father must have dampened your magic," he said, longing to brush the stray strands of hair away from her face. "So you can't use it against him."

"He does not have that right!" Mab said hotly. "That is not fair. I swore to obey him, not to be powerless."

Corvus put his hand on hers quickly, worried that she would do something rash. "Perhaps you're not powerless. Perhaps you just can't use your magic against me—my brothers and sisters?"

"So I must now obey *Astaroth?*"

"N-not obey," Corvus said. He gulped. Her icy eyes had rooted him. "Just... respect."

"The mountains will be worn to ash before I respect that—"

"If it's any consolation," Corvus interrupted, "Astaroth can't harm the leaf—the seelie. It would break the Binding. And you know Astaroth would rather lick mud off an ogre's feet than disobey Father."

Corvus risked smiling at her. After a pause, she returned it, and Corvus' heart danced in his chest.

"If I cannot use my magic, then I suppose I do need a guard after all," she said. "I am sorry for being so sharp with you earlier. I hope you can forgive me."

"Of course, my lady."

"Please," she said, her voice gentle, warm. "Call me Mab. We are friends, are we not?"

Corvus smiled. "I like to think so." He paused. "Mab."

Her name felt wonderful on his lips. He lifted his arm to drape it around her, then stopped himself. He quickly disguised this abrupt movement as running a hand through his hair. Lilith fluttered down from a rooftop to alight on his shoulder, pecking her feathers.

"Twice now you have saved me, Corvus," Mab said. "I must think of a way to repay you."

Corvus, cheeks grew warm. *I know a way.*

He opened his mouth to speak, but something stole Mab's attention. She turned her head, gazing past the balcony's edge.

A burst of golden-red light blinded him. Corvus thought for a wild moment Elphame was ablaze. He quickly shielded his eyes from this intense light. Apparently unfazed, Mab took in a deep breath as sunlight poured over Elphame and the stone cavern faded, revealing a sprawling purple moor.

A sweet-smelling breeze washed over the pair. Mab

opened her eyes again, gazing at those wild moors. The rising sun cast a red glow over Elphame and its queen.

When Corvus looked back at Mab, he felt his breath catch in his chest. She was silhouetted against the sky, purple and green gloaming surrounding her. The underside of wispy violet clouds burnt red and gold from the sunrise.

Mab drew in deep, welcome breaths. "Stone crushes the life from me."

Corvus fixed his eyes on her profile, mesmerised. He nodded, though he doubted she saw it. His heart pounded hard.

"You look sad," he said. The words escaped his mouth of their own will. Mab looked up at him sharply.

"What did you say?" she asked. About to ask forgiveness, he realised he just wanted *her*.

Corvus lightly touched her cheek. Her eyes followed his hands, and when his fingers brushed her face, she flinched.

"'Tis nothing," she brushed him off, turning away again. Corvus felt a twinge at her rebuff. He lowered his hand with a sigh. *I need to try harder.*

"*Liar!*" Lilith cawed, ruffling her feathers. Mab looked up at the bird. Her eyes widened briefly.

"Where did you find that crow?" she asked, a faint frown crinkling her brow. Corvus shrugged.

"Lilith? She's followed me since I was a boy. She's harmless, she calls everyone a liar," he chuckled. Smiling, Mab shook her head.

"Indeed," she said. "It just... she reminds me of another creature. Remarkably similar. Belonging to Idath, your father's brother."

Corvus felt a chill creep over his flesh.

"No doubt that bird is long since dead," she went on,

reaching high to stroke her fingers over the crow's gleaming feathers. "Perhaps your Lilith is a descendant?"

Corvus nodded wordlessly. His uncle's name had sapped all courage from him. Had a cloud passed over the sun? It felt cooler now.

Seeking warmth, he repressed a shiver, and fixed his eyes on Mab's face instead.

"Forgive me," Mab said. "'Tis always a grim conversation that invites Death's name."

Behind them, on a leafless, thorny tree, one pink bud glistened with dew. Above, a swallow swooped and dived, twittering an early morning song. Mab watched it jealously.

"Mab?" Corvus asked, feeling heat spread in his cheeks already. Mab made a noise to indicate she was listening.

"What... w-what do you know of... love?"

Mab froze. She looked up at him. He gazed at her.

"Has some maiden caught your fancy?" she asked, a playful emphasis to her voice.

Nervously, Corvus laughed, then nodded, "S-something like that."

Mab sighed. She didn't say anything for a long time.

"Love..." She paused again. "Love is cruel. A vicious spark. Something so complex, I confess I know little of its mystery. 'Tis a selfish creature. I do not recommend it."

Corvus stared in despair. "Surely you—you don't *believe* that?" he asked. How could her heart be so closed? So cold? Had his father done this to her? Had he made her this way?

"Love will either make you the best man in the world," she said, "or the worst."

She looked down at that shining silver ring. Taking in a deep breath, she glanced up at him. "I should go."

She turned away. *No!* Corvus wanted to stop her. He

had to ask her – *tell* her – about this new feeling that he didn't quite comprehend.

It burned, consuming him. He had to explain. He had to know what it was like to have her. Just once. Just to touch her once to satisfy this blazing hunger—

"Mab?" he asked.

She turned back to him. "Yes?"

She would understand, surely. She must have known this before. A man desiring her so much he would set the world ablaze just to keep her warm.

Corvus gulped.

No. I can't do this. Father thinks like this. He wants her this much. And she belongs to him... I have no business wanting her. She's too good, too precious. I can't... I mustn't...

His resolve melted away, words dying in his throat. Instead, he gulped and shook his head. He unbuckled a dagger sheath from his belt, handing it over to her. Mab took it, frowning in confusion.

"I can't be with you every moment," he said. *As much as I want to be.* "You should keep this with you."

"Thank you," she replied, not unkindly, and turned away again. Corvus gave an unhappy sigh, turning to watch the sunrise.

The more I'm with her, the more this feeling will grow. I'll speak to Father about relieving me of this task. Malik should do it. He's stronger. He could survive this.

Later, when Corvus had retreated to his chamber, he didn't have to wonder who had left a posy of wildflowers on his pillow.

CHAPTER 38

In which there is a rescue

WIND HOWLED FEROCIOUSLY over the moors. Face
lashed by hair caught in the wind, Alissa groggily
opened her eyes. She blinked, wildly thinking for a moment
that the bump on her head had rendered her blind. But then
the fog in her mind lessened, and she realised the darkness
meant only night. Blue stars winked at her in the sky's black
cloak. The yellow moon, almost full, offered some light to
see by.

Alissa pushed herself up with her hands, shivering in a
rough wool dress. Wind tugged off her linen hat, and it
vanished into the night, swirling into darkness like a ghost.

Looking around these dark and terrifyingly vast moors,
panic drowned her. Every shadow became a heaving
monster. Every howl of wind a groaning beast. *Thomas said
he was going back to Elphame for me! How is he going to find me
now?*

Shaking, Alissa got to her feet, heart thudding hard in
her chest. She blinked back tears of fear and panic. *Don't cry,
Alissa. Thomas wouldn't cry. Don't cry!*

She had no idea where to go or what to do. Should she
try finding Elphame? She shuddered. *No. Not back there.* The
unseelie prince had been a cruel master.

Alissa remembered the first and only time she'd seen him. Some disturbance in the castle had rattled the other slaves. She'd later heard that someone – a stranger that no one recognised – had defied the prince, and had paid for the insult with their life.

Erlik himself had appeared in slave's quarters that night. Eyes blazing, covered in dirt, twigs, and roots, as though he'd battled his way through a forest. Though no one had spoken, Erlik had dealt swift punishment to every mortal woman there.

Alissa bore scars from his lashes.

She would never see him again. Word amongst other slaves was his temper had grown worse, and something powerful stirred at the heart of Elphame.

Alissa raised her head. A still-high moon meant morning was far away. *Keep moving. Keep warm.* Yet after a few tentative steps, Alissa collapsed back down again. Where could she go? Hugging her knees close to her chest, she dissolved into tears.

"YOU LOST, LASS?"

Alissa looked up sharply. With a gasp, she scrambled to her feet. She'd no idea how long she'd been sobbing, yet she knew she hadn't heard these strangers approach. A group of hempen men now stood before her, huddling against the beating wind. She took a few steps back.

"Wh-who are you?" she shook out. Each man glanced at their leader, then offered Alissa kind smiles.

"Don't fret, lass, we're not here to hurt you," he said. "You're a thick-skin?" Alissa nodded but said nothing. She could barely understand his words under that thick accent. "What's your name?"

"A-Al—Alissa," she said. "Alissa Rhymer."

"Rhymer?"

Alissa swallowed hard. Why, why, *why* had she given her name?

"A-aye. Who are you?"

The group paused, glancing at one another. Their leader nodded.

"Just travellers. It's dangerous on these moors, lass. How are you out here alone?" he asked.

Alissa's eyes drifted, seeking confirmation these men were not dangerous. Noticed a fiddle under his arm. Minstrels, perhaps?

"I-I don't remember," Alissa paused. The bump on her head sent pulses of pain through her. She touched a finger to it, and winced.

"There's a forest nearby, just over the brow of that hill," he said, pointing. Alissa could just make out dark, feathery treetops. "We'll be setting up camp there tonight. You're welcome to join us."

Alissa hesitated. These moors were dark, cold, and lonely. She had no idea how to find Thomas, no idea how to get home. If she went with these minstrels, they could at least offer warmth and company until morning.

Or they would rape her in the forest and leave her for dead.

Shivering, she cast a wary eye over the others. She found only cheerful – if weather-beaten – faces. Something told her they meant no harm.

"I would be grateful," Alissa said. Smiling, the lead minstrel gestured for her to follow. One wrapped her in a thick woollen cloak. Warmth enveloped her.

Wind swirled ever harder around them at hill's peak.

Once their group passed over it, a wild-looking wood sprawled before them. Battling against raging wind, they headed into a dark sanctuary of trees. Here, at least, the wind didn't lash them so hard. This wild wood seemed eerier to Alissa than the moors. Yet she kept quiet, and let them lead her towards a clearing.

Alissa sat on a log, with the man who'd asked her name beside her. One gathered bracken and twigs. Within moments, a crackling fire blazed before them. Welcome heat washed over Alissa.

"You hungry?" someone asked. Alissa nodded, only now realising how long it had been since she'd last eaten.

The minstrel emptied his bag. Several apples, a few loaves of bread, lumps of cheese, and some salted meat were placed in the open on top of the bag's material. Around the circle, others leaned in and grabbed whatever they wanted. Alissa watched with mingled fascination and disgust as one roasted an apple over their fire.

While they ate, one strummed quietly on his lute. Alissa stared at him, mesmerised by his music.

"Where are you heading, Alissa?" their leader asked, making her jump and avert her eyes.

"Well," she began, unable to keep sadness from colouring her voice. "I have to find my brother. I was in Elphame, and he said he'd come for me, but—"

"You escaped from *Elphame?*" one interrupted, swallowing a mouthful of cheese. "Smith's Hammer, lass. That's not an easy task. More to you than meets the eye, hm?"

"Well, I—I didn't *escape...*" Alissa said slowly. "I was scrubbing the floor in the scullery. I heard footsteps, someone coming up behind me, but before I could turn around..." She rubbed the bump on her head again. "Everything went dark. I woke up on the moors."

The one beside her nodded; his long brown hair, she noticed, was tangled with forest debris. A minstrel sniffed and scratched his nose.

"We've heard from the merfolk there's a war brewing. We're heading for a seelie colony. You know about seelie, don't you?" he asked. Alissa nodded, having heard stories from other slaves.

"You can come with us, if you fancy," he continued. "If your brother's got any sense, he'll be with the seelie. Safest place these days."

Alissa felt a smile tug her lips. *Thomas never had any sense. But... maybe they're right.*

She stared around at this group, chewing her lip. Some were already lulled to sleep by the lute's gentle thrum. Alissa felt her own eyelids grow heavy.

"Aye," she mumbled, laying down on a mossy bed. She barely heard the minstrel bid her goodnight and tell her his name. Instead, she yawned and curled up to sleep.

✧   ✧   ✧

MORNING ROSE, PALE and cold, on the castle keep. Thomas dashed through corridors, tightly clutching something in his fist.

He burst into the small dining hall, finding Lightfoot and Thissy already there, ladling milky porridge into bowls. Thomas strode to them.

Thissy looked up at once and beamed. "Good morning, Thomas," she said brightly.

Thomas had intended to speak straight to Lightfoot, but

Thissy's warm greeting disarmed him. "G-good morning, Thissy. Did... did you sleep well?"

She nodded. Thomas returned the gesture. Silence fell as they gazed at one another.

Lightfoot awkwardly glanced between the two. He cleared his throat before saying, "Good morning, Thomas. Would you like—"

"Lightfoot," Thomas interrupted, now remembering his urgency. "I found this in my hand when I woke."

He opened his fist. A purple flower sat in his palm, half-crushed from being held so tight. Thomas stared at Lightfoot so hard he barely heard the clunk when Thissy dropped her bowl to the table in surprise.

Lightfoot lowered his own dish slowly.

"What does it mean?" Thomas pressed. Lightfoot glanced at Thissy, yet her eyes were fixed on that flower in Thomas's hand.

"It's a sign," he explained. "A rhododendron. It means danger." Thissy swallowed hard. "Purple," Lightfoot continued, taking the flower and holding it up to light. "The colour of royalty and magic. A sign from Mab."

"I dreamt of her last night," Thomas remembered suddenly, glancing between both seelie. They looked at him, Thissy's eyebrows disappearing into her hair. Thomas closed his eyes to remember his dream better. "We were in a garden."

"*Gairdín Síoraí?*" Thissy asked.

"That was it." He explained everything Mab had told him in his dream.

"That twisted bastard threatened her into it!" Lightfoot said, outraged. "Of course he did. She would never have willingly agreed."

"Milord?"

Thomas ignored the voice behind him. Thissy politely cleared her throat. Thomas looked at her.

"She means you, Thomas," she said. He glanced back, annoyed. *Would that they stop calling me that!*

"What is it?"

"You have a visitor, milord," she said, bowing. Thomas's heart immediately dived. Who could possibly...?

"Someone wants to see Thomas?" Thissy asked, her brow knitting. "Who? No one knows he's here."

"An unseelie?"

"Or worse."

"They asked for you by name, milord," the young seelie pressed. Thomas stared at her.

"*They?* Who is it?" he asked. The girl beckoned.

Thomas followed, bemused, Thissy and Lightfoot trailing behind. They reached the entrance hall, where a group of men stood; each dressed in dark tunics of green and brown, and filthy, grease-smattered breeches. Thomas immediately recognised the loud, accented voices.

"Murchadh?" he called. The warlock turned to look at Thomas, grinning. Thomas gave a startled smile in reply. "What are you doing here?"

"I think we've found something of yours, lad," he replied. "We thought we'd better return her."

He moved aside.

Her face was dirty, her wool dress poorly patched, yet Thomas felt his heart leap into his throat. He howled with joy, and, laughing, ran to her, pushing aside the warlocks in his excitement. He wrapped his arms around her and pulled her into his embrace.

At last – at long last – brother and sister were reunited.

CHAPTER 39

In which Corvus partakes of forbidden wine

MAB RAN AN ivory comb through her thick dark hair, humming to herself. She tugged at the tangles, hissing softly at the most stubborn snags, loosening her entwined jewels, undoing twisting, glittering braids. A large bath, full of steaming water, awaited her on the other side of her chamber, barely lit with a few flickering, white-flamed candles.

That hot water beckoned. Mab stood and approached the bath, its copper exterior gleaming, inviting. *To lie there and rest awhile,* she thought, *would be bliss.*

She kicked off her boots. The cold stone floors nipped at her feet. Running a finger through the scalding water, Mab wistfully sighed.

Let this heat burn away hate. Let this water wash away fury.

Humming again, Mab began undressing. Her amethyst robe dropped into a ring around her feet. She wore a simpler gown beneath, her fingers twitching at its corset strings.

Something rustled behind her. She stopped.

He is here.

Slowly, Mab turned her head, looking over her shoulder.

From behind a wooden screen dividing her room, Erlik appeared. His shirt partially open, Mab could see just a corner of a seven-pointed star tattoo that disfigured the flesh over his heart. She swallowed a lump in her throat, warmth reaching her cheeks. How long had he been watching her?

He stepped towards her, his eyes fixed on hers. Her fingers tightened on her gown strings.

"Go on," he said eagerly, in barely a whisper.

"Not when you are watching," she said softly. Erlik ran his tongue over his lips. Mab bent down and collected her heavy gown in her arms. Pulling it back around her, she fastened it tight.

A faint frown creasing his brow, Erlik sighed. Heavy silence smothered the room.

"I've a gift for you," he said at last.

Mab paused. "A gift?" she repeated.

Obviously pleased now he had her attention, he beckoned. Taking her hand, guiding her back to the dressing table, he sat her down. Confused, she glanced between her reflection and his.

"What—"

Erlik waved a hand over her face and neck. As he did so, Mab felt cold metal hang heavy around her throat and from her ears. She stared at her reflection.

A golden necklace glittered around her neck, a matching pair of earrings glinting through her hair.

She took in a slow breath. Erlik patiently awaited her response.

"Do you like them?" he asked, when she remained silent.

The golden chain around her throat choked her. The earrings: too heavy. Their expense obvious, Mab sighed.

"They are beautiful," she admitted. "But you cannot win my affection with trinkets." Looking up into his reflection's eyes, she said, "They are only illusions."

That sparkling jewellery vanished almost as fast as Erlik's smirk. His grip tightened on her shoulder, fingers digging into her flesh.

"You always liked my gifts before," he said, a hard edge in his voice now. Leaning down, bringing his head closer to hers, he brushed stray hair away from her throat.

"I do not want your gifts," she said.

"Then what would you like instead?" he breathed, now nuzzling her neck, kissing the warm flesh below her ears.

Mab paused. Her eyes closed as Erlik's hand wrapped around her throat, keeping her still. He kissed her hard. Feeling herself start to kiss him back, Mab at once pulled away.

No...

"Erlik, stop it," she said, injecting sharpness into her voice.

"Why?" he muttered, his hot, eager breath warming the softness of her throat. "Is my little wolf feeling coy?"

"You will soon feel your *little wolf's* claws if you continue," she said. Erlik tensed. He pulled away, standing straighter, looking down on her with contempt.

"I've offered you gifts; what more do you want? Am I to charm you with sweet words?" he asked. His tone clearly intending to hurt, Mab said nothing, eyes narrowed. Erlik went on, "Such a beautiful creature. You know what I adore most? Not your beauty, not your silken smile, not your baffling love for those leaf—*seelie*," he cleared his throat when Mab fired a furious look at him. "It's this—" touching the bridge of her nose, "crinkle here, when you get angry."

"Be silent, Poison-Hoarder," Mab said at last. Erlik raised an amused eyebrow and laughed. His hand rested on her shoulder, close to her neck. His fingers twitched, as though he longed to wrap them around her throat.

"How is it," he shook his head, smiling, "that you're so cruel, yet your people adore you? You're so cold, yet there's fire blazing in you. So heartless, and yet…"

Erlik reached down, his hand creeping over her heart, feeling its tempo quicken. Mab inhaled sharply.

Mab stood up, pushing his hand away. With one withering look, she pushed past him. He stumbled, her scent washing over him. Erlik inhaled, closing his eyes, groaning, breathing deep of the perfume of magic.

"Tonight, then," he said, opening his eyes again, gazing at her with a hungry expression. Mab stopped. She turned back to him, frowning. Erlik smiled innocently, raising an eyebrow.

"What happens tonight?" she asked.

"We marry, my love," Erlik said coolly, smirking once again, and reached forward to play with her hair.

"*Tonight?*"

Erlik pressed his fingers to her lips, hushing her lovingly. Mab recoiled.

"It is too soon—" she began.

"Too soon for what? For us to be together?" he snapped. "Or are you worried your little Champion won't have time to swoop in and rescue you from me? You don't *need* to be rescued from me, Mab. I am yours, just as you are mine. Why do you insist on thinking I'd hurt you?"

"Tell me honestly that you never would."

Erlik paused. His lip curled into a snarl. He huffed and looked away.

"You cannot do it," she said.

Sullen, Erlik shook his head. *Petulant child*, she thought wryly.

"I can try," he muttered, after a brief pause. "I'll try to control my temper. If you do too."

Mab narrowed her eyes again. Yet she could see his reasoning. His fits of anger could be matched only by hers. *'Tis something of a miracle we have not killed one another yet.*

"Agreed," she said.

"Won't this be interesting?" he asked, a smile tugging his lips. Mab made a noncommittal noise. Erlik touched the bridge of her nose again and cast a glance at her steaming bath. "I'll leave you now."

Mab nodded without a word. Erlik kissed her brow before walking past her towards the door. She'd already begun unfastening her gown again when she heard his voice once more.

"One more thing, Mab," he said, a sickly sweet inflection now lacing his voice. "I forbid you to visit the dungeon or the seelie district; do you understand?"

Mab frowned. Her fingers twitched. "No, I do not understand," she said in clipped tones. "Why am I *forbidden* to speak with my own people?"

"Is that disobedience, Mab?"

She halted. A flare of heat blossomed from the Binding Ring. Mab stared into those glinting eyes. Deceptive. Ancient. Deep pools waiting to drown her.

Jaw clenched tight to stop her angry retort, she shook her head. "No. I understand your... orders."

Erlik smiled, approaching her again. Mab stood her ground, sulking gaze averted.

"Good girl. Here," he took her hand, dropping three

gold coins onto her palm.

"What is this?" she asked, glancing a revolted look at him.

"Ask Corvus to escort you to market. I know you like—"

"Do you think I am your pet?" she spat. "You think you can dress me up and parade me around? Keep your blood money, *nathair!*"

She threw those coins at him and turned her back. Erlik grabbed her arm, spinning her back to face him. For a moment, she wondered if she had pushed him too far.

"Last chance, Mab," he said, voice low. "Disrespect me one more time, and *you* will choose which leaf-ear I execute."

Every ounce of her being, every last scrap of her pride screamed at her to strike him down. *Do not submit to this pusillanimous man!*

Both pairs of eyes locked onto the other. Each impenetrable darkness resisted, two black waves crashing against each other.

Can you share in my thoughts as you once could? Or has your madness taken you too far from me?

"You'll be a beautiful bride," Erlik said at last. "I'll have a seamstress sent up for your gown."

Mab sighed. "Very well. Do you have any further instructions for me?" she asked, unable to keep bitter sarcasm from her voice. Erlik's lips twitched.

"I would have you call me Master, just so I can see that exquisite stubborn fury of yours. But for now, I just want a kiss."

Mab growled. "You want me to call you—"

"Just a kiss, Mab."

She sighed again. Narrowing his eyes, Erlik impatiently

tapped his foot. He was too tall for her; Mab lifted up on her tiptoes, briefly brushing soft lips against his.

"Like you used to, sweet thing," he breathed, barely a puff of air against her mouth. He put his arms around her to pull her closer, pressing his body against hers. After a moment of delay, Mab acquiesced and kissed him hard.

Erlik responded with such enthusiasm, he forced her backwards, shoving her against a wall. The resulting thump interrupted neither.

Her teeth worrying his lower lip, she cursed the disappointed mewl that escaped her when he pulled away. Erlik chuckled at her noise. Breathless, she gazed up at him, stealing a glance at his kiss-swollen lips.

"I'll leave you now," he said. "I'll send someone to fetch you when it's time."

He brushed hair away from her eyes, kissed her brow, and left. The door snapped shut behind him.

Closing her eyes, Mab furiously muttered curses and oaths under her breath. That hot bath still awaited her, yet she no longer felt a want to sink beneath its surface.

A strange desire overtook her now. A desire to rebel, to defy. To tempt his rage. Just how far would he go to make her obey?

Chewing her lower lip, Mab quietly moved to the door and opened it. The empty hallway filled her vision. He had left her alone, as he'd promised.

Pulling a cloak around her, Mab ran down spiralling stairs. Once she'd reached the bottom, she paused to catch her breath, her face flushed with more than simple exertion. The stairs had brought her to a stone courtyard, where, in its centre, a white tree stood bold and bare. No flowers or leaves softened its sharp, crooked branches.

That arrogant swine! Mab thought to herself. *Who is he to think he can control me? I am no puppet, to dance when he pulls the strings. I will not submit.*

She stared at the ring on her left hand. Her thoughts blurred into mist, her heart thudding hard. She could still feel his hot, eager breath on her neck. Mab ran her tongue over her lower lip. Erlik's oddly soothing voice echoed in her head. Visions of him approaching her, shirtless and hungry, clouded her mind. *Dare I?*

She furiously shook her head. "Fool."

Mab sped off, heading for the seelie district.

CORVUS ANXIOUSLY PACED, twisting a posy of wildflowers into a shredded mass. He looked down, eyebrows disappearing into his hair, unaware of what he'd been doing. He sadly let the flowers drop, mutilated petals drifting away in the breeze. Morrigan bounded into the courtyard, beaming at him when she approached. Corvus gave her a weak smile.

"You should stop using Lilith to deliver your messages," she said, still smiling. "She wouldn't tell me until I'd given her food."

Corvus didn't laugh. Instead, he cast a nervous glance behind him, twisting his hands.

"What's wrong?" Morrigan pressed, eyes squinted in suspicion.

"I'm in trouble, *a dheirfiúr*," he said in a low voice. Morrigan's eyes grew round.

"You spoke seelie," she said in awe, then shook herself and looked seriously up at him. "No, leave that. What kind of trouble?" Morrigan folded her arms, cocking an eyebrow.

Corvus flushed scarlet under her stare. "It's hard to explain," he began. How should he proceed with this?

"Have you done something?"

He shook his head. "Not yet, but I fear I soon will," he said. "I think I—I'm..." Biting his lip, he didn't finish. Morrigan patiently stared at him. Corvus heaved a heavy sigh.

"I'm in love, Morrigan," he mumbled.

Her face lighting up with joy, she threw her arms around her brother. "Oh, Corvus! That's wonderful! Who is she? Is she from the castle?"

Corvus sighed and lowered his eyes, hating himself. *I shouldn't have burdened her with this. She's too young.*

"It's Mab," he said at last. Morrigan's smile vanished. Corvus thought he felt his heart stop beating.

"W-what?" Morrigan asked, then nervously chuckled. "Is this a game I don't understand?"

Sighing again, Corvus shook his head. "No, I'm sorry. I—I..." He couldn't finish.

"Corvus, how did this happen?" she asked. Corvus didn't answer. He couldn't. He didn't *know* how it had happened.

"Corvus?"

"I-I couldn't help it. I thought I could resist, but she's not what I thought. All I want is..." He trailed off, blushing.

"How do you know she didn't put you under a spell, like you said she would?" Morrigan asked.

Corvus frowned at her. "She didn't. I'd know."

"Would you, though?" she pressed, tugging his hand to walk with her. "Corvus, this... this is madness. You need to fight against—"

"It's not magic, Morrigan!" he snapped. She flinched. "It's real. I know it's real!"

Morrigan's gaze lowered.

Corvus sighed. "I'm sorry... Help me?"

"Well," she said, still looking wary. "Let's say this feeling *is* real, it's still wrong. You can't have her, she belongs to Father."

"She doesn't *belong* to anyone." He paused, chewing his tongue. "Speaking of Father, you have to promise not to tell anyone about this. If Father found out, he'd never forgive me."

"He'll do worse than that, Corvus," she said. "He gave orders to have Monstrance killed because he helped her escape. What would he do to you?" Her voice was full of ill-disguised fear. Corvus' scarred hand instinctively curled into a fist.

"Then it'll be our secret," he said, trying to inject some lightheartedness into his voice. Morrigan stared at him with weary compassion.

"Corvus, this isn't like stealing bread from the kitchens. You can't keep it a secret; he'll find out eventually. You know he will," she said.

Corvus sighed. He'd opened his mouth to reply when a furious scream echoed through the courtyard.

"What was that?" Corvus asked. Morrigan shrugged, frantically shaking her head. Grabbing her hand, he pulled her along behind him.

Rounding a corner, the pair skidded onto the same balcony where, earlier, Corvus and Mab had watched the sunrise. Now, dark storm clouds gathered, low and heavy, threatening rain on the two figures who argued there. Corvus and Morrigan scrambled behind a marble statue to watch from the shadows.

Towering over Mab, their father dragged her into the castle, his hand fisted in her hair, snarling so viciously that Morrigan trembled. Mab stumbled, her nails scratching his hand.

"Let go of me!" she screamed, trying to get her feet again. *"Let go!"*

Erlik pulled her upright. Corvus, sharp eyes could see her face, her eyes full of ice and poison. His heart leapt at her bravery.

"What did I tell you, Mab?" Erlik spat. He pulled her face uncomfortably close to his. "You're a treacherous, deceitful little whore!"

He struck her. Even from across the courtyard, that sound of flesh hitting flesh made Corvus flinch. How could Mab endure this? He had to do something—

"Come," Erlik said, dragging Mab along behind him. "It's time for you to choose which leaf-ear I kill first."

Mab pulled her arm out of his grip. "You will not touch them!" she snarled.

Erlik laughed, hard and cold. "Do you want to take their punishment, then?" he said, producing a wickedly barbed dagger. Mab glanced at it.

From their hiding place, Corvus and Morrigan watched in horror. Corvus balled his hands into fists, glaring at his father with deepest loathing.

You won't hurt her again!

"Corvus, do something!" Morrigan whispered desperately. He glanced at Mab. She'd tipped her head back. Defiant, reckless.

"You would not dare kill me," she said. Erlik paused, a sneer curling on his lip.

"You're right, Mab," he said. "I won't kill you. But you're mine. You have to learn that. You need to learn

319

obedience."

He sheathed the blade, and instead held out his empty hand. A flickering orb of fire formed on his palm. Still scowling, Mab stood straight, proud. Corvus marvelled.

"I won't kill you," Erlik said again. "But if you beg my forgiveness now, then I won't hurt you."

Corvus knew his father had asked for a miracle.

Morrigan squeezed his hand so tightly he almost lost feeling in his fingers. Mab said nothing. She gazed back at Erlik, blinking slowly and deliberately, one eyebrow cocked into her hair.

Erlik growled.

"You test me so greatly, Mab," he said, and threw the fiery sphere at her.

It struck her chest. With a gasp, she stumbled back.

"Another?" he said.

He threw another bolt of fire at her. It struck her again and she flinched. Another: this time she fell. Erlik approached her quivering, breathless form.

"This hurts me, beloved," he said, shaking his head. "It pains me to do this to y—"

"Father, stop!"

Corvus had run out before he'd realised his legs had taken him. Kneeling beside Mab, he helped her back to her feet. He could feel her shaking.

"Corvus, what are you doing?" Erlik asked, eyes narrowing.

"I'm protecting her," he replied. "That's what you told me to do."

Erlik laughed, "I didn't mean from *me*—"

"She shouldn't *need* protecting from you!" Corvus interjected, his voice beseeching. "Father, you can't treat her like this. She's going to be your wife."

"Foolish boy!" Erlik snapped. "How *dare* you speak back to me?"

Corvus ignored the slight. He glanced at Mab, who stared between them. Her wounds were already healed, though charred marks on her gown showed where Erlik's magic had struck her. She said nothing.

"Are you alright?" he asked. Mab nodded silently.

Erlik took a step closer. Corvus drew back on instinct.

"Corvus…" Erlik said, in a low voice. His eyes narrowed in suspicion. He ran his tongue over his teeth, thoughtful. "What is this?"

"I'm just doing what you told me," Corvus said, unable to hide the waver in his tone.

"No. There's something *more*," Erlik hissed, taking Corvus' scarred hand, pressing his thumb harshly onto that scar. Corvus' face twisted with pain. Erlik's eyes briefly widened. "You—"

"Erlik, enough! You are hurting him," Mab said angrily, pushing Erlik away to separate them. She took Corvus' hand, checking his scar. Corvus gazed down at her.

Erlik laughed again. A malicious, cruel laugh that Corvus didn't like. "Well," he said.

Corvus looked up sharply. *No…*

"Isn't this… *precious?*" Erlik folded his arms.

Mab threw a scowl at him. "What are you talking about?" she asked.

"It would appear my son has developed *feelings* for you, Mab," Erlik spat, glaring at Corvus with such hatred now that the lad took several steps back. Mab blinked, speechless for a moment.

"Corvus?" she said softly. "Is this true?"

Corvus gulped, glancing between Mab and his father. Mab exhaled slowly. Erlik started to laugh. Corvus backed away a few more steps, truly afraid now. Mab stood in front of him. In defence, it seemed.

"I don't even know where to begin," Erlik said, still laughing. "How do I punish you for something like this?"

A long, heavy pause.

Finally, Erlik smirked. He stepped closer.

"You want her, Corvus?" he asked, taking hold of Mab's upper arm in a tight grip. He roughly threw her at Corvus, who caught and steadied her as she stumbled. "You want her?" he said again. "Take her. Go on. Show me how much you want her. A gift from father to son. A precious little whore for you to use."

Mab hissed at him, catlike in her fury.

"What was it, then?" Erlik went on, folding his arms. "What was it that drew you to her? You've always wanted to prove yourself. Show me now that you're like me. Because when she screams, Corvus, and she struggles to be free of you, and she begs you to stop, I'll know at last that you're truly my son—"

Corvus launched forwards, releasing a blind roar of fury. Erlik stepped aside in time to deflect him.

Corvus staggered back, only to draw his sword and charge forward again. Driven by hatred. Eyes blazing, blood hot. Years of anger exploded from him in this wild assault. He didn't even care if his blows struck true.

"CORVUS, NO!"

She had to stop this. Mab ran forward and grabbed his arm as he drew back to swing his blade, pulling him back.

"I am *nothing* like you!" Corvus spat at Erlik, straining against her grip. "I hope the seelie come for you. I hope they bring your demise. You've hunted and slaughtered her people like animals! It stops *now*, Father. You're not going to hurt her or her people again!"

"Corvus, enough!" Mab put her hands on his face and turned him to look down on her. "Corvus, you must stop. You said you are not like him. Prove it to me now. Show him whatever mercy he did not show you," she said, gazing up at him.

Corvus stared at her. She brushed away the stray strands of hair from his face.

Please. Do not do this.

Corvus dropped his sword with a metallic clatter. Silence fell hard around them. Erlik pushed himself back to his feet, yet didn't speak.

"I'm sorry, Mab," Corvus said, barely a whisper. "I couldn't help it. I felt... I felt—"

"Hush, *a chara*," she soothed, pressing her cool fingers against his lips. "'Tis not your fault."

"You forgive me, then?"

"Of course."

"I, however, don't."

Both Mab and Corvus looked at Erlik. He lunged forwards, grabbing Mab's throat, throwing her aside. In one swift movement, Erlik drove his sword deep into Corvus' belly.

Corvus froze; eyes bulged in shock and pain. He made choking, guttural noises at the base of his tongue. Erlik grabbed his collar and pulled him close.

"I hope your beloved crow feasts on your carrion flesh," he snarled, twisting his blade as he tugged it free, inviting forth a torrent of blood.

"*Corvus!*"

Mab looked up to see Morrigan rushing toward them.

No, she must not see—

Morrigan pushed past her father, half-catching Corvus as he crumpled. She lowered him as gently to the ground as she could, whimpering, "C-Corvus…"

Corvus brushed fingers against her cheek, leaving a faint bloody smudge. Morrigan gave him a watery smile.

"You'll be fine," she said. "We'll fix you—" She put her hands over his wound. Nothing. She jolted her hands, as if trying to shake magic from them. Again, nothing happened.

"No!" she looked up at Mab. "Please, help me!"

Casting one filthy look at Erlik, Mab kneeled down beside Corvus. "Corvus, I am so sorry," she said. "I will avenge this, I swear it."

"No… no, you need to heal him! Please!" Morrigan squealed.

Mab shook her head slowly. "I am sorry, Morrigan. I—I cannot," she whispered, her voice breaking. Her eyes remained dry; she had no tears in her to shed. "My magic is too akin to seelie, it would poison him."

Morrigan wailed, cradling her brother's body. He shuddered, gasping as he tried to say something.

"Shh, Corvus," she breathed.

Instead, he reached to her face.

Mab raised her hand and held it over his, twining their fingers.

His face went still, a half-smile frozen on it as his hand slipped away.

Morrigan wept, long and loud, still clutching his body as if that alone would wake him. Mab closed her eyes, bowing her head and whispering a prayer of death in her native tongue.

"Be brave, Morrigan," she said at last. "He is at peace."

Gently taking hold of her, Mab held her in a motherly embrace. Morrigan shuddered, sobbing into Mab's hair.

The stillness broke. Rough hands seized Mab and dragged her to her feet, pulling her away from Corvus.

"A traitor deserves no less," Erlik snarled.

Morrigan stood and staggered back. Her young face did not suit the harsh hatred etched onto it. "You did this!" she spat, "*You* killed him!"

Mab looked at Morrigan, struck with a sudden, daring thought.

She threw out her arm, hurling a cloud of silvery magic towards Morrigan. It enveloped her head, then scattered like fireflies. Blinking, the princess nodded, then turned and ran to the balcony's edge.

Erlik wrapped his arms around Mab, pinning hers down. "Don't you dare, Morrigan," Erlik hissed.

Morrigan spat in his direction. "Farewell, *Father*."

A bright flash. A white barn owl irritably ruffled her feathers, then took off into the air.

"Morrigan! *Morrigan!*" Erlik bellowed after her. But she had already vanished into clouds.

In the deathly silence that followed, Erlik slackened his grip on Mab.

"You have only yourself to blame," Mab said coldly, approaching Corvus' still form. She kneeled, closing his eyes. Erlik sharply exhaled.

"He had no right," he said. "You aren't his."

"*Titim gan éirí ort, nathair,*" Mab stood again, glaring at him with such venom in her eyes, enough hate to disguise her anguish.

Erlik reached forward and, grabbing her arm, pulled her along behind him as he made strides to the castle. "Come with me, we're not waiting until tonight."

CHAPTER 40

In which Queen Mab tastes Dragon Fire

IN THE CENTRE of a long feasting table, Erlik drunkenly laughed, watching a dancing fool. Mab offered him a dirty look as she refilled his wine. The hall rumbled with talk and laughter, several dozen unseelie packed onto two long tables which were both laden with a magnificent feast to celebrate their prince's marriage. Platters were piled high with salted unicorn stuffed with herbs; sweet, brittle drake wings dripping with honey; roasted boar and bear; fat swan and apple pies.

Mab touched nothing.

Ever since Erlik had bound their hands with silver rope, declaring them wedded, Mab had remained silent. A moment of childish frustration, perhaps, but she had sworn an oath to herself that she wouldn't speak another word to him. She sensed Erlik's growing annoyance at her disobedience. To avoid his gaze, her eyes drifted over each unseelie.

In the hall's centre, that colourful, dancing fool had vanished. Now, two runty giants wrestled violently. As the victor snapped his opponent's neck, the unseelie cheered in approval. Erlik nudged Mab, grinning. She rolled her eyes and turned her face away.

Glancing along the table, she found Astaroth. He returned her look with a malicious smile.

So far, no one had dared ask about Corvus or Morrigan's whereabouts. But the whispers in the hall indicated his subjects knew more than Erlik would normally allow. Mab looked again along the table, avoiding Astaroth's sneering gaze, taking in those empty seats.

One dead. One banished.

Two defected.

Three left.

"You enjoy music, don't you, my love?" Erlik asked, interrupting Mab's thoughts. Taking a long draught from his goblet, he slipped his hand under the table. His fingers danced along her silk-covered thigh. Her leg twitched. Though she fired a look of disgust at him, she didn't reply. Lowering his goblet with an unnecessarily loud bang, he shifted in his seat, leaning closer and staring at her profile.

"Mab."

Again she ignored him. A few heads turned to them. Noticing their growing curiosity, Erlik narrowed his eyes, and whispered in her ear, "Don't humiliate me tonight, Mab."

Keeping a proud silence, Mab picked up her goblet and brought it to her lips, not seeing Erlik lean back, waving a dismissive hand at her.

Mab gagged, coughing, spitting sour vinegar back into her cup. Erlik laughed as Mab wiped her mouth, throwing him a filthy glare.

"Only a bit of fun, my love," he smiled, nudging her again. Erlik sniggered drunkenly into his goblet. Finding it empty, he turned away and called for a selkie slave to refill the jug.

Sighing, Mab lowered her eyes. Then, unexpectedly, another cup slid in front of her.

"Here," Malik mumbled on her other side, moving his water goblet towards her. "Don't let him see."

Her brow furrowed, Mab stared at him. Why would he do this for her? She subtly nodded her thanks. After a quick glance over her shoulder, finding Erlik for once not looking at her, she gulped down the water; the fresh liquid cool and soothing to her dry throat.

Wiping her lips, Mab handed his cup back. Malik said nothing more. He turned his back, but Mab had seen anguish in his eyes. He knew what had happened to Corvus, and Erlik had lost the loyalty of yet another child.

"Mab," Erlik said loudly. A small jolt as she looked back at him. "I have another gift for you." He gestured to a guard by the door, who nodded, vanishing with two of his comrades. "I had it captured especially. Here."

A collective gasp shivered through the hall when three guards returned, each struggling to master massive chains forged from black steel.

A giant wolf snarled, thrashing, bound by chains; dug its claws into the ground, trying to pull itself to freedom. Its eyes burnt ruby-red in the moon-white of its face. Yellow teeth dripped saliva onto matted, snowy fur.

Mab stared, silent, her insides burning with rage. She found herself on her feet, yet unable to recall standing up. Her hands had trembled into fists. Impulsive lightning and fire crackled at her fingertips.

Faolan.

This magnificent wolf – her most trusted companion, her most faithful lieutenant – belonged in the wilds. Not a captive, to be paraded like a pet dog. Mab bit her tongue hard to quell her storm of fury.

How *dare* he bring her one of her own sacred animals in chains?

"Well?" Erlik said, standing up. She could practically hear the smug smirk in his voice.

Again she pressed her lips together to stop herself from retorting. Should she speak, she feared she would set this hall ablaze. Mab closed her eyes and exhaled slowly. Sighing, Erlik leaned closer to her.

"Show them how you can tame it. I've seen you do it before," he said, his lips brushing her ear. His eyes swept over her face for any trace of affection.

It took every last scrap of her willpower to remain silent. Instead, now trembling with rage, she took her seat again.

"Take it away," Erlik growled to the guards. "Lock it in the menagerie."

They obeyed, still struggling to contain the beast. Mab watched Faolan snap at his captors, silently encouraging him.

"I've given you many gifts," Erlik said, reclining comfortably now. "I'd like one from you. In fact, I think you should dance for me." Erlik got unsteadily to his feet.

"Everyone!" he called. Across the hall, all excited chatter died away. Every head turned to him. Erlik glanced down at Mab, "My beautiful bride is to dance for me. Come! Cheer for her; she's shy."

They gave her a loud roar. Mab glowered. Smiling callously, he leaned down to her, a hand on the back of her chair. "Don't tire yourself out, my love. We still have our wedding night to attend to." He pulled her to her feet.

As Mab made her way to the hall's centre, the unseelie

applauded. *They* were respectful to her, at least.

Minstrels began their music: a slow, haunting tune. Mab closed her eyes, letting the song flow through her.

I am not here.

Instead, she imagined herself at a Beltane festival, Pagans twirling around her, her people dancing in the dark cloak of night.

You want me to dance, Poison-Hoarder? Then I shall dance. Witness the power of the Old Ways.

Opening her eyes again, she chanced a glance at Erlik, his smirk still in place.

Mab started slow, elegantly swaying to the music. Excited muttering mounted and then silenced as the music increased in tempo, and Mab picked up speed.

Twisting, spinning, her dress billowed around her feet. Waves of intoxicating scent washed over her audience. All watched with widening eyes, mesmerised by this hypnotic movement. Erlik sat up a little straighter.

A spark of fire flickered at Mab's feet.

She stepped lightly, barely touching the ground, whirling faster. More sparks appeared. Trembling higher, forming shapes: men and women.

Entranced, the minstrels played on.

Those fiery creatures twirled. Mab's shadow broke away from her feet and danced on the wall.

Fiery spirits wrapped blazing arms around her in a cocoon of flames. Billowing out, they lifted her, a queen of fire, those orange flames engulfing, yet not burning.

Braziers on walls grew dim, flickered, and died; light now came from Mab's summoned spirits. A blink; stone became wood and the unseelie now sat, not within a great hall, but a dark, stygian forest.

Those few unseelie not under Mab's spell glanced around, fearful, at the looming darkness. They gasped as the fire spirits blazed higher.

Bewitched, the minstrels played faster.

A shadow – *Mab's* shadow – flitted between tree trunks. Dancing, writhing within that encroaching gloom, beckoning. More than one shadow now darted between the flames.

One fiery spirit stepped into Mab's circle. She took its burning hand, dancing with it. The glow of its flames flickered over her pale face.

Mysteriously smiling now, Mab whirled around the spirit. It caught her in a shivering grasp. Others danced furiously around them, still in their circle, casting embers high. Heat surged from each. Moss and grass blackened beneath their feet; the pungent scent of woodsmoke stung all faces.

"She'll burn us all!" came a hysterical shout.

Mab laughed, her step uninterrupted. Gesturing, a casual flick, at the panicking unseelie. A tongue of flame whipped from her fingertips. Wrapped around his mouth. Silenced him.

Full-bodied and faceless, her shadows formed a barricade, an enclosure of interlocking arms, around the fires, protecting those fretful unseelie.

Faster. Dancing faster. Each spirit tall as any giant. Different forms, now. A man. A snake. A dragon. Fuelled by magic and ardour. Shadows danced with fire. Faster. Faster. *Faster!*

"*Woman!*"

All music stopped at Erlik's furious bellow. Spirits vanished in twirls of orange and red. Her forest melted away. Light returned to the stone hall once more.

Mab sucked in a sharp breath. She looked up at Erlik, now on his feet. Silently, he jerked his head at the empty chair beside him; an order to return to her seat. Mab exhaled slowly. She obeyed. This time, she knew, she had pushed him too far.

Around the hall, each unseelie blinked owlishly, shaking their heads, waking from dreams. Erlik looked up.

His voice rang cold in the silence. "The feast is over."

Though Mab had just taken her seat, he grabbed her arm. Erlik steered her from the hall, leaving a crowd of confused unseelie muttering to one another.

"YOU THINK YOU'RE clever, don't you?" Erlik snarled, dragging Mab through empty corridors. He yanked her back to him when she stumbled. "You think you can get away with that little game? I'll teach you a lesson, my sweet leaf-ear whore."

Throwing open his bedchamber door, he hurled Mab inside. He slammed the door shut again. Locked it with an ominous click. He slowly turned, facing her.

Erlik took a deep breath. "Mab, why did you do that?"

Her eyebrows drew together, a stubborn frown. He had wanted her to dance, and she had done so. She had done nothing to wrong him.

Still she said nothing, true to her oath.

"After everything I've done for you," he went on, "why did you *humiliate me?*"

He pounded his fists on a dresser, delicate glass bottles trembling, then swept everything onto the floor. Shattered shards danced over stone.

Mab took a wary step back, hands raised to calm him,

still not saying a word. Erlik grasped his hair, a desperate, hungry look in his eyes now, panting hard.

"Take off your gown," he said. Mab narrowed her eyes, tipping her head back. Erlik gave her a cruel smile. "This is our wedding night. Take it off, now!"

Mab turned away, approaching a chair by the fire. She sat, back rigid, hands tightly clasped in her lap.

She didn't look back at him, despite sensing that scorching gaze on her.

"Mab, it would *not* be a clever idea to test my patience."

Erlik stepped in front of her chair, filling her sight. He kneeled, gazing into her frosty eyes. She forced her gaze to look past his face, focusing on those flickering flames beneath the hearth.

I know what you are going to do.

"Say something," he said, fingers creeping around her face, to touch her cheek. "Say you will allow me." Erlik let his hand fall into her lap.

Slowly, daring to lock her eyes onto his, Mab shook her head.

Erlik's hand journeyed along her thigh. Higher.

"Very well," he said. "You've left me no choice."

Mab swallowed hard and closed her eyes. She didn't need to see him stand. She didn't need – nor want – to see that expression twisting his handsome face. Her magic dampened, unable to use it against him. The lives of her seelie at risk if she didn't comply now. *Will madness never relinquish its hold on you?*

"I've been patient for long enough."

Erlik lunged. He grasped her face, holding her still, kissing her hard. Tangling his fingers in her hair, he dragged her to her feet. Mab hissed. Ignoring her, he pulled her away from the fire, turned, and threw her down on the bed.

Mab twisted, trying to scramble away. Grabbing her ankles, Erlik pulled her to him. Spun her onto her back. He crawled on top of her, trapping her beneath him, pressing his weight down on her. He ran his tongue over her lips, down to the hollow at the base of her bruised throat.

"You still won't speak?" His voice was rough with desire. Mab squirmed away from his wine-heavy breath, recoiling from its stench, and he laughed. "It's time you were tamed, Wolf-Queen," he snarled. His knee found its way between her legs, forcing them apart. A beast now.

Mab squeezed her eyes shut, knowing struggling was futile. He always had been too strong.

Erlik planted ugly, wet kisses along her neck. Pinned her wrists to the bed, holding her down with just one hand. She heard her gown rip in his eagerness to undress her, to see all of her at once, to take her as his own.

A primal, animal instinct awoke in her. To lash out, to fight, to throw him off and incinerate him. Her breath quickened. Lightning surged through her veins.

With a guttural scream of fury, Mab forced all her strength into shoving him away. Erlik grunted and fell back, staggering. His lip curled into a snarl, and Mab growled and bared her teeth. Locks of hair fell in front of her face, fanned by her fast, short blasts of breath.

Mab flexed her coiled fingers. Erlik lunged at her again, and the last thread of Mab's control on her fury snapped. Rage powerful enough to overcome the Binding magic.

She brandished her hands, a surprisingly graceful gesture, and a circle of fire erupted around Erlik. White light flickered in his eyes, pupils blown huge and dark. He took one step, through her inferno.

Mab threw a crackling sphere of flame at him. He buckled with a groan of pain, and Mab suddenly hesitated.

Erlik looked up. Mab trembled, not with fear, but rage.

"You've broken the rules of the Binding," he said, his voice low. Quiet.

Mab's face twisted with agony and she convulsed, stumbling backwards. Clawed pain raked her body. Intense, crippling heat flared from the Binding Ring on her left hand. Biting her tongue to keep her scream contained, she clutched her shaking hand close to her chest. Her heart beat so fast it felt like it was going to burst. The fiery circle vanished, leaving the room in semi-darkness. Mab moaned and whimpered, disgusted with herself for this display of weakness.

Her vision grew darker, and through a haze, Mab could just see Erlik approaching her with an unreadable expression.

Mab shivered, caught between wanting to beg for his help and wanting to scramble away. Her back pressed against the foot of the bed, hunched over and cowering like a wounded animal.

She felt Erlik gather her up in his arms and lay her down on the bed. Her last sight before becoming engulfed by darkness was him looming over her, still wearing that impassive look.

CHAPTER 41

In which the seelie begin their battles

T HOMAS HALTED. THE broth he'd eaten earlier roiled in his belly. He staggered, collapsing against a wall. Groaning, he clutched his head, suddenly hot and heavy, full of needles. His eyes burned.

"Thomas?" Alissa's voice echoed as though from inside a long tunnel, despite being right beside him. And yet she wasn't.

Where am I?

A wildly dizzying sensation overtook him. Too hot, much too hot, he clawed at his collar. Blinking fast. Tongue too big for his dry mouth.

It took a few moments before Thomas realised he was happy. No. More than happy. *Ecstatic.* Deliriously giddy with joy. Heat coiled inside him. A surge below his waist. He needed—

His vision went black. A room. A hearth. A bed.

Self-loathing, coupled with a powerful desire to hurt, washed over him like hot water. A scent of wildflowers and woodsmoke filled his nostrils. A thick lump forming in his throat, Thomas swallowed the urge to be sick.

"Thomas, what's wrong?"

"Milord? Should I fetch someone?"

Their voices clanged invasively in his brain. He shook his head. He regretted it almost at once.

"I—I have to find—" He sped off without finishing, leaving his sister among seelie friends. Each looked as bewildered as the next.

THOUGH EVERY HALLWAY yielded no one, still Thomas searched for his quarry. At last, he found a seelie boy, his arms full of chopped wood.

"You, lad!" Thomas called, wiping sweat from his brow. The boy looked up in surprise.

"Aye, milord?"

Teeth gritted in both annoyance and discomfort, Thomas said, "Where's Thissy?"

The boy paused. "Thiss—oh!" His face brightened, apparently realising who Thomas meant. "In the stables, milord."

Thomas nodded his thanks and sped off.

SKIDDING GRACELESSLY INTO the stables, Thomas glanced around. No one. *She must have already left.*

He groaned, weary, covering his face with his hands. He fought the urge to kick over an upturned bucket and sank down onto it instead. Nearby, a horse snorted. Thomas inhaled slowly. The stench of horseshit crushed whatever ruttish desires he had.

"Thomas?"

He lowered his hands at once, seeing her there, gazing down at him, concern and fondness painted on her face.

"What's wrong?" Thissy asked, tilting her head.

Thomas squeezed his eyes shut, pressing the heels of his palms into his eyes as he pushed back tears. Breathing deep, burying his desire beneath that pungent fetor.

Not her. Don't hurt her. Not her!

"He's not well," said a voice. Not Thissy's voice.

Thomas looked up again, frowning. Thissy smiled at him. Behind her, Epona snorted, tossing her head. Thissy glanced over her shoulder at her.

"She's just returned," she said. "More of her kin are coming to help us fight. Their numbers are few, as are ours. But I have faith."

She rewarded him with a fond smile. Thomas slowly nodded, hiding his face in his hands again.

Thissy approached and sank to her knees before him. She gently took his hands, lowering them and entwining her warm fingers in his.

"You *do* look sick," she said. "You're so pale. Your wounds haven't opened again, have they? Do you need me to heal you?"

Voice shaking, Thomas explained everything he'd felt. From those waves of vicious emotion to that scent of wildflowers that still clung to him. Even as he spoke, a strong desire to laugh erupted in him. He bit his tongue to stop it.

Listening with wide eyes, Thissy's expression grew from concern to fear.

"Do you think it was... *him?*" she asked. He held back a disappointed sigh. As much as Thomas's speech had rallied the seelie, still they wouldn't speak his name.

Thomas nodded. "I'm sure of it. I don't know what caused this... feeling." He didn't elaborate.

"It must be awful for you," she went on, stroking his cheek. "I can't imagine what it must be like. To share in such evil."

Thomas lifted his arm, wrapping it around her to bring her closer. Her flowery scent tickled his nose. "I don't know what I'm going to do, Thissy," he admitted. "I'm glad you're here with me."

"What do you mean?" she said softly, her voice a caress to his ears.

"Mab wants me to be her Champion," he said. "The seelie see me as some sort of saviour. My sister wants me to take her home as soon as possible. My mother is counting on me to rescue Alissa and return home straight away. Even Erlik has some sort of bond tying me. Don't I get any agency?"

"Of course you have a choice, *a ghrá*," Thissy squeezed his knee. Thomas gazed at her, his eyes drawn to her soft lips. "What do you *want* to do?"

Gently, he wrapped his hand around the back of her head, pulling her closer. She didn't resist. Thomas's heart pounded in his throat. His lips brushed against hers.

An amused cough came from behind them. Thomas and Thissy broke apart at once, leaping to their feet.

"I hope we are not interrupting," said a curiously accented voice. Thissy cleared her throat shyly, averting her eyes. Thomas stared at this stranger and his company.

The speaker, a feral-looking man with tanned skin and a charlatan smirk, somehow looked both rugged and incredibly charming. Another man and a woman stood behind him, clutching spears. Feathers trembled in their braided and dreadlocked hair. Swirling, thorny tattoos were inked over their faces and chests. Their leader took a step forward.

"Who are you?" Thomas asked.

The stranger spoke in a proud voice, "I am Lughaid

Stronghand, Chieftain of the *Fianna*. This is Aife," he gestured at a woman behind him. She slightly inclined her head. "And Oisín." He nodded to the other warrior, who looked immensely bored, picking something out from between yellow teeth.

"Are you the Rhymer?" asked Aife, with a throaty accent. She stared at Thomas through cold, angled eyes, her head tipped back as though to look down on him.

"I'm Thomas Rhymer, yes," he replied, cautious. Smirking, an eyebrow cocked, she cast an appraising gaze over him, looking unimpressed. Was she being deliberately condescending?

Her tanned skin gleamed under dull light. Russet hair framed her heart-shaped face. The speckled grey feathers in her hair quivered when she moved.

"We heard of a war brewing like fire in your western grasslands. We want to offer our services," said Lughaid, switching his impressive spear to his other hand.

"Why do you want to fight with us?" Thissy said quietly, though maintaining her position at Thomas' side. Lughaid sniffed.

"Rumours abound, little mistress. Seelie fighting against the Dark Prince? The Dragon King himself? A fool's errand. But if you hope to defeat the *Attercop Aetheling* – the Spider Prince – then you will need us."

Behind him, Oisín loudly kissed his teeth. Clearly impatient. Thomas turned his gaze to each in turn.

"All three of you?"

Aife clicked her tongue in annoyance. "This was a waste of time, Lughaid," she said in a loud whisper. "The boy is soft-headed. He has no mind to let us fight."

"The rest of our tribe awaits my orders," Lughaid said,

ignoring Aife's disapproving sigh. "They are outside."

Thomas narrowed his eyes. "Show me."

Lughaid shrugged, beckoning him to follow. At the stable doors, bright light stung his vision. Thomas pressed a hand to his brow to shield his eyes. It took a few moments to adjust. Blinking to rid his sight of dancing pink spots, Thomas's mouth fell open and stupidly gaped.

The *Fianna* army held far greater numbers than he could have imagined. About five hundred strong, Thomas reckoned. All looked similar to their chieftain, with wild hair and tattooed faces. A barbarian army, each individual bearing as many weapons as could be carried.

Thomas stared. Oisín and Aife smirked at each other. Lughaid appeared by Thomas's shoulder. "Well?" he asked, when Thomas said nothing. A smile tugged at his lips, and he looked over his shoulder at the chieftain.

"Chieftain Lughaid," he said. "You're welcome to fight with us against Erlik."

Lughaid grinned, but Thissy hissed in his ear, tugging him away from the *Fianna*.

"Can we speak alone, please?"

Thomas nodded. Lughaid turned away to inform his company, and Thomas entered the stable again behind Thissy.

"Are you *mad*?" she asked as soon as they were alone. "Weren't you listening when Elder Lightfoot said we aren't going to ask them to fight for us? They're not soldiers, they're *mercenaries*! They fight only for coin, coin that we don't have. We can't trust them, Thomas, they're too dangerous and too many."

"What choice do we have?" Thomas asked, sadly shaking his head. "Half of our soldiers are dead. The other half are in Elphame. Thissy, we need them. We can't do this alone."

"We've managed without them so far," Thissy said. Her voice, steadily growing in volume, carried and echoed through the stable. "Thomas, you need to revoke your offer."

A surge of annoyance bubbled inside him like liquid fire.

"Quieten down, Thissy," he hissed. "This isn't helping."

"Why do you have so little faith in us?" she asked, her eyes now brimming with frustrated tears. "After everything you said? You told us we could fight and win if we had faith. Now you're selling that faith to an army of mercenaries? Thomas, this isn't right. I won't be a part of this. I have to speak to Elder Lightfoot—"

Thomas grabbed her arm, tighter than he'd expected. She flinched and bit back a cry of pain.

"Thomas, let go!"

He pulled her close, grasping both her arms now, and shook her hard. "I'm doing this for *you!* To keep you safe! Don't you see?"

With a gasp, Thissy shoved him away. She stepped back from him, her eyes wide.

"Don't you realise who you sound like?" she whispered, still backing away from him. Thomas's heart constricted. Sickness overwhelmed him again.

"Thissy, I'm sorry! I didn't mean—" he said, approaching her.

"No!" She flinched, holding her arms up to keep him back. "Stay away!"

Thomas couldn't bear to see her looking at him with such fear. "Thissy, please—" He took a step toward her, but she staggered back.

"Stay away!" she warned again. "We were foolish to think the Dragon King's poison could be so easily cured." She turned and fled, quiet sobs lancing through him like shards of glass.

Thomas couldn't move. His fingers were numb, his heart racing. He felt shameful, unclean.

Behind him, Lughaid laid a hand on his shoulder.

"We'll set up camp out here," he said. Thomas nodded. Epona nudged him with her nose as he passed, but he ignored her.

He wanted – *needed* – to see Thissy. He had to apologise, if she'd let him. Shame clawed at him. His heart beat so fast he felt it might burst.

What would he tell Lightfoot?

THOMAS WANDERED THROUGH halls, ignoring queries about his wellbeing. He passed like a ghost, blank-eyed, dead-limbed.

He looked up sharply; a whimpering bleat had caught his ear. Gaining speed, he ran through the corridors towards the sound... Until a group of playing children ran past shrieking. His heart heavy, Thomas continued drifting between rooms, searching.

AT LONG LAST – or perhaps too soon? – he found himself outside the main chamber. He pushed open its huge door and crept inside, feeling like a naughty child. The smell of ages-old incense, warm wood, and musty tapestries filled his nose.

Only Lightfoot stood by the table, his face set in an ugly look.

Thomas lowered his eyes. Coldness danced along his

arms. He stayed silent.

"She told me everything." Lightfoot's voice sounded hollow. No anger, only bitter disappointment.

"I didn't mean what I said," Thomas croaked. "I know I scared her—I hurt her. I didn't mean to, I just—"

"When you first told me that you were bound to the Dark Prince," Lightfoot interrupted. "I kept silent. I had my misgivings, but then I thought perhaps it could work in our favour. For the first time in too long, we had an advantage in our war. I should have trusted my instincts. You are too dangerous to stay here."

"Lightfoot, I'm sorry, I—"

"We will have to honour your promise to the *Fianna* that they fight with us. If we revoke that now, then we'll be fighting a war on two fronts," Lightfoot turned to face him. "They march with us. But you will not. You and your sister will leave."

"*What?*" Thomas heard a loud ringing in his ears now. "No! I won't leave, I want to fight!"

"You will not fight in our war when you're so closely bound to our enemy. I want you gone. Epona will take you and your sister. Gather your things and leave."

"I'm not going home! Thissy—"

"She is no longer your concern!" Lightfoot snapped. "I took care of her when her mother and father were killed. She's like a daughter to me, and I have never heard her speak so fondly of anyone before. But I won't let you near her again. Conduct befitting the Dark Prince begets no second chances. Leave, Thomas, and don't come back."

"But—"

"Leave."

"I want—"

"Leave!"

Thomas wordlessly mouthed. Indignation, fury, and despair robbed his speech. Lightfoot turned away again.

Thomas dazedly left, clutching furniture to keep himself upright. Suddenly realising, with a lump in his throat, that he would never see Thissy again. He'd never get a chance to say sorry, to beg her forgiveness. To tell her how much he loved her.

A fist clenched around his heart, crushing his life out of him.

HE KNOCKED ON Alissa's door. Beaming, she opened it. Then her face fell.

"What's wrong?" she asked at once.

Vervain, the sweet serving girl, appeared at her side. Alissa's new blue wool gown fitted her better than her slave's tunic.

"It's time to go home, Alissa," Thomas said quietly.

Alissa's eyes lit up, and she gave a great sigh of relief. "At last! I can't wait to see Mother. Let me just say—"

"There's no time to make your farewells," Thomas took her hand and pulled her along behind him as gently as he could manage with a snowstorm building in his head. "We're leaving now."

"Milord?" Vervain stumbled along behind them.

"Please don't call me that, Vervain," he said. "It's time Alissa and I went home." He didn't really feel like going into detail.

"But... milord—Sir Thomas, Elder Lightfoot should—"

"Elder Lightfoot already knows. I'm sorry," he said, guiding Alissa through corridors. Other seelie pointed, whispering amongst themselves as they passed.

"But..." Vervain stopped, staring at him. "Thomas, we... we need you."

With a sigh, Thomas halted. "I can't help you. This isn't my war; it never was. I don't belong here," he said. "If you see Thissy, please tell her I'm sorry. Tell her I'll think of her every day. And tell her—tell her I love her."

THE WEIGHT IN his heart growing heavier, choking his words, Thomas kept a firm hold on Alissa's hand until they'd entered the stables. Neither spoke as he saddled Epona. He wished Alissa would speak, just to ease his guilt. *Is this the right thing to do?*

Thomas climbed up onto Epona behind his sister. His sword hilt jammed against his hip. He looked down.

He saw himself reflected in the ruby pommel. His sword. His father's sword – or as close as he would get to it. The weight of shame grew unbearable. Flicking her reins, Thomas rode Epona out of the stable and through the *Fianna* camp. He ignored all shouted questions as he continued towards the moors. Until, thinking of those he'd left behind, something broke inside him, and he allowed his tears to fall.

CHAPTER 42

In which Mab makes a friend

A GENTLE TUGGING on her gown pulled Mab out of her reverie. She looked down in surprise, finding a young unseelie girl looking shyly up at her, scuffing her tiny toes.

Mab blinked. Erlik had made it clear that no one was to enter the scullery this morning. *This child is braver than most.*

Earlier, Mab had awoken to find herself lying beside Erlik. Uncertain, she had sat up to find herself in a simple shift, her body decorated with bruises. The blossoming purple marks – the size and shape of his hands – on her waist and hips unnerved her most. *I had been in no position to fight him, what had he done after I'd fallen faint?*

Erlik had woken some time after her, bleary-eyed and sickened by wine. He had dragged her down to this cold room. After dismissing the other slaves, he'd ordered her to make herself useful – no doubt in an attempt to humiliate her into compliance. Then, when she'd finished, she was to join him in his chamber. He'd staggered back upstairs after that, no doubt to sleep off his pounding head.

Too sore, too shaken to argue, Mab took as long as possible to fulfil his command. So long, in fact, that the pale autumn sun had risen high.

Now, she kneeled down to this child's height, wincing.

She ached inside and out – every movement felt like a burred branch twisting inside her.

"What is it, child?" she asked, not unkindly. The girl blushed behind the dirt on her face. A giggle and a hushing whisper came from behind the door. Mab curiously looked up. Another child peeked out from his hiding place. Followed by another, then another, and yet another. Four children crept out, joined their friend, and smiled up at Mab. She straightened, raising an eyebrow. Even the tallest child barely reached her hips in height.

"You know you are not supposed to be in here," she said, folding her arms, yet offering a warm smile.

"Yes, milady," the eldest nodded glumly, then put his hand on the smallest girl's shoulder. "Cara was hungry, and…" He trailed off, going red.

Mab's lips twitched. "You were hoping to steal some food?"

Each child shyly nodded. Mab smiled in earnest now.

"Fret not, I will tell no one. Come." She beckoned them to follow her to the scullery's far side. "You can have these."

Turning around, with a subtle wave of her hand, and a secret pulse of simple magic – one that would cause her no harm – she presented a plate of sweet-smelling buttermilk biscuits. She knelt, offering the plate forwards. Eyes gleaming, each child leapt forwards to take one. Mab chuckled.

The smallest girl – Cara – gazed up at Mab as she took the last biscuit left. Mab tilted her head as the child hesitated.

"I saw you dancing at the feast," Cara said quietly. "I wasn't supposed to be there. But I watched through a hole in the door."

Mab's smile slipped. She inhaled slowly. If her magic had terrified the unseelie, what effect would it have had on this young child?

"Were you frightened?" she asked.

Cara giggled behind her hands, and shook her head. "No," she said. "I like your magic. Can you teach me?"

Mab smiled kindly. "Perhaps when you are older." She straightened again, patting Cara's hair.

"Thank you, milady," said the eldest, starting to usher the others out.

Mab nodded, still smiling. "You are welcome. Run along and play, go on," she said. Laughing, they ran out, rushing past a figure lurking in the doorway, leaning coolly against its frame.

Unsmiling, Erlik watched the children run past. Arms folded, dark circles under his eyes, and his hair a matted mess; he looked dreadful.

"You're good with children," Erlik said softly, raising his eyes to meet hers. "You'll make a wonderful mother one day."

Mab looked up at once. She set the plate down, warily gazing at him.

"Did you bake those?" he asked, glancing behind him. Mab shook her head, remaining silent. Erlik nodded. He ran his tongue over his lips, his eyes darting around the room. Nervous, perhaps?

Erlik inhaled, then said awkwardly, "I—I have a gift for you."

Mab narrowed her eyes. The last gift he had offered had not been well received. At his tentative approach, she took a few steps back, sucking in a sharp breath. Erlik stopped. Perhaps he could sense how uncomfortable she felt in his presence. He sighed – suddenly looked younger, more vulnerable than she had ever seen him – and produced a spray of wildflowers from behind his back. No magic this time. Some stalks were bent out of shape in his tense grip.

"I... know you like flowers," he sullenly mumbled, offering them forward. Mab hesitated.

Erlik watched each step as she slowly approached him. She reached toward him, and took the spray in hand. His finger brushed against hers. She retreated again.

"Aren't you going to thank me?" he asked. Scowling, Mab bit her tongue.

Thank you? After what you did to me? Should I praise you as a murderer, next?

He averted his gaze. Twisting his hands.

"Mab, I..." he ran his tongue over his lips again, "I didn't mean for it to hurt so much. You'd made me angry. I'd had too much wine. I couldn't control myself. It'll be easier, next time. I promise. I'll be gentler."

Mab narrowed her eyes, her heart thudding painfully hard. She swallowed. *Next time? Madness or no, what you did holds no excuses. Be assured, there will be no 'next time'.*

Erlik took a step forward. Mab took one back. He frowned.

"Say you forgive me," he said. Mab shook her head, solemn and slow. Almost calm. "Say something else, then. Anything at all. It's unnatural for you to be so quiet. I want to hear your voice."

Mab stared hard at him. She swallowed again. She took a slow, deep breath and shook her head.

Sighing, Erlik ran his tongue over his lower lip. "I've been thinking," he said.

An unusual pastime for you, Mab thought. She had to bite

her lip to stop herself saying it aloud.

"Now that we're married," he went on, "I'll be protected from the Godsbane moon. You will share your power with me."

Will I?

Erlik narrowed his eyes. Perhaps he *could* still hear her thoughts?

"You swore to obey and respect me," he said. "Do you want to see the leaf-ear distract ablaze?"

Scowling, Mab turned her head away. She shook her head. Erlik approached.

"Then you will do as I say," he brushed her face with his fingers, trailing his hand down to her arm. "You will share your power with me, and we will be safe together."

Mab frowned. That word he used – *safe* – it seemed impossible. There was no such thing as safety around him. Only death and chaos. A dark and frenzied glint danced in his eyes.

"I do not know how," she said at last. A strange look overcame him. His eyes, at hearing her speak, had lit up. Yet once her words had penetrated his mind, his brow sunk into a frown, obviously thinking he'd misheard.

"What did you say?" he asked, his head tilted. His grip tightened around her arm. Mab hissed sharply, stepping back, out of reach.

"I said, I do not know how."

"You *offered*—" he began, aghast.

"No. I said I could learn, but I will not," she said coolly, her head tipped back. "Not after what you did."

Erlik bared his teeth. "I could just *take* your magic instead."

Despite herself, Mab let out a little laugh. "We both

know you would not," she breathed. *Besides, magic must be willingly given. It cannot be taken by force.*

"You *infuriating* woman," he growled. "Mab, this isn't fair!" he said. "I've already apologised."

"Apologised?" Mab echoed, throwing him her most vicious glare. "I have heard no apology from you. The words stick in your throat and choke you."

Erlik huffed – a petulant child – and narrowed his eyes. Sweeping a hand through his unkempt hair, he ran his gaze over her. She watched his eyes travelling over her face, and pressed her lips together. She recognised that hungry look.

"Very well. We'll do it my way," he said.

Mab's brow knitted. "Your way usually involves blood and fire."

Erlik smirked now. "How better to best an ice queen?" he asked. He laughed, the dark chuckle echoing through that empty room. "I have my methods, my love. There are ways to manipulate the Old Gods."

"They will see through your lies, Erlik. You cannot win this. The Old Gods will never aid you," she said. "You have no one who can—"

"I have *you!*" Erlik suddenly bellowed. He grasped at her, pulling her close. A mad frenzy danced in his eyes. Mab withheld her sharp intake of breath. *How can I ever trust your words when you are so poisoned by madness?*

"We're together now," he went on, "that's all I ever wanted. I just want to be strong enough to protect you."

"The only thing I need protection from is you."

Erlik continued as if he hadn't heard her. "You are my wife. You are the mother to my children. You will learn to love me."

"I do not need to learn."

Erlik blinked as the weight of her words penetrated the air. Silence hung between them, hot and heavy. A faint frown creased his brow. Mab turned her back on him. She could still feel his glare on her. For a moment, she thought he would plunge a blade between her shoulders.

As she repressed a shudder, Erlik spoke quietly, "Why do you have hemlock?"

She glanced over her shoulder, finding Erlik staring at a bowl on the table and the wilted flower that lay within.

Mab swallowed hard.

"Mab," he said, voice low. "Why do you have hemlock?"

Her heart pounded hard in her throat. Mab looked up at him, "An antidote to a poison you may have inflicted on me last night."

Erlik's mouth fell open. He sucked in a sharp breath, his widening eyes flickering briefly to her belly. "You... you think...?"

"I had to be sure," she said slowly. "Any child begat in hate and fear would live its life thusly."

"You could have poisoned yourself!" he said. Mab stared at him. His face twisted, not with anger, but with sorrow. Concern. His eyes glistened now. *Tears?*

She had expected fury. She had expected him to launch forwards, grab her, and shake her until she cried out.

But this? This show of sorrow and despair?

Chewing the inside of his lip, perhaps stopping himself from crying, Erlik sniffed and nodded.

"What about any lasting effects?" he asked, voice shaking. "Did you even think—"

"Do *not* speak to me about thinking before acting, Poison-Hoarder!" she growled, suddenly more wolf than woman. For a brief moment, she was pleased to see him retreat. "I will not be your chalice."

He nodded in silence. This meekness disturbed her. Mab looked away.

"And you're alright?" he asked. "You're not hurt?"

She shook her head, still gazing at the floor. "Hemlock could not kill either of us."

"Either of us?"

Mab froze. She closed her eyes. *Fool.*

"What exactly do you mean by that?"

"Nothing," she said quickly. Too quickly. "I misspoke."

And his eyes suddenly burned with rage.

And there is his fury.

Erlik lunged at her. He grabbed her wrist, twisting it behind her, pressing himself against her back. Mab grunted, trying to throw off his grip. He roughly pushed her into the table. His free hand trailing down from her throat to her belly, he pressed his fingers hard into her flesh. That twisting burr inside shattered, and shards of agony ripped through her abdomen. Mab bit her tongue to keep her groan of pain from escaping. She tasted blood.

"You were going to poison me?" he breathed into her hair, grabbing her face and turned it to look at the bowl on the table. "You want me dead?"

"Of course n—" she began. Erlik's free hand wrapped around her throat and squeezed.

"You lie," he said, his lips grazing her pointed ear. Her body stiffened. She drew in a long, shivering breath, blood pounding in her ears.

"I… I just—"

"You want to make me ill. Weak enough for your pet mortal to kill me. You don't have the courage to kill me yourself, so you want to make it easier for him to do it."

"That is not true!"

"*Liar!*" he hissed. "Is that what you want? You truly want me dead?"

Mab said nothing.

"You're too clever to be left alone, beloved," he said. "From now on, you remain at my side. You do exactly as I say. Do you understand?"

Mab shook. Not from fear, but anger. How could she ever have felt pity for him? She heard a blade being unsheathed, that metallic singing crisp and sharp, and felt its sharpness prick the small of her back.

"Do you know what this is?" Erlik whispered against her ear, running his tongue over her cheek. Mab pulled her head away in disgust. "This is a very special dagger. I'm going to use it to end the life of your pet mortal."

"You—" Mab struggled to free herself. Erlik jabbed his blade harder against her, and Mab stopped moving at once. She licked her lower lip, releasing a slow breath.

"Do you want me to hurt you as well?" he said softly. "I can. I don't want to, but I can."

"You already have hurt me."

"Then I'll hurt you again. And again. And again. Until you learn to love me and respect me as your master, your *king*."

"You are not my king. No man—"

"Can tame you? Yes, I know," he smirked. "But look at yourself, Mab. I *have* tamed you."

Mab looked over her shoulder at him. Their faces were so close, their lips almost touching; she could see herself reflected in his eyes. A smouldering silence fell. Mab matched his gaze. She longed to look away, yet something in those oceanic eyes held her. Erlik leaned forward, gently pressing his lips onto hers.

"Come," he said softly, sheathing his dagger. "It's too cold for you in here. We'll go to my chamber; you can warm yourself by the fire."

"HE'S NOT COMING for you, you know," Erlik said, several paces ahead. Mab said nothing. "He's obviously taken his fool sister and left Albion. That was what you wanted, wasn't it?"

His tone verged on patronising, clearly trying to provoke an angry response. Mab took a deep breath in through her nose and said nothing. Erlik paused, glancing back at her, and smirked to find her biting back a retort.

As he led her up some stairs, they passed that same group of children from the scullery playing in a hallway. Among them, Cara played with a stuffed doll. Seeing Mab, she beamed and waved at her. Mab sadly returned her smile, and kept following Erlik's steady pace.

MAB BARELY NOTICED where Erlik had led her. Only when she felt a chill breeze nip at her arms did she break from her thoughts, finding herself in the castle's main hall. Her eyes raked the room, finally resting on the throne she had once occupied.

"You said we were going to your chamber," she said without thinking. Erlik laughed loudly.

"Eager, aren't you?" he said. Those few courtiers who'd heard laughed with him. Mab narrowed her eyes. Their mirth died away almost at once.

"At least light a fire," she snapped. "'Tis freezing in here."

"You heard my wife, set a fire," he said sharply to a slave girl, gesturing to a banked fire pit in the middle of the hall. "My lady likes warmth."

The girl scuttled forward with an armful of firewood.

Erlik took her hand again, guiding her towards that empty throne as the fire blazed and crackled into life. "Come, sit by me," he said, indicating the floor beside him. Folding her arms, she raised an eyebrow.

"I am not sitting on the floor," she said haughtily.

Erlik grabbed her arm and yanked her closer.

"On the floor, or in my lap for everyone to see, my little pet wolf," he said, quietly enough for only her to hear. Huffing, Mab pulled her arm out of his grip. She lowered herself to the cold floor, throwing curses at him in her mind. Erlik smiled as he settled on his throne.

"I'm going to keep a closer eye on you from now on. I won you. I can do what I want with you," he said. Then, lowering his voice again, "Don't forget what I hold, Mab. I can make you hurt if I want." he whispered, a familiar mad gleam in his eye. Mab sighed.

Erlik smiled at her. He rested a hand on her shoulder, gently pulling her closer. She shifted, laying her head against his leg, while he stroked her hair.

His tamed she-wolf at last.

CHAPTER 43

In which Monstrance's world crumbles

BESIDE A *FIANNA* tent on the outskirts of their camp, a barn owl landed and ruffled its feathers. Two warriors sat there, ladling out bowls of steaming rabbit stew. More tents and horses dotted that field outside the seelie colony's castle.

One nudged his companion, pointing at the owl. It turned its head to him.

A flash, a loud yell of surprise, and an even louder curse as hot stew spilled over hands and laps. Both warriors leapt to their feet, unsheathing swords.

Morrigan stared back, eyes brimming, chin quivering. She blinked a couple of times, then burst into tears. Each warrior nervously glanced at the other.

"What's going on here?" Aife demanded, pushing through both *Fianna* and staring at Morrigan, who childishly wiped her eyes.

"C-can I see Monstrance?" she asked, her voice cracking.

Aife frowned. "What business do you have here, mothblood?" she asked unkindly. Morrigan sniffed, her breathing abnormally fast and short.

"I-I w-want to see my b-brother," she wept. Aife regarded her for a few moments, then nodded and beckoned her to follow. Morrigan rubbed her tears away again, following the *Fianna* through murmuring crowds.

"You wait here, *maegdencild*," Aife commanded when they'd reached the front steps. "I don't think these seelie will take to having you walk so brazenly through their halls."

Biting her lip to stop herself crying, Morrigan nodded. Aife threw her a judging stare, then turned away. Morrigan sat meekly on the castle's cold steps, gazing at the blooming army the seelie had gathered.

AFTER A WHILE, Aife returned. Beside her, Monstrance looked irritated at the interruption.

"What exactly—"

Aife pointed at a hunched figure on the steps. Monstrance halted and stared.

"*Morrigan?*" he gaped. "What are you doing here?"

Rushing forwards, he warmly embraced her, not noticing her tears until he'd pulled away. His smile slipped at once. "What's wrong?" he asked. His heart dropped like a stone. "Who's hurt?"

He held her at arm's length, gently rubbing tears from her cheeks. Morrigan gulped.

"It-it's Corvus," she swallowed, pushing her knuckles into her eyes.

"Hurt?"

"D-dead."

Monstrance felt a chill hand constrict his throat. Morrigan shuddered in his arms.

"F-Father killed him!" She broke into sobs again, covering her face with her hands. Monstrance dropped his arms. He staggered. Aife caught him.

"Easy, lad," she said, gesturing for him to sit before he

fell.

A group of seelie had gathered now. Each nervously stared at Morrigan and Monstrance.

"Why?" he breathed, blinking down tears. Shaking, Morrigan looked down at her brother. She sat beside him, sniffling and rubbing her face against his arm, cat-like.

"H-he fell in love with Queen Mab," she said, leaning in to wrap her arms around his waist, seeking comfort. All around, seelie glanced at each other, and even some *Fianna* looked nervous. The same question in each mouth.

If Erlik would willingly kill his own son, what more could he be capable of?

IT TOOK A long time for Morrigan to calm herself. Monstrance took her inside, leaving her with a group of kindly seelie. At first, they appeared to be wary of her, yet once they'd seen her shaking with uncontrollable sobs, they took her away to a quiet room. Monstrance rushed into the castle, seeking Lightfoot's advice.

He burst into Lightfoot's chamber, just as Thomas had once done, blurting Morrigan's story before he could stop himself. Though he struggled to keep tears from pooling as he did so. He quickly blinked them back before Lightfoot could see and cleared his throat.

"Where's Thomas?" he said quietly, looking for another subject. "He should know about this."

Fidgeting, Lightfoot sighed.

"I've sent him home."

Monstrance stared.

"Why?" Monstrance took a few tentative steps. Lightfoot said nothing. "Elder Lightfoot?" he gently prompted.

"Thomas is… blood-bound to your father," he said. "If he had stayed, if we had let him fight… if there was any chance he might be swayed to fight against us… I couldn't allow it." A pause then. "He had already shown a darkness inside him."

"Lightfoot," Monstrance approached him, laying a hand on his shoulder. "You must send for him. I know he's a stubborn ass, but you saw how much courage he gave the seelie. They need him as much as we do. Besides, Mab chose him as her champion, didn't she?"

"Aye," Lightfoot said softly. "She did. But what if she's wrong? What if he's not the champion we need?"

"Mab believes in him," Monstrance said. "So I believe in him too. Thomas had come back to Albion to save his sister, and reclaimed his heritage as a result. Don't let him run away from that. And…" He swallowed. "Thissy loves him, doesn't she?" That simple phrase jammed into his chest. "Please, send for him to come back."

Lightfoot sighed, and after a glance at Monstrance, he turned away to stare out at the *Fianna* camp, his gaze falling over the vast moors.

"It's too late," he said. "We don't have time to wait for him. The Godsbane moon rises in less than a week. When it does, we need to be at Elphame. We march today."

THOMAS FELT TEARS pricking behind his eyes. Each time he thought his misery had ended, it blossomed in him again, and he'd feel his cheeks become wet.

Epona had ridden for miles, across moors and through forests. Thomas let her guide his hand, only ever pulling her back on course when he felt her straining to turn back.

At the edge of a dark, wild-looking wood, Epona slowed to a walk. Trotting over a rough wooden bridge, Thomas felt his heart sink further, remembering the crossing into Albion. *So many days ago.*

Pulling on Epona's reins, he dismounted. "We can rest here awhile." His voice sounded hollow, even to himself. He turned to offer his hand to Alissa, but she ignored his help and slid from the horse herself.

Alissa retraced a few steps to the bridge and down the bank, kneeled by the gushing stream to splash her face with its cool spray, "How long before we reach home?"

"Not long," Thomas said miserably.

What was Thissy doing now? Were the seelie already marching to Elphame? And – a lump that he couldn't swallow formed in his throat – what would happen when they arrived?

These questions burned inside him. In his heart, he knew what would happen when they reached Elphame. Erlik would—

No. Thomas shook his head. He had to rid himself of these thoughts. *Everything will be fine. Mab will be rescued; Thissy will be safe.*

No they won't. That wicked voice in his head sounded unbearably like Erlik. *They won't be safe. You've abandoned them. They will die. They will all die.*

"It's not my fault!" Thomas suddenly shouted. Several birds skittered away through branches. Alissa looked up in alarm. With a sigh, Thomas ran a hand through his hair. "Stay here, I just need to—I won't be long." Without another word, he turned away, striding into comforting darkness.

THOMAS WISHED HE could stop those haunting thoughts. He kept hearing those awful words he'd said to Thissy. Over and over. Each time, they sounded more vicious, more spiteful. He finally understood why she backed away with such fear. Maybe she was right. *Maybe I am just like him.*

Him. Erlik.

Thomas's stomach churned. Hatred and anger rolled into a toxic pit. It was *his* fault. Everything. There was no one else to blame except him. *He* was the root of all pain, all misery, all anguish. Mab's imprisonment. Alissa's kidnap. The war. The seelie's dwindling numbers, their slaughter at *his* hands. Every bad experience Thomas had suffered or witnessed in Albion could be traced back to the Dragon King.

Thomas's hands curled into fists as something broke inside him. His eyes burned with hot, angry tears.

"Thomas?" came a soothing female voice behind him. Thomas spun, finding only Epona standing there, her beautiful, doleful eyes fixed on him. Her tail twitched, and Thomas sighed.

"I'm sorry, we'll be on the move soon," he said sadly, "You were there, Epona; did I really say such cruel things to Thissy?"

Epona silently approached and nudged him with her nose. Thomas lifted his hand, running it through his hair.

"How is it I understand you now?" he asked, desperately seeking another topic. Grateful she hadn't answered his previous question; he didn't want to hear her confirm his fears.

"You learned to listen," she said. "You accepted yourself as a seelie."

"You sound like Mab," he gave her a sad smile, patting

her nose. "I want to go back, Epona. I need to see Thissy again. I need to tell her how I—how I feel… I can't let it end this way."

He raised his eyes, staring at the closest tree trunk, though not really seeing it. Reaching out and running his hand over its bark, it took him a moment to recognise the familiar markings. He frowned.

A heart, roughly carved into the tree. Thomas felt his breath hitch. *We must be near home. I saw this tree when we first entered Albion.*

His hand dropped. He turned away. Epona stayed still, her eyes fixed on the tree.

"Thomas, wait," she said, approaching it with a nervous gait. Thomas slowly looked back.

He turned, matching her gaze on the tree, seeing something just beneath that rough carving. A splatter, something red. Paint? Or—

"Thomas!" Epona's gentle voice sounded fearful.

He followed her gaze upwards. He couldn't restrain his resulting gasp.

Hanging lifeless in the high branches of the tree before him, a dead seelie. His face swollen, head twisted at a bizarre angle, clothes torn and bloodstained. Thomas retched. How had that smell not hit him sooner? Epona backed away in fright.

"On his chest, look," she said. Thomas hadn't even noticed the note pinned to the corpse.

Thomas's heart dropped hard, squinting to read its message again and again.

"*Leaves will fall,*" he read in a slow whisper. "What does that mean?"

He looked up at Epona, then back at the message. He

read it again, his mouth silently forming those words. *Leaves. Leaf-ears. Seelie.*

"Thissy…" Thomas glanced at that swinging body. "We have to go back."

Thomas leapt up onto Epona. When he burst through foliage by the stream, Alissa jumped up in alarm, her unbraided hair dripping.

"What is it? Unseelie?" she asked, quickly casting her eyes about.

"Alissa," Thomas turned his horse and pointed. "Follow that path, it'll lead you out of the forest and back home. You're not far as long as you stick to the path. When you come to a stone bridge, you'll know you're going the right way."

"I don't—where are you going?" Alissa panicked, approaching Epona and tugging Thomas's arm. The horrified look in her eyes did nothing but confirm to Thomas of how stupid – and incredibly dangerous – his plan really was. *I can't abandon them now.*

"I'm going back," he said. "I'll come home, I promise."

"Thomas, you can't just—" Alissa protested.

Thomas cut her off sternly, "Go home, Alissa. I'm not putting you in danger again."

Alissa stood her ground, hands planted on her hips. "Thomas, I—"

"Go home, Alissa."

Epona whinnied in fright. Thomas looked up. He, too, had heard shrieks of mournful crying high above.

Ghosts of dead elves flickered like silvery fish, darting between clouds that formed and swiftly darkened. Rain began to patter through the trees. A lightning flash illuminated the forest, now Thomas could see properly around them. Though thankfully no more bodies swung hidden in the darkness, most trees had been stained with threatening messages against seelie, or even Mab herself.

Burn the district.

Skin the wolf.

Death to the leaf-ears.

His heart thumped faster.

"Come, Epona," Thomas said, flicking her reins. Galloping through woodland, Alissa's annoyed shouts ignored, he kept on course. Back from whence he'd come, back to fight in a war that he'd been part of since before he'd been born.

CHAPTER 44

In which his march begins

THE SECOND DAY'S sun was already sinking into its horizon as Epona ran hard across moorland. A cold autumn wind cruelly lashed Thomas's face. He urged her faster, though he knew he would be too late, even riding an Elvish horse. Every seelie would have already left, marching across the moors to Elphame with Monstrance, able to sense its location, leading them. Thomas pushed such thoughts aside, fixing his eyes instead on the sprawling purple moors before him.

A DARK SHAPE emerged through the gloaming. Thomas blinked before he realised it was their castle. No light shone from behind its windows and the *Fianna* camp had cleared out. Thomas trotted right up to the front gates, dismounted, rushed up a set of steps, then burst into the castle, breathless.

"Lightfoot?" he desperately called, knowing it was futile. He ran through the atrium and up a stairwell, his footsteps bleakly echoing around the empty halls. "Firestrider? Monstrance? *Thissy?*"

A soft sniff behind him. Thomas spun.

"Thiss—oh." His smile dropped.

Her eyes red, Morrigan emerged from a corridor.

"They're gone," she said quietly. "They bade everyone who couldn't fight to stay here."

"I thought so." Thomas sighed, still out of breath. "What are you doing here, Morrigan?"

He tried not to sound accusatory, but found difficulty trusting her. *Unless she's been banished too?*

"My father—he d-did something terrible," she said thickly. "Queen Mab told me to come here." Despite her bloodshot eyes and blotchy, tearstained face, an embarrassed blush crept up her cheeks. "Y-you were brave, to stand up to my father the way you did. When we—when you first met him…" She averted her eyes.

"Are you well?" Thomas asked, feeling awkward. Morrigan sniffed, nodding. Unconvinced, Thomas gave her a few moments to wipe her eyes before pressing on.

"Can you show me the way to Elphame?" he asked. Morrigan hiccoughed, gazing up at him.

"Well… I suppose, but Monstrance—"

"Morrigan, please," he took her hand. Morrigan stared into his eyes. "Tonight is our only chance, the moon will be rising soon."

"I-I know, b-but—"

For a brief moment, he considered telling her about those messages scrawled on the trees, then decided against it. If she knew of what he had seen, she'd likely never help him.

"Think of Mab. What would she do? She wouldn't run and hide, would she?"

Morrigan blinked. She hesitated, gazing at Thomas with a strange expression. "I like her," she said softly. "She's always kind to me. I… I want to try and help her." She smiled up at him, eyes glistening.

Thomas grinned, then nodded his head back the way he'd come, trusting the unseelie to walk by his side with no more cajoling. In the courtyard, Epona patiently waited for him.

"Epona—Morrigan, can you lead Epona to Elphame?" he asked. Morrigan nodded.

"Are you sure about this?" Epona asked softly. Thomas grinned, patting her neck.

"I've never been so sure."

Epona tossed her head and snorted. Thomas smiled; it almost looked as though she'd rolled her eyes at him.

After a confused glance between them, Morrigan clambered up into the saddle, Thomas climbing up behind her.

MOORLAND RUSHED PAST. A faint track of foot- and hoof-prints stretched out below them, already fading thanks to the morning mists and light drizzle. Passing a familiar loch, Thomas felt a question fall from his mouth.

"Morrigan," he called over pounding hooves. "Why does your father move Elphame?"

"Father is afraid," she called back. "He's afraid that someone will come to take his throne, just as he stole it from Queen Mab."

Thomas found it difficult to imagine Erlik as afraid; he struggled to picture him as anything other than arrogant and domineering.

"THERE!" MORRIGAN POINTED ahead, yet Thomas saw only stretching moors. No city. Night had properly fallen now, and the moon had begun rising, a fat yellow coin rolling into a velvet sky.

"Look, Thomas."

Straining his eyes, the air began to waver like a hot summer's day. A tingle of fear and excitement prickled his scalp. Elphame rose up out of darkness, looming over the moors with an ominous presence.

He could see the castle's whitewashed walls. *Mab is in there,* he thought, then shivered. *So is Erlik.*

He focused instead on Elphame, and more emerged into view. Smoke rose from within the walls; a large shouting crowd had gathered outside the gates.

"*Damnú air,*" he muttered.

"What is it?" Morrigan asked at once.

"Something's wrong, look," Thomas said. That crowd outside Elphame's gates, as he'd suspected, were seelie. Though those gates were thrown wide open, none were entering.

Someone shot an arrow through the open gates. It struck an invisible wall and vanished, a flame in water. Neither Mab nor Erlik could be seen.

"My father has hexed the gate," Morrigan said over the clamouring crowd they now rode through.

"So we can't enter?" Thomas dismounted as soon as Epona had drawn to a halt, with Morrigan sliding from the elvish horse far more gracefully than he had done in his haste.

"No, wait!" Morrigan grabbed his arm, tugging the fabric of his tunic until he got the message to follow her. "I know another way, follow me!"

Instead of guiding him towards the gates, Morrigan led the way to a towering wall that surrounded Elphame's outer reaches.

"Father had this built in case he ever needed to flee the city," she said. "No one knows about it. He killed the architect afterwards."

"How do you know about it, then?"

Morrigan grinned. "I was his favourite. He wouldn't have left *me* behind." She led him towards a discoloured stone in the wall. "Here, help me." She pushed hard on that stone, and it flickered. *Magic?*

Thomas momentarily glanced over his shoulder at the seelie crowd now congregated some way off. He pulled a face as the set of stones shimmered into nothing, revealing a cobwebbed tunnel.

"This comes out at the *gard—gaird*—that seelie garden," she said. Thomas nodded.

"Thank you, Morrigan." He smiled at her. "For everything."

"Please be careful, Thomas. You know how tricky my father is," she said. He cuffed her chin, smiling still.

"Stay safe," he said, winking at her. Despite everything, Morrigan gave a genuine – albeit small – smile. She turned, making her way back to Epona.

With a nervous swallow, Thomas drew his sword, then headed into the tunnel, sweeping aside cobwebs, trying not to break his ankle as he blindly stumbled through the blackness.

AFTER AN UNCOMFORTABLY dark journey – during which he'd bumped his head more than once – Thomas emerged into a faded echo of the empty *Gairdín Síoraí*. Finding a gravel pathway slicing through withered grass, he followed it until he reached a wide balcony.

He approached the balcony's edge, looking out into

Elphame and beyond.

Still, seelie struggled at the gates. Though too far away to make out individuals, he imagined Thissy among them. The *Fianna* stood in ranks behind them, patiently watching, waiting for the seelie to break in.

He turned back to the castle, taking a deep breath. The moon climbed slowly higher. Thomas remembered Mab's words, as clear in his head as the day she'd spoken them:

When that golden moon rises, magic rests. All faekind become powerless.

Her voice echoing in his head, he walked up the steps to the entrance, drawing his sword and continuing to look around him for any movement which could betray danger.

His hands slippery with sweat, Thomas pushed hard on those ominous white doors.

CHAPTER 45

In which sibling rivalry reaches its peak

IRESTRIDER AT ITS head, the seelie army stood in defensive ranks, weapons drawn. Unseelie forces marched towards Elphame's gates. Seelie archers stood at the fore, bowstrings taut, as the unseelie began forming their own ranks. Each *Fianna* warrior stood patiently behind the seelie rows, listening to Lughaid's stirring speech in their native tongue.

The unseelie army stretched out, ranked, bolstered by pride, beating their swords against their shields.

Deathly calm descended. Eyes furiously blinked under helms. Hands tightened on hilts. Metal ground on metal whenever someone shifted beneath weighty armour.

The ground trembled. A massive black cloud, echoing with baying hounds and thundering horses, galloped with fierce, powerful force.

On the peak of a hill, watching from a safe distance, Morrigan had mounted Epona again when she felt the Wild Hunt drawing near.

"Morrigan!" A shout from the crowd broke the heavy silence. Morrigan looked to the side in time to see Monstrance running at her. She stared at the sword clenched in his hand. "*Gods*, Morrigan, what are you doing here? I told you to stay behind!"

"Thomas—Thomas told me to bring him here," she stammered, quaking under her brother's horrified look. "I'm sorry—I wanted to help!"

"Thomas is here?" he asked, brow creasing. Morrigan nodded. "Why—no, leave that. Do you have a weapon?"

She nodded, jabbing a thumb at her white bow and quiver of arrows on her back.

Monstrance withheld his huffy exhale. He'd been hoping she'd be defenceless, just for an excuse to send her away. Chewing his lip, he sighed.

"Monstrance, what should I do?" Morrigan asked as she slid from the horse. He gazed down at her. Her chin held high, her brow set fierce. He almost smiled. His youngest sister, now fighting for the *seelie*. His heart swelled with pride.

With a glance at the approaching Wild Hunt, Monstrance espied the familiar figure leading them; black horse snorting, sword raised high, conjuring lightning to slash the skies and rally his hunters.

"Go to the seelie, Morrigan," he said. "You know how our army fights. Get a high vantage. The hill would be best, or atop the wall. The unseelie will try to flank them. Stop that before it happens. Try to avoid killing when you can. Fly, little owl."

She nodded. Her flash of magic almost blinded him for a moment. She took to her wings as a barn owl and soared into darkness. Monstrance stood foolishly still for a fraction too long, then leapt up onto Thomas's elvish horse.

"I know you're not used to an unseelie rider, Epona," he said, feeling daft for addressing a horse. "But I need your help now."

She snorted. Monstrance – no seelie blood in him to understand – took this as affirmation, flicked her reins and galloped towards the Wild Hunt.

The horde drew nearer. Monstrance could now see a twisted mask of hatred on his beloved brother's face. Had it truly come to this? Must he lose yet another sibling? *First Kali, then Corvus, now Malik.* Monstrance pulled Epona's reins to slow her. Steadying her, she stamped as he drew his unfamiliar sword.

Huntsmen thundered past Monstrance, the scent of seelie blood fresh in their nostrils. Hounds bayed, leaping to tear at exposed flesh. A tremendous crashing of steel against steel almost drew Monstrance's gaze. But Malik had stopped before him, and the sight of his brother now filled his eyes.

Malik and Monstrance faced each other. Both on horseback. Both clutching swords. Both eyeing the other with wary respect.

"You shouldn't have come here, brother!" Malik shouted over the din.

"Malik, please don't do this!" Monstrance yelled back. "We can't lose anyone else!"

Malik took in a sharp breath, slightly lowering his sword. Monstrance saw a glimmer of tears, though Malik blinked them away when Monstrance carefully approached on his horse.

"Morrigan told me about Corvus," he said. "We can't fight, Malik, please. Our brothers and sisters—we're dwindling. Morrigan is fighting with the seelie. Corvus is dead. Kali is dead. And if I go back to Father now, he'll kill me too."

Malik glared, his eyes darting. He raised his sword again. Quietly, he said, "Kali, too?"

Monstrance nodded. A hot, hard lump formed in his throat. "Madness had taken her," he said, gazing in anguish at his elder brother. "I tried to help her, but... please, Malik, lay down your sword. I don't want to fight you."

"I don't want to fight you either," Malik said. "But don't you understand, Monstrance? It's too late. Father's won. He has everything now. Mab, the kingdom, an army. Soon he'll regain his place as an Old God. Before tonight is over, this war will end."

"Malik." Monstrance took hold of his brother's arm. A brave, bold, foolish attempt at reaching him. "I know you have no love for seelie kind. But if you have any love for me, come with me to Father, beg him to *stop* this madness."

Malik hesitated. Monstrance tightened his grip without realising. Malik's gaze drifted past his brother, resting on that swarm of battling soldiers.

"I can't... I'm sorry, Monstrance," Malik said, face screwed up in anguish. He straightened, shrugging his arm out of his brother's grip. He raised his shaking voice now, "I, Prince Malik, first-born of the Dragon King, by the might of Tír-Na-Nóg and all its domains, command you to withdraw your army and *stand down*."

Monstrance shook his head.

Malik nodded. "Then this is how it must end." He lifted his sword skyward, turning his horse and retreating a few paces. "Forgive me, brother."

A heavy cloud formed overhead, lightning crackled across the sky, striking Malik's raised blade. He kicked his horse. Charging forward, Malik swung his sword in a cruel arc, bringing it crashing down on his brother, a scream of self-loathing ripping from his lips.

Monstrance parried at the last moment. His arm

shuddered.

Both horses snorted, and had to be steadied by their riders.

Malik grabbed Monstrance's wrist, trying to pull him from his steed. Dangerously close to falling, with a grunt Monstrance managed to kick himself back up into his saddle. The air grew hot. A bolt of lightning struck somewhere close beside them and both horses reared up in fright. Monstrance slipped from his saddle, seizing Malik's arm and dragging him to the ground with him.

Both brothers landed heavily, groaning, and with no riders to soothe their fright, the horses galloped away into darkness.

Staggering to his feet, dragging his sword, Malik stood tall over Monstrance and prepared to plunge his blade through his chest. Monstrance quickly rolled away, scrambling to his feet.

"Malik, listen to me, stop—"

Malik thrust his sword forwards again and again. Monstrance twisted aside, sword hanging limply by his side. Malik stumbled with his clumsy lunge, and a tiny part of Monstrance, a part perhaps born from slaying Kali, saw an opening to attack. Yet he held back. *Not again.*

"Fight back!" Malik screamed, driving his sword forwards in crescents. Monstrance knocked Malik's thrust away with the flat side of his blade, shaking his head as he sidestepped.

"I don't want to lose you too, Malik!" he replied. The elder brother growled in frustration. Each swing too wide, Monstrance managed to dodge his attack. But Malik's blade finally caught his shoulder, biting into flesh through his pauldron – part of only a few pieces of armour Monstrance had deigned to wear. Blood stained his tunic, red pearls running in sluggish rivulets down between the metal and his arm. Monstrance felt its cruel sting, and retreated with a shout of pain, dropping his sword, clutching his arm. Malik froze, eyes wide and mouth trembling.

"Pick up your sword!" he shouted, taking a few steps back. "I—I won't fight you unarmed, Monstrance. *Pick it up!*"

Monstrance lifted his gaze, staring at his brother. The clamour of battle raged behind him. Blood warmed his sleeve and chest as a sharp, nettled sting coursed through. Brother stared at brother, neither wanting to fight, neither willing to surrender.

THISSY MOVED BETWEEN fighting soldiers, ghost-like, to reach those wounded or fallen. Her sword, still strapped to her waist, hadn't yet tasted blood. Dodging a heavy blow, she ducked and jabbed an unseelie foot with a short knife. Screeching, the soldier dropped his axe, and Lightfoot leapt forward to drive him away from her.

Thissy kneeled beside a wounded seelie, healing gaping wounds as best she could with already-leaden arms.

"We still need you," she encouraged. "You can't fall yet."

He rose, his injuries half-healed, enough for him to return to battle. Breathing hard and fast, Thissy held onto this brief moment of reprieve. She had lost count of how many she'd healed now. Would this battle never end?

As though the gods had heard her, a golden light illuminated the field around them. One by one, every seelie and unseelie, each Huntsman and *Fianna*, both ally and enemy, looked to the sky.

An immense equinox moon cast all in a benign, calming, sallow light, sapping everyone of whatever magic they possessed.

Thissy lowered her gaze from the sky, tired eyes seeking the mounted Wild Hunt. Their shadows stripped away. Each Huntsman looked at themselves and each other, seeing their defences melt away beneath the moonlight. Her heart pounded hard. *Men.* Ordinary, scared men: unmasked and vulnerable. But this was not the time for mercy.

The *Fianna* roared with exhilaration, weapons raised, and charged towards the terrified former Huntsmen with renewed vigour. Overwhelming them, dragging them down from horses, slaughtering their snarling, corporeal hounds as they leapt.

MALIK AND MONSTRANCE circled each other like cautious wolves. His sword thrown aside, Malik nervously flexed his hands. Monstrance ran his tongue over dry lips. Neither knew nor cared that they no longer possessed magic.

Malik's resolve broke first.

With a low, defiant growl, he dived forwards, tackling his brother around his middle. They fought in the mud as though they were children again, and this only a game.

Monstrance delivered a strong punch to his brother's belly, then struggled to his feet. Winded, Malik wheezed and retched, clutching his stomach, still kneeling in the mud.

"Black Heart!"

A bellow of wild, bloodthirsty laughter immediately followed the scream from somewhere in the battling throng.

Monstrance spun to see Astaroth charging towards him,

mounted on his enormous black steed, war axe held out to the side. His face was twisted into a hideous, manic grin. Laughing, Astaroth galloped forwards. Monstrance stepped in front of Malik, not taking his eyes from their youngest brother. Astaroth dismounted before his horse had fully stopped, using the momentum to run forwards in a show of intimidation.

"You're back, traitor?" he sneered, casually swinging his axe.

Before Monstrance could speak or move, Astaroth raised his axe and, easily cleaving the leather buckles of Monstrance's armour, slammed the blade into his chest. A gasp, a flinch when the axe was tugged free, and Monstrance rapidly blinked in fright and horror. His plated pauldron fell, squelching in the mud at his feet.

"You should've stayed where you were safe, *leaf-lover*," Astaroth turned, returning to furore of battle.

"*NO!*" Malik's scream didn't register.

At first, there was no feeling. Monstrance looked down at his shoulder and chest. Blood throbbed out of a neat slash wound at an alarming rate, staining his tunic in a slow red waterfall. Then the pain hit him, both sharp and blunt, as though the axe stroke had come again.

"*Brother…*"

His world slowed; Monstrance felt his hands shaking, and he fell to his knees, still staring down. Coughing blood, he fell back into the mud with his legs bent under him. Through a haze, he saw his eldest brother lean over him. Cradle him. Whisper to him.

"Monstrance… I'm sorry. I'm sorry, I'm so sorry…"

Unable to speak, Monstrance poured his last strength into a smile – his last smile – and closed his eyes.

MALIK REGAINED HIS feet, raising his eyes to gaze at this battle before him. He approached the crowd, dreamlike, dragging his feet, dripping with mud and Monstrance's blood. Deadened by the loss of yet another he loved.

He watched Morrigan on high, firing her arrows into the press of bodies. *Defending the seelie? Morrigan, little sister, you brave girl.*

He watched her leap down from her post, standing over a wounded seelie so none would attack. Behind her, a fair-haired girl helped him to his feet so he could return to battle. He vaguely recognised her, yet nothing mattered to him now.

Then, black hair dripping seelie blood and gaunt face twisted in a sneer, Astaroth pushed through the throng of bodies, heading for little Morrigan. She hadn't seen him.

I have to reach her first.

Few people paid attention to Malik as he waded through bodies. As he neared the heart of the crowd, there came yet another cry from within.

"Dragon King! He's here!" That hysterical scream rang with terror.

Malik spun, seeking his father. His mind was awhirl with confusion. *Father never leaves the castle, let alone the city, why would he be—*

Then he understood. As an arm wrapped around his chest, a dagger biting deep between his shoulder blades, the last thought passing through his mind made him sadly smile, even in his death throes.

They think I'm my father.

Malik slumped into the mud, a knife handle sticking out of his back.

THE ASSASSIN KICKED over the body. Seeing her mistake – just a princeling, not the Dragon King – Aife shrugged and sniffed. One more dead: what did it matter? She entered the fray once more, crouching to retrieve a spear from a fallen companion, lunging for the nearest unseelie.

MORRIGAN STOOD OVER Thissy as she helped up a soldier and checked his wounds would not prevent further action.

"Are you nearly done?" she shouted, firing an arrow into someone's eye socket. "I don't—"

"There! My thanks, Morrigan!" Thissy stood, she and the seelie disappearing into the crowd once more. Morrigan smiled, retreating, meaning to return to her post. No archer should be so close to the fray.

A volley of screeching laughter echoed from the crowd. Astaroth approached, his eyes fixed only on her. "Little sister," he sang, mocking. Morrigan's eyes widened. Her grip on her bow tightened.

Firestrider dashed from the crowd, crashing into Astaroth and tackling him to the ground. "Go, Morrigan! We need you higher!"

A deep cut above his eyebrow bled into his eyes, blinding him to Astaroth's returning attacks.

"Filthy leaf-ear!" Astaroth roared in frustration. He thrust Firestrider away with the handle of his axe, grabbed his throat, and threw him bodily into the crowd. Firestrider landed in the mud and didn't move again.

Morrigan's hands acted of their own accord. An arrow drawn, fletched, and fitted flew through the air and embedded in Astaroth's shoulder. Just above his heart.

A meaty thump, and Astaroth stopped laughing at once, staring at that trembling arrow. He staggered, then raised his head, seeking the archer who'd struck him. He found Morrigan, bowstring still quivering, glaring at him with pure hatred. Astaroth grinned maniacally, and yanked her arrow out.

A torrent of blood followed. Astaroth screwed up his face in agony, snapped the arrow in two, and tossed it away. He approached his little sister, his painted smile more menacing for the pain it hid.

"You should run, little girl," he sneered as he got closer, twisting his axe in his hand. "I love a moving target."

"*Enough!*" Morrigan screamed, fitting another arrow and firing it so fast it became a blur. Laughing, Astaroth lifted his axe to block it. The arrow careened away, useless.

"Morrigan," he scoffed, twirling his axe round, still laughing. "You're a weak little gi—"

Morrigan's third arrow sailed under his outstretched arms and pierced his heart.

His laugh froze on his face. He staggered back. His fingers lost their grip, his axe splattering in the mud below.

Morrigan lowered her bow. Fighting soldiers behind Astaroth bumped him, and he fell to his knees, groaning.

He lifted his gaze to Morrigan. "In our next life, then, little sister?" A bubble of blood burst in the corner of his lips. He fell back, his eyes hollow, staring at stars, his final sneer still twisting his mouth.

CHAPTER 46

In which his last battle begins

"**M**AB, COME ON. Come with me. *Now*," Erlik said, Mab struggling against his grip. He dragged her towards a wall, brandishing her like a ragdoll.

"Let go of me!" she demanded. "I need to be with them!"

"It's not safe for you out there," he snapped. "Do it now!"

"I will not—"

"Yes, you will! *Do it!*"

He threw her towards the wall. A stumble and she righted herself, raising her eyes to stare at a large symbol he'd scrawled there.

A seven-pointed star filled her eyes. Usually, her mark would be a warm and welcome sight. Yet now she felt only dread writhing inside her belly like a swarm of snakes.

"Erlik, this is madness. You know—"

"I won't ask again, Mab," he said. He took a few steps back, glaring. "Swallow your pride. Do it now!"

"You cannot make me do this!"

Erlik narrowed his eyes at her. His lip curled into a snarl. Twisting his hand, an ornate dagger appeared there in a flurry of black smoke. Mab sharply inhaled. *I know that blade. I gifted you that blade.* Her name still shone bright, carved upon its metal.

Erlik lunged at her, grabbing her hand. "Stubborn…" he muttered to himself. He pressed the blade into her palm, slicing downwards. Erlik ignored her wince of discomfort and slammed her bleeding hand against the wall, smearing her blood onto stone.

A wet, red stain on the seven-pointed star now, Erlik threw Mab aside. The symbol began to glow red.

"See? That wasn't so bad."

Mab threw him an ugly look, flexing her bleeding hand. *"Nathair."*

Erlik pressed the blade against his own palm now. A sharp breath – *it hurts, does it not?* – running his tongue over his teeth, and he sliced the flesh. Wiped his blood over the symbol, across hers.

He ran his tongue over his lips and twisted his hand again. Flames wreathed his fingers. Gesturing to each candle stood proud around them, the dark hall soon flickered with dim, dancing light.

"They're coming, listen."

A chilling chime of echoing song. Mab suppressed her shiver. Graceful, swimming through air, empyreal spirits of slain elves floated like flowers on water towards that painted star on the wall, their haunting song almost too sorrowful to bear.

Mab watched the first ethereal spirit touch the symbol, its light fading into stone. One by one, each phantom vanished into the wall, absorbed by the stone to serve as a conduit of magic; a gateway between worlds.

The star pulsed brighter. Lips parting, wary and anxious, Mab backed away. Erlik took her arm, pulling her towards him. Mab glanced at him. He, too, looked cautious and perhaps even a little afraid. He swallowed hard.

"Don't be afraid, my love," he whispered to her. "I'm here with you."

"What have you done?" Mab breathed.

"I want us to go home, Mab."

She looked to that shining star in fear, yet also quivering with anticipation.

Two glistening silver figures formed there, hoary beings of incomprehensible power. So familiar to Mab, her heart ached to rush to them, to embrace them. To allow herself to be vulnerable, if only for a moment.

"*Máthair… Athair…*" she whispered.

Two of the beings who gave her form and breath, gave her *life*, took shape. Her most familiar, her most beloved. Those she regarded as her mother and father above any other.

Danu, the Mother-Goddess of magic, and Cernunnos, the Horned God of the forest.

Mab blinked her suddenly wet eyes. "Why have you come?" she asked, almost accusingly.

Danu's eyes crinkled into a warm smile. "We heard your suffering call, *chroí iníon*," she said. "We have waited so long for our prison to be opened. We are here for you, *peata*."

Mab lowered her eyes again. "You should not have come, *Máthair*. He—"

"Enough!" Erlik's voice rang cold, sharp and clear. He pulled Mab closer to him. "Look, here," he took her hand, lifting it to show the ring gleaming there, "Mab and I can come home now."

Danu and Cernunnos glanced at each other, then

frowned at Erlik. He glared back, his expectant gaze flickering between both.

Danu spoke first, coldly, "Marrying the Heart of Magic Itself does not bring an end to your banishment, Dragon King. You struck down a fellow god, your own kin no less. You will not return to the House of the Old Gods until you have atoned."

Erlik scoffed.

"Even then, you will not be welcomed back with good grace," Cernunnos added, his voice icier even than Danu's. "Perhaps one day you *will* redeem yourself. Perhaps one day you will return to us in shining glory. But you will always be shunned. An outcast among brethren. Join your brother in Annwyn, *nathair*."

A muscle twitched under Erlik's eye. Yet, somehow, he managed to keep his voice calm when he spoke. "I could raze Albion to the ground if I wanted to," he said, slow and dangerous, "but I won't. I'm giving you this one chance to help me."

"Why would we help you?" Cernunnos laughed. Cold. Mocking. Erlik clutched Mab tighter.

"I can force your hand."

"Then you are a bigger fool than we believed," Danu said. She seemed to glow brighter. A goddess of magic to rival even Mab herself. "Show us then, Dragon King. Prove your worth."

Mab closed her eyes, shaking her head a fraction. *Please, Máthair, do not taunt him like this.*

Erlik sniffed once. Gazing down at Mab, he swallowed hard. He yanked her closer to him, pressing the point of his dagger to her throat. He jammed it hard into her soft flesh. Mab drew in a sharp breath.

"Erlik, please—" she breathed, as the blade sat cold against her skin. He ignored her plea.

"Let me come home. Give me back my power."

"No, *Máthair*—" Mab began.

Erlik pressed a hand over her mouth. "Be silent," he growled, looking to the Old Gods again. "Well?"

Frowning, Danu started forwards. Erlik drew back at once, dragging Mab with him. Pressing that dagger deeper into her throat. Drops of blood slid down the blade. Mab hissed a whine, her breathing fast and sharp.

Silence fell. Moments clicked past. Mab swallowed past the point of the blade. *Surely they are not considering….*

Cernunnos looked down at Erlik.

"Very well."

"*No!*" Mab screamed, desperate to struggle against Erlik's grip. "*Máthair*, stop him! Do not let him return!"

"You're coming too, Mab," Erlik kissed her temple, his blade still jammed against her throat, eager gaze fixed on the portal home. "Don't fret, my love."

"I am not leaving!"

"I said, be silent!" Erlik snarled. Those few drops of blood became a trickle creeping down her white throat. Danu restrained a gasp, while Cernunnos raised his hands in defeat.

"Erlik, halt your blade," he said, his voice low. "We will give you back your place amongst us, but Mab must stay here in Albion."

"No," Erlik said at once. "She stays with *me*. We're both coming home."

Cernunnos hesitated. He glanced at Danu, yet she seemed unable to speak. Her eyes remained on Mab, pensive and afraid.

"You would take magic away from this world?" the Horned God asked.

"In a heartbeat," Erlik said. "She deserves better than this wasteland you sent us to. She stays," he lowered his voice, "with me."

Danu laid a comforting hand on Cernunnos' arm. Again they exchanged a glance, and held a silent conversation between their eyes. Joining hands, they muttered together in an ancient language.

A cool breeze swept around Erlik and Mab, still pressed together. He lowered his blade. Mab's eyes heavy with disappointment, she let him snake his fingers into hers and gently kiss her brow.

The doors swung open and cold night air rushed in. Each candle flame flickered, died, and both Erlik and Mab looked up in surprise.

Danu and Cernunnos vanished with those candle flames, returning to the House of the Old Gods. That seven-pointed star dimmed: its magic, its ritual, broken.

"WHAT ARE *YOU* doing here?" Erlik asked loudly, momentarily too stunned for harsh words or wicked sarcasm. His hand clenched tighter around Mab's.

Thomas approached, sword drawn and ready. "Release my queen, *nathair*."

Erlik glanced down at Mab, finding a smile tugging her lips.

His composure regained almost at once, he released her fingers from his. He glanced at the star where Danu and Cernunnos had vanished. His brow sunk low, face darkening with fury, Erlik turned his gaze on Thomas.

"Do you have *any* idea what you've just done, *amadán?*"

Thomas took another step, but Erlik hissed, brandishing his knife and looking sideways at Mab – his intentions clear.

"Let her g—"

"Lay down your sword," Erlik interrupted.

Thomas hesitated, eyes narrowing.

Feeling Mab shake her head, he drew the blade across her collarbone to the dip of her throat. "Now, now, beloved," he said. "Don't help him. The boy needs to learn."

Thomas lifted his sword slightly higher. Erlik's mouth twisted into a sneer at the blank, helpless look on his face.

"Oh, I almost forgot. Thomas Rhymer, pitiful and weak mortal being, I'd like to introduce you to my wife." He withdrew his blade, grabbed her left hand and thrust it forward.

Instinctive fire fluttered from her fingertips.

A Binding Ring still glimmered there, now gleaming golden. Thomas balked at the sight.

Erlik laughed; he couldn't help himself.

"You're too late, boy," he said, holding Mab before him. "Lower your sword and I'll let go of her. Then we can settle our differences."

Mab slowly inhaled. Thomas hesitated.

"Do not trust him, Thomas," she said. "He lies. Do not lower—"

"Hush," Erlik pressed his mouth against her head when he spoke, so his words came muffled. His eyes never left Thomas's face. "There's a time and a place for you to speak, my love."

Erlik saw Thomas clench tighter, then lean forwards, lowering his sword to lay it at his feet. Erlik smirked wider at him.

Foolish boy.

In a breath, he tossed Mab aside – out of harm's way – and threw his dagger at Thomas.

THAT BLADE HUNG, shining, for a brief second. A metallic bolt of lightning.

Instinct awoke. A flinch, and Thomas grabbed the dagger handle midflight. Barely a hairsbreadth from his throat.

He blinked, stunned. Yet his bemusement couldn't last.

Erlik uttered a low growl of fury. "Leaf-ear tricks won't save you," he snarled. With a guttural roar, lunging forwards, he unsheathed his sword.

Thomas threw Erlik's hated dagger away, hooked his foot under his sword's blade, kicking it into the air and catching it just as Captain Bonney had taught him. He pointed it at Erlik, but the prince gave a cold and mocking laugh.

"You have skill, I'll admit," he said, circling him. "But this isn't a wise venture. I'm the Dragon King; you can't best me."

Thomas felt sweat drip down his back. He hated how Erlik looked so calm.

Erlik gently tapped Thomas's sword with his own, stepping back. Thomas swallowed his fear. His heartbeat raced, sweat stinging his eyes.

Erlik's attack came in a vicious arc. Thomas raised his sword in barely enough time, and Erlik's blade crashed against his. Thomas strafed, thrusting back clumsily.

But Erlik had years of training, impossible strength, and cunning finesse. Thomas had tricks taught by a pirate, and youthful skill against a straw dummy.

The screeching of metal on metal rang hard through the chamber. Knocking Thomas's blade away, Erlik grabbed his throat and crushed hard.

Thomas felt his flesh grow hot. Burning, blisteringly hot. Erlik yelled in pain and withdrew, staring at his hand. Thomas gasped, clutching his cooling throat.

"Enough!" Mab's scream gave both men pause.

Thomas looked at her. So did Erlik.

That same icy fury she'd displayed against Abarta now burned bright in her eyes. Approaching, her face was a harsh mask of anger.

"Stop this," she said in a low voice, looking between them. Erlik stared at her, his arm lowering in shock.

"Mab?" his voice sounded childish for a moment.

"I will not help you in this," she said.

Erlik's lips twisting into a snarl, he narrowed his eyes at Thomas. "You turned her against me," he growled. He pushed Mab aside, raising his sword and charging at Thomas.

Just before Erlik brought his blade down, Thomas ducked. He slashed his sword. Erlik grunted, staggering, a deep wound on his left leg now freely bleeding.

Erlik stared at the wound, as though he'd never seen his own blood before. Then his eyes sought Mab, seeking whatever pity and comfort he could beg from her. She shook her head.

"You would have him try to kill me?" he asked her quietly. Thomas glanced at her. His sword felt hot and heavy in his hand.

"I would have him *stop* you," she said. Thomas took that as affirmation. *Do not kill him. Cripple him any way you can.*

Somewhere, far away, the drumming of red thunder rattled through the sky. War drums.

Erlik held out his hand, uncurling a fist. On his palm there hung a crackling ball of black fire.

"Let him stop this, then!" he bellowed, throwing those flames at Thomas.

His eyes shut in reflex. A dull blow struck his chest, and he staggered back, groaning.

And yet...

Nothing more.

No agonising sensation of being consumed by flame. No pungent smell of burning flesh.

Tentatively, he opened his eyes. Blinked. He looked down at himself. Not even a mark where the blow had struck him.

"Impossible," Erlik breathed.

The chamber filled with warm, yellow light. All three within looked up. An oculus above allowed light from the harvest moon to flood in.

Thomas stared at that yellow orb, outlined in a velvet cloak of night by a circle of burning red.

Erlik's gaze grew fearful. "No..."

"I gave you this warning," she said as she approached him. "Now, you are powerless."

Erlik grabbed her arm. "I'll show you *powerless*," he growled, raising his fist and unclenching it again. Nothing.

Erlik tried again and again to shake some magic from his hands. Nothing came.

"Erlik," Mab said softly, laying her hand on his arm. "It is over."

"No!" he screamed. "It's not over!" Madness dancing in

his eyes, Erlik raised his sword against the Queen of the Old Ways.

Whether he truly intended her harm or not, Thomas didn't care. Without pausing to think, he leapt forwards, between Erlik and Mab.

Thomas steadied Mab, then looked deep into her eyes, "Please, help me!"

She gazed at him, lips parting in both surprise and apprehension. Thomas could have sworn a flicker of pity erupted in the fiery hollows of her eyes until her sight darted over his shoulder, and her eyes widened.

"Erlik, no!"

But he'd already grabbed Thomas's collar and dragged him away from her. With a snarling growl, Erlik threw him against a wall, fingers wrapped around his throat, mercilessly choking him.

Mab immediately appeared by Erlik. He gave a roar of annoyance, striking her face backhand before she could so much as touch him. She staggered away, a large purple bruise already blossoming across her temple.

Thomas took the chance to duck out from Erlik's grip and punch him hard in the stomach. Erlik stumbled back, coughing and grunting, while Thomas staggered to Mab. He wheezed, clutching his throat again. "You need to go, it's not safe—"

"I cannot leave him," she said at once.

Once more, her eyes flickered to something behind him. She pulled him away, standing there in his stead. Thomas caught sight of Erlik lunging forward with a gleaming obsidian dagger.

Once Mab had stepped in front of Thomas, Erlik stopped short. As though afraid of harming her with this blade.

"Leave him," she commanded, her voice ringing clear in the silence. "You swore you would not harm him. You have broken the law of the Binding."

"Mab, it no longer matters!" Erlik shouted. "Don't you understand? Once he's dead, we can go *home*."

He rolled his wrist, the dagger flashing. Mab didn't move.

"I will not let you hurt him," she said, adamant. Erlik paused. Each stared at the other, silence filling the hall. Mab swallowed hard. "He is one of my own; I will protect him as I protect the others."

"I hurt you, Mab," Erlik said softly, reaching out to her cheek with a soft expression on his face. Thomas blinked. *Does he truly love her as she says he once did?*

"I don't mean to," Erlik went on, "I just want us to be together. I want us to go home. And you must understand, my love. You're *mine*. Everything you own is mine. I can destroy it if I wish."

Erlik sidestepped Mab, reaching out past her. Seizing Thomas's shoulder, he stepped in and plunged the brittle dagger deep into his belly.

CHAPTER 47

In which moonlight aids Thomas

T HOMAS CHOKED, GASPING for air. His throat felt tight and wet. Breathing too fast—no, unable to breathe at all. Shards ripped through his insides. Burning pain spread from that dagger to the extremity of every limb.

His legs buckled, but Erlik held him up. Almost fatherly in his action. Erlik twisted his knife. Thomas screamed.

At last, Erlik let him fall, yanking the dagger free as he did so.

"Thomas!"

LIGHT RETURNED. A scent of woodsmoke and wildflowers crept into Thomas' nostrils. Vision sharpening – *even sharper than before, how?* – Thomas saw Mab leaning over him, her face breaking into a genuine smile.

"Welcome home," she breathed.

He looked down at himself, heartbeat quickening. Unharmed. Unmarked. Nothing to suggest he had even been wounded.

Mab stepped away, allowing Thomas room to regain his feet. His eyes were suddenly sharper, his ears now more attuned to each noise around him. He could see every floating dust mote in the hall. Hear every furious beat of his own heart. Smell the fear that hung heavy in the air.

"What..." Erlik stared, brow creased.

For a moment, Thomas wanted to tell him he shared this surprise.

"*No!* I won't have this!" Erlik screamed. He glanced at his dagger in disgust, then threw it down in a fit of frustration. The brittle blade shattered on impact. Its handle spun, useless, on the ground.

Erlik pointed petulantly at it, "That blade was enchanted to steal the life of any human it pierced. Why do you *still* live?"

Erlik took a few menacing steps, hands twitching, but Mab put herself between them again.

"Let me kill him, Mab," Erlik said quietly. "Please."

"Do you remember those stories we used to tell each other?" she asked. "Stories of the moonstate of Godsbane?"

Erlik paused, narrowing his eyes at her insolence. Mab looked over her shoulder at Thomas. He returned her gaze, flexing his newly empowered hands.

"What about it?" Erlik snapped, pacing before her. A slow, dangerous, big cat.

A slight smile twitched Mab's lips, "The stories say that when a Champion chosen by magic, a Son of the Old Ways, accepts himself, he is changed under the Godsbane moon. He cannot be hurt by your blade because he is not human."

Thomas's lips parted in shock. "Not..." he whispered.

Erlik lunged. Swatting Mab aside, he struck Thomas across the face with the heel of his hand.

His nose popped. Thomas howled in pain, twisting back, clutching his face. Blood began to drip into his mouth. The hot, metallic taste made him feel sick.

"I can't kill you with magic," Erlik spat, circling him

again. "I can't kill you with my blade. What will it take to be rid of you!"

Thomas watched Erlik carefully, seeking any moment, any brief window where he lowered his guard.

"This *Champion*, Mab—"

There!

Thomas swung, his new extraordinary speed aiding him. Eyes widening, barely raising his sword in time, Erlik clumsily parried the strike. But Thomas still felt his sword make contact.

A scream of pain and surprise ripped from Erlik's mouth. He staggered back, clutching his face.

The dripping blood painted Erlik's hand. He stared at his shaking fingers, eyes taking in that red stain. A long, deep slice marred his cheek now, replacing his usual smirk.

Erlik hissed, something furious, insulting in an ancient language that Thomas didn't understand.

Spurred by his successful attack, Thomas roared – a wild battle cry – and lunged again. But Erlik raised his sword, ready for him this time, snarling. Enraged and frustrated.

Again and again their swords struck. Sparks flew and the haft grew hot in Thomas's grip.

Unlike before, when Thomas's arms ached and sweat poured from his brow, his newly acquired magic and power pushed him further. He'd never felt calmer. Courage swelled inside him.

Thomas delivered a powerful parry against a mighty but clumsy swing, and Erlik fell, dropping his sword. Though he scrambled to reach it again, Thomas pointed his blade at him. Erlik abruptly stopped, withdrawing, panting.

"T-Thomas, wait!" he said quickly, for Thomas had pressed his sword into his chest. "You wouldn't kill your own father, would you?"

Silence.

The loudest silence Thomas had ever heard. It pressed hard into his ears. Pressure building in his head.

No—

He stared at Erlik, an odd ringing in his ears. His hands shook.

Erlik gazed back, still panting but slower now. Eyes wide. Cautious. Hesitant. Even Mab stared between both, mouth open.

"What madness is this?" Mab breathed at last. Thomas shook his head.

He whispered, "No... my—m-my father... my father is dead." His voice grew to a shout, then. "You're *not!*"

His words echoed back at him, mocking, in the huge hall.

Thomas's head swam. He swallowed hard, breathing fast. Mouth too dry for words.

No. No no no no no!

Groaning, sighing, Erlik propped himself up on his elbows. He stared at Thomas with that same miserable, pitiful look. It was far too strange to see such emotion in him.

Erlik reached out and took Thomas's hand, which had been limp at his side. At once, his grip tightened. He pulled down as he stood, his knee connecting with Thomas' face. Thomas grunted and reeled back. Sword dropped, abandoned.

Laughing, Erlik regained his feet. "Of course I'm not!" he sneered, picking up his sword while Thomas lurched unsteadily.

Though the room spun and Thomas could barely see through a red haze, he suddenly felt huge, meaty hands spin him round.

His gaze met a torso.

Thomas raised his eyes to the unsmiling face of a giant of a man. He inhaled and quickly backed away. The giant's single eye stared down at him in remorse.

"Thomas Rhymer," came Erlik's voice in wicked victory. "Meet my son, Balor. Balor, destroy him."

Still reeling from the kick in the face, Thomas hadn't prepared himself for the punch. The blow landed hard, knocking him against a wall. Crumpling, landing in a painful, groaning, dizzy heap on the floor. Weakly, Thomas threw out his arm to grab at his discarded sword.

Mab made a move towards him. Erlik raised his sword, pointing it at her.

"Don't touch him, Mab," he said. "Go upstairs. I'll join you s—"

"No…" came Thomas's weak voice, struggling to his feet. Every breath burned in his chest as he panted hard; he suspected his already injured ribs had fractured. Through hazed eyes, Thomas glared at Erlik. His grip on his sword weakened.

Balor's footsteps stomped closer, arms hanging heavy at his sides. Still the giant said nothing. Another punch, and Thomas ducked – a challenge with the crippling agony in his chest.

Yet Balor was slower, heavier. Thomas had agility on his side for however long it lasted. Thomas knew his sword was useless steel against that mighty beast of a man.

"Destroy him!"

Erlik's voice rang with impatience. Spittle flecked his

mouth when he screamed at his son. Foolishly, Thomas took his eyes off Balor and glanced at Mab.

The sight of her at Erlik's side filled Thomas with such protective rage – usually a feeling reserved for Alissa – he didn't even realise he had taken steps towards them.

Only when Erlik lifted his sword did Thomas stop moving.

"Erlik," Mab said softly. She rested her head back on his shoulder, gazing up at him, weariness aging her. "Please, stop this."

Erlik lowered his gaze to her. He lowered his sword without smirk or sneer. They stared at each other. Thomas suddenly wished he could read minds.

Erlik's brow lowered, scowling at Mab.

"I do what I must, my love," he said quietly, then pressed a kiss to her forehead.

Balor suddenly swung upwards, and Thomas felt that massive fist collide with his shoulder. Once more thrown across the room, spinning with the force and smashing against a white column. His body screamed.

Balor approached, his heavy footsteps shaking the ground. Coughing, tasting blood, Thomas weakly scraped to his knees and raised his sword: a needle against a giant.

Then, from somewhere high above, a horrid shriek pierced the night. An enormous, screeching bird. Or a screaming, wailing woman—

With a great rush of wings, the harpy crashed through the oculus, shattering its glass dome, scattering shards like rain all around them. The great, feathered beast slammed heavily down between Thomas and Balor.

The harpy batted away the giant with one rush of its massive wings.

Erlik's eyes widened in surprise, then immediately narrowed with dislike, glaring at the dismounting figure.

"How about we make this a fairer fight, hmm?" Captain Bonney brushed glass off herself and smirked at Thomas, unsheathing a cutlass. More keening cries came from outside, blood-curdling screams echoing in the night, announced the arrival of a battalion of harpy-riding pirates to the fray.

"Balor," Erlik growled, "kill that interfering sea-rat."

Balor regained his feet – thunderous and slow – and firmly shook his head. The harpy snapped at him.

"I will not fight a woman, Father," he said, voice weirdly quiet for his size. Thomas blinked. Erlik heaved a sigh, hands balling into fists.

"She's dressed as a man, use your imagination," he said coldly.

Turning away, he didn't see Balor shaking his head. Thomas swallowed, running his tongue over dry lips.

"I will not fight a woman," Balor repeated, stepping away from Captain Bonney. She raised an eyebrow, looking pleased with herself.

"That was easy," she said, and lowered her cutlass.

Erlik's eyes travelled between each as he chewed his tongue. Thomas thought he felt the air crackling.

"You will do as you are *told!*" he screamed suddenly, his eyes burning with wild madness. "Balor! Kill that ship-dwelling bitch! Mab!" She flinched. "Go upstairs! And *you!*" Erlik snarled now at Thomas, used the side of his foot to push himself back, even as the prince approached.

Screaming, growling like the dragon of his crest, Erlik threw all of his weight behind his swing, eyes burning bright.

There was no fighting this, Thomas realised. It was too wild. Too fast. *Too strong!*

Madness had taken Erlik, just as it had taken his daughter.

Out of the corner of his eye, Thomas could see Balor grabbing Captain Bonney and pulling her aside, gently guiding her towards Mab. He stood guard by the two women, unwilling to harm either.

Erlik knocked Thomas' sword aside as he blocked a vicious swing. Defenceless now, Thomas dodged Erlik's next strike, but wasn't fast enough to see and avoid a large shard of glass from entering the side of his foot as he shuffled out of reach.

Thomas fell. Spat blood onto the floor. Sweat dripped from his hair, tiny cuts stinging his face. He heard Mab suck in a sharp breath.

Erlik kicked Thomas's sword away, raising his own. Prepared to plunge it into Thomas's chest.

Gasping for breath, Thomas stared back.

"Do you know what it's like?" Erlik said quietly, eyes thin with hate. Thomas swallowed. *What's this game now?*

"Do you know how it feels to have the woman you love look at you with such contempt? Such *hate?* You have no *clue.* I treasure every scrap of love she gives me, because I have to fight for it like a hound. I love her more than you could ever realise. And she… she loves those… those filthy *animals!* Those leaf-ears! She loves them more than she loves *me!*"

"Then why do you hurt her?" Thomas asked quickly. Erlik hesitated, and Thomas ploughed on, "If you love her so much, why do you make her suffer?"

Another pause.

"Because she's mine. She needs to learn that." Erlik said, pressing his blade tip against Thomas's throat.

His flesh broke. Erlik smirked. His pupils huge. Black. Empty.

"You might have seelie blood, *amadán*, but you've got an unseelie heart." He laughed again. "Farewell, Thomas Rhymer."

Erlik gripped Thomas' collar to hold him still as he drew back his sword an inch. Thomas tipped his head back. Glanced once at Mab. She closed her eyes. Lowered her head. Despair, shame, and regret clouded her face.

I failed you. I am sorry.

"TAKE YOUR FILTHY mothblood hands off him." Wearing a victorious smile, Thissy's voice rang over the sound of the mighty doors crashing open. Dried blood had caked in her dishevelled hair. Her battle tunic was ripped.

Somehow, she had never been more beautiful to Thomas.

Lightfoot appeared beside her, moonlight making his grey hair shine like quicksilver. Despite bleeding from several wounds, he too wore a smile.

More seelie emerged, blooming from behind Thissy. Even a fair few unseelie soldiers – each looking amazed at their own daring – stood among them.

Erlik stared at each one, dropping his grip on Thomas's collar. Straightening, he took a few steps back.

"That… this… how did you—"

"Malik is dead," Lightfoot said, his voice cool and clear. "Astaroth is dead. The Wild Hunt has scattered. You are defeated, Dragon King."

Erlik's glare could have incinerated him. He cast his

eyes around the still-growing crowd.

"Balor!" he called, pointing. "K-kill them!"

"No, Father," Balor shook his head. Erlik snapped his head round to stare. "They've won. It's time this finished."

He stepped away from Captain Bonney and Mab, kneeling before the latter.

"Forgive us, my lady," he said.

Erlik stared at Balor as he knelt, eyes wide and hands trembling. He turned back and cast his eyes into the crowd.

"Morrigan!" he called. "Morrigan, my little girl, where are you? You'll help me, won't you?"

Morrigan stepped from the crowd, a bloody smear across her cheek. Her face set in a harsh, unforgiving glare. "No, Father," she said. "Not this time."

Thissy ran to Thomas as he got to his feet, hooking her arm around him and letting him rest on her. Erlik turned around to gaze at Mab instead.

"Mab..." his voice a whisper now, "please..."

Their eyes met. Thomas could have sworn she gave Erlik a small, sad smile, even as she shook her head. Approaching him, she laid her hand on his arm.

"Erlik," she said, something that looked like pity in those glittering midnight eyes. "It is over."

With a quiet growl, Erlik snatched his arm out of her gentle grip, running his tongue over his teeth. His eyes darted. The muscles in his throat rolled as he swallowed. He glanced at the seelie crowd. Each face stared back at him, each expression different. A vein pulsed in his temple.

Turning, Erlik walked away from the crowd, approaching Mab's throne. He raised his eyes to stare around the great hall, as though he was taking it all in one last time. Then, finally, he released a heavy sigh, eyes closed, head lowered. He turned and faced the seelie again.

A clattering of metal against stone; he threw his sword at Thomas's feet. Erlik's eyes found Mab again.

They gazed at one another. Mab took in a deep breath. Slowly she raised her hand, tugging the ring from her finger. With no magic left to bind it there, it slid off easily, dulling back to silver. She threw it at him; it sparkled in midair for a moment, and he caught it deftly. Staring down at this small, gleaming piece of metal, he smiled. When he raised his head again, he winked at Mab, her roguish prince once more.

"This isn't over, my love," he said softly.

Erlik walked into the crowd with heavy footsteps, tightly clutching the ring, ready to meet his punishment, finally accepting his defeat.

CHAPTER 48

In which Thomas finds peace

THOMAS STARED AT the little house, cool within the shade of trees. It seemed to have changed so much in so little time. Ivy had crept around its windows. Thatch had fallen from its roof in places. The once carefully patched scarecrow hung limply off his perch.

Thomas felt a strange sort of sorrow for everything he had witnessed, suffered, experienced. A feeling that perhaps he didn't *want* to go home. That he wanted to stay in Elphame, where his seelie heart now yearned to remain.

Epona softly whinnied. Thomas patted her neck, glancing at Mab. Mounted beside him on a powerful white stallion, she was resplendent in a gown of grass-green silk, a mantle of finest velvet around her shoulders.

Softly, laying a hand on his arm, she spoke, "I know what you are thinking, Thomas. But it is time for you to go home."

"Why must I?" he asked. "Why can't I stay with you?"

Even as he spoke, a figure left the little house and scanned the trees with weary hope. Thomas's heart ached.

"Mother…" he breathed, without realising. Mab smiled warmly again.

"A time will come when you and your kin will return to

Albion. Even now a shadow is growing in the east, and the Iron Keep is being rebuilt."

Thomas frowned briefly.

"But for now," Mab went on, "you must go home. Go home. Live, laugh, love, and be loved."

Thomas gazed at her with adoring respect. With a sigh, he looked back at his mother as she returned inside.

"There is… one other thing, Thomas," Mab said, twisting her horse's reins. "When you cross the threshold into your world again…" She paused. "You will have been gone for seven years."

A loud thumping in his ears jolted Thomas to her words.

"*Seven years?*" he yelped.

Mab nodded grimly. "Time passes differently in Albion. Our realm is a strange shadow land, lying beyond the fields you know."

Thomas's head ached just thinking about it. Finally, trusting her, he nodded with a soft sigh. "I understand," he said. A horse behind him snorted, and he glanced over his shoulder.

A large gathering of seelie stood watching him. Though they were past the bridge, their forms were tall and proud. Mab's magic could protect them here, allowing each one to bid Thomas a proper farewell. Thissy approached on a palomino gelding, looking at his little house with a strange expression.

"Do you remember when we first met?" she asked, smiling. "It seems like so long ago now."

"I remember," he took her hand, squeezing it. "You bit me."

Thissy chuckled, and Thomas grinned.

"Only in self-defence."

They laughed together, more like children. Sweethearts in love.

"You must swear to take care of her, Thomas," Mab said. Thomas frowned for a moment, pleasantly confused.

"I… what?" he said, glancing between both women.

Thissy beamed. "I can, then?"

Mab graciously nodded. "It is time I learned that not all love is as bitter and twisted as that I have felt," she said.

Thomas blinked. "I don't understand."

"I can come back with you," she said, then her cheeks turned pink. "That is, if you want me to, of course."

Thomas gaped. "Of course I want you to!" He laughed, then took her gloved hand in his and pulled her closer. He pressed his lips against hers at last. Warmth filled him up inside. His heart beat so fast he thought it might burst.

Mab cleared her throat, though he could hear the smile in her voice. Finally, he broke away from Thissy, gazing at her. She seemed, for a moment, to glow.

"Thomas," Mab said from behind him. "It is time for you to go home."

Thomas nodded. Smiling, Mab kissed both in farewell.

"Thomas Rhymer, we shall see each other again. For wherever men walk, there shall faekind be. Farewell, my Champion."

That crowd of seelie lowered themselves to their knees, bowing before him.

His cheeks burning, Thomas beamed and nodded. "Thank you, Mab."

Though a wave of sadness billowed inside him – he would miss her dearly – Thomas gently flicked Epona's reins. Heading through the trees, back to his home with

Thissy by his side.

As looked over his shoulder one final time, Mab raised her delicate hand in a fond farewell.

One by one, her seelie departed, until finally only Queen Mab stood gazing after him.

Her Champion, her defender.

The Son of the Old Ways.

EPILOGUE

His Final Resting Place

ERLIK SAT ALONE, staring at the forest floor, hands resting in his lap. Leaves crunched, and he looked up.

Dressed in shadows of moonlight, her midnight cloak glittering with starlight and magic, Mab approached his cage. Her eyes, now rimmed with black, sparkled. Fire and ice and power. She stood before him, gazing down on him with a strange, unreadable expression. Soft flurries of snow began to fall.

"Come to bask in your victory?" he asked sullenly.

"No," she said softly. "To say farewell."

Erlik's face broke out in a slow smile. "Such sweet sentiment." He tilted his head slightly, raising an eyebrow as Mab kneeled down to his level.

"Erlik," she said quietly, gazing into his eyes. "It did not have to be this way. But you forced my hand. Because of your actions, you are to remain here, bound to this prison without magic, without power, to fade from memory and existence." Her voice held no coldness. Only sorrow. Regret, even. A snowflake landed on her lips, yet didn't melt away.

"I'll never be forgotten," he replied. "Not least because you'll think of me every day."

Mab rewarded him with a smile, though she lowered her eyes. "*A múirnín*, I can make you hurt with the simplest words. Please do not make me say them," she said.

Erlik smiled at her, not unpleasantly. "Tell me, then," he challenged. "Tell me that you don't love me. Tell me you never loved me. Break me."

Mab breathed a sigh. "Quite the opposite, *a múirnín*," she whispered. "I love you. I have always loved you. I will never *stop* loving you."

Erlik closed his eyes, head bowing. Mab swallowed hard and slowly drew back, gazing at him.

"How?" he murmured to his knees. "How can you love me?"

"How can I not?" she reached through the bars. She had no fear of cold iron here. These bars were meant to contain, not to harm. A cage meant to soothe his poisoned mind, and cure the madness within. "There are not enough lifetimes to explain my love for you."

"Then why did you fight me?"

"I had no choice. If I had succumbed…" She paused, drawing a slow breath. "You would have destroyed everything, and I would have let you. I would have been so blinded by my love for you, I would have willingly turned away as you ripped Albion apart."

"My love—"

"What chance does a wolf have before a dragon, when the dragon commands it to yield?"

Erlik stared at her, aghast, and reached out, hoping to stroke her cheek. To kiss her. Just to touch her one last time.

But Mab quickly stood.

"You sat idly on my throne, fulfilling your own selfish desires, and ignoring a greater threat that hangs over our land. Could you not feel it? Romans have brought the New Religion to Britain's shores. Even now they slaughter Pagans and tear down our shrines. Britain is soaked with the blood of *our* people, while you sat obsessing over a pointless pursuit. I had to push aside my love for you because I had to be selfless."

"Mab, please—"

"I must repair what damage they have caused, and battle the foes that you were too afraid to face. I must bring our people back to the Old Ways. Farewell, *a múirnín*." She paused, then sadly added, "Farewell, my love."

She turned away.

"Mab, wait," Erlik called after her, reaching for her through the bars of his prison. "Mab, please—wait! *Mab!*"

But she ignored his cries. Raising her head, she kept a dignified silence and walked away from him, then mounted her horse with an easy grace.

Erlik stared after her, distraught.

Mab looked over her shoulder – one final, long, lingering look – before riding away, leaving him to his final resting place.

Translation Guide

Word/Phrase – Meaning

Tarrthála! – Help me!/Rescue!

Titim gan éirí ort – May you die in battle (lit. "may you fall without rising")

Cosain mé – Protect me

Nathair – Snake

Amadán – Foolish boy

A chara – My friend

A ghrá – My love

A rúnsearc – My secret love

Damnú air – Shit/Damn it

A sheanchara – My old friend

Cosantóir – Protection

Lonsaigh! – Attack!

Gairdín Síoraí – Eternal Garden

A dheirfiúr – My sister

Máthair – Mother

Athair – Father

Chroí Iníon – Beloved Child (lit. "Heart Daughter")

Peata – Pet

A múirnín – My honey/My sweet one

Twpsyn* – Idiot

Attercop Aetheling** – Spider Prince

Maegdencild** – Little girl

*   Waelisc, the language Ceridwen speaks.

**   The language of the Andrastans, which is different to that of the seelie.

Lightning Source UK Ltd.
Milton Keynes UK
UKHW01f0023020618
323605UK00001B/3/P